among
others

TOR BOOKS BY JO WALTON

The King's Peace

The King's Name

The Prize in the Game

Tooth and Claw

Farthing

Ha'penny

Half a Crown

Among Others

What Makes This Book So Great

My Real Children

The Just City

The Philosopher Kings

Necessity

An Informal History of the Hugos

Lent

Or What You Will

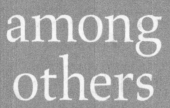

among others

—

jo walton

TOR ESSENTIALS

A TOM DOHERTY ASSOCIATES BOOK
New York

This is a work of fiction. All of the characters, organizations, and events portrayed in this novel are either products of the author's imagination or are used fictitiously.

AMONG OTHERS

Copyright © 2010 by Jo Walton

"Jo Walton: Among Others" copyright © 2013 by Ursula K. Le Guin.
First appeared in *The Guardian* in March 2013, and then in *Words Are My Matter,*
published by Small Beer Press in 2016. Reprinted by permission of Curtis Brown, Ltd.

A Tor Essentials Book
Published by Tom Doherty Associates
120 Broadway
New York, NY 10271

www.tor-forge.com

Tor® is a registered trademark of Macmillan Publishing Group, LLC.

The Library of Congress has cataloged the hardcover edition as follows:

Walton, Jo.
Among others / Jo Walton.—1st ed.
p. cm.
"A Tom Doherty Associates book."
ISBN 978-0-7653-2153-4 (hardcover)
ISBN 978-1-4299-9152-0 (ebook)
1. Young women—Fiction. 2. Mothers and daughters—Fiction. 3. Magic—Fiction.
4. Books and reading—Fiction. 5. England—Fiction. I. Title.
PR6073.A448A825 2011
823'.914—dc22
2010036108

ISBN 978-1-250-23776-7 (trade paperback)

Our books may be purchased in bulk for promotional, educational, or business use.
Please contact your local bookseller or the Macmillan Corporate and Premium Sales
Department at 1-800-221-7945, extension 5442, or by email at
MacmillanSpecialMarkets@macmillan.com.

First Edition: January 2011
Second Trade Paperback Edition: March 2020

Printed in the United States of America

D 0 9 8 7 6 5 4 3

jo walton: *among others*

by Ursula K. Le Guin

This beautifully titled novel is, I suppose, a fairy tale, since there are fairies in it, or, anyhow, beings called fairies. They aren't visible to everyone, yet can affect the lives of people who don't see, or don't believe in them. In that, they play in modern industrial England something like their role in the folklore of the past. They don't, however, fit conventional notions of what a fairy looks like: they aren't the tall, fair ones who carry you off under the hill, nor yet the tiny Peaseblossoms and sprites the Victorians loved, and they are most definitely not Tinker Bell. Walton's descriptions suggest that the great illustrator Arthur Rackham was one of the people who could see them: "In the same way that oak trees have acorns and hand-shaped leaves, and hazels have hazelnuts and little curved leaves, most fairies are gnarly and grey or green or brown, and there's generally something hairy about them somewhere. This one was grey, very gnarly indeed, and well over towards the hideous part of the spectrum."

Mori, the protagonist and narrator of the novel, has always seen and known the fairies. Though she'd like them to be Tolkien's elves, they aren't gracious and powerful, but frustrated, marginal, somehow diminished. Some of them are probably ghosts. They are untamed, uncivilised, and unpredictable. They speak Welsh, mostly. They don't answer to any name, but if asked properly they can grant wishes. They are like fragments of the wild, surviving only where a trace of woodland survives, haunting whatever remains of the unhuman: old parks, pre-industrial, untilled places, forgotten roads out past the edges of towns and farms.

Among Others does not, however, make the trite equation of wilderness with magic, for several quite commonplace-seeming human beings in the story also have supernatural powers. The knowledge of how to ask the fairies to grant a wish is one kind of magic, but there are others, some much nastier.

Bringing supernatural events into ordinary modern life—in this case, Oswestry in 1979—isn't an easy business for a novelist. The realists left us with the notion that "fantasy" is acceptable only when presented as about, or for, children. But there is nothing inherently childish about the overlapping of the natural with the supernatural, and many novels written for adults even in the heyday of realism involve that overlap. The first that came to my mind was the subtle and charming *Lady into Fox*. In David Garnett's story, as in many others, the supernatural element is simply there, not explained, not discussed—a good aesthetic ploy, for if it is discussed, the author has to tackle both plausibility and causality head-on.

Most fantasies evade opportunities to make the impossible plausible, to give magic accountability in a realistic setting and moral and emotional weight in a modern novel. Jo Walton accepts the double challenge and meets it with courage and skill. She shows how easily the effects of a magic spell can be seen and explained away, and how every action that brings about real change must be paid for—a reciprocity as absolute in the world of three wishes as it is in the world of Newton's third law.

The narrative is the diary of fifteen-year-old Mori, but Mori as an adult is implicitly present, and this greatly enriches the book. Mori writes with style and reads obsessively, mostly science fiction, though given the chance she devours Plato as eagerly as she does Heinlein or Zelazny. Her critical notes, delivered with the energetic conviction of her age, are a delight. I was glad to learn that T. S. Eliot is "brill."

Having suffered a lot of major damage, physical and psychic, Mori sees her reading as "compensatory." In fact, books give her passion and fierce intelligence access to larger realities of art and thought. Books are almost enough to get her through separation from everyone she has loved, the pain of a smashed pelvis, the suffocating pettiness of the girls' boarding school that her three very respectable and very strange aunts have sent her to, and the uncanny attacks of an insane witch, her mother. But even reading fails her at last, and in search of some companionship, some human warmth in her life, she resorts to working magic.

Among Others is a funny, thoughtful, acute, and absorbing story all the way through, but in the magic parts it is more than that. When Mori realises that perhaps her new friends did not choose to offer her friendship but were forced to do so by the spell she laid upon them, her moral anguish is that of anyone who honestly faces the responsibility of power; and it is not soon or easily resolved.

The heart of the book is a scene in the Welsh hills where Mori obeys the fairies' command to help the souls of the dead go into the darkness on All Souls' Eve. In the crash that crippled Mori, her twin sister was killed, and the sister's soul comes to the gate of darkness now and clings and clutches and will not let Mori let her go. In this passage, haunting in its reticence and its drama, all the anguish of loss and need gathers almost intolerably, and, as in old ballads, the quiet, factual narration deepens the inexplicable experience, making strangeness real.

This is for all the libraries in the world,
and the librarians who sit there day after day
lending books to people.

thanks and notes

I'd like to thank Aunt Jane, who accepted axiomatically that I would grow up and write, and her daughter Sue, now Ashwell, who gave me both *The Hobbit* and Le Guin's Earthsea trilogy. I'm also grateful to Mrs. Morris, once my Welsh teacher, who worried about me for thirty years.

Mary Lace and Patrick Nielsen Hayden encouraged me while I was writing this. My LiveJournal correspondents were excellent at providing random required information, especially Mike Scott, without whom this would have been impossible. Some people have full-time research assistants who aren't as speedy or as well informed. Thanks again, Mike.

Emmet O'Brien and Sasha Walton and, quite often, Alexandra Whitebean, put up with me when I was writing. Alter Reiss bought me a DOS laptop so I could keep on writing, and Janet M. Kegg found a battery for it and delivered it. My next-door neighbour René Walling found this book a title. I have the best friends. Seriously.

Louise Mallory, Caroline-Isabelle Caron, David Dyer-Bennett, Farah Mendlesohn, Edward James, Mike Scott, Janet Kegg, David Goldfarb, Rivka Wald, Sherwood Smith, Sylvia Rachel Hunter, and Beth Meacham read the book when it was done and made useful comments on it. Liz Gorinsky, and the hardworking production and publicity people at Tor, always do a great job paying attention to my books and helping get them into people's hands.

People tell you to write what you know, but I've found that writing what you know is much harder than making it up. It's easier to research a historical period than your own life, and it's much easier to deal with things that have a little less emotional weight and where you have a little more detachment. It's terrible advice! So this is why you'll find there's no such place as the Welsh valleys, no coal under them, and no red buses running up and down them; there never was such a year as 1979, no such age as fifteen, and no such planet as Earth. The fairies are real, though.

Er' perrehnne.

　　　　　—Ursula K. Le Guin, *The Lathe of Heaven*

What one piece of advice would you give to your younger self, and at what age?

Any time between 10 and 25:

It's going to improve. Honest. There really are people out there that you will like and who will like you.

　　　　　—Farah Mendlesohn, LiveJournal,
　　　　　　　　　　　　　23rd May 2008

Thursday 1st May 1975

The Phurnacite factory in Abercwmboi killed all the trees for two miles around. We'd measured it on the mileometer. It looked like something from the depths of hell, black and looming with chimneys of flame, reflected in a dark pool that killed any bird or animal that drank from it. The smell was beyond description. We always wound up the car windows as tight as tight when we had to pass it, and tried to hold our breath, but Grampar said nobody could hold their breath that long, and he was right. There was sulphur in that smell, which was a hell chemical as everyone knew, and other, worse things, hot unnameable metals and rotten eggs.

My sister and I called it Mordor, and we'd never been there on our own before. We were ten years old. Even so, big as we were, as soon as we got off the bus and started looking at it we started holding hands.

It was dusk, and as we approached the factory loomed blacker and more terrible than ever. Six of the chimneys were alight; four belched out noxious smokes.

"Surely it is a device of the Enemy," I murmured.

Mor didn't want to play. "Do you really think this will work?"

"The fairies were sure of it," I said, as reassuringly as possible.

"I know, but sometimes I don't know how much they understand about the real world."

"Their world is real," I protested. "Just in a different way. At a different angle."

"Yes." She was still staring at the Phurnacite, which was getting bigger and scarier as we approached. "But I don't know how much they understand about the angle of the everyday world. And this is definitely in that world. The trees are dead. There isn't a fairy for miles."

"That's why we're here," I said.

We came to the wire, three straggly strands, only the top one barbed. A sign on it read "No Unauthorised Admittance. Beware Guard Dogs." The gate was far around the other side, out of sight.

"Are there dogs?" she asked. Mor was afraid of dogs, and dogs knew it. Perfectly nice dogs who would play with me would rouse their hackles at her. My mother said it was a method people could use to tell us apart. It would have worked, too, but typically of her, it was both terrifyingly evil and just a little crazily impractical.

"No," I said.

"How do you know?"

"It would ruin everything if we go back now, after having gone to all this trouble and come this far. Besides, it's a quest, and you can't give up on a quest because you're afraid of dogs. I don't know what the fairies would say. Think of all the things people on quests have to put up with." I knew this wasn't working. I squinted forward into the deepening dusk as I spoke. Her grip on my hand had tightened. "Besides, dogs are animals. Even trained guard dogs would try to drink the water, and then they'd die. If there really were dogs, there would be at least a few dog bodies at the side of the pool, and I don't see any. They're bluffing."

We crept below the wire, taking turns holding it up. The still pool was like old unpolished pewter, reflecting the chimney flames as unfaithful wavering streaks. There were lights below them, lights the evening shift worked by.

There was no vegetation here, not even dead trees. Cinders crunched underfoot, and clinker and slag threatened to turn our ankles. There

seemed to be nothing alive but us. The star-points of windows on
the hill opposite seemed ridiculously out of reach. We had a school
friend who lived there, we had been to a party once, and noticed the
smell, even inside the house. Her father worked at the plant. I wondered if he was inside now.

At the edge of the pool we stopped. It was completely still, without
even the faintest movement of natural water. I dug in my pocket for
the magic flower. "Have you got yours?"

"It's a bit crushed," she said, fishing it out. I looked at them. Mine
was a bit crushed too. Never had what we were doing seemed more
childish and stupid than standing in the centre of that desolation by
that dead pool holding a pair of crushed pimpernels the fairies had
told us would kill the factory.

I couldn't think of anything appropriate to say. "Well, un, dai,
tri!" I said, and on "Three" as always we cast the flowers forward into
the leaden pool, where they vanished without even a ripple. Nothing
whatsoever happened. Then a dog barked far away, and Mor turned
and ran and I turned and pelted after her.

"Nothing happened," she said, when we were back on the road,
having covered the distance back in less than a quarter of the time it
had taken us as distance out.

"What did you expect?" I asked.

"The Phurnacite to fall and become a hallowed place," she said, in
the most matter-of-fact tone imaginable. "Well, either that or huorns."

I hadn't thought of huorns, and I regretted them extremely. "I
thought the flowers would dissolve and ripples would spread out and
then it would crumble to ruin and the trees and ivy come swarming
over it while we watched and the pool would become real water and
a bird would come and drink from it and then the fairies would be
there and thank us and take it for a palace."

"But nothing at all happened," she said, and sighed. "We'll have
to tell them it didn't work tomorrow. Come on, are we going to walk
home or wait for a bus?"

It had worked, though. The next day, the headline in the Aberdare *Leader* was "Phurnacite Plant Closing: Thousands of Jobs Lost."

I'm telling that part first because it's compact and concise and it makes sense, and a lot of the rest of this isn't that simple.

Think of this as a memoir. Think of it as one of those memoirs that's later discredited to everyone's horror because the writer lied and is revealed to be a different colour, gender, class and creed from the way they'd made everybody think. I have the opposite problem. I have to keep fighting to stop making myself sound more normal. Fiction's nice. Fiction lets you select and simplify. This isn't a nice story, and this isn't an easy story. But it is a story about fairies, so feel free to think of it as a fairy story. It's not like you'd believe it anyway.

Very Private.
This is NOT a vocab book!

Et haec, olim, meminisse iuvabit!

—Virgil, *The Aeneid*

Wednesday 5th September 1979

"And how nice it'll be for you," they said, "to be in the countryside. After coming from, well, such an industrialised place. The school's right out in the country, there'll be cows and grass and healthy air." They want to get rid of me. Sending me off to boarding school would do nicely, that way they can keep on pretending I didn't exist at all. They never looked right at me. They looked past me, or they sort of squinted at me. I wasn't the sort of relative they'd have put in for if they'd had any choice. *He* might have been looking, I don't know. I can't look straight at him. I kept darting little sideways glances at him, taking him in, his beard, the colour of his hair. Did he look like me? I couldn't tell.

There were three of them, his older sisters. I'd seen a photograph of them, much younger but their faces exactly the same, all dressed as bridesmaids and my Auntie Teg next to them looking as brown as a berry. My mother had been in the picture too, in her horrid pink wedding dress—pink because it was December and we were born the June after and she did have some shame—but *he* hadn't been. She'd torn him off. She'd ripped or cut or burned him out of all the wedding pictures after he'd run off. I'd never seen a picture of him, not one. In L. M. Montgomery's *Jane of Lantern Hill*, a girl whose parents were divorced recognised a picture of her father in the paper without knowing it. After reading that we'd looked at some pictures, but they never did anything for us. To be honest, most of the time we hadn't thought about him much.

Even standing in his house I was almost surprised to find him real, him and his three bossy half-sisters who asked me to call them Aunt. "Not aunty," they said. "Aunty's common." So I called them Aunt. Their names are Anthea and Dorothy and Frederica, I know, as I know a lot of things, though some of them are lies. I can't trust anything my mother told me, not unless it's checked. Some things books can't check, though. It's no use my knowing their names anyway, because I can't tell them apart, so I don't call them aunt anything, just Aunt. They call me "Morwenna," very formally.

"Arlinghurst is one of the best girls' schools in the country," one of them said.

"We all went there," another chimed in.

"We had the jolliest time," the third finished. Spreading what they're saying out like that seems to be one of their habits.

I just stood there in front of the cold fireplace, looking up under my fringe and leaning on my cane. That was something else they didn't want to see. I saw pity in one of their faces when I first got out of the car. I hate that. I'd have liked to sit down, but I wasn't going to say so. I can stand up much better now. I will get better, whatever the doctors said. I want to run so much sometimes my body aches with longing more than the pain from my leg.

I turned around to distract myself and looked at the fireplace. It was marble, very elaborate, and there were branches of copper birch leaves arranged in it. Everything was very clean, but not very comfortable. "So we'll get your uniforms right away, today in Shrewsbury, and take you down there tomorrow," they said. Tomorrow. They really can't wait to get rid of me, with my ugly Welsh accent and my limp and worst of all my inconvenient existence. I don't want to be here either. The problem is that I don't have anywhere else to be. They won't let you live alone until you're sixteen; I found that out in the Home. And he is my father even if I'd never seen him before. There is a sense in which these women really are my aunts. That makes me feel lonelier and farther away from home than I ever had. I miss my real family, who have let me down.

The rest of the day was shopping, with all three aunts, but without him. I didn't know if I was glad or sorry about that. The Arlinghurst uniform had to come from special shops, just like my grammar school uniform did. We'd been so proud when we passed the Eleven plus. The cream of the Valleys, they said we were. Now that's all gone, and instead they're forcing on me this posh boarding school with its strange requirements. One of the aunts had a list, and we bought everything on it. They're certainly not hesitating about spending money. I've never had this much spent on me. Pity it's all so horrible. Lots of it is special games kits. I didn't say I won't be using them any time soon, or maybe ever. I keep turning away from that thought. All my childhood we had run. We'd won races. Most of the school races we'd been racing each other, leaving the rest of the field far behind. Grampar had talked about the Olympics, just dreaming, but he had mentioned it. There had never been twins at the Olympics, he said.

When it came to shoes, there was a problem. I let them buy hockey shoes and running shoes and daps, for gym, because either I can use them or not. But when it comes to the uniform shoes, for every day, I had to stop them. "I have a special shoe," I said, not looking at them. "It has a special sole. They have to be made, at the orthopaedic. I can't just buy them."

The shop assistant confirmed that we can't just buy them in the school pattern. She held up a school shoe. It was ugly, and not very different from the clumpy shoes I have. "Couldn't you walk in these?" one of the aunts asked.

I took the school shoe in my hands and looked at it. "No," I said, turning it over. "There's a heel, look." It was inarguable, though the school probably thinks the heel is the minimum any self-respecting teenage girl will wear.

They didn't mean to totally humiliate me as they clucked over the shoes and me and my built-up sole. I had to remind myself of that as I stood there like a rock, a little painful half-smile on my face. They wanted to ask what's wrong with my leg, but I outfaced them and they didn't quite dare. This, and seeing it, cheered me up a little. They gave in on the shoes, and said the school would just have to understand. "It's not as if my shoes were red and glamorous," I said.

That was a mistake, because then they all stared at my shoes. They are cripple shoes. I had a choice of one pattern of ladies' cripple shoes, black or brown, and they are black. My cane's wooden. It used to belong to Grampar, who is still alive, who is in hospital, who is trying to get better. If he gets better, I might be able to go home. It's not likely, considering everything, but it's all the hope I have. I have my wooden key ring dangling from the zip of my cardigan. It's a slice of tree, with bark, it came from Pembrokeshire. I've had it since before. I touched it, to touch wood, and I saw them looking. I saw what they saw, a funny little spiky crippled teenager with a piece of tatty wood. But what they ought to see is two glowing confident children. I know what happened, but they don't, and they'd never understand it.

"You're very English," I said.

They smiled. Where I come from, "Saes" is an insult, a terrible fighting word, the worst thing you can possibly call someone. It means "English." But I am in England now.

We ate dinner around a table that would have been small for sixteen, but with a fifth place laid awkwardly for me. Everything matched, the tablemats, the napkins, the plates. It couldn't be more different from home. The food was, as I'd expected, terrible—leathery meat and watery potatoes and some kind of green spear-shaped vegetable that tastes of grass. People have told me all my life that English food is awful, and it's reassuring that they were right. They talked about boarding schools, which they all went to. I know all about them. Not for nothing have I read Greyfriars and Malory Towers and the complete works of Angela Brazil.

After dinner, *he* asked me into his study. The aunts didn't look happy about it, but they didn't say anything. The study was a complete surprise, because it's full of books. From the rest of the house, I'd have expected neat old leatherbound editions of Dickens and Trollope and Hardy (Gramma loved Hardy), but instead the shelves are chockablock with paperbacks, and masses of them are SF. I actually relaxed for the first time in this house, for the first time in his presence, because if there are books perhaps it won't be all that bad.

There were other things in the room—chairs, a fireplace, a drinks tray, a record player—but I ignored or avoided them and walked as fast as I clumsily could to the SF shelf.

There was a whole load of Poul Anderson I haven't read. Stuffed on the top of the As there was Anne McCaffrey's *Dragonquest*, which looks as if it's the sequel to "Weyr Search" which I read in an anthology. On the shelf below there was a John Brunner I haven't read. Better than that, two John Brunners, no, three John Brunners I haven't read. I felt my eyes start to swim.

I spent the summer practically bookless, with only what I took with me when I ran away from my mother—the three-volume paperback *Lord of the Rings*, of course, Ursula Le Guin's *The Wind's Twelve Quarters, Volume 2*, which I will defend against all comers as the best single author short story collection of all time, ever, and John Boyd's *The Last Starship from Earth*, which I'd been in the middle of at the time and which hadn't stood up to re-reading as much as one might hope. I have read, though I didn't bring it with me, Judith Kerr's *When Hitler Stole Pink Rabbit*, and the comparison between Anna bringing a new toy instead of the loved Pink Rabbit when they left the Third Reich has been uncomfortably with me whenever I've looked at the Boyd recently.

"Can I—" I started to ask.

"You can borrow any books you want, just take care of them and bring them back," he said. I snatched the Anderson, the McCaffrey, the Brunners. "What have you got?" he asked. I turned and showed him. We both looked at the books, not at each other.

"Have you read the first of these?" he asked, tapping the McCaffrey.

"Out of the library," I said. I have read the entire science fiction and fantasy collection of Aberdare library, from Anderson's *Ensign Flandry* to Roger Zelazny's *Creatures of Light and Darkness*, an odd thing to end on, and one I'm still not certain about.

"Have you read any Delany?" he asked. He poured himself a whisky and sipped it. It smelled weird, horrible.

I shook my head. He handed me an Ace Double, one half of it *Empire Star* by Samuel R. Delany. I turned it over to look at the other half, but he tutted impatiently, and I actually looked at him for a moment.

"The other half's just rubbish," he says, dismissively, stubbing out a cigarette with unnecessary force. "How about Vonnegut?"

I have read the complete works of Kurt Vonnegut, Jr., to date. Some of it I have read standing up in Lears bookshop in Cardiff. *God Bless You, Mr. Rosewater* is very strange, but *Cat's Cradle* is one of the best things I've ever read. "Oh yes," I said.

"What Vonnegut?"

"All of it," I said, confidently.

"*Cat's Cradle*?"

"*Breakfast of Champions, Welcome to the Monkey House . . .*" I reeled off the titles. He was smiling. He looked pleased. My reading has been solace and addiction but nobody has been pleased with me for it before.

"How about *The Sirens of Titan*?" he asked, as I wound down.

I shook my head. "I've never heard of it!"

He set down his drink, bent down and got the book, hardly looking at the shelves, and added it to my pile. "How about Zenna Henderson?"

"*Pilgrimage*," I breathed. It is a book that speaks to me. I love it. Nobody else I've met has ever read it. I didn't read it from the library.

My mother had it, an American edition with a hole punched in the cover. I don't even think there is a British edition. Henderson wasn't in the library catalogue. For the first time, I realised that if he is my father, which in some sense he is, then long ago he *knew* her. He married her. He had the sequel to *Pilgrimage* and two collections. I took them, very uncertain of him. I could hardly hold my book pile one-handed. I put them all in my bag, which was on my shoulder, where it always is.

"I think I'll go to bed and read now," I said.

He smiled. He has a nice smile, nothing like our smiles. I've been told all my life that we looked like him, but I can't see it. If he's Lazarus Long to our Laz and Lor, I'd expect to have some sense of recognition. We never looked anything like anyone in our family, but apart from the eye and hair colour I don't see anything. It doesn't matter. I have books, new books, and I can bear anything as long as there are books.

Thursday 6th September 1979

My father drove me to school. In the back seat was a neat suitcase I never saw before, in which, one of the aunts assured me, was all the uniform, neatly laid out. There was also a leather satchel, which she said is school supplies. Neither of them were scuffed at all, and I think they must be new. They must have cost the earth. My own bag held what it had held since I ran away, plus the books I have borrowed. I clutched it tightly and resisted their attempts to take it from me and put it with the luggage. I nodded at them, my tongue frozen in my mouth. It's funny how impossible it would be to cry, or show any strong emotion, with these people. They are not my people. They are not like my people. That sounded like the first lines of a poem, and I itched to write them down in my notebook. I got into the car, awkwardly. It was painful. At least there was room to straighten my leg once I was in. Front seats are better than back seats, I've noticed that before.

I managed to say thank you as well as goodbye. The aunts each kissed me on the cheek.

My father didn't look at me as he drove, which meant I could look at him, sideways. He was smoking, lighting each cigarette with the butt of the last, just like her. I wound down my window to have some air. I still don't think he looks the least bit like us. It isn't just the beard. I wondered what Mor would have made of him, and pushed the thought away hard. After a little while he said, puffing, "I've put you down as Markova."

It's his name. Daniel Markova. I've always known that. It's the name on my birth certificate. He was married to my mother. It's her name. But I've never used it. My family name is Phelps, and that's how I've gone to school. Phelps means something, at least in Aberdare, it means my grandparents, my family. Mrs. Markova means that madwoman my mother. Still, it will mean nothing to Arlinghurst.

"Morwenna Markova is a bit of a mouthful," I said, after rather too long.

He laughed. "I said that when you were born. Morwenna and Morganna."

"She said you chose the names," I said, not very loudly, staring out of the open window at the moving patchwork of flat fields full of growing things. Some of them are stubble and some of them have been ploughed.

"I suppose I did," he said. "She had all those lists and she made me choose. They were all very long, and very Welsh. I said it would be a mouthful, but she said people would soon shorten it. Did they?"

"Yes," I said, still staring out. "Mo, or Mor. Or Mori." Mori Phelps is the name I will use when I am a famous poet. It's what I write inside my books now. Ex libris Mori Phelps. And what has Mori Phelps to do with Morwenna Markova and what's likely to happen to her in a new school? I will laugh about this one day, I told myself. I will laugh about it with people so clever and sophisticated I can't imagine them properly now.

"And did they call your sister Mog?" he asked.

He hadn't asked me about her before. I shook my head, then realised he was driving and not looking at me. "No," I said. "Mo, or Mor, both of us."

"But how could they tell you apart?" He wasn't looking at all, he was lighting another cigarette.

"They couldn't." I smiled to myself.

"You won't mind being Markova at school?"

"I don't care. And anyway, you're paying for it," I said.

He turned his head and looked at me for a second, then back to the road. "My sisters are paying for it," he said. "I don't have any money except what they allow me. Do you know my family situation?"

What is there to know? I knew nothing about him apart from the fact that he was English, which has caused me no end of playground fights, and that he married my mother when he was nineteen and then ran off two years later when she was in hospital having another baby, a baby that died because of the shock. "No," I said.

"My mother was married to a man named Charles Bartleby. He was quite wealthy. They had three daughters. Then the war came. He went off to fight in France in 1940 and was captured there and put in a prisoner of war camp. My mother left my three little sisters with their grandmother Bartleby, in the Old Hall, the house we've just left. She went to work in an RAF canteen, to do what she could for the war effort. There she met and fell in love with a Polish flying officer called Samuel Markova. He was a Jew. I was born in March 1944. In September 1944 Bartleby was liberated from the camp and came home to England, where he and my mother obtained a divorce. She married my father, who had just learned that his entire family in Poland had been killed."

Had he had a wife and children too? I felt sure he had. A Polish Jew! I am part Polish. Part Jewish? All that I know about Judaism comes from *A Canticle for Leibowitz* and *Dying Inside*. Well, and the Bible, I suppose.

"My mother had some money of her own, but not very much. My father left the RAF after the war and worked in a factory in Ironbridge. Bartleby left his money, and his house, to my sisters. When I was thirteen my mother died in an accident. My sisters, who were grown up by then, came to her funeral. Anthea offered to pay to send me to school, and my father accepted. They've been subsidising me ever since. As you know, I married partway through university."

"What happened to Bartleby?" I asked. He couldn't have been much older than my grandfather.

"He shot himself when the girls turned twenty-one," he said, in a tone of voice that closed off further questions.

"What do you . . . do?" I asked.

"They hold the purse strings, but I manage the estate," he said. He dropped the butt of a cigarette into the ash tray, which was overflowing. "They pay me a salary, and I live at the house. Very Victorian really."

"Have you lived there ever since you ran off?" I asked.

"Yes."

"But they said they didn't know where you were. My grandfather went there and talked to them, all this way." I was indignant.

"They lied." He wasn't looking at me at all. "Did it bother you so much that I ran away?"

"I've run away from her too," I said, which didn't answer his question but seemed to be enough.

"I knew your grandparents would look after you," he said.

"They did," I said. "You needn't have worried about that."

"Ah," he said.

So then I realised guiltily how my very presence in his car was actually a huge reproach. For one thing, there is only one of me, when he abandoned twins. For another, I am crippled. Thirdly, I am there at all; I ran away. I had to ask for his help—and worse, I had to use the social services to ask for his help. Clearly, the arrangements he made for us were far from adequate. In fact, my existence there at that moment demonstrated to him that he is a rotten parent. And, truth be told, he is. My mother notwithstanding, running out on babies isn't an acceptable thing to do—and in fact, as an abstraction, abandoning babies with her is particularly and unusually irresponsible. But I have run away from her too.

"I wouldn't have grown up any other way," I said. My grandparents. The Valleys. Home. "Truly. There was so much about it to love. I couldn't have had a better childhood."

"I'll take you to meet my father soon, perhaps at half term," he said. He was signalling to turn, and we turned between two elms, both dying, and onto a gravel drive that crunched under the car wheels. It was Arlinghurst. We had arrived.

The first thing that happened in school was the fight about chemistry. It's a big gracious house in its own grounds, looking stately and Victorian. But the place smells like a school—chalk, boiled cabbage, disinfectant, sweat. The headmistress was well-mannered and distant. She didn't give my father permission to smoke, which wrong-footed him. Her chairs are too low. I had trouble getting out of mine. But none of that would matter if it wasn't for the timetable she handed me. First, there are three hours of games every day. Second, art and religious education are compulsory. Third, I can have either chemistry or French, and either Latin or biology. The other choices were very simple, like physics or economics, and history or music.

Robert Heinlein says in *Have Spacesuit, Will Travel* that the only things worth studying are history, languages, and science. Actually, he adds maths, but honestly they left out the mathematical part of my brain. Mor got all the maths. Having said that, it was the same for both of us: We either understood it instantly or you might as well have used a drill to get it into our heads. "How can you understand Boolean algebra when you still have problems with the concept of long division?" my maths teacher had asked in despair. But Venn diagrams are easy, while long division remains challenging. Hardest of all were those problems about people doing incomprehensible things with no motivation. I was inclined to drift away from the sum to wonder why people would care what time two trains passed each other (spies), be so picky about seating arrangements (recently divorced people), or—which to this day remains incomprehensible— run the bath with no plug in.

History, languages and science pose me no such problems. When you need to use maths in science, it always makes sense, and besides, they let you use a calculator.

"I need to do both Latin and biology, and both French and chemistry," I said, looking up from the timetable. "But I don't need to do art or religious education, so it'll be easy to rearrange."

The headmistress went through the roof at this, because clearly timetables are sacred or something. I didn't listen all that much. "There are over five hundred girls in this school, do you propose I inconvenience them all to accommodate you?"

My father, who has no doubt also read Heinlein, backed me up. I'll take Heinlein over a headmistress any day. Eventually we ended up with a compromise in which I'll surrender biology if I get to take all three of the others, which can be arranged with a little shuffling between classes. I'll take chemistry with a different class, but I don't care about that. It felt like enough of a victory for now, and I consented to be shown my dorm and meet my housemistress and "new friends."

My father kissed my cheek when he said goodbye. I watched him out of the front door and saw him lighting a cigarette the second he was in the open air.

Friday 7th September 1979

It turns out to be a joke about the countryside.

Well, it is true in a way. Arlinghurst stands alone in its playing fields, surrounded by farmland. There isn't an inch of land within twenty miles that someone isn't using. There are cows, stupid ugly things, black and white like toy cows, not brown like the real cows we'd seen on holiday. (How now, brown cow? Nobody could talk to these.) They mill about in the fields until it is time for milking then they walk in a line into the farmyard. I figured it out this afternoon, when they let me take a walk around the grounds, that these cows are stupid. Bovine. I knew the word, but I hadn't quite appreciated how literal it could be.

I come from the Welsh Valleys. There's a reason they're called "the Valleys." They're steep narrow glaciated valleys without much flat land at the bottom. There are valleys just like them all over Wales. Most of them have a church and a few farms, maybe a thousand people in the whole valley. That's what they can naturally support. Our valley, the Cynon Valley, like its neighbours, has a population of more than a hundred thousand, all living in Victorian terraced houses, terraced up the hillsides like grapes, stuck together in rows with barely room between to hang out washing. The houses and the people are jammed together, like in a city, worse than a city, except that it isn't a city. But away from those rows, it was wild. And even in them, you could always lift up your eyes.

You could lift up your eyes to the hills from whence cometh your help—a psalm that always seemed self-evident to me. The hills were beautiful, were green and had trees and sheep, and they were always there. They were wild, in the sense that anyone could go there at any time. They didn't belong to anyone, unlike the flat farmed fenced-in countryside around the school. The hills were common land. And even down in the valleys there were rivers and woods and ruins, as the ironworks ceased to be used, as the industrial places were abandoned. The ruins sprouted plants, returned to the wild, then the fairies moved in. What we thought would happen with the Phurnacite really did happen. It just took a little longer than we'd imagined.

We spent our childhood playing in the ruins, sometimes alone and sometimes with other children or with the fairies. We didn't realise what the ruins were, not for a long time. There was an old ironworks near Auntie Florrie's house where we used to play all the time. There were other children there, and we'd play with them sometimes, wonderful games of hide and seek, chasing through. I didn't know what an ironworks was. If pressed, I'd have worked out the etymology that someone must have once worked iron there, but nobody ever pressed me. It was a place, a thing. It was all over rosebay willow-herb in the autumn. It was unusual that we knew what it was.

Most of the ruins where we played, in the woods, didn't have names and could have been anything. We called them witch's cottage, giant's castle, fairy palace, and we played that they were Hitler's last redoubt or the walls of Angband, but they were really old crumbling relics of industry. The fairies hadn't built them. They'd moved in with the green things after people had abandoned them. The fairies couldn't make anything, not anything real. They couldn't do anything. That's why they needed us. We didn't know that. There were a lot of things we didn't know, that we didn't think to ask. Before the people came I suppose the fairies would have lived in the trees and not had houses. The farmers would have put out milk for them, perhaps. There wouldn't have been so many of them either.

The people had come to the Valleys, or rather their ancestors had, at the beginning of the Industrial Revolution. Under the hills there were iron and coal, and the Valleys were the boom towns of their day, filling up with people. If you've ever wondered why there wasn't a Welsh immigration to the New World on the scale of the Irish or Scottish ones, it isn't because the people didn't need to leave their farms in the same way. It's because they had somewhere of their own to go. Or at least, they thought it was their own. English people came too. The Welsh language lost out. Welsh was my grandmother's first language, my mother's second language and I can only fumble along in it. My grandmother's family had come from west Wales, from Carmarthenshire. We still had relatives there, Mary-from-the-country and her people.

My ancestors came like everyone else, after iron was discovered, and coal. People started building smelters on the spot, railroads to take it out, houses for workers, more smelters, more mines, more houses, until the valleys were solid strips of habitation up and down. The hills were always there between, and the fairies must have huddled in the hills. Then the iron ran out, or was cheaper to produce somewhere else, and while there was still coal mining it was a pitiful remnant of the boom of a hundred years before. Ironworks were abandoned. Pits closed down. Some of the people left, but most stayed. It was home by then. By the time we were born, chronic unemployment was a fact of life and the fairies had crept back down into the valleys and taken over the ruins that nobody wanted.

We grew up playing freely in the ruins and had no real sense of this history. It was a wonderful place for children. It was abandoned and grown over and ignored, and once you slipped away from the houses it was wild. You could always go up the mountain into real countryside, which had rocks and trees and sheep, grey-coated from coal dust and unappealing. (I can't understand how people are sentimental about sheep. We used to shout "Mint sauce!" at them to get them to run away. Auntie Teg always winced at that and told us not to, but we kept on doing it. They'd come down into the valley and knock over dustbins and destroy gardens. They were the reason you had to keep gates shut.) But even down in the valley, running through everything were the seams of trees and ruins. They were everywhere, through and under and parallel to the town. It wasn't the only landscape we knew. We went to Pembrokeshire on holiday, and up to the real mountains, the Brecon Beacons, and to Cardiff, which is a city, with city shops. The Valleys were home, they were the landscape of normality, and we never questioned it.

The fairies never said they built the ruins. I doubt we asked, but if we had they'd just have laughed, as they did at most of our questions. They were just inexplicably there or, some days, inexplicably not there. Sometimes they would talk to us, and other times flee from us. Like the other children we knew, we could play with them or without them. All we really needed was each other and our imagination.

The places of my childhood were linked by magical pathways, ones almost no adults used. They had roads, we had these. They were for walking, they were different and extra, wider than a path but not big enough for cars, sometimes parallel to the real roads and sometimes cutting from nowhere to nowhere, from an elven ruin to the labyrinth of Minos. We gave them names but we knew unquestioningly that the real name for them was "dramroads." I never turned that word over in my mouth and saw it for what it was: Tram road. Welsh mutates initial consonants. Actually all languages do, but most of them take centuries, while Welsh does it while your mouth is still open. Tram to dram, of course. Once there had been trams running on rails up those dramroads, trams full of iron ore or coal. So empty and leaf-strewn, used by nobody but children and fairies, they'd once been little railroads.

It wasn't that we didn't know history. Even if you only count the real world, we knew more history than most people. We'd been taught about cavemen and Normans and Tudors. We knew about Greeks and Romans. We knew masses of personal stories about World War II. We even knew quite a lot of family history. It just didn't connect to the landscape. And it was the landscape that formed us, that made us who we were as we grew in it, that affected everything. We thought we were living in a fantasy landscape when actually we were living in a science fictional one. In ignorance, we played our way through what the elves and giants had left us, taking the fairies' possession for ownership. I named the dramroads after places in *The Lord of the Rings* when I should have recognised that they were from *The Chrysalids*.

It's amazing how large the things are that it's possible to overlook.

Tuesday 18th September 1979

School is awful, as expected. For one thing, as I'd known from all the school stories, one of the most important things about boarding schools is the games. I'm not in any shape to be doing games. Also, all the other girls are from the same background. They are almost all English, from not too far away, products of the same landscape as the school. They vary a little in size and shape, but most of them have the same voice. My voice, which was posh for the Valleys and immediately marked my class origins to everyone there, here brands me an outlander barbarian. As if being a crippled barbarian isn't bad enough, there's also the fact that I was coming late for the year into a class that has known each other for two years already, with enmities and alliances drawn up across lines I know nothing about.

Fortunately, I figured this out quickly. I'm not stupid. I've never gone to a school before where everyone didn't already know me, or know my family, and I've never gone into a new school as a singleton, but I've just been through three months of the Children's Home, and this can't possibly be any worse. Using the clue of voice, I identified the other barbarians, one Irish (Deirdre, called Dreary) and one Jewish (Sharon, called Shagger). I do what I can to befriend them.

I glare at the other girls when they try to tease me or patronise me or pick on me, and I'm glad to see that my glare works as well as ever. I get called names a lot, "Taffy" and "Thief" and "Commie," as well as slightly more justified things like "Crip" and "Suck-up." Commie is because they think my name is Russian. I was wrong in thinking it would mean nothing to them. They pinch me and thump me when they think they can get away with it, but there's no real violence. It's nothing, absolutely nothing, after the Home. I have my stick and my glare, and soon I started to tell ghost stories after Lights Out. Let them fear me as long as they leave me alone. Let them hate me as long as they fear me. It's a pretty good strategy for boarding school, however it worked out for Tiberius. I said this to Sharon, and she looked at me as if I was an alien. What? What? I'll never get used to this place.

I quickly rose to the top of the class in everything but maths. Very quickly. More quickly than I'd expected. Perhaps these girls are not as clever as the ones at the grammar school? One or two there gave us some competition, but here there doesn't seem to be any of that. I soar above the others. My popularity, bizarrely, goes both up and down slightly because of the marks. They don't care about lessons, and they hate me for beating them, but you get house points for exceptional marks, and they care a lot about house points. It's depressing how much boarding school is just like Enid Blyton showed it, and all the ways it's different are ways it's worse.

The chemistry class, with a different set of girls, is a lot better. It's taught by the science master, the only male teacher in the school, and the girls seem a lot more engaged by the subject. It's the best thing on the curriculum, I'm really glad I fought for it. I don't care that I miss art—though Auntie Teg would care. I haven't written to her. I've thought about it, but I don't dare. She wouldn't tell my mother where I am—she'd be the last person to do that—but I can't risk it.

Then yesterday I found the library. I've got permission to spend time here when I'm supposed to be on the playing field. Suddenly, being crippled starts to feel like a benefit. It's not a wonderful library, but it's so much better than nothing that I'm not complaining. I've finished all the books my father lent me. (He was right about the other half of *Empire Star*, but *Empire Star* itself is one of the best things I've ever read.) On the shelves here there's *The Bull from the Sea* and another Mary Renault I've never heard of called *The Charioteer*, and three adult SF novels by C. S. Lewis. It's wood-panelled and the chairs are old cracked leather. So far it seems to be deserted by everyone except me and the librarian, Miss Carroll, to whom I am unfailingly polite.

I'll have a chance to keep up my diary now. One of the worst things here is how impossible it is to be alone and how people ask you all the time what you are doing. "Writing a poem" or "Writing in my diary" would be the kiss of death. After the first couple of days I stopped trying, even though I really wanted to. They already think I'm weird. I sleep in a dorm with eleven other girls. I'm not alone even in the bathroom—there are no doors on the toilet or shower cubicles, and of course they think lavatory humour is the height of wit.

Out of the library window I can see the branches of a dying elm. Elms are dying all over the place, it's Dutch elm disease. It isn't my fault. I can't do anything about it. But I keep thinking maybe I could, if the fairies told me what to do. It's the kind of thing where there might be something that would make a difference. The dying trees are very sad. I asked the librarian and she gave me an old copy of *New Scientist*, and I read more detail about it. It came from America on a load of logs, and it's a fungal disease. That makes it sound even more as if it might be possible to do something. The elms are all one elm, they are clones, that's why they are all succumbing. No natural resistance among the population, because no variation. Twins are clones, too. If you looked at an elm tree you'd never think it was part of all the others. You'd see an elm tree. Same when people look at me now: they see a person, not half a set of twins.

Wednesday 19th September 1979

After prep and before supper, we have a free half hour. Yesterday it wasn't raining, so I went out in the dusk. I walked down to the bottom of bounds, the edge of the school grounds. There's a field there with black-and-white cows in it. They stared at me apathetically.

There's also a ditch and a straggle of trees. If there are any fairies here, this looked like where they'll be. It was chilly and damp. The sky was losing colour without any noticeable sunset.

It's hard enough to find fairies on purpose even when you know where they are. I've always thought fairies are like mushrooms, you trip over them when you're not thinking about them, but they're hard to spot when you're searching for them. I hadn't brought my key ring, and everything I was wearing was new and had no connections, so I couldn't use that. But my cane was old, and wooden, and might work. I tried to think about the elm trees and whether I could help. I tried to calm my mind.

I closed my eyes and leaned on my cane. I tried to ignore the pain, and ignore the huge hole where Mor ought to be. The pain is hard to put aside, but I knew it would scare them off like nothing else. I remembered them scattering and bounding away like startled sheep when I cut my hand up behind Camelot that time. The normal pain in my leg is in two parts, a sharp tug and a slow grind. If I stand still and balanced the grind goes down to an ache, and the tug doesn't come unless I shift my weight, so I tried that and got it down. I tried to think of what would we do if we wanted to call them. I opened my mind. Nothing happened. "Good afternoon?" I said, tentatively, in Welsh. But maybe fairies in England would speak English? Or maybe there aren't any fairies here. It's not a landscape with much room for them. I opened my eyes again. The cows had wandered away. It must have been milking time. There was a bush and a little stunted mountain ash and a hazel tree on the school side of the ditch. I put my left hand on the smooth bark of the hazel, not really hoping for anything now.

There was a fairy up in the branches. It was wary. I've always noticed how much more fairies are like plants than anything else. With people and animals you have one standard pattern: Two arms, two legs, one head, a person. Or four legs and wool, a sheep. Plants and fairies, though, there are signs that say what they are, but a tree might have any number of branches, growing out anywhere. There's a kind of pattern to it, but one elm tree won't look exactly like the next, and might look completely different, because they'll have grown differently. Fairies tend to be either very beautiful or absolutely hideous. They all have eyes, and lots of them have some recognisable sort of head. Some of them have limbs in a roughly human way, some are more like animals, and others bear no resemblance to anything at all. This was one of that kind. It was long and spindly, its skin like rough bark. If you didn't see its eyes, which are kind of underneath, you'd take it for some kind of creeper draped with spider's web. In the same way that oak trees have acorns and hand-shaped leaves and hazels have hazelnuts and little curved leaves, most fairies are gnarly and grey or green or brown and there's generally something hairy about them somewhere. This one was grey, very gnarly indeed, and well over towards the hideous part of the spectrum.

Fairies don't go much for names. The ones we knew at home we gave names, and they answered to them or not. They seemed to think they were funny. They don't name places either. They don't even call themselves fairies, that was us. They're not big on nouns at all, come to think, and the way they talk . . . Anyway, this fairy was completely strange to me, and I to it, and I didn't have any names or passwords to give it. It was just looking at me, as if it might go bounding away at any moment, or fade back into the tree. Gender's another iffy thing with fairies, except when it isn't because they have long trailing hair full of flowers or a penis as big as the rest of their body or something like that. This one didn't have any indication in that direction, so I think of it as it.

"Friend," I said, which should be safe.

And then from total stillness it exploded into motion and speech. "Go! Danger! Find!" Fairies don't exactly talk like other people. It doesn't matter how much you want them to be Galadriel, they're never going to make that kind of speech. This one said that and then vanished, all at once, before I could tell it who I was or ask it anything about the elms and if there was anything I could do. It felt as if I'd blinked, but I hadn't. It's always like that when they go quickly— gone between one heartbeat and the next, gone as if they've never been there.

Danger? Find? I have no idea what it meant. I didn't see any danger, but I headed back to the school, where the bell was ringing for supper. I was one of the last in the line, but the food isn't worth eating even when it's hot. Danger didn't find me and I didn't find danger, at least not tonight. I drank my watery cocoa and hoped the fairy was all right. I'm pleased it's here, even if it isn't very communicative. It's like a little piece of home.

Thursday 20th September 1979

This morning, I discovered what the fairy meant by "find" and "danger." The post brought a letter from my mother.

I don't know how finding the fairy let her know where I was. The world doesn't work in a nice logical way. The fairies wouldn't have told her, and while there were people who might have, they might have done it at any time. What I think is that she was looking for me. Being in a strange landscape and with all new stuff I'd have been hard to catch hold of—I have nothing but the cane and a handful of things of my own here, and the things of mine that she has will mostly be fading by now. But by opening my mind to call the fairy, I drew her attention. Maybe that made someone give her my address, or maybe she came to know of it directly. That doesn't matter. You can almost always find chains of coincidence to disprove magic. That's because it doesn't happen the way it does in books. It makes those chains of coincidence. That's what it is. It's like if you snapped your fingers and produced a rose but it was because someone on an aeroplane had dropped a rose at just the right time for it to land in your hand. There was a real person and a real aeroplane and a real rose, but that doesn't mean the reason you have the rose in your hand isn't because you did the magic.

That's where I always went wrong with it. I wanted it to work in a magical way. I expected it to work like it did in the books. If it's like books at all, it's more like *The Lathe of Heaven* than anything. We thought the Phurnacite would crumble to ruins before our eyes, when in fact the decisions to close it were taken in London weeks before, except they wouldn't have been if we hadn't dropped those flowers. It's harder to get a grip on than if it did work the way it does in stories. And it's much easier to dismiss, you can dismiss all of it if you have a sceptical turn of mind because there always is a sensible explanation. It always works through things in the real world, and it's always deniable.

My mother's letter is like that too, in a way. It's barbed, but with barbs that wouldn't really show if I showed it to someone else. She offers to send me pictures of Mor after I write back. She says she misses me but it was my father's turn to look after me for a while, which is a construction of the situation that makes me want to strangle her. And the envelope is neatly addressed in her inimitable writing to Morwenna Markova, which means that she knows the name I am using.

I am frightened. But I would like the pictures, and I am fairly sure I am out of her reach.

Saturday 22nd September 1979

Raining today.

I went into town, Oswestry, not much of a town, and bought shampoo for Sharon. She can't use money on Saturday, because of being Jewish. I found a library, but it shuts at noon. Why would you have a library that shuts at noon on Saturdays? That's just so English, honestly. There's no bookshop, but there's a Smiths with some books, just bestsellers but better than nothing.

I came back and spent the rest of my free afternoon in the library, being shocked at *The Charioteer*. It hasn't struck me before that the men in Renault's ancient Greek books who fall in love with each other are homosexuals, but I see now that of course they are. I read it furtively, as if someone would take it away from me if they knew what it was about. I'm amazed it's in the school library. I wonder if I'm the first person to actually read it since 1959, when they bought it?

Sunday 23rd September 1979

We are supposed to write home on Sunday afternoons. I have been writing to my father, Daniel, fairly long letters all about books except for a cursory hope that he and my aunts are well. He has written back in similar style, and sent me a parcel of the one book I really didn't need, a hardcover three-volume edition of *The Lord of the Rings*. The paperback one I have was a present from Auntie Teg. He also sent me *Dragonflight*, which was "Weyr Search" and what happened immediately afterwards, Le Guin's *City of Illusions* and Larry Niven's *The Flight of the Horse*. It's okay, but not as good as *Ringworld* or *A Gift from Earth*.

Today I composed a letter to my mother. I said I was well, and that I am enjoying lessons. I gave her my marks and class standing. I told her how my house is doing in hockey and lacrosse. It was a model letter, and in fact it is modelled on the letter my Irish friend Deirdre, who finds writing laborious, has written to her parents. I let Deirdre, whom I never call Dreary, copy my Latin translation in return. She's actually very sweet—not very bright, and always using the wrong word, but very kind. She'd have let me copy her letter without any compensation, I think.

Tuesday 25th September 1979

My letter brought results, by almost the next post. As she promised, she sent a photograph. It is one of the two of us on the beach, building a sand castle. Mor has her back to the camera, patting down the sand. I had been looking at the camera, or at Grampar who had been holding it, but you could no longer see anything but my silhouette, because I have been carefully burned out.

Wednesday 26th September 1979

School, as normal. Top of class in everything except maths, as normal. I went down to the ditch to look for fairies, because horses, stable doors, but didn't see anything. The elms are still dying. Reading *Out of the Silent Planet*, which isn't a patch on the Narnia books. Another awful letter. Stomach cramps.

Saturday 29th September 1979

You can never be sure where you are with magic. And you can never be sure if you've really done anything or if you were just playing. And in any case, I shouldn't do anything at all like that, because it will draw her attention and I have too much of it already.

Mor and I would go out on a summer day when it wasn't raining and play. We'd play that we were knights, making desperate last stands to save Camelot. We'd play that we were on a quest. We'd have long conversations with the fairies where we knew we were saying both parts. It would be perfectly possible to edit the fairies out of these memories—though not of course Mor so I still couldn't talk about them. I can't talk about my childhood at all, because I cannot say "I" when I mean "we," and if I say "we" it leads to a conversation about how I have a dead sister, instead of what I want to talk about. I found that out in the summer. So I don't talk about it.

We would go out along one of the dramroads, talking and singing and playing, and when we came close to one of the ruins we'd sneak up on it, as if that gave us a better chance of catching them. Sometimes the one we called Glorfindel would be peeping around the ruins to catch us out, and we'd have a glorious game of chase with them. Other times they'd want us to do things. They know a lot, but they can't do much, not in the real world.

It says in *The Lord of the Rings* that the elves have dwindled and are living in secret. I don't know if Tolkien knew about the fairies. I used to think so. I used to think he knew them and they told him the stories and he wrote them down, and that would mean it was all true. Fairies can't exactly lie. But whether or not, they don't speak his elvish languages. They speak Welsh. And they're not as human-looking as his elves, mostly. And they never told us stories, not real stories. They just assumed we knew everything, that we were part of everything, like they were.

Until the end, knowing them brought us nothing but good. And in the end, I don't think they understood. No, they did. They were as clear as can be. It was we who didn't understand.

I wish magic was more dramatic.

Sunday 30th September 1979

On the horse/stable door front, I wrote to Auntie Teg today.

My family is huge and complex, and perfectly normal in all ways. It's just—no. If I think about trying to explain it to somebody well-meaning who doesn't know anything about it, I'm daunted in advance.

My grandmother didn't have any brothers or sisters, but she was brought up by her Auntie Syl because her mother died. Actually it's even more complicated than that. I should start in the generation before if I want this to make sense. Cadwalader and Marion "Mam" Teris moved from West Wales, where they left a great deal of family, and came to Aberdare. There he worked in the mines and she ran a Dame School and they had five children, Sylvia, Susannah, Sarah, Shulamith and Sidney. I feel sorry for poor Shulamith, but what could they do, once they'd started with a series of matching names like that and had so many girls?

Sylvia never married, and brought up all of everyone's children.

Susannah married a man who was a Bad Lot. He was a miner. He beat her and she ran away from him, taking both her daughters with her. In those days it was the running away that was considered a disgrace, not the beating, so she left her daughters Gwendolen and Olwen with Auntie Syl and went off to London to go into service. Auntie Gwennie grew up to be appalling, and to marry Uncle Ted and have two daughters and five grandchildren who were, to hear her talk about them, so perfect you couldn't help but hate them. Auntie Olwen became a nurse, and lived with another nurse, Auntie Ethel, from the nineteen-thirties on. They were just like a married couple and everyone treated them like one.

Sarah married a clergyman called Augustus Thomas. This was a social step up for her. They met when he was a curate in St. Fagans, which was our local church, but they married when he acquired a living on the Gower, near Swansea. He took Sarah off there, and there she had a son, also called Augustus, but always known as Gus, who his father brought back to Auntie Syl to bring up after poor Sarah died. Uncle Gus was a hero in the war, and he married an English nurse called Esther who didn't like any of us. He was my grandmother's favourite cousin, and she never saw as much of him as she'd have liked.

Shulamith married Matthew Evans, who was a miner. She was my grandmother's mother, and she was a teacher before she married, like her mother before her. It was actually illegal to be a proper teacher after you were married, but it was all right to keep a Dame School where the children came to learn in your house. She had a baby who died, and then my grandmother, Rebecca, and then died herself.

Sidney kept a draper's shop in the village, and later became Mayor. He married a woman called Florence, who died giving birth to Auntie Flossie. Auntie Flossie herself had three children and then her husband died of the Black Death, which he caught from a rat. Auntie Flossie then went back to teaching and gave her children to Auntie Syl as a new generation to bring up, so my cousin Pip, who was only six years older than me, born in 1958, was the last of Sylvia's babies, when the first of them, Auntie Gwennie, was already sixty, born in 1898.

You'd think there was a terrible lot of dying going on, and you'd be right, but they were Victorians, and they didn't have antibiotics or much in the way of sanitation and they only just had the germ theory of disease. However, I think in a way they must have been sickly, because you've only got to look at the Phelps family to see the difference. I'll write about them another day. My Auntie Florrie, my grandfather's sister, blamed it on all the education the Terises went in for. I don't see how it can have killed them—and Auntie Syl, who was as educated as any of them, lived into her eighties. I remember her.

It seems so more complicated written down than it really is. Maybe I ought to draw a diagram. But it doesn't matter. You don't have to remember who these people are. All I really want to say about them is that when you belong to a big family like that, where you know everyone and you know all the stories about everyone, even the stories that happened long before you were born, and everyone knows who you are and knows the stories about you, then you are never just Mor but "Luke and Becky's Mor" or "Luke Phelps's granddaughters." And also, when you need someone, someone will be there for you. It might not be your parents, or even your grandparents, but if you have a catastrophic need for someone to bring you up, someone will step in, the way Auntie Syl did. But she was dead before my grandmother died, and when I needed someone, somehow that net of family that I counted on to be there for me, the way you might bounce down to a trampoline, disappeared, and instead of bouncing back I hit the ground hard. They wouldn't admit what was wrong with my mother, and they'd have had to do that to help me. And once I had to use social services to get away from her, they couldn't do anything, because to social services an auntie you have known all your life is nobody compared to a father you haven't even met.

He has a family too.

Tuesday 2nd October 1979

Actually, James Tiptree, Jr.'s *Warm Worlds and Otherwise* gives *The Wind's Twelve Quarters, Vol II* a run for its money. I'd say the Le Guin is still ahead, but it's not as clear-cut as I thought it was. The other two books in the package from my father today are both Zelazny. I haven't started them yet. *Creatures of Light and Darkness* was awfully peculiar.

Thursday 4th October 1979

Nine Princes in Amber and *The Guns of Avalon* are absolutely brill. I've done nothing but read them for the last two days. The concept of Shadow is amazing, and the Trumps too, but what makes them so good is Corwin's voice. I have to read more Zelazny.

A letter from Auntie Teg came today, sounding very relieved to know I am well. She sent me a pound note, inside the letter. There's lots of family news. Cousin Arwel is starting a new job with British Rail in Nottingham. Auntie Olwen is on the list for a cataract operation. Cousin Sylvie's having another baby—and Gail's not two yet! Uncle Rhodri's getting married. She doesn't say anything about my mother. I didn't expect her to. I didn't either. I didn't tell her about abandoning art for chemistry. She teaches art; she wouldn't understand. Chemistry and physics and Latin are my three favourite subjects, though my very highest marks are in boring old English, as usual. We're reading *Our Mutual Friend*, which I secretly call *Our Mutual Fiend*. You could re-write it with that title to make Rogue Riderhood the one they all know.

Friday 5th October 1979

My grandfather's father was French. He came from Rennes in Brittany, and his mother was Indian, from India. He was very dark-skinned, from all accounts, and my grandfather and his sisters were also quite dark—all dark-haired and dark-eyed, and with skin that tanned browner than any European skin. My mother was the same. Grampar despised our skins for burning in the sun. Alexandre Rennes changed his name to Phelps when he married my great-grandmother Annabelle Phelps, because she wouldn't marry him on any other terms. He worked in the mines. She was one of eight children, had seven children herself, of whom five survived to adulthood, lived to be ninety-three, and was a tyrant all her life. She died the year before I was born, but I grew up on stories of her.

Because Alexandre was French, they spoke English at home, unlike my grandmother's family, who always spoke Welsh by choice. Their five surviving children all married and had children of their own.

The eldest boy, Alexander, married on the eve of the Great War, and left his new wife pregnant when he went to the trenches. He never came back, and they had a telegram saying he was missing in combat. His young wife, my Auntie Bessie, moved in with her parents-in-law, had the baby, my Uncle John, and was generally, along with Auntie Florrie, treated as my great-grandmother's unpaid servant. Then, years later, in 1941, a young woman got off the bus in Aberdare with two solemn-eyed little boys, my uncles Malcolm and Duncan. She went to my great-grandmother's house, claiming to be the widow of her son Alexander. He hadn't died at all, he'd stayed in the army and gone off to India, where he'd married again without the formality of a divorce from Auntie Bessie.

His second wife, Lillian, was English, had grown up in India and had a little money of her own. She was used to living in a hot country and having servants. My great-grandparents took her in, which some people thought very good of them in the circumstances, but she found living with them very difficult. After a while, she talked to Auntie Bessie, who had a small widow's pension, and they discovered that between the two of them they could afford a tiny house of their own. By the time I was born the scandal was old news—I knew that they were both the widows of the same man, but what could you say? He was dead, after all. The two widows got on very well. They spent the war knitting socks for soldiers, then after the war opened a wool shop in their front room, where they sold wool and home-knitted items. It had a strange animal smell, which they tried to hide with bowls of dried lavender from Auntie Florrie's garden, the first potpourri I ever saw.

My grandfather had three sisters, who all married and had children. One, Auntie Maudie, disgraced herself by marrying a Catholic and going off to live in England, where she had eleven children, the last a Mongol, and adopted four more, two of them African. I do not regard this as shocking, if she could care for them all, which she could. She had been my grandfather's favourite sister, but now they couldn't be together without quarrelling. She was a lot like her mother. I didn't see what was so utterly shocking about being a Catholic, compared to being a bigamist, which everyone forgave dead

Alexander, or a lesbian, like Auntie Olwen, which people didn't talk about but quietly accepted.

Auntie Bronwen had three sons and a daughter, and her husband worked in the pit. Auntie Florrie lived very near us and we saw her all the time—my grandmother used her for babysitting. Her husband, who had been a miner, died in the war. She had two little boys, my Uncle Clem, who went to prison for forgery, and Uncle Sam, who never seemed to come home. She had seen the devil in her house one day and chased it upstairs with a prayer book and shut it in the box room. Afterwards, she asked my grandfather to brick up the door to the box room so the devil couldn't get out. Years later, after she died, he unbricked the door and we went in, consumed with curiosity, to find a printing press. He threw it out, but not before we helped ourselves to a number of blank calling cards and some of the leaden letters.

My grandfather, Luke, was the youngest, and he married my grandmother, Becky, and they had two children, Elizabeth and Tegan. My mother, Liz, married my father and had us. Auntie Teg never married anyone, because she was always busy helping to bring us up. In most ways she was more like a much older sister than an aunt.

I miss her a lot, and Grampar too.

Saturday 6th October 1979

Beautiful day today, best day since I got here.

I got into town before the library closed and tried to join it. They wouldn't let me. I was remarkably restrained and didn't cry or raise my voice or anything. They said they needed a parent's signature, and they needed proof of residence. I told them I was at Arlinghurst, as if they couldn't see that for themselves from the uniform. When outside we have to wear a navy gymslip, a navy blazer, a school raincoat (if raining, but it's always raining, except today the sun was shining) and a school hat. The winter hat is a beret. There's a straw boater for summer. The hat is entirely penitential for me; it always wants to fall off my head when I move.

The librarian, who was a man, quite young, said that if I was at Arlinghurst I should use the school library. I said that I did, and that it was inadequate to my needs. He actually looked at me then, pushing his glasses up his nose, and for a moment I thought I'd won, but no. "You need a parent's signature on this form, and a letter from the school librarian saying you need to have the use of the library," he said. Behind him were all these shelves of books, stretching out. He wouldn't even let me in to browse.

However, I found a bookshop, and a little bit of wild ground. The shopping bit of Oswestry is basically two streets with a market cross at the top, with a market. The library, which is a typical Victorian library building, is just off there. Last time, that's all I saw—the bus stops at the bottom of the hill and the library is essentially the top of it. But there's a road that curves down to the left and I thought it might go around to where the bus stop is. It didn't, and it got very residential and I thought I was going to have to go back, but then there was another curve and a pond, with mallards and white swans on it and trees around, and on the other side of the road, a little parade of shops, and one of them a bookshop.

I bought Samuel Delany's *Triton*. I don't know if my father has it already, I don't care. It was 85p. The lady in the bookshop was really nice. She doesn't read SF, but she tries to keep a good selection. It was nothing to a really good selection like Lears in Cardiff, but it wasn't bad at all. I'm going to ask my father for pocket money so I can buy books. I'm also going to ask him to sign the library form. I'm pretty sure he will. I'm not so sure about Miss Carroll writing a letter.

Next door to the bookshop is a junk shop with three shelves of secondhand books, all of them old and battered. I bought Dodie Smith's *I Capture the Castle* for 10p. I liked her Dalmatians books, especially *The Starlight Barking*, or "Klothes that Klank" as Mor used to call it. I didn't know she'd written any historical fiction. I'll keep it until I'm in the mood for a good siege.

That left me with 5p. There wasn't anything there for 5p. The third little shop in the row is a bakery and cafe. I went in, because Sharon had asked me to buy buns. Now this is a thing people do. The way it works is that you buy the buns yourself, or get someone to buy them for you. Then you give the bag to the kitchen staff with instructions, and they get sent to the designated recipients after lunch on Sunday. The rule is you have to buy at least two, you can't just buy for yourself. Popular girls have whole piles of different buns every week. Usually I don't have any. Deirdre doesn't have much money, and Sharon's Jewish. But Sharon's doing it this week, because she's nice. I mean, it's especially nice of Sharon to do it because she can't even eat them. Jewish people have to have special food. Sharon's special food seems much nicer than our school food. It comes on trays. I wonder if they'd give it to me if I told them I was Jewish? But what if I'm not Jewish enough and it killed me or made me sick? I should talk to Sharon about it before trying it. Anyway, Sharon wanted me to buy buns for me and Deirdre and Karen, who's her other friend. So I bought buns, and they were 10p each or four for 35p, so I bought four, using my own fivepence. They were honey buns, and they were still warm from the oven and I walked over by the pond and ate one. It was absolutely delicious.

There's a bench by the pond, and grass growing around it, and willows by the water, dipping down over it. The leaves on the trailing branches are turning yellow. I always think weeping willows is a good name for them, but then so is "sally willows." Willows love water and alders hate water. There's a road over Croggin Bog called Heol y Gwern, the Alder Road, because people planted alders along it to make a safe dry path. Neolithic people, they think. Certainly it was there before the Romans. It was a shock, reading the history of the valley. When I go back, I don't know if I'll be able to take it for granted the same way.

I sat on the bench by the willows and ate my honey bun and read *Triton*. There are some awful things in the world, it's true, but there are also some great books. When I grow up I would like to write something that someone could read sitting on a bench on a day that isn't all that warm and they could sit reading it and totally forget where they were or what time it was so that they were more inside the book than inside their own head. I'd like to write like Delany or Heinlein or Le Guin.

I only just caught the bus back to school. I could see it at the bottom of the hill, and I wanted to run to catch it, I remember how it feels to run full pelt, and I wanted to do that, to lean down and just take great running strides. I almost did take one step like that, but when I put my weight on my leg wrong it feels like being stabbed. The bus driver saw me coming and recognised the uniform and waited. Lots of other girls from the school were on the bus, most of them from other forms. They nearly all know, or think they know, that I walk with a stick because my mother sticks voodoo pins into a doll. I got a seat to myself, but then Gill Scofield, who's in my chemistry class, came and sat by me.

"What have you been doing to make you late?" she asked.

"Reading," I told her. "I forgot the time."

"Not meeting boys?"

"No!"

"Don't sound so shocked, that's what half the other girls on this bus have been doing. More than half. Look at them." I look. Lots of them have the skirts of their gym slips folded down, and their lips are suspiciously red.

"That's so tacky," I said.

Gill laughed. "I want to be a scientist," she confided.

"A scientist?"

"Yes. A real one. I was reading the other day about Lavoisier. You know?"

"He discovered oxygen," I said. "With Priestley."

"Well, and he was French. He was an aristocrat, a marquis. He was guillotined in the French Revolution, and he said he'd keep blinking his eyes after his head was off, for as long as he had consciousness. He blinked seventeen times. That's a scientist," Gill said.

She's weird. But I like her.

Sunday 7th October 1979

Finished *Triton*. It's amazing. But the more I think about it the less I understand why Bron lied to Audri.

I used today's letter writing time to send a "Good Luck" note to cousin Arwel Parry and a congratulations note to Uncle Rhodri.

Why *did* Bron lie to Audri?

Monday 8th October 1979

On the one hand, Gramma and Grampar never mentioned sex at all. They must have done it, or they wouldn't have had Auntie Teg and my mother, but I don't think they did it more than twice. Then there's the way they talk about sex in school and in church. And there's no sex, hardly any love stuff at all, in Middle Earth, which always made me think yes, the world would be better off without it. Arwen's just a sop to propriety. Or just a vessel for future half-elven High Kings of Gondor and Arnor. A prize. It would have been better for him to have married Eowyn—who was a hero, after all, in her own right— and just let the Numenoreans dwindle. (After all, look at us now!) So sex, necessary evil to produce children. That's normal.

And when you look at those girls on the bus, and my mother and her boyfriends, and the girls who creep into each other's beds at night and, well, *ach y fi*.

But on the other hand, I do have sexual feelings. And *Triton*, and Heinlein, and *The Charioteer* have made me think that actually sex itself is neutral, and it's society demonizing it that makes it icky. And the whole sex-change thing in *Triton*, there must be a sort of spectrum of sexuality, with most people somewhere in the middle, drawn to men and women, and some off on the ends—me at one end and Ralph and Laurie at the other. One of the things I've always liked about science fiction is the way it makes you think about things, and look at things from angles you'd never have thought about before.

From now on, I'm going to be positive about sex.

Wednesday 10th October 1979

If the school was going out of their way to try to detach us from magic, they couldn't organise things better. I wonder if that was someone's original intention. I'm sure nobody here now knows a thing about it, but Arlinghurst has been running like this for more than a hundred years.

We do no cooking, we're completely cut off from the food we eat, and the food is incredibly awful. Yesterday, for instance, dinner was spam fritters, totally tasteless mashed potatoes, over-boiled cabbage. For pudding, we had a dish of set custard with a half walnut in the middle, between six people. That's called Hawaiian Delight. There's a similar one we have at least once a week called Hawaiian Surprise, which is set custard with a half glace cherry. I don't like glace cherries or walnuts, so I'm marginally popular for a moment whenever it's served for not joining in the squabble over who gets it. I don't like custard either, but sometimes I'm hungry enough to eat it. You couldn't get worse food, or food more detached from nature, if you tried. If you have an apple, you're connected to an apple tree. If you have a dish of set custard and half a glace cherry you're not connected to anything.

Still on the subject of eating, we don't have our own plates, or our own knives and forks or cups. Like most of what we use, they're communal, they're handed out at random. There's no chance for anything to become imbued, to come alive through fondness. Nothing here is aware, no chair, no cup. Nobody can get fond of anything.

At home I walked through a haze of belongings that knew, at least vaguely, who they belonged to. Grampar's chair resented anyone else sitting on it as much as he did himself. Gramma's shirts and jumpers adjusted themselves to hide her missing breast. My mother's shoes positively vibrated with consciousness. Our toys looked out for us. There was a potato knife in the kitchen that Gramma couldn't use. It was an ordinary enough brown-handled thing, but she'd cut herself with it once, and ever after it wanted more of her blood. If I rummaged through the kitchen drawer, I could feel it brooding. After she died, that faded. Then there were the coffee spoons, rarely used, tiny, a wedding present. They were made of silver, and they knew themselves superior to everything else and special.

None of these things did anything. The coffee spoons didn't stir the coffee without being held or anything. They didn't have conversations with the sugar tongs about who was the most cherished. (We always felt they might at any moment.) I suppose what they really did was psychological. They confirmed the past, they connected everything, they were threads in a tapestry. Here there is no tapestry, we jangle about separately.

Another letter. I haven't opened it. I really notice it though, because of this stuff. It's pulsing with significance—malign significance, but significance all the same. Everything else is muted around it.

Thursday 11th October 1979

Miss Carroll agreed to write a library letter without any hesitation. "I saw you were reduced to reading Arthur Ransome," she said.

Actually, I like Arthur Ransome. I wouldn't call it reduced. I've read them all before, of course, years ago, but I've been enjoying them. There's something nice about out-and-out children's books with no sex and a happy ending—Ransome, Streatfeild, that kind of thing. It isn't very challenging, and you know what you're getting, but what you're getting is a nice wholesome story about children messing about in boats, or learning ballet or whatever, and they'll have minor triumphs and minor disasters and everything will work out fine in the end. It's cheering, especially after reading Chekhov yesterday. I'm so glad I'm not Russian.

Still, anything that'll get me closer to a library ticket, so I just smiled. If only *he*'d send the form back, I could get one this weekend. I shouldn't call him "he" that way. But it's difficult to know what to call him. What do you call your father when you've only just met him? "Dad" would be ridiculous. But though it's his name, it feels a bit odd to call him Daniel.

Friday 12th October 1979

The letter from my father came first post, with ten pounds (!) and the form, signed. He says the money is to buy books, but I'm also going to buy some buns.

I had a talk with Sharon about Jewish food. She says it's what God told them to eat, or not to eat, and it's special but it wouldn't harm anyone else. She says the trays she gets are nice. She gets lots of roast beef and fish, and it's well cooked but always cold, because it can't even be heated up with our food. She says the bread she gets is lovely, but always slightly stale because it comes all the way from Manchester. It seems like being Jewish is a lot of trouble, and I'd hate not being able to spend money on Saturdays, especially when it's the only time we're allowed out. But it might be worth it.

It was hard to get her to talk about it. She's been teased about it a lot, and also she uses it as a kind of thing for other people to be afraid of, so she quite sensibly doesn't want people to know too much. I had to tell her about my father's Jewish father. She says that doesn't make me Jewish at all, you can't be part Jewish, and you get it through your mother. She says if I wanted to be Jewish, I'd have to convert.

I remember when a missionary came to Church and told us about converting the heathen. He said some of them pretended to convert for the free food, and then changed back to their old heathen gods as soon as there was some crisis. He called them "rice Christians." I suppose I could be a rice Jew.

On the other hand, Grampar would have an absolute fit if he found out. My mother would be sure to tell him in the hope of making him have another stroke.

Saturday 13th October 1979

The weather has changed completely in the last week. Last Saturday was mild and sunny, autumn looking reluctantly back over its shoulder towards summer. Today it was wet and blustery, autumn barrelling forward impatiently into winter. The ground was slippery with dead leaves. Oswestry looked even less appealing than ever. Now Gill has pointed it out to me, I noticed the girls on the bus passing around a forbidden lipstick and giggling. They remind me of Susan in *The Last Battle*. I went off into a daydream about meeting C. S. Lewis, though I know he's dead. Much too embarrassing to recount.

I went to the library, armed with my letter and my signed form, and was greeted by a friendly cheerful female librarian who I'm sure would have let me join without them. She hardly looked at them. I now have a little nested set of eight cards which will let me take out eight books at any time—or in fact, on any Saturday morning I can get into town before noon. Also, she told me that if I need anything they don't have, interlibrary loans are free to people under sixteen. So I could order whatever I wanted to read and they'd get it for me. I only have to know author and title. So I started with all the Mary Renault books listed in *The Charioteer* that I've never heard of. I'm going to make a list of books listed in the front of other books and take it in next week. She said they can get anything published in Britain, ever, it doesn't matter about out of print. She said they'd send me a card, but I said it was all right, they could save the stamp money to buy books, and I'd just come in every week and collect whatever they had.

Interlibrary loans are a wonder of the world and a glory of civilisation.

Libraries really are wonderful. They're better than bookshops, even. I mean bookshops make a profit on selling you books, but libraries just sit there lending you books quietly out of the goodness of their hearts.

I then spent a happy hour among the stacks, which are like the school library in that they contain a few gems, but only a few. Also, the SF is shelved in with everything else, which makes things slower. With eight books weighing me down and rain slashing in my face, I considered going straight back to school and reading them in my own comfortable library. But I wanted to check the bookshop, and eight books sounds (and feels!) like a lot, but it isn't as if they'll last me all week. I normally read now in the early morning if I wake before the bell, for the three hours of compulsory games, during any boring classes, in prep after I've finished my prep, in the half-hour free time after prep, and for the half hour we're allowed in bed before lights out. So I'm getting through a couple of books most days.

So I walked slowly down the hill to the bookshop. The wind was whipping the willow branches out across the water. Most of the yellow leaves were down and floating on the surface. There was no sign of the swans. But I could see that beyond the pond there were more trees.

I bought a couple of things. I wish I knew how long this ten pounds is supposed to last. Most books are 75p, with thick ones being more. I left a lot of books when I ran away. I could replace them, but I also want new things to read. Re-reading's all very well. I bought a new Tiptree collection. This one has an introduction by Le Guin, so she must like him too! It's lovely when writers I like like each other. Maybe they're friends, like Tolkien and Lewis. The bookshop has a new biography of all the Inklings, by Humphrey Carpenter who wrote the Tolkien biography. It's in hardcover. I shall order it from the library.

After the bookshop, I checked out the shelves in the junk shop and bought a couple of things there too. I had so many books I could hardly walk at this point, and of course my leg was terrible. It always is when it rains. I didn't ask to have my good leg replaced by a creaky rusty weathervane, but then I suppose nobody does. I would have made much greater sacrifices. I was prepared to die, and Mor *did* die. I should think of it as a war-wound, an old soldier's scars. Frodo lost a finger, and all his own possibility of happiness. Tolkien understood about the things that happen after the end. Because this is after the end, this is all the Scouring of the Shire, this is figuring out how to live in the time that wasn't supposed to happen after the glorious last stand. I saved the world, or I think I did, and look, the world is still here, with sunsets and interlibrary loans. And it doesn't care about me any more than the Shire cared about Frodo. But that doesn't matter. My mother isn't a dark queen who everyone loves and despairs. She's alive, all right, but she's trapped in the nets of her own malice like a spider caught in its own web. I got away from her. And she can't ever hurt Mor now.

I went into the bakery and sat down on one of the tables by the window and ate a Cornish pasty and a honey bun and played with a pot of tea. I don't like tea, and coffee is worse, it smells fine but it tastes disgusting. In fact I only drink water, though if I absolutely have to have something I can drink lemonade. I prefer water. But a pot of tea is fiddly and nobody can tell if you've finished it, especially if you haven't drunk any, and it gives you an excuse to sit and read and rest for a while.

So I did that, and then I bought four honey buns to go, with my own money this time. One for Deirdre, one for Sharon, though of course she won't be able to eat it so I'll get that one too, one for me, and one for Gill. Last week I had Sharon's bun, and this week she'll have mine. It's more for the symbol than the actual bun, though goodness knows the actual buns are nice. I'm not buying one for Karen, because Karen calls me Hopalong, which I hate more than any of the other names. Commie's almost affectionate, and Taffy's inevitable, but using Crip or especially Hopalong means hostility.

Then I asked the bakery girl about the pond. "Is it a park?"

"A park, love? No, it's the edge of the estate."

"But there's a bench by the pond. A park bench."

"Council put that there for people to sit, like. By the road, that belongs to the council, so I suppose it might be a park, but not a proper park with flowers. But what you see behind, those trees and that, that's part of the estate, and you'd find a No Trespassing sign before long, reckon, because there are pheasants. We hear them banging away over there in August."

So it's an estate with a country house, managed and with game keepers and things, but left half-wild for the pheasants. I bet there are fairies all over it.

Sunday 14th October 1979

I got a telling-off after lunch, and an Order Mark, my first. Apparently it's not done to give buns to girls not in your house or form, unless they're a relation. And Gill, while she is in my chemistry class, isn't in my house or form, so I'm not supposed to be friendly with her, and my giving her a bun is considered deeply suspicious, and possibly lesbian. I think from the way some of this got said that Gill may well be a lesbian. Fine. I have no problem with that. I'm not one, but I'm definitely with Heinlein and Delany on this.

Even Deirdre and Sharon thought I shouldn't have given Gill the bun. Deirdre tried to make excuses for me, saying I didn't understand because I hadn't been here long enough, and maybe all the chemistry had addled my brain.

I will never understand this place.

Monday 15th October 1979

I didn't write back again. But she keeps on writing to me and sending photographs like that. I get one or two every week. I am so desperate for the glimpses of Mor that I keep opening the letters, and I can never quite not read them. I save them until I am in the library, because I can't bear everyone to see me reading them. Then today Lorraine Pargeter had a bad cold and came into the library and saw me looking at one of the cut-out photographs. Lorraine is a big-boned blonde stupid girl, captain of the form hockey team and a fly half for the house one. She's certainly called me names and pinched me, but she stopped the others trying to trip me coming out of the showers, so I don't feel especially antagonistic to her. Today her nose is very red and she looks truly miserable not to be out on her favourite games pitch. I heard her asking the teacher if she could wrap up and go out and watch.

"What's that, Morwenna?" she asked. I didn't want her to know I cared, which she would if I hid it, so I flicked it across the table to her. She picked it up and looked at it. It was a picture of the two of us getting prizes at school speech day, except with me burned out, as usual.

"My mother's a witch," I said, casually.

Lorraine gasped, and dropped the picture. "Is it voodoo?" she whispered.

I have been wondering that myself. I don't know how these things work, and well, you just try looking it up. What does it mean to burn someone out of a picture? What could it do? What consequences could it have? I reached for my wooden charm, but of course it isn't there, I can't wear it with my uniform. I have a rock in my pocket and I reached for that. I don't know if it helps, but it certainly is comforting. I touched the wooden library desk, which has been smoothed by time and hundreds of hands.

"Sort of," I said, quietly. "She burns me out, but I seem to be all right."

"But you're right there," Lorraine objected, loudly enough that Miss Carroll glanced over at us.

Lorraine, naturally, doesn't know about Mor. I haven't mentioned her because firstly it's personal, secondly I can't stand sympathy, and thirdly I can't stand teasing about it even more. People teasing me about Mor could cause me to lose my temper with them. "Oh, really?" I said, and reached for the picture. "I hadn't looked at that one yet. Usually it's me she burns. But I'm protected. It would be awful if she started going after my friends."

Lorraine gasped and moved away from me to sit on the other side of the library, pretending to read *Gone with the Wind*. For the rest of today, "Let them fear me as long as they obey me" has been working even better than normal, but Deirdre and Sharon have been keeping their distance too, which is going to get awfully lonely.

Tuesday 16th October 1979

You know, class is like magic. There's nothing there you can point to, it evaporates if you try to analyse it, but it's real and it affects how people behave and makes things happen.

Sharon probably has more money than any of the other girls in our form. We're the Lower Fifth, which is so meaningless in any normal context that it makes me cross to think about it. They start counting at "Upper Third." In theory, there exists some platonic Lower School that starts at First, with seven-year-olds. In fact, there's no such thing, and I deduce it only from the existence of these ridiculous numbers. By the time they get to the sixth, lower and upper, they're on the same system as the rest of the world that goes from one to four in Junior School and one to six in Secondary School. Arlinghurst is, you notice, running from one to six like an ordinary Secondary School, just counting stupidly.

We're specifically Lower VC. There's an A and a B too, but we're not streamed, heaven help us, that would be wrong. Only in fact we are, because Gill and the whole chemistry group is A, and they are definitely brighter. I should be in A on my marks, but they don't move people except at the end of term. Miss Carroll, the librarian, has told me they have said I would be moved to A at Christmas, except for having upset the timetable, which means I'll stay where I am with the dunces until next September. She said this as if I'd learn a valuable lesson about keeping my place, but I'm glad I fought for chemistry. I wish I'd held out for biology as well.

The house system is separate from the forms. The forms run horizontally, the house systems run vertically. Girls from all three forms in each year are in all four houses. The houses compete with each other for cups—perfectly real silver cups that are kept in the Hall. The houses are called after Victorian poets. I'm in Scott. The others are Keats, Tennyson and Wordsworth. No Shelley and no Byron, I suppose because they have faintly disreputable auras. Gramma was fond of all of those poets except, ironically, Scott. The form system controls lessons, and the house system everything else—games particularly, but also the system of points gained or lost for behaviour. We're supposed to care intensely about our houses and their relative standing, and look out for other people in our houses, whatever their form. Needless to say, I do not give a damn about this. It's a granfalloon in the purest sense, and I am enduringly grateful to Vonnegut for giving me the word.

Anyway, I was trying to talk about class. In Lower VC, which are the only girls I know well, Sharon's family have the most money. She goes on foreign holidays more often than most girls, her father is a surgeon, they have a big house and a big car. But classwise, she rates quite low, because she's Jewish and that makes her different, and because of the other intangible class thing that's like magic. She doesn't have a pony, though they could easily afford one. They have a swimming pool, but not a pony, because her parents' priorities are different. She goes skiing at Christmas, but she goes to Norway, because her parents won't go to Germany or Switzerland.

Julie's parents don't have much money at all. Her uniforms were her sister's. They have an old car. But her sister is Head Girl, and her mother was a prefect, and won a tennis cup for Wordsworth, which is her house too. They put Julie in Wordsworth because her mother and her aunts and her sister were in Wordsworth. There's an old black-and-white photograph of Julie's mother and the cup in the Games Room. And the label under that picture says "The Hon. Monica Wentworth," because Julie's mother's father is a viscount. Julie isn't an Hon., but she scores higher classwise than anybody else because her mother is. It's not just that, it's the combination of the Hon. and the cup and the school tradition. And Julie's not all that clever, but she's good at games, which is a lot more important.

There's a fat giggly girl in the Upper Fourth who's Lady Sarah. Her father is an earl. I think Julie would defer to her opinion, but I'm not

sure. Class isn't pure snobbery, it's lots of things. But everyone cares
about it madly. One of the first questions they asked me was about
what kind of car my father has. "A black one" didn't go down too
well. They couldn't believe I didn't know. I didn't say I'd only seen it a
couple of times and I didn't like cars much anyway. It turns out it's a
Bentley—I wrote and asked—which is an acceptable kind of car. But
why do they care? They want to be able to place everyone very precisely. Of course, they quickly saw that I came nowhere—no pony,
no title, and Welsh. I got points for the kind of house my father lives
in—it's fathers they're interested in. Some of the girls have divorced
parents—poor Deirdre does, for instance—but even if they live with
their mother, it's the father that counts.

Class is entirely intangible, and the way it affects things isn't subject
to scientific analysis, and it's not supposed to be real but it's pervasive and powerful. See; just like magic.

Wednesday 17th October 1979

When I am grown up and famous, I will never admit to having
attended Arlinghurst. I'll pretend never to have heard of it. When
people ask where I was educated, I'll leave it out.

There are other people like me out there. There is a karass. I know
there is, there can be.

Thursday 18th October 1979

This school is enough to make anyone a communist.

I read *The Communist Manifesto* today—it's very short. It would
be like living on Anarres. I'll take that over this any day.

Friday 19th October 1979

I loved Mor, but I never appreciated her enough. I never really understood how wonderful it was to always have someone to talk to who would know what you were talking about, and someone to play with who understood the kind of things I wanted to play.

Only one more week of school before half term.

Saturday 20th October 1979

Blessed interlibrary loan. They've found *Purposes of Love* and *The Last of the Wine* for me!

I took back last weeks's eight books. I also got out five other things by authors I know and *The Magus*. I've never heard of the author (Fowles) but hey, a book about a wizard!

I ordered twenty-eight books, from lists on title pages. The librarian, the man, looked a little taken aback, but didn't make a fuss about it.

It was raining stair-rods, and almost all the leaves are off the trees. I went to the bakery cafe again, because the other girls don't go there and they're all over the proper cafes in town. Afterwards I walked over to look at the water and the swan hissed at me. My shoes were sinking into the mud at the edge, but I went on under the trees, looking for fairies. There were one or two, but hard to see, and not inclined for conversation, which is a pity, because apart from a letter from my father I haven't had any at all this week.

Sunday 21st October 1979

James Tiptree, Jr. is a woman! Gosh!

I never would have guessed though. My goodness, Robert Silverberg must have egg all over his face. But I bet he doesn't care. (If I'd written *Dying Inside* I wouldn't mind how much of a fool of myself I made about anything ever again. It might be the most depressing book in the world, I mean it's right up there with Hardy and Aeschylus, but it's also just so brilliant.) And the Tiptree stories are good, too, though none of them quite up to "The Girl Who Was Plugged In." I suppose I can see doing that so as to get respect, but Le Guin didn't, and she got the respect. She won the Hugo. I think in a way Tiptree was taking the easy option. But think how fond her characters are of misdirection and disguise; maybe she is too? I suppose all writers use characters as masks, and she was using the male name as another layer. Come to that, if I was writing "Love Is the Plan, the Plan Is Death" I might not want people to know where I lived either.

I was the only person not to get a bun today, not that I care. Even Deirdre got one from Karen. Deirdre looks at me in a strange puzzled way, which is actually worse than anything. I understand Tiberius' reliance on Sejanus much better now. I also understand how he became peculiar. Being left alone—and I am being left alone—isn't quite as much what I wanted as I thought. Is this how people become evil? I don't want to be.

I wrote to Auntie Teg, trying to sound cheerful. I also wrote to my father, hoping I might persuade him to take me to see her, maybe, and see Grampar in hospital. They're the only people I have left now. *He* wouldn't want to see them, but I could and he could wait in the car. It would be really nice to see some people who like me. Five more days to half term and getting out of this place for a week.

Monday 22nd October 1979

In chemistry today, Gill came and sat by me. It was very brave of her, actually, considering how everyone has been behaving. "So you don't think I'm a voodoo leper?" I asked straight out at the end of class.

"I'm a scientist," she said. "I don't believe in any of that. And I know you got in trouble for sending me a bun."

It was lunchtime, so we went to the dining hall together. I don't care what people think. She says she doesn't read fiction much at all, but she'll lend me a book of Asimov's science essays called *The Left Hand of the Electron*. She has three brothers, all older. The oldest one is at Oxford. They're all scientists too. I like her. She's restful.

The Magus is very weird. I'm not sure whether I like it, but I can't wait to get back to it and I keep thinking about it all the time. It's not about magic, not really, but the atmosphere is just like. It's an odd thing to read, because he's always walking for miles across the thyme-scented island, like we used to do. We'd think nothing of walking miles on the dramroads, up to Llwydcoed, or to Cwmdare. We'd usually get a bus to Penderyn, but once we were there we'd walk out across the tops for hours. I loved the views from up there. We'd lie down on the grass and stare up to see the skylarks, and we'd pick up bits of wool the sheep had dropped and card them and give them to the fairies.

Tuesday 23rd October 1979

Leg very bad today. I have days when I can sort of walk, and then other days. I suppose I could say days when stairs are bad and days when stairs are torture. Today is definitely one of the second kind. I got another letter, dammit. I need to burn them or something. They're so malign they almost glow with it. I can see them out of the corner of my eye, though it might just be the pain doing odd things to me. Friday is half term. My father's going to pick me up at six. He didn't say where we're going, but it'll be away from here. I can't take the letters, though of course I can't leave them either.

I'm not at all sure about the end of *The Magus*. It's even more ambiguous than *Triton*. Who would write the last two lines in Latin, which almost nobody can read? It's a library book, but I have lightly pencilled in the translation over the page:

> Tomorrow shall be love for the loveless, and for the lover, love.

So Alison will love him, I suppose, for whatever that's worth. It wasn't enough before. He only really wanted her when he thought she was dead.

In the last part of the book, back in London, when Nicholas wants back into the mystery, whatever it is, is just how I don't want to be. I should never have tried to talk to that fairy. Let someone else do something about Dutch elm disease. It isn't my problem. I have finished with saving the world, and I never expected it to be the slightest bit grateful anyway. I've got this stupid boring one-note pain droning on at me, and I understand Nicholas only too well there, because who wouldn't want that? But also, I don't want to be pathetic like him.

Thursday 25th October 1979

It wasn't raining, for the first time in ages, and my leg was feeling a bit better, so I went out in the half hour after prep. I went down to the edge of the playing field by the ditch, where I saw the fairy before, and made a bonfire out of all the letters. It was almost dark, and it burned up very brightly at once, with only one match. I suppose it might have been the photograph paper, because she'd burned part before so it longed for fire. "Oft evil will doth evil mar," as Gandalf put it. Oft, not always. You can't rely on it, but it does seem to happen quite often.

I felt much better once they were on fire. A few fairies came out and danced around the flames, the way they always do. We used to call them salamanders, and igneids. They're an amazing colour, where blue flicks over and becomes orange. Most of them were acting as if they couldn't see me, or I couldn't see them, but one of them was looking at me, kind of sideways. She turned the yellow of the spots on the elm bark when she saw me looking, so I knew she knew what I'd asked before. "What can I do?" I asked, pathetic, despite what I said yesterday about Nicholas.

They all vanished when I spoke, but they came back after a moment. They're not quite like our home fairies. Maybe it comes of not having ruins to live in. Fairies always seem to prefer places the wild has crept back into. We did Enclosure in history recently. The whole country used to have shared wild common places—like Common Ake, I suppose, where the peasants could graze their animals and gather wood and pick blackberries. They didn't belong to anyone in particular, but to everyone. I bet they were full of fairies. Then the landlords got the people to agree to enclose them and make them into proper tidy farms, and they didn't realise how squeezed they'd be without the commons until the commons were gone. The countryside is supposed to have those veins of wild running through it, and without them it suffers. This countryside is deader than cities in some ways. The ditch and the trees are only there because this is a school, and the trees by the bookshop are the edge of an estate.

The fairies didn't speak to me, not even a few words like the one on the tree. But the yellow one kept looking at me, cautiously, so I knew she had understood. Or rather I knew she had understood *something.* I can't be sure what. Fairies are like that. Even the ones we knew well, the ones we'd given names and who talked to us all the time, could be odd like that sometimes.

Then they all vanished again, and the papers were going to ash—they burned fast, being paper—and Ruth Campbell caught me and gave me ten order marks for starting a fire. Ten! It takes three house marks to cancel out one order mark, which is unfair to begin with if you ask me. But over this whole term so far, I've earned forty house marks, for coming top or for excellence in marks. And I've had eleven order marks, so that's the equivalent of cancelling out thirty-three of them. It's a stupid system and I don't care about it, but *honestly* does that seem fair by any measure?

The oddest thing is that Ruth was more upset about it than I was. She's a prefect, and she's Scott, so in giving me ten order marks she was hurting her own house, and she cares about it much more than I do. If you have ten order marks you get gated the next Saturday and can't go to town, but as this week is half term that doesn't count. I'd be all right anyway, as I have enough house marks to cancel out, but I'd better make sure that I don't get caught like that again.

Oh, and I couldn't have burned the school down. It was a tiny fire, under control, and I've been making little fires for years. I knew what I was doing. Even if I hadn't, I was a long way from any buildings, the ground is waterlogged from all the rain, and the ditch is full of water. There were also a lot of wet leaves I could have scuffed over it if there had been the slightest danger, which there wasn't. I accepted the order marks, because I definitely didn't want the matter to be passed on to a teacher. Better to keep them out of it. Ruth also confiscated my matches.

It's a great relief the letters are destroyed. I feel lighter altogether without them being there.

Friday 26th October 1979

All day in school there was an almost tangible sense of suppressed excitement. Everybody wants to get away. They were all talking about their plans for the week, showing off. Sharon got to leave this morning, lucky pup, because another thing Jews can't do is travel on Friday nights or Saturdays. What happens if they do? It's like having a pile of geasas.

A few girls got picked up straight from afternoon school. The others were watching out of the library windows to see what kind of cars they had and what their mothers—mostly mothers—were wearing. Deirdre got picked up by her older sister in a white mini. I don't suppose she'll ever live it down. The thing mothers are supposed to wear, it seems, is a Burberry with a silk headscarf. A Burberry is an upmarket brand of mackintosh.

Nobody asked me what my mother wears, because nobody is speaking to me. But it's just as well. She wears every third thing in her wardrobe, and she cycles her clothes through it in some strange order only she understands. I don't know if she does this because it's magical or if she does it because she's mad. It's very hard to tell the difference. Sometimes she looks an absolute guy, and other times she looks perfectly normal. The normal times do usually seem to coincide with times when it would be useful—she looked demure and respectable in court, for instance, the last time I saw her. A long time ago when she kept the nursery school she always looked reasonable for a teacher—but Gramma was still alive then, and could keep her in check. But I've seen her wear her wedding dress to go shopping, and a winter coat in July, and be barely covered in January. Her hair is long and black and even combed and tamed it looks like a nest of snakes. If she wore a burberry and a silk scarf it would look like a disguise, a cloth dragged over an altar where something had been sacrificed.

My father arrived in a rush of parents, and nobody remarked about him to me. He looked like himself. I was back to glancing at him sideways I'm afraid. I don't know why, it's absurd really when we've been writing to each other like human beings all this time. He drove me back to the Old Hall.

"We'll stay there tonight, then tomorrow I'll take you to meet my father," he said. The headlights lit the road far ahead. I could see rabbits bounding out of the way, and the skeleton tracery of branches illuminated for an instant and then dropping back into dark. "We'll stay in a hotel. Have you done that before?"

"Every summer," I said. "We'd go down to Pembrokeshire and stay in a hotel for two weeks. It was the same one every year." I felt my voice thicken with a sob at the back of my throat thinking about it. It had been such fun. Grampar would drive us to different beaches, and to castles and standing stones. Gramma would tell us the history. She was a teacher, all my family were, though I was determined I wouldn't be. She loved the holidays, when she didn't have to cook, when she and Auntie Teg could relax and laugh together. Sometimes my mother came, and sat in cafes smoking and eating peculiar things. It was better on the years she didn't come, obviously. But she was much more avoidable in Pembrokeshire, and smaller somehow. Mor and I had our own special games, and there would always be other children staying in the hotel who we'd organise into our games and into putting on an entertainment for the parents.

"Was the food good?" he asked.

"Wonderful," I said. "We'd have special things like melon, and mackerel." Delicious things we never had at home.

"Well, the food will be good where we're going, too," he said. "How's the school food?"

"Appalling," I said, and made him laugh with my description of it. "Is there any chance I could get down to South Wales?"

"I can't take you down as you suggested. But if you want to go on the train for a couple of days, that would be all right."

I wasn't sure, because on the train I'd be trapped there and she was there, after all, and if she physically grabbed me I didn't know what I'd do. But probably she wouldn't come near me. She wouldn't know. I wouldn't do anything magic.

At the Old Hall, when we finally got there, the aunts were all sitting in the drawing room. It's not a room where people draw, with easels, it's short for "withdrawing room," where people withdrew for quiet conversation. They were hardly talking though. I kissed them, then a stop at Daniel's bookshelves, and retired to bed with *The End of Eternity*.

Saturday 27th October 1979

I had no idea London was so big. It goes on for *ever*. It sort of creeps up on you and before you know it, it's everywhere. There are outlying bits, with gaps in between, and then it gets just more and more built up.

My father's father's name is Sam. He has a funny accent. I wonder if they call him Commie? He lives in a bit of London called Mile End, and he wears a skullcap but doesn't look the slightest bit Jewish otherwise. His hair—and he still has a lot of it, even though he's old—is all white. He wears an embroidered waistcoat, very beautiful but a bit threadbare. He's awfully old.

All the way in the car, my father and I had been talking about books. He hadn't mentioned Sam except to say that's where we were going. I was more thinking about the hotel and about London, so it was almost a surprise when he got there. My father tootled the horn in a pattern, and the door opened and out Sam came. My father introduced us on the pavement, and he hugged me, and hugged my father too. I was a little alarmed at first, because he really isn't at all like anyone I know, and not the faintest bit like Grampar. With my father and his sisters it's quite easy to keep them at arm's length, and even to keep thinking about them at arm's length somehow, because they're English, I suppose. But Sam isn't English, not at all, and he just instantly seemed to accept me, whereas with them I always feel horribly on probation.

Sam took us in, and introduced me to his landlady as his granddaughter, and she said she saw the resemblance. "Morwenna favours my family," he said, as if he'd known me for years. "Look at the colouring. She looks like my sister Rivka, *zichrona livracha*."

I looked blank, and he translated, "May her memory be a blessing." I like that. That's a nice way to say that somebody's dead that doesn't stop the conversation. I asked him how to spell it and what language it was. It's Hebrew. Jewish people always pray in Hebrew, Sam says. Maybe one day I'll be able to say "My sister Mor, *zichrona livracha*," just normally like that.

Then he took us up into his little room. It must be odd to live upstairs in someone else's house. I can tell he doesn't have any money. I'd know even if I didn't know. The room has a bed and a sink and one chair, and books all piled up everywhere. There's a dresser, all piled with books, with a kind of electric samovar and glasses. There's a cat, too, a big fat ginger-and-white cat called Chairman Mao, or maybe Chairman Miaow. She took up half the bed, but when I sat down on it, perched on the edge, she came and sat on my lap. Sam said—he said I should call him Sam—that meant she liked me, and she didn't like many people. I stroked her, carefully, and she didn't scratch me after a minute the way Auntie Teg's Persimmon always does. She curled up and went to sleep.

Sam made tea, for him and me. My father had whisky. (He drinks an awful lot. He's gone down to the hotel bar now, drinking. He smokes a lot too. It would be unkind to say he has all the vices, in the circumstances, as he did help me get away and he is paying for me to go to school. It's not as if he wanted me.) The tea came in glasses with metal holders, and didn't have milk or sugar, which made it a lot nicer. It had a pleasant sort of flavour. I was surprised, because I don't usually like tea at all and I was only drinking it to be polite. He got the water from the electric samovar, which he said kept the water at the right temperature.

After a little while, I was looking at the books, and I saw *The Communist Manifesto* on top of one of the piles. I must have made a little noise, because they both looked at me. "I just noticed you have *The Communist Manifesto*," I said.

Sam laughed. "My good friend Dr. Schechter lent me that."

"I was reading it recently myself," I said.

He laughed again. "It's a lovely dream, but it would never work. Look at what's happening in Russia now, or Poland. Marx is like Plato, he has dreams that can't come true as long as people are people. That's what Dr. Schechter can't understand."

"I've been reading about Plato too," I said, because he's in *The Last of the Wine* of course, and Socrates too.

"Reading about Plato?" Sam said. "How about reading Plato?"

I shook my head.

"You should read him, but always keep arguing with him," he said. "Now, I must have some Plato in English somewhere." Then he started moving piles of books, with my father helping him. I would have helped too, but I couldn't move with Chairman Miaow asleep on my knees. He had Plato in Greek, and Polish, and German, and I realised as he muttered his way through the piles that he could read all those languages, as well as Hebrew, and that even though his English was funny and quite strongly accented and he lived in this little rented room, he was an educated man. Seeing my father help him go through the piles, I saw that they were fond of each other, though they didn't do much to show it. "Ah, here," he said. "*The Symposium*, in English, and a good place to start."

It was a slim black Penguin Classics volume. "If I like it I can order more from the library," I said.

"You do that. Don't be like Daniel here, always reading stories and no time for anything real. I'm the opposite. I have no time for stories."

"I have a friend in school who's the same," I said. "She reads science essays for fun."

It turned out that Sam has read some of Asimov's science essays, and also owns a book he wrote about the Bible! "It's a Jewish Atheist book about the Bible, so of course I own it," he said.

When it got dark, my father bustled up and insisted he'd take us out to eat. We went to a place quite near by, where we ate little pancakes called blinis with smoked salmon and cream cheese, which was absolutely delicious, perhaps the most delicious thing I've ever had. Then we had lovely dumplings with cheese and potato in them, which would have been the nicest thing I'd had for months if they hadn't come after that lovely salty salmon, and then another sort of pancakes with jam inside. Everyone there knew Sam, and kept coming over to say hello and be introduced. It was a bit embarrassing at first, but I soon got used to it because Sam acted as if it was normal. I saw that he lived among these people as if they were family, he lived in community with them.

I like Sam. I was sorry to say goodbye. I wrote down his address and gave him mine in school. I wanted to talk to him about being Jewish and what Sharon had said, and about my thought about being a rice Jew, but I didn't want to with my father there. He made it awkward. It's easier with Sam. For one thing, I don't have to feel grateful to him, and for another, he doesn't have to feel guilty about me.

We drove to this hotel. It's not a patch on the one where we used to stay in Pembrokeshire. It's very anonymous. We're sharing a room, which I didn't expect, but as he went down to the bar almost at once, I've had the place pretty much to myself. The clocks go back tonight, so an extra hour of sleep!

The Symposium is brill. It's just like *The Last of the Wine*, though earlier, of course, when Alkibiades was young. That must have been a great time to be alive.

Sunday 28th October 1979

I'm on the train, the big intercity train from London to Cardiff. It goes indiscriminately through countryside and towns, running along its inevitable rail. I sit in the corner of the carriage and nobody takes any notice of me. There's a cafe car where you can buy awful sandwiches and horrible fizzy drinks or coffee. I bought a Kit Kat, which I am eating very slowly. It's raining, which makes the countryside look cleaner and the towns dirtier.

It's also great to be wearing my own clothes. I was yesterday too, but I didn't notice so much. But sitting here, on my own, looking out of the window, it's really nice to be wearing jeans and my Tolkien T-shirt instead of that awful uniform.

It's funny, I write this whole thing mirror, so nobody could read it, but I want to write this next bit double mirror or something, in case, upside-down as well as backwards. The notebook locks. I'm lucky I can write mirror by just using my left hand. With all the practice I get, I'm almost as fast as I am right-handed.

Anyway.

Last night, after I finished writing in here, I read for a bit (*World of Ptaavs*, Niven) and then put the light out. I fell asleep, but then later *he*, my father—I really should call him Daniel, it's his name, and that's what Sam calls him—Daniel came in, putting the light on and waking me. He was drunk. He was crying. He tried to get into my bed and kiss me, and I had to push him away.

I know I said I was going to be pro-sex, but.

In one way, it's nice to think that somebody wants me. And touch is nice. Also sex, well, there is no privacy in school, so, but I'd had a chance the night before. (How long does it take? Masturbation is five, ten minutes tops. It never says, in books, how long. Bron and the Spike were at it for hours, but that was exhibition sex.) And I know from *Time Enough for Love*, which is very explicit on that, that incest isn't inherently wrong—it's not as if it really feels as if he's family. I can't imagine wanting to with Grampar, ugh! Ugh!!!

But with him, Daniel, it really is just the consanguinity thing, because we're strangers really. And that just means contraception, which I would want anyway. I'm only fifteen! And it's illegal, I think, and it wouldn't be worth going to prison for. But he seemed to want me, and who else is going to want me, broken as I am? I don't want to be depraved, but I suppose I probably am. *Anyway*, I said no before I thought about it, because he was drunk and pathetic. I pushed him away, and he went to sleep in the other bed and snored, loudly, and I lay there thinking about Heinlein and that Sturgeon story in *Dangerous Visions*, "If All Men Were Brothers, Would You Let One Marry Your Sister?" Great title.

This morning, he acted as if it had never happened. We were back to not looking at each other, eating floppy bacon and cold fried eggs in the breakfast buffet in the hotel. He gave me the trainfare and another ten pounds for books. Even if I use some of it for food and busfare, I should be able to buy ten books at least. He's very odd about money, sometimes acting as if he has none and then just handing it out like that. I have to go back to Shrewsbury next Saturday, because I have to be in school next Sunday night. But that is a week, a whole week away. He's going to meet me in Shrewsbury station. And Auntie Teg is going to meet me in Cardiff station today. I rang her from Paddington. Meanwhile, I am between, between everything, between worlds, eating a Kit Kat and writing in here. I like trains.

Monday 29th October 1979

Half term is not the same time here as it is at Arlinghurst, everyone here was off school last week. Typical. So Auntie Teg is teaching, and all my friends are in school. I got here last night, ate one of Auntie Teg's cheese pies, and fell asleep straight after dinner.

Today I went into Cardiff and bought books. The thing about Lears is that it has American books. Chapter and Verse is very nice, and I always go there too, but they don't import. Then there are a number of secondhand bookshops. There's the one in the Castle Arcade, the one on the Hayes, and the one by the casino that has porn in the back. I think I'm the only person who ever buys the books from the front. They always glare at me, as if I wanted to go into their stupid back room and buy their stupid porn. Or maybe they don't want to sell the normal books from the front because now they'll have to get more? I got *The Best of Galaxy Volume IV* for 10p, and it has a Zelazny story in it.

Then in the evening we went up the valley to see Grampar. He's out of hospital and in a nursing home called Fedw Hir. Everyone else there is a loony, practically. There's a man who sits going "Blubba, blubba, blubba," with his lips, and another one who cries out at intervals. It's the most horrible depressing place I've ever seen in my life, all those old men with their jaws sunken and their eyes dull, sitting on their beds in pajamas and looking as if they're in death's anteroom. Grampar is one of the best there. He's paralysed all down one side, but his other side is as strong as ever, and he can talk. His mind is all there, though his skin isn't the right colour. His hair has always been grey, ever since I can remember, but now it's white and there's a patch in it that looks the colour of curdled milk.

He can talk, though he didn't have much to say. He's hoping to come home soon, but Auntie Teg doesn't think so, though she hopes to have him out for the day at Christmas. She wants me to come, and I said I only would if I don't have to see my mother at all. I don't know if we can manage that. Grampar was absolutely thrilled to see me, and wanted to know all about me and what I was doing, and that was awkward, of course. He won't have Daniel's name mentioned, not at all ever, he hasn't let anyone mention it since Daniel abandoned my mother. So of course I can't say anything about him. But I told him about school, leaving out quite how awful it is and how everyone hates me. I told him about my marks and about the library. He wanted to know if my leg was getting better, and I said it was.

It isn't. But I realise now it's nothing. All right, it hurts, but I can walk about. I'm mobile. He's just stuck there, though he gets some physical therapy, Auntie Teg says.

When we were walking out, Auntie Teg, who goes there often, was saying goodnight to some of the other men, who she knows, and who either didn't respond or responded inappropriately with howling and stammering. I couldn't help thinking about Sam, who must be around the same age as these men, and his nice warm room and the piles of books and the electric samovar. He was a person, and these men were just refuse, really, the remains of people. "We have got to get Grampar out of there," I said.

"Yes, but it's not that easy. He can't manage on his own. I could come up at weekends, but he'd need a nurse. It's very expensive. They're hoping maybe in the spring."

"I could live with him and help," I said, and for a moment it hung there like a little star of hope.

"You need to be in school. And anyway, you couldn't help him walk. He leans all his weight on the person supporting him."

She's right. I'd fold up under that, my leg would give way and we'd both be on the floor.

I should write to him. I can do that, nice cheery letters. Auntie Teg can read them out, it'll give them something to talk about at visiting time. We have got to get him out of there. It's incredibly grim. And I thought school was bad.

Tuesday 30th October 1979

I went up the valley on the red-and-white bus today. It's interesting. It goes on the old road all the way, up through the narrow streets of terraced houses, through Pontypridd, and all the way I could see horrible coal tips and slag heaps and ugly houses crammed together, and above them, the hills. When I got to Aberdare, I got off and walked up the cwm to the ruins we call Osgiliath. I don't know what they really were. The trees were practically leafless, and there were a lot of wet leaves on the ground. It wasn't actually raining, which was good, as I urgently needed to sit down by the time I got there. I hadn't remembered how far it was. Or rather, I'd remembered it was about half a mile, the nearest of any of them to a bus stop, but still a long way for me to walk now.

I wasn't looking for fairies, especially. I just wanted to go there. But the fairies were there. Glorfindel was. They were waiting for me.

I'd like to report our conversation as if it were like talking to Tolkien's elves. "Long we have missed you and awaited your coming, Mori, long we have sought you in vain among the trees and palaces. Word came to us from a far country that you still walked the world, riven from your twin, so we waited yet in hope until today the breeze brought us news of your coming. Be welcome among us, for we have great need of you."

But it wasn't like that. Sometimes Mor and I would play over a conversation with the fairies with me saying what they should have said in language like that. That speech is essentially what Glorfindel said, what he meant to say, only most of it wasn't in words at all, and what was, was in Welsh and not that kind of words.

Glorfindel's beautiful. He looks like a young man, nineteen or twenty, dark-haired and grey-eyed. He wears a cloak of leaves that swirls around him, except that it isn't really a cloak. It isn't as if he could take it off.

The fairies are very wise. Or rather, they know a lot. They've had a lot of experience. They understand better than anyone else how magical things work. That's why it would have been such a disaster if my mother had got control of them. She would have used that knowledge to make herself powerful. They wouldn't have been able to help doing it for her. I don't know how it would have played out in the real world. I don't suppose she'd really have become a dark queen, not exactly. But while she can't ever try that again, she's trying something else. I should have known.

What Glorfindel wants is for me to go, tomorrow, up through Ithilien to Minos's labyrinth, where he says the dead will walk. Tomorrow *is* Halloween. He said I need to take oak leaves and make a door for them to pass through. That will stop her getting hold of them. Fairies know a lot, but they can't do a lot, they can't really interact all that much with the world, they can't affect things. They have to get other people to do it for them, and that means me. According to Glorfindel, he'd done as much as he could in making me get here this week. He hadn't known where I was until I spoke to the fairy, and he couldn't reach out until I'd burned the letters. But then he arranged things to bring me to him. (He rearranged the school timetable? All the school timetables? He arranged for Daniel to agree to let me come? He made me want to come to the cwm today? Sometimes I hate magic.)

He said it would be easy, not like last time. No risk. The difficult thing is that I'll have to be there at dusk. I thought that would be really hard, but when I lied to Auntie Teg and said I wanted to have tea with Moira from the Grammar School, she said she'd pick me up at seven and take me to Fedw Hir to see poor old Grampar again.

Reading Marion Zimmer Bradley's *The Spell Sword*, which is fun so far.

Wednesday 31st October 1979

Near thing, but not the way I expected at all.

So the first thing was, it was a long loooong walk. No fairies were anywhere near me as I walked it. They hate pain, I don't know why, but I've known it as long as I've known anything about them. Even a skinned knee or a turned ankle will send them scattering. The pain screaming out every step from my leg must have been enough to scare them off for miles around. It's a good thing I set off early, to give it time to subside after I got there.

King Minos's labyrinth is right up the mountain, the Graig. It's one of the highest ruins. It was a very old ironworks, one of the first, and an iron ore mine, not a deep one, just a scratching and mostly filled in. What's left of it really does look like a labyrinth, or a maze anyway. You have to thread your way through the walls, and though none of them are more than shoulder-height it does feel like following a maze pattern. The bit where the entrance to the diggings used to be is in the centre, and it's a bit sunken, and there's a kind of lane that leads down to it. I sat on the wall there and rested, leaning my cane up against the wall. It was spotting with rain, so I couldn't read, though I'd brought my book, of course. It was Delany's *Babel 17*, I'd been reading it on the bus. I'd brought oak leaves too, I picked them up on the way up through heavily wooded Ithilien. Glorfindel hadn't said how many, but I'd kept stuffing them into my bag as I went. Oaks hang onto their leaves all winter, like mallorns, so it's easy to find them.

I was wearing my school coat, because I don't have another any more. I hadn't brought my coat when I'd run away. My school coat has the Arlinghurst badge on it, a rose, with the motto *Dum spiro spero*, which actually I rather like—while I breathe I shall hope. I heard a joke about a school deciding to have "I hear, I see, I learn" which translates as "Audio video disco." I spent a little while thinking about that. At this distance, I could kind of like the motto. When I'm there, I feel I have to hate everything about it or I'm giving in. School seemed very far away as I sat there, coat notwithstanding. There's something real and essential about the landscape in the valleys that makes everything else seem like a distant distraction.

After a while the sun came out, feebly. The clouds were scudding across the sky at a tremendous pace, and I was looking across the valley from almost as high as they were. There aren't many trees up there, just two spindly rowans clinging by the entrance to the old diggings. There were flocks of birds circling about, probably deciding which direction to migrate, marking patterns across the sky. After the sun came the fairies, peeping out at me behind walls, and at last Glorfindel.

It's very unsatisfactory writing down conversation with a fairy. Either I put it into proper words, which really is making it up, or I try to represent something that's only partly in words with just those few words. And if I write it down like I did yesterday, it's a lie. I'm saying what I want him to have said, when in fact what he said was a few words and a whole lot of feeling going along with that. How do you write that down? Maybe Delany could.

We didn't talk all that much, anyway. He sat beside me, and I could almost feel him. Then I could feel him next to me, which is beyond unusual, and then I started to have sexual feelings. I know, unthinkable, with a fairy. All the fairies came closer, then, which worried me and once I'd started worrying about it Glorfindel was as insubstantial as ever, though still right next to me.

I remembered then that I do know stories about women who had sex with fairies, and every single one of those stories is about pregnancy. I looked at Glorfindel, and yes, he's beautiful and . . . ineluctably masculine . . . and he was looking at me soulfully, and yes I would like to, but not if it means that. No way! Even if all the normal men I meet look at me as if I am dogmeat. And in a way, that would be incest too, with Glorfindel. More so.

"Untouched?" he said, or something like that, I'm never absolutely sure what that word means. But I knew what he was talking about.

"So far, I've fought off everyone who's tried," I said, sounding much fiercer than I intended, though it's nothing but the truth, not that Daniel needed fighting exactly. "You know about Carl."

"Dead," he said, with gloating finality. Carl is dead. He was a policeman, and he went to Northern Ireland, because the pay was better, and he got blown up. Or, to put it another way, I had asked Glorfindel how to get rid of him, and I stole his comb and sank it in Croggin Bog. That was when he was staying with my mother and he came into my room and sat too close and kept trying to touch me. I bit him, hard, and he hit me, but he backed off. I knew that wasn't the end of it. I was still fourteen then. Dropping someone's comb in a bog isn't murder. I thought it had worked when he went away.

Glorfindel just looked at me, and I knew he was my friend, as much as any of the fairies are, as much as they can be, being what they are. Lots of them don't care about people or the world at all, and even the ones that do aren't like people. I don't know what it meant to him for desire to be in the air between us. His name isn't really Glorfindel, he doesn't even really have a name. He isn't human. I felt very aware of that.

The sun was sinking behind the hill we were sitting on, but it wasn't really set yet; in the next valley it was still full daylight. But I suppose there's always a next valley, all the way around the world until you get to tomorrow. Our shadows were very long. Glorfindel got up and told me to scatter the leaves in a spiral through the maze, ending at the two rowan trees. I did, and then I sat and waited as the light faded. I wasn't sure if I was going to see anything, or whether it would be one of those times when I do what I've been told and it makes no sense and I never know whether it worked or what it did. The sky faded until it got to that point where there's no colour left in anything but it isn't dark. I started to think about how awful going back was going to be.

Then they came walking up the dramroad out of the valley through the twilight. They were ghosts, I suppose, the procession of the dead. They weren't pale kings and pale maidens, they were work-worn men and women—perfectly ordinary people, except for being dead. You'd never mistake them for living people. You couldn't quite see through them, but they were even more drained of colour than everything else, and they weren't quite as solid as they ought to be. One of the men I recognised. He had been sitting in Fedw Hir near Grampar making blubbing sounds with his mouth. Now he strode along easily with a spring in his step. His face was grave and composed, he was a man with dignity and purpose. He bent and picked up one of my oak leaves from the path and offered it like a ticket at the cinema as he passed between the two trees. I didn't see anyone take it. I couldn't see into the darkness at all.

Some of the others were milling about at the entrance, they had come this far and were unable to get in, because of whatever my mother had done. When they saw the old man give the leaf, they started picking up the leaves. Then each passed through, one at a time. They were all very earnest and dignified, not speaking at all, taking their turns to go between the trees and vanish into the darkness. I don't know whether they were going into the ground or under the hill or to another world or down to Acheron or what. There was a fat woman and a young man with a motorcycle helmet, who seemed to be together. All the dead saw each other, but they didn't seem to see me or the fairies, who crowded to each side of the path, watching. The young man gestured for the woman to go ahead, and she did, solemnly, as if they were in church.

Then I saw Mor. I hadn't been expecting it at all. She was walking along quite unconcerned, a leaf in her hand as if she was playing some serious part in a game. I shouted her name, and she turned and saw me and smiled, with such gladness that it broke my heart. I reached out for her, and she for me, but she wasn't really there, like a fairy, worse than a fairy. She looked afraid, and she looked from side to side, seeing the fairies, of course, lining the path.

"Let go," Glorfindel said, almost in my ear, a whisper so warm it moved my hair.

I wasn't holding her, except that I was. Our hands reached out and did not touch, but the connection between us was tangible. It glowed violet. It was the only thing with colour. It wasn't visible normally, but if it had been for the last year it would have been trailing around me like a broken bridge. Now it was whole again, I was whole again, we were together. "Holding or dying," he said in my ear, and I understood, he meant that I could hold her here and that would be bad, and I trusted him about that although I didn't understand it, or I could go with her through that door to death. That would be suicide. But I couldn't let her go. It had been so very hard without her all that time, such a rotten year. I'd always meant to die too, if dying was necessary.

"Halfway," Glorfindel said, and he didn't mean I was half dead without her or that she was halfway through or any of that, he meant that I was halfway through *Babel 17*, and if I went on I would never find out how it came out.

There may be stranger reasons for being alive.

There are books. There's Auntie Teg and Grampar. There's Sam, and Gill. There's interlibrary loan. There are books you can fall into and pull up over your head. There's the distant hope of a karass sometime in the future. There's Glorfindel who really cares about me as much as a fairy can care about anything.

I let go. Reluctantly, but I let go. She clung. She held on, so that letting go wasn't enough. If I wanted to live, I had to push her away, through the connection that bound us, though she was crying and calling to me and holding on as hard as she could. It is the hardest thing I have ever done, worse than when she died. Worse than when they dragged me off her and the ambulance took her away and let my mother go with her, smiling, but not me. Worse than when Auntie Teg told me she was dead.

Mor was always braver than I was, more practical, nicer, just generally a better person. She was the better half of us.

But she was afraid now, and lonely and bereft, and dead, and I had to push her away. She changed as she clung, so she was like ivy, all over me, and seaweed, tendrils clutching, and slime, impossible to shake off. Now I wanted to get her off I couldn't, and even though she was changing I knew she was still Mor all the time. I could feel that she was. I was afraid. I didn't want to hurt her. In the end, I put my weight down on my leg. The pain broke the bond, the same way it frightens the fairies. The pain was something my living body could do, the same as picking up oak leaves and bringing them up a mountain.

She went on, then, or tried to but the twilight had became darkness, and couldn't go through the door, it wasn't there any more. She stood by the trees looking like herself again, and very young and lost, and I almost reached out for her again. Then she was gone, in an eyeblink, the way fairies go.

It was a long walk back in the dark, alone. Every step I was afraid of meeting my mother, come to see what had gone wrong with her plan to get them all. It was because of Mor she could try it, I see that now, because Mor was her daughter, her blood. I kept thinking that I couldn't run, and she could. Mor felt further away than ever. The fairies had all fled the pain, naturally. Even *Babel 17*, which was right there in my bag, felt a long way away. But Auntie Teg was waiting with the car, and Grampar at Fedw Hir, so pleased to see me, he'd have been heartbroken if I'd gone on. The bed was empty where the man had been making the blubba blubba noises, they'd already taken his empty body away. He was lucky to be able to go tonight. People who die in November have to wait a whole year. Like Mor. What happened to her? Will she have to wait until next year?

Thursday 1st November 1979

The more I think about it, the less I understand about what happened. Does every valley have an opening like that? How about people who die in flat places? Is it actually old, older than the ironworks, or did the ironworks open it up where before it was smooth hillside? And where did they go? And was that really them, all of them? And what about Mor? Where is she now? Did my mother get her after all? Will the fairies help her? What about the rowan trees? I never heard that the rowan is the tree of death—that's supposed to be the yew, the graveyard yew. But it was oak leaves, dry gold oak leaves. There's one left in my bag. It doesn't mean someone got left out, Mor had one, and there were still leaves crunching on the ground when I left, I brought more than enough. I thought I shook them all out, but there was one inside the back cover of *Babel 17*. What an *odd* book! Does language really shape the way it's possible to think? I mean, like that?

I only seem to have questions today.

I was knackered, and my leg was unmentionable, so I stayed in and read all day. Then I made dinner for Auntie Teg for when she came home from school—baked mushrooms with onions and cheese and cream, and jacket potatoes with more cheese, and peas. She said how nice it was, and that she supposed men got that every day, if they had a wife, and what she needed wasn't a husband who would expect that but a wife who would do it. It was lovely to be cooking with actual food. There's something so grounding about it. It's not that I was doing any magic, beyond the magic it is to take big flat mushrooms and raw potatoes and turn them into something totally delicious. I was just making dinner. But I wonder how much of cooking for someone else is magic anyway, more than I know about. I think it might all be. Auntie Teg's dishes don't like me any more than Persimmon does. The knives and peelers don't cut me, but they turn awkward in my hands. They know I'm not the person supposed to be using them.

There's supposed to be a Heinlein fantasy novel called *Glory Road*. That would be something! I wonder if Daniel has it? If not, there's always blessed interlibrary loan.

Friday 2nd November 1979

I went up to Aberdare again on the bus today. There wasn't so much as a sniff of Mor or any fairy, though I kept getting the feeling they were disappearing as soon as I looked for them and appearing just where I couldn't see them. That's a game, of course, but I didn't want to play it. I wanted answers, though I should know how impossible it is to get straight answers from them, even when they want something, which clearly they don't just at the moment.

I went to Grampar's house. I still have the front door key, though it's stiffer than ever, and terribly hard to get in. Auntie Teg keeps it clean, but it was kind of dusty and unused-smelling even so. It's a very little house, crammed in between two others. When Auntie Florrie lived there it didn't have a bathroom, the bath was in the kitchen, and the toilet was a *ty bach*, outside. It was like that when my great-grandparents lived there too. My grandfather put in proper plumbing when he moved back in. I quite liked the bath in the kitchen, next to the coal fire. It was surprisingly cosy. But I used to hate going outside to the toilet, especially at night.

He moved in there after Mor died to get away from my mother. Everyone runs away from her. I didn't officially ever live there. I officially lived with her. I even sometimes spent some time living with her, when she insisted, but mostly I didn't, while Grampar was all right. I had my own bedroom, with my bed from home and the blue box. Most of my books and clothes were in her house, but I found a woolly jumper of Mor's and my denim shorts with a lion on, and a copy of *Destinies*. *Destinies* is an American science fiction magazine that comes in paperback books, and they stock it in Lears and I love it. I bought the new one—"April–June"—there on Monday. I'm saving it to read on the train.

So I left a few books. I know I won't be able to get them until Christmas, but they're really piling up, and I'm pretty sure I won't want to re-read the ones I left any time soon. There isn't much room at school. Anyway, even if I miss them, I like them being there. If Grampar gets well enough to come out of Fedw Hir and go home, I can go home too. Daniel doesn't actually care, I'm sure he wouldn't mind. I feel as if I don't actually live anywhere, and I hate that. The thought that there are eight books on the windowsill in my room in alphabetical order is comforting. It's magic, too, it's a magic link. My mother can't get in there, and even if she could, they're books. You can't do magic with books unless they're very special copies—and if she could, she already has all the rest of mine. She has all too much of mine, but there's no way of getting it from her.

If I defeated her again, and I think I did, will she want revenge? It wasn't at all like last time. It's weirdly anticlimactic, especially since I can't find Glorfindel to ask him the nine million questions I have.

I couldn't lock the front door again. I locked it from inside and went out the back, then put the back door key in through the letterbox. I've told Auntie Teg, who'll be the next person to come in.

I saw Moira and Leah and Nasreen after they got out of school this afternoon. They asked me what Arlinghurst was like, and I didn't tell them, except for superficial things. Leah has got a boyfriend, Andrew who used to be so good at maths in Park School when we were all little. I said that and Moira said some of us were still little. She's had a growth spurt. I wonder if I will. I've been the same height since I was twelve, when we were the tallest in the class, but now almost everyone has passed me. They told me all the gossip. Dorcas, who always used to be top in French and Welsh and whose parents are some kind of nutty religion, Seventh-day Adventists or something, has got pregnant. Sue has left because her parents were moving to

England. It felt really normal, but also really weird, as if I was just
pretending.

Back to Shrewsbury tomorrow, just when they're going to be out
of school and we could have done something together.

Saturday 3rd November 1979

The Crewe train is much smaller than the London train. It has a corridor and little carriages that seat eight, on sort of benches across
from each other. There's a luggage rack up above, and black and
white photographs of places—in my carriage Newton Abbot, which
I've never heard of. I wonder where it is? It looks nice. For most of
the way I had the carriage to myself, though a middle-aged lady and
her two children got on in Abergavenny and off in Hereford. They
didn't bother me much. Most of the time I alternated looking out of
the window and reading, first my *Destinies* and then I started Spider Robinson's *Callahan's Crosstime Saloon*, which I also bought in
Lears.

The train runs up the Welsh border. Once it gets away from Cardiff and Newport it's all hills and fields as it goes up through the
borders. The sun was in and out, in a fitful autumnal way, with that
odd autumn afternoon light that looks almost like an underwater
colour. The clouds made patches of darkness on the mountains, and
when there was a patch of sun the grass seemed almost luminous,
as if you could read by it. You can see the Sugarloaf from the train.
Well, it's a very distinctive mountain. We used to go to Abergavenny
sometimes, and there was a song we'd sing in the car, "Over the hills
to Abergavenny, hoping the weather'll be fine." It gave me a warm
feeling to see it, even just the railway station and the hills behind.
I'll mention going through it to Grampar when I write. After Abergavenny the train crosses the border into England somewhere, because Hereford is in England, and Ludlow definitely is. Ludlow is a

little market town. It looks a lot like Oswestry, from the train, but a
bit warmer.

The last stop before Shrewsbury is Church Stretton. A lot of people
came into my carriage then, and my beautiful corner where I'd felt
so comfortable all the way became a bit crowded. My heart sank a
bit too. I'd managed to enjoy the journey up to that point without
thinking about where I was ending up.

Daniel wasn't waiting in Shrewsbury station. I'd thought he'd be
on the platform, but he wasn't. I went out through the barrier and
stood in the car park. I thought about getting a bus but I didn't have
the faintest idea what bus I'd want or where it would go from. That's
another thing, in the Valleys I know where all the buses go, and their
routes, and which ones are useful to me. Red-and-whites go to Cardiff,
and the dark-red ones are locals. It's easy to think about knowing
the dramroads and the way things fit together, but I'd never thought
how useful it is to know buses, until I was standing there and felt
so stuck. I had my bag, and a bag of books too, and I wasn't exactly
weighed down with luggage but it wasn't nothing.

I had two pounds ten left of the ten pounds. (That might not
seem like much, but I had bought a lot of books.) I went back into
the station, where there's a W. H. Smiths and bought a map, a pink-
covered one inch to the mile Ordnance Survey map of Shrewsbury
and district. (I always thought it was "ordinance," but apparently not.
Ordnance. What a funny word, and what a funny concept too. They
surveyed the whole country for military logistics, and now they sell
anyone the maps. Well, I wasn't planning to invade.) I went back out
into the car park and sat down on a bench. I found Mickleham, where
the Old Hall is, and thought that a bus to Wolverhampton would
probably go near there, when Daniel got there after all. I was relieved
to see the black Bentley draw in. I folded the map up and put it away,
but he saw it.

"I see you've bought a map," he said.

"Maps are very interesting, really," I said, embarrassed, though it was him who ought to be embarrassed, being late. I got into the car. He threw a cigarette butt out of the window and drove off. He shouldn't do that, even in a car park. It's a bad habit. It could start a fire. I felt thoroughly disapproving of him.

I think I'll buy as many Ordnance Survey maps as I can. They're arranged in logical squares. I could collect the set and get the whole country, eventually. Then I'd always be able to find my way, and know where places are in relation to other places. Though they wouldn't do me much good if they were at home when I happened to be somewhere. I'll just have to be organised and put the map for where I'm going, and the maps around it maybe, into my bag when I go out.

Shrewsbury is where we bought my uniform. It's a town, not a city, and it all seems to be built of the same rose-pink-coloured stone.

We went back to the Old Hall for high tea. It's afternoon tea if you have tea and cakes and scones and little sandwiches, but high tea if there's something hot and substantial as well. In this case it was a hot dish with pasta and cheese and ham, but everything else was cold. The sandwiches were tuna and cucumber, ham and parsley, and cheese and pickle. I liked them a lot. The scones were as dry as the Kalahari. They also fell to crumbs when you put butter on them. I could make better scones when I was four. I didn't say so, but maybe next time I'll tell one of the aunts (I still can't tell them apart) that I'd like to have a try at making some. It seems the sort of thing they might approve.

They talked about nothing but school, and expected me to contribute with current news about teachers and how the houses are doing. They were in Scott, all three of them, and they care a lot more about it than I do. I don't understand them one bit. They're grown up and they have their own house—and it's a jolly nice house too. But they don't do anything. They don't read, and they don't work and they don't make anything. They organise jumble sales for church. Gramma used to do that, and she was teaching full time as well. They keep the house nice, but that's not a full-time job for three people. They pay my father to manage the estate and the money, so they don't do that. They're rich, reasonably rich, I think, but they don't go anywhere or do anything, they just sit there eating awful scones and talking with real enthusiasm about the time Scott won the Cup. I'm not sure exactly how old they are, but they were born before 1940, so they're at least forty, and they still care about a stupid house they were in at school. They weren't just pretending, so as to be interesting to me. I can tell the difference. They were talking to each other far more. Why do they stay there? And why didn't any of them get married? Maybe they hate children. They certainly seem to find me a trial, but that doesn't count; if they'd wanted to they could have had nice upper-class English children of their own and trained them not to be surly.

Daniel has *Glory Road* and *Waldo and Magic, Inc.*, which he says are both Heinlein fantasies. He has also lent me Poul Anderson's *The Broken Sword*. I'm still reading the Callahan stories, which are amazingly sweet, not much like *Telempath*, but I'm enjoying them.

Tomorrow church, then lunch with the aunts, then back to school, dammit.

Monday 5th November 1979

I remember how far away school felt from the labyrinth, but the second I got back it was totally pervasive and as if I'd never been away.

It's funny how insignificant the reportable parts of my half term are. It was only a week, but so much happened in it compared to a school week that it might have been a year. But when I was asked about it in French Conversation first period this morning I could only say *"Je visite mon grandpere dans Londres et je visite mon autre grandpere dans Pays de Galles."* Two visits to grandfathers, that's all, and all Madame said was that it should be *en* not *dans*. I sink into school as into a warm bath, and it closes over my head. Even if I could tell them about Halloween and Glorfindel and the dead I wouldn't.

Glory Road is deeply disappointing. I hate it. I stopped reading it and read Gill's book of Asimov science essays in preference, that's how much I hate it. I love Heinlein but he clearly doesn't *get* fantasy. It's just stupid. And nobody saying "Oh, Scar" would be heard as "Oscar," it's not even plausible. It's almost as bad as its cover, and that's saying something, as the cover is so bad that Miss Carroll raised her eyebrows at it from her librarian desk on the other side of the room. It's funny how *Triton*, which is all about sex and sociology, has a cover of a spaceship exploding, while *Glory Road*, which does mention sex here and there but is actually a stupid adventure story, has a cover like that.

There's some poetry competition thing. Everybody seems to think I'll win it as a foregone conclusion.

I miss the mountains. I didn't miss them before, except in thinking how unattractively flat it was here. But now I have been home and had them around me for a while, I miss them actively, more than my living family, more than being able to shut the toilet door. It's not really flat here, it rolls, and I can see the mountains of North Wales in the distance when it's clear. But I miss having the hills tucked up around me.

Tuesday 6th November 1979

Fireworks and a bonfire last night in the school grounds. I saw some of the fire-fairies clustering. Nobody else saw them. You can only see them if you already believe in them, which is why children are the most likely to. People like me don't stop seeing them. It would be *insane* of me to stop believing in them. But lots of children do when they grow up, even though they've seen them. I'm not a child any more, though I'm not grown up either. I have to say I can't wait.

But my cousin Geraint, who's four years older than me, saw the fairies when playing with us in the cwm. He was eleven or twelve, and we were seven or eight. We told him he should close his eyes and when he opened them he'd see them, and he did. He was amazed by them. He couldn't talk to them, because he only spoke English, but we translated what he said, and what they said. We must have been eight, because I remember freely translating what they said into purest Tolkien, and we didn't read *The Lord of the Rings* until we were eight. At that point, when we were about that age, we were always looking for someone else to play with, and preferably a boy, because in books that's the group you have to have to go into another world. We thought the fairies would take us to Narnia, or Elidor. Geraint seemed like a good candidate. He saw the fairies, and he was awed by them. He liked them, and they liked him. But he lives in Burgess Hill, near Brighton, and he only spent summers in Aberdare, and the next summer he couldn't see them, he said he was too old to play, and he remembered what had happened as if it had been a game where we'd been pretending to be fairies. All he wanted to do was play football. We ran away and left him in the garden with his stupid ball, disconsolate, but he didn't tell the grownups we'd abandoned him. He said at dinner that he'd had a very nice day playing. Poor Geraint.

I had a letter this morning, which I haven't opened, and also a letter from Sam. He asked how I liked the Plato, and if I'd found any more, and he writes just the way he speaks. I'll write back on Sunday. There isn't any Plato in the school library. I asked Miss Carroll, and she says they don't teach Greek so there's no call for it. I might have a problem with interlibrary loan, as I don't know translators, or even all the titles. But I can order the ones listed in *The Symposium* of course, so I'll do that.

Penguin are the best of any publisher about listing other titles, even if they didn't publish them. I have a whole pile of things to order on Saturday, because *Up the Line* has a whole long list of Robert

Silverbergs. Also, I am going to order *Beyond the Tomorrow Mountains*. Sylvia Engdahl wrote this totally brilliant book called *Heritage of the Star*, and Puffin, who are Penguin, brought it out and I read it. It's about people living with lots of superstitions but also some technology they think is magic, and they're oppressed by Scholars and Technicians and anyone who thinks wrongly is called a Heretic. And actually they're colonists on another planet but they don't know, and it's just brilliant. In the story, there's a promise that when they can know, when everything will be all right, they'll go "Beyond the Tomorrow Mountains," and there's a sequel with that title, but I've never seen it anywhere, though I've been looking for a long time.

The poetry competition is nationwide. Everyone in Arlinghurst has to write a poem, then they'll pick the best from each form to send in. I can't believe people really think I'll win. All right, realistically, I'd win out of Lower VC, or even all of Form V, probably, because the academic standards here are not especially high. But out of all the fifteen-year-olds in the whole country? No way. The best one in the school is going to be awarded fifty house points. That's made everyone as keen as mustard. The best hundred in the country are going to be published in a book, and the best one wins a hundred pounds and a typewriter. I'd really like a typewriter. Not that I can type, but you have to send typewritten submissions to magazines.

Deirdre came sidling up to me at lunch, and sat down one seat away from me, as if casually, but doing it so badly that lots of people noticed. She looked frightened, poor dab, but resolute. "My mother told me I should stick up for you," she whispered.

"Good for your mother," I said, in a normal tone.

"Will you help me with my poem?" she asked.

So I'm going to help her write a poem at prep, which will probably mean writing it. I haven't written mine yet, though there's plenty of time, I have until Friday.

Thursday 8th November 1979

I wrote Deirdre's poem, and I was quite pleased with it. But yesterday as I was sitting here reading *Waldo and Magic, Inc.* (which are two quite different novellas), Miss Carroll came over with a pile of modern poetry books, which she said she thought I might like to look at.

It seems poetry has moved on since Chesterton. Who knew? Clearly not Gramma, and nobody in any schools I've been to. I'd seen one stanza of one poem by Auden, that Delany quoted, and not even heard T. S. Eliot's name, or Ted Hughes's either. I got quite drunk on Eliot and was late for Latin and got an order mark. I got revenge by translating Horace just like Eliot, and she couldn't say anything, because it was also accurate.

I've written a poem for the competition. I don't feel very confident of it. I've mastered the Chestertonian, I really have, but I don't feel as if I've had time to master this. It's about nuclear war and Dutch elm disease and how we should actually be getting into space while we can.

There's apparently a long T. S. Eliot poem called *Four Quartets* which the school doesn't have. I'll order that on Saturday as well. According to Miss Carroll, T. S. Eliot worked in a bank when he was writing *The Waste Land* because being a poet doesn't pay.

"Oh dark, dark, dark . . . those are pearls that were his eyes . . . With these fragments have I shored up my ruins."

Friday 9th November 1979

It doesn't seem so terrible that the elms are dying when it's autumn and all the trees seem dead.

Another letter. I'm going to have to burn them again. I almost want to know if she's said anything about what I did. I'd like to have confirmation. Though I know it worked.

I handed my poem in. Miss Lewes looked at it but didn't say anything. Miss Gilbert, who teaches English to the Sixth Form, will be judging.

I'm hoping there'll be some books waiting for me at the library tomorrow, because I'm almost through with what I have. I'm reading *Nine Princes in Amber* again.

I keep dreaming about Mor. I dream she's drowning and I don't save her. I dream I push her in front of the car instead of trying to pull her away. It hit both of us. I have a reminder of that in every step I take, but not in my dreams. I dream I'm burying her alive in the centre of the labyrinth, throwing earth down on top of her while she struggles and it gets in her hair.

It was a year ago today. I've been trying not to think about it, but it keeps ambushing me.

Saturday 10th November 1979

Going into town on the bus, the anticipation of the library filled me with delight. It almost made the wet grey streets nice, but not quite. It was drizzling, and the sky was very low and flat.

The librarian, the man, was a little startled at how many books I wanted to order, but he just gave me a pile of blanks and had me fill them in myself. Lots of books were waiting for me! Then I went down to the bookshop and bought *Four Quartets*, Ted Hughes's *Crow* and Anne McCaffrey's *Dragonsinger*. I also bought a box of matches.

I did not buy a book called *Lord Foul's Bane* by Stephen Donaldson, which has the temerity to compare itself, on the front cover, to "Tolkien at his best." The back cover attributes the quote to the *Washington Post*, a newspaper whose quotations will always damn a book for me from now on. How dare they? And how dare the publishers? It isn't a comparison anyone could make, except to say "Compared to Tolkien at his best, this is dross." I mean you could say that even about really brilliant books like *A Wizard of Earthsea*. I expect *Lord Foul's Bane* (horrible title, sounds like a Conan book) is more like Tolkien at his worst, which would be the beginning of *The Silmarillion*.

The thing about Tolkien, about *The Lord of the Rings*, is that it's perfect. It's this whole world, this whole process of immersion, this journey. It's not, I'm pretty sure, actually true, but that makes it more amazing, that someone could make it all up. Reading it changes everything. I remember finishing *The Hobbit* and handing it to Mor and saying "Read it. It's pretty good. Isn't there another one of these around here somewhere?" And I remember finding it—stealing it from my mother's room. When the door was open, the light from the corridor fell on the shelves R and S and T. We were always afraid to go further in, in case she was hiding in the darkness and grabbed us. She did that once, when Mor was putting back *The Crystal Cave*. When we took one of her books, usually, we ruffled the shelf so it wouldn't show. But the one-volume *Lord of the Rings* was so fat that it didn't work. I was terrified she'd see. I almost didn't take it. But either she didn't notice or she didn't care—I think she might have been away with one of her boyfriends.

I haven't said what I wanted to about the thing about it.

Reading it is like being there. It's like finding a magic spring in a desert. It has everything. (Except lust, Daniel said. But it has *Wormtongue*.)

It is an oasis for the soul. Even now I can always retreat into Middle Earth and be happy.

How can you compare anything to that? I can't believe Stephen Donaldson's hubris.

Sunday 11th November 1979

I climbed out of the dorm window in the middle of the night last night and made a circle and burned the letters in it. Nobody saw me. I made the circle out of things that were lying around, leaves and twigs and stones, and I put in the oak leaf, my piece of wood, and my pocket rock, which comes from the beach in Amroth. I could feel it working, I felt as if I was under an umbrella. I read the letters first. I wanted to know what she'd said. I might as well not have bothered. The only thing she said about what I did was "You were always the one who was most like me," which is—well, a snowman is more like a cloud than a lump of coal, but neither of them are much alike. I folded the letters into a pagoda and set them on fire. I didn't look at the pictures, but I saw there were some.

I stirred the ashes, so there was nothing left at all. Then I took the pocket rock and held it up under the moon (a three-quarter moon, I don't know if that's right) and tried to make it a protection against bad dreams. I don't know if it worked. I took the leaf and my piece of wood back.

I climbed back in and got into bed. Everyone else was asleep. The moonlight was on Lorraine's face. She looked strangely beautiful, and also distant, as if she was dead, as if she'd been dead for centuries and she was a marble statue of herself on her tomb.

The only problem with this is that if she keeps sending letters, I'm going to have to keep burning them. But late at night is definitely safer, from a school point of view, than when people are around.

Deirdre gave me a bun—an iced bun from Finefare, really sticky and sweet. They come in a packet of six, so she gave them to quite a lot of people, but I really appreciated the gesture. It's nice not to feel like a total pariah.

I wrote to Daniel about Callahan's Place and Stephen Donaldson's hubris. I wrote to Sam about Plato, and told him about ordering more. I told him about *The Last of the Wine* as well, because even if he doesn't like novels usually he might like that. I wrote to Grampar about going through Abergavenny and about missing the mountains and about all the ball games they play here and how I'd enjoy them if I could run. I can *remember* running. My whole body remembers. It's a kinetic memory, if that's the word. It was a bit of a lie to say I'd enjoy the games. I enjoy sitting in the library reading, and I hate the way the games are so important to the girls while being totally trivial really. What I enjoy is throwing a ball and running and catching, not agonising about the score.

What is it with me and Anne McCaffrey and getting the second book first? *Dragonsinger* is the sequel to something I've never seen called *Dragonsong*! I read it anyway. It's oddly light compared to the other two. It's set in Pern, rather than being about Pern, if that makes sense. I would like a fire-lizard. Or a dragon, for that matter. I'd come swooping in on my blue dragon and she'd breathe fire and burn down the school!

Monday 12th November 1979

Deirdre's poem has won the school level of the competition.

Despite the fact that I wrote it, I am mortified. Everyone expected me to win, and I expected it myself. What was wrong with my poem? I suppose Miss Gilbert is a traditionalist. Nobody has said anything, and I congratulated Deirdre with everyone else, but I feel publicly humiliated. (On the other hand, I did actually write it, and Deirdre at least knows that.)

Tuesday 13th November 1979

Deirdre came up to me after prep and dragged me out into the grounds where we could talk without being heard. She started crying and being incoherent almost at once, but what she wanted, I think, was to say that I shouldn't have given her my best work. Well, I didn't. But she thinks I did because it won. It's the first time she's ever won anything. I don't think she's ever earned a house mark before, except maybe for scoring a goal. I told her she deserved it. She sat right next to me at breakfast and nobly offered me her sausage, which I accepted, not because it would have been an insult but because I was hungry.

Wordsworth are jolly proud of her. Sandra Mortimer, the House Captain of Wordsworth, a redhead whose eyes are pink-rimmed and watery, personally spoke to Deirdre, who almost died of the honour.

Reading *The Shockwave Rider*, Brunner. It's very good, but it isn't *Stand on Zanzibar*. I wonder what it's like to have written your masterpiece, and to know you'll never do it again?

Wednesday 14th November 1979

This is the true and complete story of how Deirdre and I each got an order mark this morning.

We were in the shower, which is a long trench of tile with a dozen showerheads, with fairly feeble pressure and variably warm water. Give me a bath any day. There's hot water, meaning water that isn't icy cold, between seven and eight in the morning, and between seven and eight at night. There are also showers in the gym, which are obligatory after games, but they're cold and mostly the girls just run through them and splash off any mud. Any serious washing gets done first thing in the morning or last thing at night. It must be les-

bian paradise then, because there are always acres of female flesh jig-
gling about.

There were probably fifteen girls in there this morning, compet-
ing for the limited water. Deirdre and I had a showerhead and were
relying on my leper status to keep it to ourselves. I saw Shagger casting a few glances towards us, as if she might be repenting her shunning. As I stepped out of the water flow to shampoo my hair, Deirdre
said, laughingly, "You're getting breasts."

"Am not!" I said, automatically, even before looking down. Then
I looked down, and saw that I sort of am. I've had sort of breast
buds for ages, behind my nipples. Now that's all my mother has, so
I thought that would be all I had, but now they were swelling out
and kind of pouching. Lots of the other girls in VC have quite jiggly
breasts already. It doesn't make as much of a distinction as whether
you have pubic hair, which I have, much darker than the hair on my
head, and periods, which almost everyone does by now. I've had periods for two years. I was afraid they'd stop me being able to see fairies, but they made no difference at all, whatever C. S. Lewis thought
about puberty.

"You need a bra," Deirdre said.

"Do not," I riposted feebly. I pushed her out of the spray and rinsed
my hair. As the shampoo was running down, I looked down at my
incipient breasts. "Hey Dee, do you think they're an awfully funny
shape?"

She was laughing so much she could hardly catch her breath. People
were starting to look to see what was so funny.

"No, really," I said, quietly but vehemently. "They're sort of pear
shaped. Other people's aren't like that." I looked around the girls in
the showers, and none of them had breasts shaped the way mine were.

"They're fine," Deirdre said.

"Hey Dreary, what's so funny?" Lorraine asked.

"Commie just made a great joke," Deirdre said.

Some of the girls finishing in the shower and wrapping themselves in towels started to sing "Jake the Peg." I glared at them, but it didn't work because of the water.

Deirdre and I stood together under the falling water. "They're fine," she whispered. "They just look funny because you're seeing them from on top. If you could see them straight on the way you see other people's you'd see they're the same."

"In a mirror," I said.

"You should say 'looking glass,' Karen says," Deirdre said.

"Crap," I said, using another word that school didn't approve.

The only mirror is above the row of sinks in the toilets where we brush our teeth, and our hair. It's a long strip of mirror fixed on the wall, with the light strip above it.

"Come on," I said.

Deirdre giggled and grabbed her towel, and I grabbed mine and wrapped it around me like a cloak. I put my soap and my shampoo back into my sponge bag, because otherwise someone would steal it, or open the shampoo and pour it down the drain, that happened to me with my shower gel my first week, when I left it in the shower.

We went into the toilets, which were right next to the shower room. There was nobody there, which was easy to see because none of the toilet cubicles has doors. I put the sponge bag down and wrapped my towel around my head like a turban. That's a useful skill which Sharon had taught me. If you give it a tuck, it just stays there. Sharon has long unruly hair and it keeps even that in place. So my towel was here and Deirdre's was around her shoulders, and we were otherwise naked.

We saw at once that the strip of mirror was useless. It reflected our faces and necks, but nothing as low as our breasts.

"Maybe if we stood on something," Deirdre said, looking around.

"There's nothing," I said. "Unless we stood on the toilet seats, and then we'd be too high."

"Let's try it," she said.

So we shut two of the toilet seats and climbed onto them, and saw that we were too high, so we tried crouching to get the right angle, pretty much naked and balancing precariously and giggling, because it really was very funny. And that's when one of the prefects came in to see what the noise was about.

Thursday 15th November 1979

Either my dream-protection didn't work, or she isn't sending the dreams, they're just coming out of my subconscious.

I dreamed last night that my mother had a plan to separate us. She was going to live in Colchester in Essex and take Mor with her, because, she said, Mor was more biddable and I didn't do what I was told, and because I'd argued so hard to stay. We were protesting and fighting and she was dragging Mor away physically and I was crying and clinging to her. In some ways it was the opposite of what happened in the labyrinth. I was trying to hold on to her and my mother was trying to drag her off, and she started changing into different things and I had to hold on to her. I couldn't bear the thought of the separation, and I was planning to complain to everyone, the whole family, that it was unendurable and they couldn't let it happen. They let my mother get away with so much because they don't want to face the fact that she's mad, I was thinking, and Mor was howling and holding on to me, when I woke up. For a second there was a huge sense of relief that it had all been a dream, and then an instant later the memory that the reality was far worse. People can come *back* from Colchester. (No idea why Colchester.) I don't know what it means to be dead.

I'm reading Arthur C. Clarke's *Imperial Earth*. It has so many lovely science-fictional reversal moments. It isn't *Childhood's End* or *2001*, but it's just what I want today. There are a couple of Clarkes I've never found, and I've put them on this week's list.

I wonder if there will be fairies in space? It's a more possible thought in Clarke's universe than Heinlein's somehow, even though Clarke's engineering seems just as substantial. I wonder if it's because he's British? Never mind space, do they even have fairies in America? And if they do, do they all speak Welsh, all over the world?

Friday 16th November 1979

Letter this morning. I haven't opened it, and won't.

In prayers today Deirdre said "resur-esh-kun" instead of "resur-ection" at the end of the Creed. Thinking about that during the hymn, I was wondering about "the resurrection of the body and the life of the world to come," and how that relates to what I saw on Halloween. On the one hand, how much more likely resurrection if the dead process through the valley and descend into the hill. On the other, where is the religion? Where is Jesus? The fairies were there, but I didn't see any saints or anything. I've been mouthing the Creed without ever thinking about it properly.

To tell the truth I've been pretty angry with God since Mor died: He doesn't seem to do anything, or to help at all. But I suppose it's all like magic, you can't tell if it does anything, or why, not to mention mysterious ways. If I were omnipotent and omnibenevolent I wouldn't be so damn ineffable. Gramma used to say that you couldn't tell how things would work out for the best. I used to believe that when she was alive, but then after she died, and Mor died, I don't know. It's not that I don't believe in God, it's just that I haven't felt very inclined to get down and worship someone who wants me to think "no doubt the universe is unfolding as it should." Because I don't. I think I ought to do something about the way the universe is unfolding, because there are things that need obvious and immediate attention, like the fact that the Russians and the Americans could blow the world to bits at any moment, and Dutch elm disease, and famine in Africa, not to mention my mother. If I just left the universe for God to unfold, she'd have grabbed a chunk of it last year. And if God's plan for stopping her involves us and the fairies and Mor dying and me getting mashed up, well, if I were omnipotent and omniscient I think I could have come up with a better one. Lightning bolts never go out of fashion.

I was reading *The Broken Sword* and there are times I think gods like that would be easier to worship. Not to mention they're more on a human scale. Meddling like that. More like fairies. (What are fairies? Where do they come from?)

But I do not want to give Grampar another stroke, so I continue to go to church and to school prayers and take communion even though I don't know how it fits together. It's not something I can imagine talking to a vicar about, somehow.

With fairies it isn't a matter of faith. They're right there. They might not take any notice of you, but they're right there where you can argue with them. And they know a lot about magic and how the world works, and they're in favour of intervening in things. I could do some magic. I can think of all sorts of things that would be useful. I could make a better dream-ward. And I'd really like a karass.

Saturday 17th November 1979

Seven books waiting for me in the library. I wonder what happens if there are more than eight? The woman librarian was there today, and she let me fill my own interlibrary loan cards out. If I keep ordering fifty or so books a week, there may well be more than eight on any given Saturday. I wonder if I could get permission to go into town on a week night. Some girls go in for music lessons. Maybe I could start learning an instrument so I could go to the library, though as I am so pathetic at music it might not work. I wonder if there's any other kind of extracurricular thing they'd let me in for. I could ask Miss Carroll.

I didn't have any money, but I went down by the bookshop anyway. I've discovered the wood across from it is called Poacher's Wood— it's on the map—and I went in there to burn the letter I got yesterday. I went a way in, and made a circle. Nobody saw me except a couple of indifferent fairies. I didn't read the letter either. I didn't even open it. Because it was only one, and solid like that, I didn't make a fire, I just set fire to the bottom corner and dropped it. I nearly burned my hair when it caught more quickly than I'd expected, so I won't try that again.

It was cold but not raining, the first time I'd been outside without it being rainy for ages. I tried sitting on the bench where I read *Triton* to read *Born with the Dead* but the wind was too cold. I don't mind the cold all that much, what I do mind is the way the days are so short. It was getting dark before it was time to go back to school.

I looked around the bookshop and saw some things I want to buy when I have some money again, or if not, order from the library. There's an adult book by Alan Garner called *Red Shift*. I wonder what it's about? It has a weird cover with a standing stone and a light, which doesn't mean anything. If I tell Daniel I want to buy it, he'll probably send me some more money, unless that ten pounds was supposed to last me until Christmas. Well, if I tell him I want it and it was supposed to, then he can say that, and I can just order it.

Afterwards, because it was dark but I didn't want to go back, and I didn't have money to sit in a cafe pretending to drink tea, I looked around the other shops in town. I went into Woolworths where I pinched a bottle of talc and a Twix. There was a girl called Carrie in the Home who pinched things all the time, and she showed me how to do it. It's quite easy as long as you keep calm. Nobody pays any attention to me. I wouldn't take a book though, or rather, I would from Woolworths, if they had any, but I wouldn't from a bookshop, not unless I was *desperate*.

I went into *C&A* and looked at bras. I didn't try any on. They're more expensive than I would have thought, and the sizing is very complicated. Auntie Teg would know about them.

In Smiths I saw Gill looking at records. I don't care about records at all, in fact I associate being interested in pop music with the stuff she was talking about despising, trying to get boys interested in you. But I went to say hello. She was looking at a record called *Anarchy in the U.K.* by a group called the Sex Pistols. It was a very ugly cover, but I am quite interested in anarchism because of *The Dispossessed*. I think it would be much fairer to live on Anarres. Gill said we wouldn't like it because our parents wouldn't have money and we wouldn't have advantages. I said everyone would have the same advantages. I didn't say my family weren't as rich as everyone else's anyway. I said why should we have a better education than someone who can't afford Arlinghurst?

Gill bought the record, though she's not going to be able to play it until Christmas so I don't see the point.

On the way back, we talked about Leonardo. Apparently, as well as painting the Mona Lisa, he was a scientist and invented helicopters and studied fossils and kept a notebook. Gill has a book of lives of scientists which she offered to lend me, which is kind of her, though it isn't at all my thing. She's a bit—I don't know. She's not stupid, which is refreshing, and she's not afraid to talk to me, but she seems a bit overeager somehow, which is off-putting. I get the feeling she wants something.

I shared the Twix with Deirdre. I didn't tell her I pinched it.

Sunday 18th November 1979

I wrote to Grampar. When I next have some money I'll buy him a get well card. I told him about my marks (boringly top in everything except maths as usual) and about the weather. I wrote to Daniel, mostly about *Imperial Earth* and *The Shockwave Rider*, but mentioning the

Garner. I wish he'd give me pocket money like most of the girls get, and then I'd know how much I was going to get. I also wrote to Auntie Teg about the bra problem, very carefully not asking for money, in fact saying specifically not to send any, because that wouldn't be fair, just wanting to know how the sizing works. There's a number and a letter. I suppose I could ask Deirdre, or even Gill, but I'd rather not.

No buns today.

Tuesday 20th November 1979

Parcel from Daniel this morning, with Clifford Simak's *City* and Frank Herbert's *Dune*, neither of which look all that immediately appealing. It's so great having plenty to read. Also, another ten pounds. I don't know, if he's going to send me ten pounds every time I mention wanting to buy a book I suppose it's good, but it's very unreliable. I talked to Deirdre about this, though it was hard to get her to open up, as money, and pocket money, is one of those taboo subjects which you're supposed to talk about in oblique ways. But when she did start to talk, I could hardly shut her up.

"I get two pounds whenever we come back here. My mother says I don't need any money because it's all provided, but that's daft. I know you've noticed I'm always borrowing your soap. There's soap and shampoo and all that, and if you want anything at all at the tuck shop, even an apple. And if you don't buy buns ever, everyone says you're mean, or worse, knows you're poor and patronizes you. Karen bought me a bun last term and said 'I know you won't be able to pay me back, but don't worry about that at all' in such a smarmy way. So I bought buns the first week after half term."

I had noticed, because she bought me one too. "You don't have to buy me a bun back, really," I said. "Though of course it's nice to have one."

"Most of the girls have a pound every week, or even two pounds, some of them. I don't know how they'll manage if they ever really do change the pound notes to coins, because they send it in letters. Nobody talks about exactly how much they get, because it's vulgar to mention specifics about money."

Vulgar to mention specifics about money, but what kind of car your father has and what job he has and what kind of house and what kind of fur coat your mother has are common topics of conversation. I didn't even know there were different kinds, let alone which are good. The first time they asked me I said fox, just at random, which seems to be plausible, though Josie asked me if I meant silver fox or just plain red fox. It was so obvious from the framing of her question that silver fox was good that I didn't hesitate. Of course, my mother doesn't have a fur coat at all, and if she did she'd probably torture the poor thing. Anyway, I think fur is wrong, and I said so. I said I'm never going to have a fur coat, not ever, because it's wrong to kill animals just for the fur. I'm not a vegetarian, I think it's all right to kill animals to eat them, because that's different. They'd do that to us. There's no need for us to take their fur just to show off.

There are five school weeks until Christmas, so if I divide this ten pounds into two pounds a week that would work pretty well. Though I might anticipate on it to buy a bra this weekend, because now I've noticed that I have breasts I can't seem to stop noticing them, and it would be nice to have a harness to get them out of the way.

Wednesday 21st November 1979

Letter.

I didn't open it, but just touching it seemed to bring on the pain in my leg, it's been very bad indeed today.

This morning I finished *Up the Line* as I was sitting here, and I didn't have anything else with me, so I was going to get something off the shelf. Miss Carroll was bustling about shelving a consignment of new books that had come in, mostly in nonfiction, and I was sitting in my usual corner, where I have panelling on two sides and a bookshelf in front of me. Sometimes I sit one seat along, where I can see out of the window, but there's nothing worth seeing today, grey sky and bare branches and endless rain.

I was about to get up and go to the shelves, when Miss Carroll came over. "I remember you were asking about Plato," she said, and put down a brand-new copy of the Everyman edition of Plato's *Republic*. She also casually left two other books on the table nearby, a most intriguing book by Josephine Tey called *Daughter of Time* and Nevil Shute's *An Old Captivity*, which I have read, of course, it's the Leif Erickson one.

The Republic isn't as much fun as *The Symposium*. It's all long speeches, and nobody bursting in drunk to woo Socrates in the middle. But it's very interesting all the same. I keep thinking that it wouldn't work, though, like Sam said. Human nature is against it. People just tend to behave in certain ways because they are people. And if Socrates thinks ten-year-olds would be blank slates for him to work with, it must have been a long time since he was ten! Put me and Mor in *The Republic* and we'd turn it upside-down in five minutes. You'd have to start with babies, like *Brave New World*, which I see now is influenced by Plato. You could have a lovely story about two people in Plato's Republic falling in love and messing up the entire plan. Falling in love would be a perversion. It would be like being queer is for Laurie and Ralph. I prefer Triton or Anarres if I want a utopia. You know what I'd love to read? A Dialogue between Bron and Shevek and Socrates. Socrates would love it too. I bet he wanted people who argued. You can tell he did, you can tell that's what he loved really, at least in *The Symposium*.

When I came back this afternoon and sat down here again, I noticed the Shute and the Tey were still there. She mostly doesn't move my things, and if she does she tells me where they are, or gives them to me. But these were hers. All the same I started reading the Tey. I think she meant it for me. I think she noticed moving around was hard today and brought it over so I'd have something. I'm positive she ordered *The Republic* for me. I suppose I am the only person who actually uses this library for the purpose to which it is intended—no, that's not fair, some of the sixth-form girls do use it to get books out for essays. I've seen them. But I suppose Miss Carroll must have taken notice of me sitting here all the time reading and done something nice for me.

I should do something nice for her. People sometimes buy teachers buns. Does Miss Carroll count as a teacher? Or maybe I could think of something to get her for Christmas.

Thursday 22nd November 1979

My leg's still not great. I wonder if I should go to the doctor again about it. Nurse has the prescription for Distalgesic, I could go to her and have one. I would, except it's down two flights of stairs and then up one.

Who would have thought Richard the Third didn't actually kill the princes in the Tower?

Letter from Auntie Teg, full of news. And now I understand the bra system, though if I have to be measured I don't know about that. Maybe I should just try on some likely sizes and refine from that.

Friday 23rd November 1979

I went to Nurse in the end yesterday, and she gave me a painkiller and said I ought to go to the doctor and she was making an appointment for me. I don't see the point, considering, but I didn't argue.

I got Gill to put the letter in the kitchen dustbin for me. Having all the scraps and grounds and everything dumped on it will stop it being so strong, and soon it will be taken away altogether. I asked Deirdre first, but she wouldn't touch it. Sensible of her really.

No wonder fairies run away from pain. They like to be entertained, and it's awfully boring.

Tomorrow, I have to be fit to go to the library.

Saturday 24th November 1979

Only three things for me at the library. I picked them up and bought a get well card for Grampar and came straight back. *Red Shift* and a bra can wait until next week.

Sometimes I'm not sure whether I'm entirely human.

I mean, I know I am. I shouldn't think my mother is beyond sleeping with the fairies—no, that's not how you say it. "Sleeping with the fairies" means dead. I shouldn't think she's beyond having sex with fairies, but if she did she'd boast about it. She's never so much as hinted. She wouldn't have said it was Daniel and made him marry her. Besides, Daniel does kind of look like us, Sam said so. And children of fairies in songs and stories are always great heroes—though come to think I never heard what happened to Tam Lin's Janet's child. But look at Earendil and Elwing. No, that's not what I mean.

What I mean is, when I look at other people, other girls in school, and see what they like and what they're happy with and what they want, I don't feel as if I'm part of their species. And sometimes—sometimes I don't care. I care about so few people really. Sometimes it feels as if it's only books that make life worth living, like on Halloween when I wanted to be alive because I hadn't finished *Babel 17.* I'm sure that isn't normal. I care more about the people in books than the people I see every day. Sometimes Deirdre gets on my wick so much I want to be cruel to her, to call her Dreary the way everyone does, to yell at her that she's stupid. I only don't out of sheer selfishness, because she's practically the only one who talks to me. And Gill, sometimes Gill gives me the creeps. Who could help wanting to Impress a dragon in preference? Who wouldn't want to be Paul Atreides?

Sunday 25th November 1979

Wrote to Auntie Teg, gratefully. She asked about whether I'd be there for Christmas, so I wrote to Daniel and asked about that. I expect he'll be fine with it, it'll get me out of the way. I also wrote to Sam about *The Republic*, at length. And I wrote in the card to Grampar too—it's nice, it has an elephant in bed, with a thermometer sticking out beside his trunk.

I miss Grampar. It's not that I'd have a lot to talk to him about really, like Sam, it's just that he's an essential part of life. He fits into my life. Grampar and Gramma brought us up, and they didn't need to really, they could have left us with my mother, only they never would.

Grampar taught us about trees, and Gramma taught us about poetry. He knew every kind of tree and wildflower, and taught us to tell trees from their leaves first, and later from their buds and bark so we would know them in winter. He taught us to plait grass too, and to card wool. Gramma didn't care about nature so much, though she'd quote "With the kiss of the sun for pardon and the song of the birds for mirth, one is nearer God's heart in a garden than anywhere else on Earth." But it was the words she loved really, not the garden. She taught us to cook, and to memorise poetry in Welsh and English.

They were a funny couple in a way. They didn't agree about all that much. Often they exasperated each other. They didn't even have all that many interests in common. They met doing amateur dramatics, but she loved plays and he loved being on the stage. Yet they loved each other. The way she used to say "Oh, *Luke!*" in a fond and exasperated way.

I think she felt confined by her life. She was a teacher, and a mother and a grandmother. I think she would have liked more poetry in her life, one way or another. She certainly encouraged me to write it. I wonder what she would have thought of T. S. Eliot?

Monday 26th November 1979

I woke up in the night—this was not a dream. I woke up and I couldn't move at all, I was absolutely paralysed, and she was in the room, hovering over me, I know she was. I tried to cry out and wake someone but I couldn't. I could feel her coming nearer, coming down over my face. I couldn't move or speak, there was nothing to use against her. I started repeating the Litany Against Fear from *Dune*, in my head, "Fear is the mind killer, fear is the little-death," and then she was gone and I could move again. I got out of bed and went to get a drink of water and my hand was shaking so much that I poured half of it down my front.

If she can get in, another time she might kill me.

The fairies here won't talk to me, and I can't write to Glorfindel or Titania and ask them how to stop her. Even if Daniel lets me go there for Christmas, that's a month, well, close enough.

I have got two little stones I used in part of the circle last time I burned letters, and I have put them on the windowsills. I think that if she tried to come through the stones would rise up as sheets of rock and block the way, making the windows solid with the wall. Really it should be a whole row of stones, or a line of sand or something. The real trouble with that is that there are eleven other girls sleeping in this dorm, and any of them will see just a little odd pebble and not care about disturbing it, or actively want it gone. I'll have to check them every night before I go to sleep, and somebody is going to notice sooner or later. I suppose I could tell them, but all this scary stuff has worked all too well already.

She couldn't get through stained glass, for what good that is.

I am going to have to get some stuff together and do some real protection magic, even without talking to the fairies first. I'm afraid to, but not as afraid as I am of her coming into the room when I'm asleep and holding me frozen like that. I couldn't move at all, and I really tried.

Tuesday 27th November 1979

It's funny how it's hard to concentrate on reading in a waiting room. On the one hand, I really want nothing more than to pull down inside a book and hide. On the other, I have to keep listening for them to call my name, so every sound distracts me. Everyone here is sick, which is very depressing. The notices are about contraception and diseases. The walls are a bilious green. There's a leaflet about getting your eyes tested. Maybe I should.

Looking out of the window, a list of everything I see while waiting:
2 scruffs.
1 man with sheepdog—a lovely sheepdog, in beautiful condition.
6 people on bikes.
12 doughy housewives with 19 kids.
4 unaccompanied school age kids.
4 young couples.
1 baby in a pushchair, pushed by a woman in a puce dress.
1 tatty old man in jeans—what was he thinking? Jeans are for young people.
1 man parking a motorbike.
Millions of cars.
2 businessmen.
1 taxi driver.
1 man with a moustache and his wife.

2 blonde women in matching green coats, who came past twice,
   once in each direction. Maybe sisters?
1 pair of middle-aged twins. (I sort of hate to see twins, though
   I know it doesn't make sense.)
1 pompous man in a dinner jacket. (At lunchtime?)
1 man in a pink shirt. (Pink!)
A skinhead carrying a dragon tankard. (He stopped outside the
   window and I got a good look at it.)
1 business woman, in a pin-striped suit with a briefcase. (She
   looked very groomed. Would I like to be her? No. But most
   of everyone I saw.)
6 teenagers in gym clothes running a race.
8 sparrows.
12 pigeons.
1 unaccompanied black-and-white dog, probably mostly terrier,
   that lifted a leg against the motorbike. He went off alone,
   looking jaunty and sniffing at everything. Maybe I'd like to
   be him.

People who notice me:
   1 man in a denim shirt, who waved.

Funny how unobservant people are generally.

When it finally got to be my turn, the doctor was very gruff. He
didn't have much time for me. He said he'd recommend me to the
Orthopaedic Hospital and get my x-rays sent there. I had to wait all
that time surrounded by snuffling children and decrepit old people
for two minutes of the doctor's attention. I missed physics for that?

However, I bought two apples and a new bottle of shampoo, and
I went back via the library and managed to return three books and
pick up four, so I count it a successful trip to town.

Waiting for the bus back to school, I was thinking about magic. I
wanted the bus to come, and I wasn't exactly sure when it was due. If

I reached magic into that, imagined the bus just coming round the corner, it isn't as if I'd be materialising a bus out of nowhere. The bus is somewhere on its round. There are two buses an hour, say, and for the bus to be coming right when I wanted it, it must have started off on its route at a precise time earlier, and people will have caught it and got on and off at particular times, and got to where they're going at different times. For the bus to be where I want it, I'd have to change all that, the times they got up, even, and maybe the whole timetable back to whenever it was written, so that people caught the bus at different times every day for months, so that I didn't have to wait today. Goodness knows what difference that would make in the world, and that's just for a bus. I don't know how the fairies even dare. I don't know how anyone could know enough.

Magic can't do everything. Glory couldn't help Gramma's cancer, though he wanted to and we wanted him to. It may reach back into time, but it can't make Mor alive again. I remember when she died and Auntie Teg told me and I thought, *She knows, and I know, and other people are telling other people and more and more people know and it spreads out like ripples on a pond and there's no undoing it without undoing everything.* It's not like falling out of a tree and nobody seeing but the fairies.

Wednesday 28th November 1979

Gill sneaked into the dorm last night to bring me her scientist book. She sat on my bed, and as we were talking she put her arm behind me, as if casually, but I could see how carefully she was doing it, and that she was looking at me all the time. I jumped up and said she ought to go, but Sharon gave me a very strange look afterwards and I think she saw. Could I have done something to encourage Gill? Or anyway, to make her think I might be interested in her in that way? It's very awkward, as she's one of the very few people who are actually talking to me. I think I need to talk to her, but not in the dorm! And I'm afraid to say I want to talk to her privately in case she takes that for more encouragement, which would be hurtful when it turned out not to be.

In *I Capture the Castle*, which isn't what I expected it to be at all, there's a bit where the heroine is in love with one man and a different man is in love with her, and she thinks she'll make do with him, maybe, but she also knows it won't work and it's pointless and she doesn't want to hurt him. The way she feels about it and not wanting to hurt him is a bit like I feel about Gill and this. I honestly don't think it would be any different if it was a boy who was my friend. I'll say this to Gill when I get the chance. Maybe Saturday, or tomorrow after chem?

One of the stones was knocked off the windowsill, but I put it back. This is only a temporary fix, but it's holding for now. No more visitations.

Thursday 29th November 1979

Terrible dreams. I really do need to do something about this. I can't go on this way. I'll do it tonight if it's not raining.

Why aren't I like other people?

I look at Deirdre and her life is completely unruffled. Or does it just seem that way to me? She came up to me at break and drew me aside and said, "Shagger said that she saw Gill coming on to you," and she looked at me entirely trustingly.

"Shagger may have seen that, but I'm not interested in Gill and I mean to tell her so," I said.

"It's wrong," Deirdre said, utterly sure.

"I don't think it's wrong if both people want it, but in this case, I don't."

Deirdre looked confused and backed away, but later she offered me a Polo mint to show there were no hard feelings. I should buy her a bun for Sunday.

No chance to talk to Gill after chem. I think she may have been avoiding me. Maybe we don't need to have a conversation after all.

Friday 30th November 1979

I got up in the deep heart of night and did magic. I climbed down the elm into the grounds, found the circle I'd made last time, and put it back together. The moon was making fitful appearances through the clouds. I didn't make a fire this time.

I don't want to write down what I did. I have a superstitious feeling about it, that it would be wrong, that I shouldn't even have said so much as I have said. Maybe I should write it not just backwards but upside-down and in Latin? I think I know now why people don't write real magic books. It's just too difficult to put words around it when you've made it up yourself. Even so, even at the end I still felt as if I didn't really know what I was doing and I was improvising like mad. It's so different from doing what you've been told to do and you're pretty sure will work. The moon has always been my friend. But even so.

Always before, they'd told us what to do. Glorfindel had told us about throwing the flowers in the water, told me about sinking the comb in the bog. Standing there in my circle I felt very inexperienced, and as if I was half playing and it couldn't possibly work. Magic is very weird. I kept looking up through the bare branches at the moon in the clouds and waiting until it was clear for a moment. I made up a sort of poem to sing, which at least helped me get into the right frame of mind.

I was using things I remembered and things I was making up and things that seemed to fit. I was trying to do a magic for protection, and to find a karass. I had an apple—I'd had two and kept them

together for a few days so they were used to each other, even if they
didn't come from the same tree, and then I ate one of them, so it
was part of me, and I used the other one. Apples connect to apple
trees and the tamed growing world, and to Eden and the Garden of
Hesperides and Iduna and Eris—and also once I kept an apple in my
desk, in the grammar school until it got ripe and riper and then soft
and bruised and was a sweet-smelling sack of sap, and only when
it started to mildew on the outside did I throw it away. That was a
strong connection. In Ancient Persia, and now in some parts of India
I think, they practice "sky burial" where they put dead bodies out
on platforms and the birds eat them and they decay in sight. It must
make for strong magic, but it must be terrible when there's someone
you know and you can watch them falling apart like that. Cremation
might not be magical, but at least it's clean.

Anyway, I also cut my finger a little bit and used blood, I know it's
dangerous, but I also know it's powerful.

I saw the fairy who spoke to me that first time here, up in the tree.
There were other eyes in the branches, but I didn't recognise any
of them and they didn't speak. I don't know how to make friends with
them and get them to trust me. They're different from our fairies,
wilder, further from people.

Even with all that feeling like left luggage I have, even with Halloween, I have never felt so much like half a person as I did last night.
It felt as if an arm had been cut off, as if I was accustomed to holding
things in both hands and now I had to struggle along with one, only
magically. And yet—I didn't try to do a healing on that. I didn't even
think of it until now. Or on my leg either. I wonder if I could? It feels
as if it's dangerous to try, that even trying what I did was dangerous,
trying for a karass. Maybe I shouldn't have extended it beyond the
protection, which I really *needed* to do. Doing magic for things you
want yourself isn't safe. Glorfindel told me that. Most of what I want
I can't have for years, if at all. I know that. But a karass shouldn't be
impossible, should it? Or too dangerous to try for?

Of course, it's impossible to know whether it worked. That's always the problem with magic. One of the problems. Among the problems . . .

I'm exhausted today. I nearly fell asleep over Dickens in English. Mind you, he's snoozeworthy at the best of times. I keep yawning. But maybe tonight I will sleep without dreams. We'll see.

Saturday 1st December 1979

Today in the library, the male librarian stopped me. "You ordered *Beyond the Tomorrow Mountains*?" he asked.

I nodded.

"There's never been a British edition, so I'm afraid we can't get that for you."

"Ah," I said, disappointed. "Thank you anyway."

"I've noticed you've been doing a lot of interlibrary loans," he said.

"She said, the librarian said it would be all right," I stammered. "She said it was free because I'm under sixteen."

"There's no problem, you order as many books as you want and we'll get them for you," he said.

I relaxed and smiled at him.

"I just noticed that a lot of them are SF, and I wondered if you'd like to join our Tuesday evening SF book club."

A karass, I thought. Magic does work. My eyes filled up with tears and I couldn't speak for a moment because I was choking on them. "I don't know if they'll let me come in from school," I said, ungraciously. "What time is it?"

"We start at six, and usually go on until about eight. It's right here in the library. I understand that the process for girls from Arlinghurst who want to go to outside classes or educational activities is that they need a parent's signature, and a teacher or a librarian's signature."

"They agreed about the library," I said.

"They did." He smiled at me. He's going a bit bald on top, but he's not very old, and he has a lovely smile.

"And it would be very educational," I went on.

"It certainly would," he agreed. "I don't know if you could get a signature by this Tuesday, when we're discussing Le Guin, but the Tuesday after we're discussing Robert Silverberg, who I've noticed you seem to like."

I wrote down the information about it and collected my books and went and sat in the bakery cafe so happy I could sing. A karass, or the start of one! Oh I hope I can get there this Tuesday! I only haven't ordered any Le Guin from the library because I've read it all already, or at least I think so. I'd have a lot to say about her. A karass! Epic! I could sing with delight.

Sunday 2nd December 1979

Miss Carroll has signed the form for me to leave school for the book club! She says I'd have to have all my prep done ahead, but that's no trouble. She said they'd see it would be no trouble from my marks, but my marks had better not drop because of the book club. I said they certainly wouldn't. She asked if I'd liked the Tey, and I said I had enjoyed it a lot, which is true.

Carpenter says in the Inklings book that Lewis meant Aslan to be Jesus. I can sort of see it, but all the same it feels like a betrayal. It feels like allegory. No wonder Tolkien was cross. I'd have been cross too. I also feel tricked, because I didn't notice all this time. Sometimes I'm so stupid—but Aslan was always so much himself. I don't know what I think about Jesus, but I know what I think about Aslan.

I wrote to Grampar and Auntie Teg, telling them about the book club. And I wrote to Daniel begging him to sign the book club thing. I'm pretty sure he will. I also told him about the Aslan/Jesus conflation thing because it would be interesting to see what he thinks, and I asked him *again* about going home for Christmas. I told Grampar I'd try to.

I had a conversation with Gill, finally. It was pouring buckets, so people were doing dancing in the hall instead of games this afternoon, and she was hanging back instead of going to change afterwards, while I was coming out of the prep room where I'd been writing letters. She didn't say anything directly, but I said "Gill, I don't know if I've got the wrong idea here, but I wanted to say I like you as a friend, but I'm not interested in a physical relationship with you."

"You said you didn't like boys," she said.

I had too, I remembered it. "That doesn't mean I like girls," I said. "I don't think there's anything wrong with it, I think most people are interested in both, but I don't seem to be. Sorry. I expect I'm just peculiar."

This was all in the doorway to the prep room, and someone came up behind me and pushed past then, and Gill just waved and ran off to change. I hope it's all right. It does make things so complicated!

Monday 3rd December 1979

Letter from Daniel with another ten pounds and saying they want me at the Old Hall for Christmas but I can go down to South Wales for a few days afterwards. Feh. Why do they want me there? What good am I to them? I'd much rather go and help Auntie Teg with Grampar, especially if he really can come out for the day. They've never shown any sign at the Old Hall of anything but wanting to be rid of me as soon as they can. Daniel, well, I don't know what to think about him. I'm grateful he took me out of the Children's Home, but school isn't all that much better. He seems to want a connection, after not having one all that time. But I'm sure he and his sisters would have a better time if I wasn't there. And what on earth can I give them? I can't just give them a box of chocolates if I'm actually going to be there on Christmas Day. It'll be excruciating. Oh well, at least I can go down to South Wales afterwards I suppose.

Tuesday 4th December 1979

Of course no letter from Daniel with the signed form. It's unfair to even expect it, because the post would hardly have had time to get the form there and back. But it's my karass, and it's happening without me tonight, and they're going to be talking about *The Dispossessed*, so I can't help feeling cross. I suppose it's been happening every Tuesday all the time I've been here, but I didn't know, and now I do. That is unless the magic made it happen, instead of just making him ask me. The more I think about magic, what it does and how it influences things, the less I think I ought to mess with it.

School is being particularly tedious. I'm used to the girls calling me names, but some of them have started singing a little song about "Jake the Peg" when I pass by, or just humming it if there are teachers near. They want to infuriate me, so I just ignore them, which is much easier to do outwardly than inwardly. They do the same to Deirdre with "Danny Boy" and sometimes reduce her to tears. The awful thing about Deirdre is that she's such a cliche. She's Irish, and she's not the brightest bulb in the box. Karen gave her a bite of a muesli bar and she said it tasted like uncooked Christmas tree. She meant to say cake, of course, because that is what they taste like, but now everyone makes jokes about them cooking Christmas trees in Ireland. I had to laugh when I heard it, just because it's so surreal. I mean she laughed herself. That wasn't unkind. It's going on and on about it that's unkind, and of course that's what they're doing, because they see it hurts her. I have to make sure they don't see that I care about the stupid "Jake the Peg with his extra leg" nonsense.

I still can't forgive Lewis for his allegory. I understand now why Tolkien said in the prologue that he hated them. You can't take something that's itself and make it stand for something else. Or you can, but you shouldn't push it. If I try to think of it as a retelling of the gospels, that diminishes Narnia. I think I'm going to have trouble re-reading them without thinking about it. That's so annoying! However, Carpenter says Lewis wrote some books directly about Christianity—overtly about it, I mean. Maybe I should try them. I have to say I feel horribly mixed up about religion. And RE is no help. We're droning through the Journeys of Paul, and I'm reading my way slowly through the Bible. There are some good stories in it, in between all the tedium. But most of it is history, not so much theology, and I'd be very interested to know if Lewis says anything about fairies—because he has the maenads in *Prince Caspian* and they always remind me of fairies a bit. There's nothing here but the Interplanetary books, but I'll see if they have *Mere Christianity* in the town library, and if not, well, that's what interlibrary loan is for.

Just as I was writing that, Miss Carroll came over.

"Has your father signed the form for the book club?" she asked.

"Not yet," I said. "I'm sure he will, but there hasn't been time yet."

"If you like, I could take you tonight. If I'm there the whole time, *in loco parentis*, that would be all right. It would be like taking girls to the theatre. I've checked with Miss Ellis, and she says it would be fine." She smiled at me.

"But do you want to go?" I asked. I can't help being such an ungracious lump when people are nice to me. It isn't what I mean, it just comes out before I think.

"It should be interesting," she said.

"Do you even read SF?"

"I try to read a sample of what's in my library, so I can recommend things to people. I've certainly read some SF. It isn't my favourite, like it is yours, but I have read some. I've even read some Ursula Le Guin; I've read *A Wizard of Earthsea*."

"Did you like it?" I asked.

"I thought it was excellent." Miss Carroll sat down opposite me across the wooden table and looked at me quizzically. "What is this? I didn't expect to be interrogated on my suitability for the book club, I thought you'd be pleased."

"I am pleased," I said. "Thank you. I really want to go. I'm just not used—I mean I can't quite believe you're giving up your evening for me." She's quite young really. She must have boyfriends, or at least somewhere she lives and cooks herself dinner and reads her book without being disturbed. To be honest, I find it quite hard to imagine her life away from the school. But whatever it is, she could be doing it tonight, and instead she's going to the SF book club because I want to. Why would she do that? I didn't know magic worked this well. It's frightening.

"It'll be an interesting experience," she said. "It'll be nice to see how they do these things at the town library. And I always like hearing about books. Maybe we could start a book club here. Some of the older girls might be interested. Besides," she leaned forward and lowered her voice, even though we were the only people in the library, as usual. "One of the things they tell you in library school is that you have to consider the needs of the clients and keep them happy. Now you're definitely my best client, and one of the few people who is really using this library, so keeping you happy is important."

I laughed. "Thank you," I said. "Thank you very much."

So I am going to the book club tonight! Miss Carroll is going to pick me up after supper.

Wednesday 5th December 1979

Of course they didn't instantly decide they were my karass and welcome me to their bosoms. That would be too much to expect. But it was brill anyway.

I was so afraid we were going to be late that we were actually early. The library was just closing when we got there. The librarian looked quite surprised to see me coming in with Miss Carroll. "Ah, Miss Markova," he said, which is literally the first time anyone has ever called me that. I've been called Miss Phelps before occasionally, but never Miss Markova. It felt weird. "You made it after all."

"This is Miss Carroll, she's the librarian at the school. And this is, um . . ." I floundered.

"Greg Mansell, but do call me Greg."

"Then I'm Alison," Miss Carroll said, to my total surprise, and they shook hands. I'd stupidly never thought of her as having a first name, maybe because Carol is a first name.

I knew that I should have said my name, that they were both looking at me waiting for me to say it, but my tongue clotted in my mouth and I couldn't get it out. It wasn't that I'd forgotten my name, so much as I wasn't sure what form of it to use. "Mori," I said, after way too long. "My friends call me Mori."

Then two other people arrived, both middle-aged guys but one tall, Brian, and one short and stout, Keith. Greg took out his key and let us into a room at the back of the library.

The library must have been built about a hundred years ago. It's Victorian, with stone windows in brick walls. The room where they have the meetings was once a reading room, but now the reading room is the reference library upstairs and this is kept locked. It has wood panels to about elbow height, and above that it's painted cream between the windows—there are lots of windows on one side, but I couldn't see what was outside because it was dark. On the other long wall there's a huge dark Victorian painting of people sitting in a library reading, looking down at their backs as they sit at little tables among rows of bookshelves. This room isn't like that at all—there's one big old table in the middle with old wooden chairs around it. There are two busts, one at each end of the rectangular room. One is

Descartes, who I don't know but who has a wonderful face, and the other is Plato, yes!

I sat on the side of the table facing the picture, with my back to the windows, and Miss Carroll sat down next to me. The men, who all knew each other of course, were standing up talking. Some more men came in, some of them younger, but none of them much under thirty. Then two boys came in, wearing the purple school blazers of the local comprehensive school. I'd guess they were sixteen or seventeen. I was starting to think there weren't going to be any women when a stout grey-haired woman bustled in and sat at the head of the table. She had a big pile of Le Guin books in hardcover editions and she put them down next to her in a businesslike way. Seeing this, the others started to take seats. I was wishing I'd brought copies, but of course I didn't have any except my dear old *Wind's Twelve Quarters, Volume 2*. My mother still has all my books, but books are replaceable.

Miss Carroll was looking at the pile of books a bit nervously. "Have you read all those," she asked me quietly.

I looked at them properly, and I had, all except one called *The Eye of the Heron*. "All but one," I said. "And I've read one that isn't there, *The Word For World is Forest*."

"You really do read a lot of sci-fi," she said.

Just then the grey-haired woman took a deep breath as if she were about to begin, and as she did the door opened and a boy—a young man—practically fell into the room. He's the most gorgeous thing I ever saw, with longish blond hair flopping about his head, extremely blue eyes, a passionately intense gaze, though I didn't see that at once, and a kind of casual grace of movement even when tripping over his own feet. "I'm sorry I'm late, Harriet," he said, favouring the woman with a dazzling smile. "The bike had a puncture."

It seemed a cruel trick of the gods that such a glorious creature should have to go about on a bicycle. He sat down directly opposite me, so close that I could see the raindrops beading on his hair. He must be eighteen or nineteen. I wonder why he isn't in university? He has somewhat the look of a lion, or of a young Alexander the Great.

"I was just going to start, but you're not late," Harriet said, smiling at him. (Harriet! I've never met anyone called Harriet in real life. I had a brief fantasy about her being Harriet Vane, because she'd be about the right age for that, except that Harriet Vane would be addressed as Lady Peter, and anyway she's fictional. I can tell the difference, really I can.)

The door banged open again and a teenage girl came in. She was wearing a purple blazer, which looked appalling with her ginger hair. She sat with the two boys in blazers, who, I saw now, had kept a seat for her between them. I felt . . . not exactly jealous, but I felt a sort of pang when I saw that.

Then Harriet started to talk about Le Guin. She talked for about fifteen or twenty minutes. After that the talk became general. I talked far more than I should have. I knew it even at the time. I just couldn't stop myself. I didn't actually interrupt anyone, which would be unforgivable, I just didn't hold back enough to give other people a turn. Miss Carroll didn't say anything the whole time. The gorgeous boy said some very perceptive things about *The Lathe of Heaven*. One of the men, Keith I think, said it was like Philip K. Dick, which is *nonsense*, and the gorgeous boy said that while there were certain superficial similarities you can't compare Le Guin to Dick because her characters are like people in ways his just aren't, which is exactly what I'd have said. There's also apparently a film of it, which nobody has seen.

He also said that maybe she writes about the scientific process so well in *The Dispossessed*, despite not being a scientist, because she understands that creativity isn't all that different across fields. He and Brian agreed that she did get the scientific process right, and everyone deferred to them about that, so they must be something scientific. I didn't like to ask what. I'd already been talking too much, as I said. I kept thinking of things to say and ask, and thinking I'd said too much and should let other people speak, and then thinking of more things I just had to say, and saying them. I hope I didn't totally bore everyone.

The gorgeous boy—I must find out his name next time!—kept his eyes fixed on me when I was talking. It was quite disconcerting.

The most interesting thing anyone said though was said by one of the boys in purple blazers. I had said that Le Guin's worlds were real because her people were so real, and he said yes, but the people were so real because they were the people the worlds would have produced. If you put Ged to grow up on Anarres or Shevek in Earthsea, they wouldn't be the same people, the backgrounds made the people, which of course you see all the time in mainstream fiction, but it's rare in SF. That's absolutely true, and it's very interesting, and I couldn't help jumping in again to say that it fit back with *The Lathe of Heaven* and what happens to people in the different worlds, and whether a grey person in a world of grey people was inherently a different person from a brown one in a mixed race world.

I don't know when I had such a good time, and if it wasn't for worrying that I talked too much I'd say it was a total success. There's a thing—I've noticed it often. When I first say something, it's as if people don't hear me, they can't believe I'm saying it. Then they start to actually pay attention, they stop noticing that a teenage girl is talking and start to believe that it's worth listening to what I'm saying. With these people, it was much less effort than normal. Pretty much from the second time I opened my mouth their expressions weren't indulgent but attentive. I liked that.

Afterwards, Keith asked who was coming to the pub. The gorgeous boy went, and Harriet, and Greg, but not the teenagers in school blazers, and not me, because I had to go back to school. Everyone said goodbye to me, but I got all awkward and tongue-tied again saying goodbye and hoping to see them next week.

Miss Carroll had a word with Greg, and then we got back into her car and she drove back to school. "You don't get a lot of chance to talk to people about things that matter to you, do you?" she asked.

I stared out at the night and the dark. In between the traffic lights at the bottom of town and the school, there's nothing to make light but the occasional farmhouse, which means car headlights seem an intrusion of brightness. I saw mice and rabbits and the occasional fairy scurrying off as the beams lit them. "No," I said. "I don't get a lot of chance to talk to people at all."

"Arlinghurst is a very good school in its way," she said.

"Not for people like me," I said.

"The last bus that runs past the school leaves at eight-fifteen," she said. "They finished closer to nine tonight. I asked Greg as one librarian to another if he'd be able to give you a lift back regularly, and he said he would. As long as you're in bed by lights out, that should be all right."

"It's very nice of him. He's very kind to ask me at all. You don't think I talked too much?"

Miss Carroll laughed, as the car swung between the elms into the school drive. "Maybe a little too much. But they certainly seemed interested in what you had to say. I wouldn't worry about it."

I do worry about it though.

Thursday 6th December 1979

The days are getting awfully short. It seems to be dark all the time. It's dark until well after nine, which keeps me inside in the morning. I had been in the habit of going outside for a moment before breakfast, just to breathe. I didn't go anywhere, just stepped outside by the cloakrooms and breathed for a moment before coming back into the din of breakfast. Breakfast is bread and margarine, as much as you want, and overcooked watery English scrambled eggs, with tinned tomatoes, which I don't eat. On Sundays, and just occasionally on

other days, we also have sausages, which seem like ambrosia. The
staff don't attend breakfast, so everyone always talks at the top of
their voice, and of course that means everyone has to if they want to
be heard. It sounds like a bear pit, but more high-pitched. Sometimes
I stand outside the cloakroom and I can hear it down the corridor,
like those Eighteenth-century madhouses where people would go for
entertainment to hear the lunatics howl. Bedlam.

It's also dark, or almost, by the time we've finished lessons. The
lights are on, and the sun is well down. There's still a little light in
the sky, but there's no doubt it's night rather than day. I like to walk
away from the school building and turn around and look at the
lights, which seem orange in the twilight. It reminds me somehow of
coming home from school with Gramma and Mor on some special
day near Christmas, one of us holding each of her hands. Maybe her
school had finished a day before ours and she'd come to meet us. We
were still in the Infants, I expect we were about six. I just remember
holding her hand and looking back at the lights with the sky not
quite dark.

It makes me melancholy to remember, but a little bit of the secu-
rity and excitement comes through from the way I was feeling in the
memory. Memories are like a big pile of carpets, I keep them piled
up in one big pile in my head and don't pay much attention to them
separately, but if I want to, I can get back in and walk on them and
remember. I'm not really there, not like an elf might be, of course.
It's just that if I remember being sad or angry or chagrined, a little
of that feeling comes back. And the same goes for happy, of course,
though I can easily wear out the happy memories by thinking about
them too much. If I do, when I'm old all the bad memories will still
be sharp, because of pushing them away, but all the good ones will
be worn out. I won't really remember that day with Gramma, which
I already don't remember properly, I'll just remember all these short
winter days in school, walking out alone and looking back at the lit
windows.

I'm sick of the dark. I know the turning year is part of life. I like seasons and seasonal fruit. The apples must be nearly done, and I expect there are bright orange tangerines in their fascinating purple wrappings with Spanish writing in Mrs. Lewis's shop even now. (If I could smell a tangerine! Maybe on Saturday.) But I'm getting to hate the darkness at this time of year. I'm not allowed outside at lunchtime, which is the one time it is reliably light, even if it's always grey and usually raining.

The days will get longer again. Spring will come. But it seems a long time to wait.

Friday 7th December 1979

Letter back from my father with the book club permission, and about time too! So I can go next week.

I was thinking about the book club, and wondering who among them is in my karass, really. The gorgeous boy? (Must find out his name!) He looked at me seriously with his beautiful eyes. And even if he's wrong about some fairly fundamental things, he is prepared to listen. I feel a little shiver when I think about him looking at me. How about those three with the purple blazers, who are my own age? (Must find out their names too, but with a less burning urgency.) I'd certainly like to get to know them better, and they are interested in books. I'll try to talk to them next time. Harriet? I didn't connect with her much, but she's very intelligent. Brian? Keith? I don't know. The others, who I didn't really meet properly? Too early to tell. Greg? Maybe. Miss Carroll? (Alison . . .)

I looked up at her as I wrote her name. She's puttering about sticking labels in books at her desk. For all that she said she's keeping her clients satisfied, she took me to the book club because of the magic. I know she did, and it makes me feel a little sick. Magic works on what's there, so probably she liked me a little anyway, and noticed me. She got me *The Republic.* Though magic can make things happen before you do it. It can make things have happened. Maybe if I hadn't done that magic, she wouldn't have ordered the Plato. I don't know if she likes me, really, or if it's only the magic making her. If she doesn't really like me, how can I like her back? How can it mean anything?

And of course, the same goes for the others, really. Is it really a karass, if I used magic to make it happen? It's like making the bus come, all those people, all those days, all those lives changed, just to make the bus be coming at the moment I want it. Only it's more than that, making them like me. Making them be my karass.

I didn't think this through enough. I was thinking about a karass in too abstract a way, I didn't think enough about the people, about manipulating them. I didn't even know them, and I was doing it.

Is this how she started? My mother, Liz?

I wish I could talk to Glorfindel about this, or somebody who would understand. I don't know if he would or not, but he's the most likely to. I don't understand why the fairies here are so unfriendly—uncaring is more like it. They should be getting used to me by now. When I go home after Christmas, I'll find him and talk to him no matter what.

Is using magic inherently bad? Is it if it's for yourself? Am I supposed to leave myself totally vulnerable to her using it against me, then? Or was it only the karass magic that was bad, and the protection was okay? Or—always the trap with magic—was it all going to happen anyway and I only think the magic did it? No, look at the timing. It was my karass magic, and I think maybe it brought the whole book club (that's been meeting for months) into existence. I never saw anything about it before, and I go to the library all the time. Maybe those people wouldn't even exist. Maybe Harriet—who is the oldest—maybe her parents wouldn't have had her, maybe her whole life, sixty years or more, exists just so there could be a book club and I could have a karass, so we could sit there discussing *The*

Lathe of Heaven, which is the perfect book for this, and whether it's like Dick.

Gosh I do hope it isn't like Dick. Like Dick doesn't bear thinking about.

I don't want to be like her.

I won't use magic any more, or anyway, just to protect myself and other people and the world. It's better to be like George Orr than have her win. I don't know what she's doing. There have been no more dreams, and no more poisonous letters either. I'm sort of worried that this means she's planning something worse.

What she really wants is to set herself up as a dark queen. I don't know how that would have worked, but that's what she wants. (She has read LOTR, and I don't know if she read it identifying with all of the evil people and hoping the good ones wouldn't resist their temptations, but I know she has read it because the first time I read it, it was her copy. This proves that just reading it isn't enough. After all, the devil can quote scripture.) She wants everyone to love her and despair. That's not a sane goal, but it's what she wants. This is not what I want. What would be the point? It's bad enough thinking about making Miss Carroll (who stopped shelving to smile at me when she saw me looking over at her) like me.

How could anyone want a world of puppets?

We were so right to stop her, and it really was worth it, worth dying, worth living on broken. If she'd done it, it would always have been the case that we'd loved our mother, that everyone did. I thought I knew how important it was, but I didn't really.

Morally, magic is just indefensible.

I was going to say I wish I'd known that before, but I did really. I knew what happened after I threw the comb in the bog. I had thought about the bus. I knew about her. I should have applied that.

Saturday 8th December 1979

Greg wasn't in the library this morning, and only three books I'd ordered, none of them very exciting. It felt a bit flat. I walked down to the bookshop. It was spitting icy rain from a very low sky, the sort of rain that seems to come from all directions. An umbrella's no use against it, not that I can use an umbrella anyway with a cane in one hand and a bag in the other. Going down the hill towards the bookshop and the little pond the wind was blowing directly into my face. It kept blowing my hat off. It wasn't the sort of rain you can enjoy, you just have to squinch your face up and endure that kind of thing.

At the bookshop I saw the ginger-haired girl. She was looking at the children's books. She saw me as soon as I came in, because the door banged in the wind and so of course she looked up. She was carrying a huge canvas bag over her shoulder, and clutching a pile of carrier bags as well. "Hi," she said, taking a step towards me. "I saw you at the book club but I didn't get your name."

"Likewise," I said, trying to smile and look friendly, trying not to think about what the magic might have done to her, to the world to make her like me. I could feel her looking at me and wondered what she thought about me. She didn't look quite as awful with a black coat instead of the purple blazer. Her hair was still ginger, and very unruly, but it just looked like a bit of a mess instead of an explosion at a paint factory.

"I'm Janine," she said.

"I'm Mori."

"Brill name. What's it short for?"

"Morwenna," I said.

Janine laughed. "That's a bit of a mouthful. Is it Welsh?"

"Yes it is. It means a breaking wave." Actually, literally it means *white sea*, but that's what it must mean, that's what white sea is, the foam on the breaking wave.

We stood there for a moment in amity but without anything to say. Then she said "I'm Christmas shopping. Only two weeks to go."

"I haven't bought anything yet!" I said, suddenly realising. "Are you buying everyone books?"

"Most of my family wouldn't appreciate them," she said. "But I thought I might buy the Earthsea books for Diane, after all the talk about them the other night."

"Don't you have them already?" I asked.

"Nope, read them out of the kids' library," she said. "Besides, I've had to make a rule about the others never touching my stuff, so I'm not about to start lending them books just when I've got it into their heads."

"I could buy my father a book," I said. "I certainly have to buy him something. But it's so hard to know what he has."

"What does he like?" Janine asked.

"Oh, SF," I said.

"Is that how you started liking it?"

"No. I didn't meet him until quite a short time ago, and I've been reading it for ages."

"You didn't meet your—" she began, and then stopped and looked away. She shifted her bags to her other hand, and when she spoke it was in a falsely casual tone. "Oh, you mean divorce?"

"Yes," I said, though in fact the actual divorce is only now going through. Daniel had disappeared without bothering with any of the legalities.

"It's nice that he likes SF," Janine said, diplomatically.

"Yes. It gives us something to talk about. It's so weird meeting someone who is your father and a stranger at the same time." This was the first time I'd said anything about this to anyone.

"You must have been really small."

"Just a baby really," I said.

"My parents are getting divorced," she said, very quietly, looking not at me but at the shelves. "It's awful. They were fighting all the time, and now Dad's living at Gran's and Mum cries into the soup."

"Maybe they'll make it up," I said, uncomfortably.

"That's what I'm hoping. Dad's agreed to come home for Christmas Day, and I'm hoping being in the family, seeing us all, Christmas, he'll realise he loves her and not Doreen."

"Who's Doreen?"

"She's a girl that works on the petrol pumps in his garage," Janine said. "She's his girlfriend. She's only twenty-two."

"I really hope he decides to come back," I said. "Look, why don't we go next door and sit down and get a cup of tea? We can come back in here and buy books afterwards."

"Okay," Janine agreed.

We sat in the window where I usually sat. There's never anyone in there on a Saturday morning, I don't know how they keep going. I ordered tea and honey buns for both of us, and two honey buns to take back to school for me and Deirdre tomorrow. "How did you find out about the book club?" I asked.

"Pete told me about it. Pete's the dark-haired boy, you must have seen him. He used to be my boyfriend, sort of, but we sort of broke up, only we're still friends." She poured herself tea and stirred in sugar.

"Are you going out with the other one now?"

Janine snorted. "Hugh? You're kidding. He's shorter than I am, and he's only fifteen. He's still in the fourth form."

"How old are you?" I asked.

"Sixteen. How about you?"

"Oh, I'm only fifteen too, and in what a sensible school would call the fourth form, but which Arlinghurst calls the Lower Fifth." I fussed with the tea and made mine mostly hot water. It's not so bad like that.

"I thought you were older," she said. "You certainly have read a lot for fifteen."

"It's about all I have done," I said. "Did Pete get you reading SF?"

"Yes, though I always liked things like that. He used to lend me books, well, he still does, and he took me to the club. My mum says SF is childish and for boys, but she's just wrong about that. I tried to get her to read *The Left Hand of Darkness*, but well, she doesn't read much and when she does she likes a nice romance. I've just found one for her called *The Kissing Gate*. Just her kind of thing." She sighed at the thought of it.

"How many of you are there?" I asked.

"Sixteen people I have to buy presents for," she said promptly. "Three sisters, Mum and Dad, four grandparents, two aunties and one uncle and four cousins, one of them a baby. I've got him a teddy. How about you?"

I hesitated. "It's all so different this year. My grandfather, my Auntie Teg, another aunt, three cousins, my father, his sisters I suppose—I don't know what I can get for them."

"What about your mum?" she asked.

"I'm not buying her anything," I said, fiercely.

"Like that, is it?" she said, though I had no idea what she imagined it was like.

"Oh, and there's Sam," I said, thinking of him belatedly. "Except Sam's Jewish, so I don't know if a Christmas present would be quite the thing."

"Who's Sam?" she asked, through a mouthful of honey bun.

"My father's father," I said.

"He's your grandfather then," she said.

"Sort of," I said.

"Are you Jewish, then?"

"No. You have to have a Jewish mother to be Jewish, apparently."

"I don't think Jewish people celebrate Christmas. Probably better just to get him something really nice when it's his birthday," she advised.

I nodded. "I really ought to buy something for Miss Carroll too because she's been really good to me, taking me to the book club and getting books for me specially."

"Is that who you were with? She was very quiet. Who is she?"

"She's the school librarian. She won't be coming with me normally, I can come on the bus and Greg's going to take me home."

Janine considered this, chewing. "You should get something for Greg too, then," she said. "Greg's easy. He likes dark chocolate. You could get him some Black Magic or something."

"I don't suppose a book would be quite right for a librarian," I said.

"Talk about coals to Newcastle," she said, and laughed. "You should probably get chocolates for your Miss Carroll too. I expect you've got lots of money."

"I do, just at the moment," I said, and then I realised what she'd said. "I'm not—I know I go to Arlinghurst, but that doesn't mean I'm rich. The opposite. My father's paying for me to go there, or really his sisters are. They're rich, and stuck up too I think. My family, my own family, are from South Wales and they're all teachers."

"Why are your aunties sending you to Arlinghurst then?"

"I really don't feel as if my father's relations are my family," I said. "It feels really weird when you call them my aunties, or Sam my grandfather." I bit my honey bun and felt the honey squirt on my tongue. "They're paying for me to go away to school so they can get rid of me, I think. They know Daniel's stuck with me now, and this way they don't have to see me very much. But they want me there for Christmas, which I don't understand. I could go to Auntie Teg's. But they don't want me to."

"I never thought of boarding schools as dumping grounds before," she said, licking honey off her lip.

"That's just what it is," I said. "I hate it. But I don't have any choice."

"You could leave next year when you're sixteen," she said. "You could get a job."

"I've thought of that. But I want to go to university, and how can I do that without any qualifications?"

She shrugged. "You could do A Levels part time. That's what Wim's doing."

"Who's Wim?" I asked.

"Wim's the long-haired bastard who was sitting opposite you on Tuesday night. He got thrown out of school, our school, Fitzalan, and now he's working in Spitals and finishing his A Levels at the college."

"He's a bastard?" I asked, disappointed. He was so gorgeous, it didn't seem possible.

She lowered her voice, though there was nobody else in earshot. "Yes he is. I saw you looking at him, and I agree he's easy on the eyes, but he's a double-dyed bastard. He got thrown out of school for getting a girl pregnant, and they say she had to have an abortion. And that's what I broke up with Pete over, because he's still friends with Wim after all that, and he said it was Ruthie's fault. That's the girl, Ruthie Brackett."

"What's she like?"

"Nice enough. Not as clever as Wim, not interested in poetry and books and that kind of thing. I don't know her very well. But I do know that when a girl falls pregnant, you don't only blame her."

"Good point," I said. I had finished my honey bun without noticing. "I think it was very moral of you to break up with Pete over that."

"We're still friends," she said quickly. "But I wasn't going to keep going out with him if that's what he thinks."

"How old is Wim?" I asked.

"Seventeen. His birthday's in March and he'll turn eighteen then. You keep away from him."

"I will. Not that he'd look at me anyway," I added.

"He might think you don't know. None of the girls who do know are going to spend any time with him. And anyway, he was looking at you last week. You're not so bad. If you let your hair grow a bit and tried some mascara maybe. But not for Wim!"

I was about to tease her back, when I remembered about the magic, and that maybe I'd inadvertantly made all these things happen so there'd be a place for me. The honey bun felt like iron in my stomach and I couldn't talk naturally.

Janine didn't notice. "Come on, I'll help you find some presents if you like," she said.

We went back into the bookshop, and then up the hill to a little shop where I bought pretty Indian silk scarves in different colours for Anthea, Dorothy and Frederica, and a dressing gown with a dragon on it for Auntie Teg, and a little brass elephant paperweight for Grampar. Then we went to British Home Stores and Janine helped me buy a bra—she was very knowledgeable about it. I couldn't bear some of them with seams and lace, but we managed to find a sports bra with a plain cup and no frills. Sports is a laugh. She didn't ask me about the stick at all, not a word, as if it was normal. I don't know if that's tact or magic or just obliviousness.

I had to rush to catch the bus. Gill was on it, but she was sitting at the back and she didn't come up to me or speak to me at all.

Apart from the magic thing, which it is too late to change, but which worries me a lot, I like Janine. It was like shopping with my friends at home, only better, because she has read a lot of things I've read. She wishes she could Impress a dragon. She said she'd see me at the book club and if I wanted she'd meet me next Saturday and we could finish our Christmas shopping. It's so nice to spend an afternoon with someone who isn't a moron for a change. Coming back in to the dorm to put things in my locker I overheard a chorus of "Dreary Dreary Drip Drip . . ." followed by poor Deirdre running out with her hands over her face.

I went after her of course, but I couldn't help contrasting her with Janine.

It's a pity about Wim.

Sunday 9th December 1979

If church—if religion—if Jesus, Aslan ... but I don't think it is. There's a way it's true, but it's a layered way, not a literal way. It isn't a way that's going to help. Otherwise I could just have gone to the vicar about her, and said "Reverend Price, do something about my mother!" And he wouldn't have said "Eh, what? What's that? Maureen isn't it, or are you the other one? How's your grandmother, eh?" He'd have taken up his crozier, well, he doesn't have a crozier, he isn't a bishop, maybe he'd have snatched up the churchwarden's staff and gone out to cast demons out of her. It's hard to imagine.

I had another even worse thought about magic. What if everything I do, everything I say, everything I write, absolutely everything about me (and Mor as well) was dictated by some magic somebody else will do in the future. The absolute worst would be if it was my mother, but I don't think it could be, as so much of what we've done has been directly about stopping her. But if it was somebody in the future where she won and was Dark Queen Liz, and they did a magic to make us oppose her to make their world better. Well, I suppose I don't mind that too much, though I don't like the thought of being a puppet any more than making other people puppets.

I wrote to Grampar and Auntie Teg and told them I couldn't come for Christmas but I'd come down the day after Boxing Day, as that's the first time there are trains. I wrote to Daniel, mostly about the book club and what everyone said.

Monday 10th December 1979

Exams. Chemistry this morning and English this afternoon. Not as much time as normal for library, I'm writing this in prep. I'd kind of forgotten about the exams, or rather, I knew about them and have been working for them, but they seemed rather further away. Never mind. I can write down chemical formulae and witter on about Dickens even half asleep.

Tuesday 11th December 1979

Exams. Maths and French.

Wednesday 12th December 1979

So last night, after dinner, I signed out for the book club, showing my permissions, and took the bus into town. It was strange going in on my own in the dark. There were only two other people on the bus, a fat woman in a green coat and an old man in a cloth cap. Normally the bus is full of Arlinghurst girls when I go in. I felt conspicuous in my uniform and my silly hat. I was a little bit later than last week, but got there before things really started. Janine was earlier. She came in not long after me, and we sat together. The boys, Pete and Hugh, came and joined us.

All the same people were there as last time except for Wim. I half-thought he'd come in late, but he didn't show up at all.

Brian led the meeting. He mostly wanted to talk about what an incredible range Silverberg has—well, he has. But let's face it, some of it is hackwork. It's still fun, but you can't put *Stepsons of Terra* next to *Dying Inside* and take it seriously. Hugh hadn't read any Silverberg before, and he read *Up the Line* and *Voyage to Alpha Centauri* for the meeting. "You keep saying 'you should have read this, you should have read that,' but all I could read was what was on the shelf," he said. "And from the random sample that was on the shelf, I don't think I'll bother with any more."

Now I like *Up the Line*. I do have a weakness for time travel though. One of the first SF books I ever read was time travel, Poul Anderson's *Guardians of Time*. (There is something to be said for alphabetical order.) But even so, I could see what he meant. Everyone agreed that Silverberg was variable, and people were talking about what his best books are, and then Keith mentioned *The World Inside* and we talked for ages about overpopulation, that book, and *Stand on Zanzibar* and *Make Room! Make Room!*, and whether it was a real problem or not, and whether Brunner's view of it as something awful or Silverberg's vision of it as something people would embrace was more plausible. It was epic! Brian didn't get us back on topic the way Harriet had the week before, and the funny thing was that Harriet was one of the worst for going off topic and tossing out tangents.

I was trying not to talk too much, but I probably did anyway.

"Do we want to have a meeting next week?" Greg asked. "Or should we leave it until after Christmas?"

"We should have a meeting, but how about a Christmas theme?" Harriet suggested.

"Christmas-themed SF?" Greg asked. "What is there?"

"There's *The Dark Is Rising*," Hugh said. "It's fantasy and it's a children's book, but it's all about Christmas."

"All right, do you want to lead discussion about that?" Greg asked.

Everyone looked at Hugh, and I realised something in that moment, which is that they took him totally seriously, even though he was only fifteen. They didn't just let him come to the meetings, they thought he could lead one. They're the same with me, they don't look at me as a remarkable dancing bear, they listen to what I say.

"I'm not sure there'd be enough discussion material for a whole meeting," Hugh said. "But there are the other books in the series."

"If we run out of things to say early, we can always adjourn to the pub," Harriet said.

"I think it's a good idea. We haven't talked about a children's fantasy since we did the Narnia books," Greg said.

"I suppose they have Father Christmas in," I said, and everyone groaned.

"Worst thing in them," Keith said.

"Tolkien hated that," someone else said, a little dark man. "He said it wasn't internally consistent. Father Christmas and Bacchus and boarding schools and everything all mixed in like a Christmas pudding with raisins and candied peel and sometimes breaking your teeth on a sixpence."

I joined in the general laughter, and then it was time to go.

I thought I might be a bit shy with Greg on his own, but I wasn't. We talked about *Dying Inside*, which we hadn't talked about properly in the meeting. Greg said it was impressive how Silverberg had taken an idea other people had always seen as a blessing and made it into a curse.

Friday 14th December 1979

Exams, and Wednesday and yesterday too. It took me until today to finish writing up Tuesday night.

Saturday 15th December 1979

I met Janine as arranged. Hugh was there too. He looked a little self-conscious at first. He also looked a lot more like a human being out of that purple blazer. I wish I could wear my own clothes on a Saturday. Or at all, really. Wearing a uniform seven days a week is like being in prison.

"Hope you don't mind if I tag along," Hugh said, sounding like someone in a book, and also as if he'd been rehearsing saying that. Janine and Hugh—and Pete, and Greg, and everyone who goes to the book club except Harriet—have local accents. The Shropshire accent isn't a pretty one, but it's nicer than the Received Snob I have to listen to all the time at school.

"Not at all," I said. "Though we're just going to do some shopping."

I had six books at the library, all heavy hardbacks, which was actually a bit of a drawback as far as shopping goes. I couldn't leave them there until afterwards, because of course the library closes at noon. I put them in my bag, sighing, and then Hugh offered to carry it. "No," I snapped, not declining politely at all and clutching my bag as tightly as I could. "I always carry this bag, it's mine, I don't feel comfortable without it," I explained.

Janine looked at me sideways. "How about if Hugh carried the library books in a carrier bag?" she asked.

"That would be all right," I said. "I mean that would be very kind of you, Hugh."

Hugh blushed. He's got sort of sandy hair and freckles, and his blushes show up. Janine and I ignored it. I transferred my library books to a carrier bag Janine produced and Hugh carried it as if it weighed a feather instead of half a ton. We went down the hill to the bookshop, sort of automatically, as if that's the way all our feet wanted to turn. I said that to them.

"Bibliotropic," Hugh said. "Like sunflowers are heliotropic, they naturally turn towards the sun. We naturally turn towards the bookshop."

In the bookshop I bought *The Mote in God's Eye* for Daniel. I don't know whether he's got it or not, but in any case I want to read it. I was going to buy *The Dark Is Rising* so I could read it before Tuesday, but Janine offered to lend me her copy instead. We went and had buns, but we didn't talk about anything personal this time, probably because Hugh was there. We talked about reading children's books when you weren't a child any more, and what Lewis and Tolkien had said about it, and Hugh's embarrassment at having mentioned one at the book club and his astonishment when Greg thought it was a good idea.

"Is this the first time you'll have led a meeting?" I asked.

"Yes. But Pete's done it twice, and Janine's done it once, and Wim's done it several times."

"What did you do?" I asked Janine.

"The Pern books. Did you know there's a third one coming out soon? It's called *The White Dragon*. I can't wait."

"Do you like them?" I asked Hugh.

He looked uncomfortable. "Sort of," he said. "There were things that made me uncomfortable, in *Dragonquest* in particular. I love the world and the dragons."

"Perhaps they're books that appeal more to girls," I said.

"No, Pete loves them," Janine said. She stirred her tea, although it couldn't need stirring.

"You should get back together," Hugh advised. "It's silly the two of you breaking up over something Wim may or may not have done."

"He did," Janine said.

"We don't have all the evidence," Hugh said. "Wim refuses to talk about it, so we only have Ruthie's side, and that not directly from Ruthie but garbled through what she supposedly told Andrea. That's hearsay. You and Pete—"

Janine was looking very cross, so I interrupted. "What books did Pete do? When he led the group I mean?"

"The Flandry books, and Larry Niven," Janine said.

"And Wim did Dick and Delany," Hugh put in.

Delany! They've already done Delany without me, and of course it would have been Wim.

"I think it's better when we have one book, or one series of books. That way you can read them before the meeting and not get into a situation like Hugh last week," Janine said.

Hugh shook his head. "I agree actually, it makes it easier and more focused, but there is something nice about discussing all of an author. It works better for some than others."

I bought a set with soap and shampoo and a fluffy flannel in Boots for Deirdre, all matching and primrose yellow, tied up with a ribbon. I didn't know if she'd get me anything, but she'd had a rotten time in the exams and these would be useful. I looked at Black Magic in Woolworths and decided to get Greg and Miss Carroll boxes of Continentals in Thorntons. They're just much nicer. I bought a bag of toffee for Sam, in case I am going to see him. If I don't I won't send it, I'll give it to Grampar along with the elephant.

Then we went to Janine's house. It was an ordinary little house, the sort of place you'd expect someone to live whose father owned a garage—modern, pebble-dashed, with a lawn in the front with one little tree in the middle. The only unusual thing about the outside was the fairy who was leaning against the tree. It was like a dog, apart from the wings. It looked at me almost insolently and then it disappeared. The others didn't seem to see it at all.

Inside, the sitting room seemed very cluttered, and full of her sisters, though there are only three of them. They were playing with Barbies and taking up the whole sofa and both chairs. The sideboard and mantelpiece were filled with ornaments. Her mother was in the kitchen, which was also very cluttered and messy. "I'm taking Mori and Hugh up to my room, all right?" Janine said.

"All right," her mother said, hardly even looking up from her ironing. She has lank ginger hair, quite different from Janine's vibrant bush. The sisters are also gingery.

We went upstairs. Janine's door has a sign on it that says "Private, Keep Out, This Means You!" She held it open for us to indicate that it didn't in fact mean us. Her room was a complete contrast to the rest of the house. All the other rooms were papered in fussy papers; hers was painted pale green. There were no ornaments or toys at all, only a bed with one faded and eyeless toy dog, and a bookshelf with all the books in rigidly alphabetical order. There was one chair, a wooden upright chair painted in a darker green than the walls, the same colour as the skirting board. The window had a blind in a very similar colour. There was a huge black office typewriter with a very small bedside table underneath it supporting it precariously.

"Did you do this yourself?" I asked.

"You bet," Janine said, sitting on the bed. Hugh took the chair, and after a moment I sat beside her on the bed. "Actually Dad helped with the actual painting. But I designed it. I wanted something different."

"I wish I had a room like this," I said. I do, too, only maybe not green. What I'd really like would be a panelled study like Daniel's.

"It's nice to be able to shut the door and keep people out," Janine said.

"It must be," I said.

"Do you sleep in a dormitory?" she asked.

"Yes I do, but no we don't have midnight feasts or anything fun you may have read about," I said.

"I share a room with my brother," Hugh said.

"What does he do?"

"He's mad about Manchester United. So his half of the room is all football, and mine is all books." Hugh looked uncomfortable saying this.

Janine bounced up and found me *The Dark Is Rising*, and she and Hugh started squabbling about whether I should read the whole series or whether it would put me off to start with the first one because it was kind of childish. Hugh didn't seem to think I'd have time to read five books between now and Tuesday night.

"I will," I explained. "I don't have much to do except lessons and reading. At Arlinghurst the emphasis is on sport, and I can't do sport of course. So I spend all my time in the library reading. I have hours every day, normally. I didn't this week because of the exams, but they're over now, so it'll be back to normal."

"Pretty dim of your family to send you to Arlinghurst in the circumstances," Hugh said.

"Yes, wasn't it," I said.

"What is wrong with your leg anyway?" he asked.

Normally I hate that question, but the way he asked—just as it had come up in conversation, and as if he was mildly interested, in the same way Janine wanted to know if I slept in a dorm—I didn't mind at all. "It was a car accident," I said. "My hip got all mashed up, and my pelvis. It's not so bad now. It doesn't hurt all the time."

"Is it getting better?" Hugh asked.

I should have just said no, it's not, either that or that I hoped it would, but burning tears came out of my eyes for no real reason and I hid my face in a tissue. Janine fussed around and changed the subject and then it was time for me to go.

Hugh came with me to the bus stop, still carrying my library books. I had my shopping and also the Susan Cooper books I'd borrowed from Janine.

"About Wim," he said, as we were turning the corner by KwikSave.

I looked at him enquiringly. My leg was hurting—Janine's bed was too low for me to sit on comfortably, and getting up again had jolted it.

"We don't know what happened. Wim has never talked about it. Wim has refused point-blank to talk about it. And I see people condemning him and—this is a small place. Reputations are strange things. It's a case of giving a dog a bad name and you might as well hang him. He dropped out of school, you know."

"I know. He's doing his A levels part time. Janine told me."

"Janine. Janine thinks the feminist thing to do is to believe the woman all the time. But I think it means treating everyone the same as much as you can. I don't know what happened. But I know I don't know. I do know Wim's making his life much harder because of it." Hugh looked terribly serious. He's shorter than I am and a tiny bit plump, and he has that freckle-face, so it's easy to think of him as a little boy and a clown, but he isn't like that at all.

"Why do you care?" I asked. We were nearly at the bus stop, but the bus wasn't there yet. A whole scrum of Arlinghurst girls were milling about waiting for it. Hugh sat down on a wall, and I lowered myself onto it next to him.

"Wim saved my life," he said, quietly. "Well, my sanity. He stopped a group of boys beating me up and instead of walking away afterwards he stayed and talked to me. He lent me *Citizen of the Galaxy*. I was twelve and he was fifteen, but he treated me like a human being and not like a snot rag. I think he deserves the benefit of the doubt?"

"Whatever he did to Ruthie?"

"No, not whatever he did, but until we know what it was he did." Hugh shrugged, and blushed again. "For what it's worth, I think they probably, well, did it, by mutual agreement. They were careless with contraception and Ruthie had a scare and panicked. That's not something to condemn someone to the outer circles of Hell for."

I didn't know what to say. My father had been made to marry my mother because she got pregnant, and look how well that worked out. Fortunately the bus came around the corner and saved me from saying anything. I took my bag from Hugh and moved towards the queue.

"See you Tuesday," I said, as I got on the bus.

Gill was just ahead of me. She turned around and gave me a look of utter contempt.

Sunday 16th December 1979

As long as I don't think about them being puppets, I can have a really good time with them. Mostly yesterday I didn't think about it at all. The whole thing with what I'd done, with the magic, just wasn't in my mind, and I could act as if they were perfectly naturally part of my karass, both of them.

But today, thinking about it, of course I can't help thinking about that.

When we were young, Auntie Lillian once bought us a doll that could really talk. Her name was Rosebud, and she was just the kind of doll little girls are supposed to want. Her eyes closed when you laid her down, and opened when you picked her up. She had a bland pretty face with no personality and a white dress covered in a rosebud pattern. She had pink shoes that slipped on and off and golden hair that you could really comb. She also had a string in her chest, and when you pulled it she spoke. She could say two things. "Hello, my name is Rosebud," and "Let's play schoo-ul!" If you pulled the string slowly, she'd say them in a deeper voice, and if you pulled it really fast, she'd squeak.

The problem with Rosebud and her really talking was that our other dolls could pretend talk, and that was better. Our collection of dolls (who mostly had some disadvantage like one arm or leg, or were animals rather than being humanoid) had epic adventures surviving after nuclear wars or rescuing dragons from evil princesses. Battered old Pippa, with her one arm and her ragged hair (Mor cut it when she was disguising herself as a soldier) could stand there vowing defiance and revenge against the evil Dog Overlord (the toy dog had a moustache which could be twirled, so he often got the bad-guy parts) and Rosebud couldn't compete when all she could say was "Let's play schoo-ul."

I don't want a karass like Rosebud.

I mean I don't want a karass like Pippa and Dog and Jr. and the others either, so this isn't a very good analogy. (I do not miss my toys. I wouldn't play with them anyway. I am fifteen. I miss my *childhood*.) Jr. was a plastic boy on a motorbike, one of our few human male toys. His name came from Ward Moore's "Lot." I thought it daring and American to have an odd name like that with no vowels. We pronounced it Jirr. I was mortified for whole minutes when I found out what it really meant.

When Hugh mentioned that Wim had done a session on Delany, my first thought, my very first thought, though I know I didn't write this down yesterday but that's because I was ashamed, was that I could do a magic to make that not have happened yet. I could do a magic that would mean he'd do it so I could be there for it. I didn't do the magic, or even really mean to, but I thought it. If I did it, I'd be making them into Rosebud. I'd also be risking what happened to George Orr, because so far, I might have made it all happen but I might not. I didn't see it without. It could have been there all the time. If I didn't exist, or if I had died with Mor, they could still have had a session on Delany. Maybe all the magic did was make me see the group was there and find them. I can't tell. I won't ever be able to tell. Deniable magic. If I did that, I really would be treating them as Rosebud, to say the same things when I pulled a string. And that's if I even could do that. I think actually I couldn't, it would do that thing Glory talked about where too many people create too much weight and you can't change what's happened.

But even thinking about it.

I don't want to be evil, I really don't. The worst of anything she could do to me would be to make me like her. That's why I ran away. That's why the Children's Home was better, why this is better.

I hereby solemnly swear to renounce the doing of magic for my own benefit, or for anything but protection against harm.

Morganna Rachel Phelps Markova, 16th December 1979.

Monday 17th December 1979

I hadn't realised that with the exams over this week would be given over relentlessly to fun.

In English, I played Scrabble with Deirdre. I beat her by 600 points, but it wasn't any fun. It would be a good game with someone who could spell and had some vocabulary. I made "torc," Celtic necklace. She suggested shyly that it should be spelled "talk." Then we played Snakes and Ladders, which she won.

Apart from that, I've been reading pretty much all day, generally in the middle of complete pandemonium.

I'm onto *The Grey King*.

There's a thing in *The Dark Is Rising*, the Christmas one, which is definitely the best of them, where Will does magic in a church, and the vicar asks about the magic crosses and they say they're before Christ, and he says "But not before God." The magic generally is pretty well written but conventional, the battle of Dark and Light, and you learn it from grimoires and then you can fly and time travel and whatever you want. Nothing like magic really is, much less confusing. In children's books with magic everything is always very black and white, though not of course in Tolkien. But "not before God" made me think.

Tuesday 18th December 1979

Exam results, Winter Term 1979
    Chemistry: 96%—*2nd*
    English Literature: 94%—*1st*
    English Language: 92%—*1st*
    History: 91%—*1st*
    Physics: 89%—*1st*
    Religious Education: 89%—*1st*
    Latin: 82%—*1st*
    French: 79%—*2nd*
    Mathematics: 54%—*19th*
    Gym: *excused*
    Games: *excused*
    Dancing: *excused*

    Average: 85%—*3rd*

I just don't have a mathematical brain, I never have. But at least I scraped a pass. I was afraid they were going to give me a zero for gym and games and dancing and then count them into my average. Gill beat me in chem. Good. And Claudine beat me in French, which isn't surprising as her mother is French. She pronounces it, which none of the rest of us know how to do. They should have Claudine teach the class. The maths brought me down more than I was expecting, so Claudine and Karen are both ahead of me overall. But it's otherwise pretty good.

I wish I could show it to Gramma. Grampar will be pleased, I expect everyone will be pleased, but it isn't the same.

I had a letter from Auntie Teg this morning. She's very upset indeed about me not coming home for Christmas. I did already say it wasn't my fault. I wish I could go.

Deirdre rushed out of the room when she saw her marks. I'm assuming they're terrible. Shagger's fourth. She deigned to say "Well done," to me, which is the first thing she's said to me for ages.

Wednesday 19th December 1979

Pretty good meeting last night. Everyone was there. Hugh did very well at leading it, gently getting people back on topic when they wandered away. We had a great talk about the seasonal nature of the books, and about their very specific locations. Greg's been to North Wales and walked on Cadfan's Way and says that Craig yr Aderyn is just like that. Everyone agreed that the end of *Silver on the Tree* is a cop-out and we'd all hate it if that happened to us. It's funny, the younger people were, the more vehement they were about how much they'd hate it. Harriet almost thought the children ought to have their memories wiped, but Hugh and I would rather have died, with everyone else falling on a spectrum by age. Hugh's nice. And I did like the feeling of being vehemently in agreement. Harriet, who really could be Harriet Vane grown up, I keep seeing her that way, stopped saying "I can see it might be kinder," and came around to our point of view as far as "I do understand what a loss it would be."

We finished early and all went to the pub. "I'll buy you an orange juice," Greg said to me. I didn't say I hate Britvic orange, I said "Thank you." Who says I have no social graces?

The pub is called the White Hart, which I said had a very Narnian sound. We'd been talking about Narnia a bit, in comparison, so it wasn't just out of the blue. We'd been comparing the ends. It really is odd how two children's fantasy series should both have such problematic ends. It isn't an inherent genre problem, because look at *The Farthest Shore*! Maybe it's a problem with books about children from our world, or British writers—but no, there's Garner. He doesn't exactly write series, but he certainly has no problem with ends! That reminds me, I never went back and got *Red Shift*.

The White Hart is an old pub with beams and horse-brasses hanging up on leather belts and a big oak bar with pumps for different beers. It stinks of smoke, like all pubs, and the supposedly white plaster between the beams is yellow because of it. I had an orange juice, and gave Greg his chocolates. He opened them right away and handed them around. I got a Viennese truffle, which felt a little mean as they were my present. Delicious though.

I found myself sitting next to Wim. Honestly, I didn't do anything to arrange it! He remains disconcertingly gorgeous close up. It's not just the long blond hair or the very blue eyes, it's something about the way he holds himself. I like Hugh much better, but Hugh is like a solid piece of treetrunk, while Wim is like new branches of blossom waving in the breeze, or a rare butterfly that lands near you and you hold your breath watching it in case it flies away. It's the same sort of breathlessness.

"So, you like Susan Cooper as well as Le Guin?" he said.

"I'd never read them before this week," I said. "I borrowed Janine's, and I've just given them back."

"You read all five books this week?" he said, tossing his head a little so his hair fell back out of his eyes. "You must have a lot of free time."

"I do," I said, quite coldly.

"I'm sorry," he said. "I hate it when people imply that people only read because they have nothing better to do, and here I am doing it."

I liked that. "What could be better?" I asked.

He laughed. He has a nice laugh, very natural. When he laughed, I could imagine doing all the stupid things girls do when they have a crush on someone, keeping a stub of pencil and a piece of sticking plaster like Harriet Smith in *Emma*, or kissing a photograph before bed like Shagger and Harrison Ford.

"How about films?" he suggested, and instantly just like that the whole group was involved in a passionate discussion about *Star Wars*.

Everyone either loves it or hates it. Middle ground is not permitted. My general feeling that it was fun to see actual robots and spaceships but that it was a bit childish compared to real SF didn't seem like a possible position.

A bit later, when people had stopped shooting fish in a barrel or passionately defending, I turned to Wim again. "I heard you did a meeting about Delany."

"Do you like Delany?" he said. "You have very broad-ranging tastes."

"I love Delany," I said, pleased that he had not said I had broad-ranging tastes *for my age*, the way so many people always do. "But there's something I've been wondering about the end of *Triton*."

"Do you think *Triton* was intended as a response to *The Dispossessed*?" he asked, interrupting me. I hadn't thought about it, but I did then, and I could sort of see it.

"Because *The Dispossessed* is an ambiguous utopia and *Triton* is an ambiguous heterotopia?" I asked.

"I wonder if he looked at Anarres and said, why does it have to be so poor, why does it have to be in famine, why is their sexuality so constrained, what other sorts of anarchy could you have?"

"What a fascinating thought," I said. "And also how brilliant of him to show all that complexity of choice through the eyes of someone who isn't happy with it."

"There would be people who drifted about like that even in paradise," Wim said. "Bron's always looking for something he can't have, sort of by definition."

"Why did Bron—" I started.

"Time to go now, Mori," Greg said.

"See you after Christmas," Wim said as I got up, carefully.

On the other side of the table, Keith and Hussein were still arguing about Princess Leia.

Thursday 20th December 1979

I can't believe I'm leaving here tomorrow. Suddenly it seems so soon. We had to clear out our lockers this morning. I wasn't expecting that. In addition to my bag and the satchel and the neat anonymous case I came with, I have six carrier bags of books and two of Christmas presents. I had to go down to the laundry, the first time I've ever been there. The school employs someone full time to wash and iron our stupid uniforms. Usually they're delivered back to our dorms and put on the ends of our beds, and I'd scarcely thought about it before. But today Deirdre didn't have all her shirts, and we need to take everything home. She wanted me to come with her, so off we went to the bowels of the building to a room with six heaving washing machines and four roaring tumble-dryers and a girl only a year or two older than we are pulling the clothes out of one machine and tossing them into the other. I'd hate us if I were her. It was hot in there today; I can't imagine it in June.

Deirdre's going to Limerick for Christmas. There's really a place called Limerick! Of course, as soon as she said, I couldn't help saying "There was a young lady from . . ." but I stopped as soon as I saw her face.

I'm all ready to go as soon as Daniel comes for me tomorrow. I can't wait.

Friday 21st December 1979

First thing this morning was the Prizegiving. I won a copy of W. H. Auden's *Selected Poems* for English, and Isaac Asimov's *Guide to Science* for chem, and Winston Churchill's *A History of the English-Speaking Peoples* for history. As everyone who got over ninety in anything got a book for it, it rather dragged on. I suspect Miss Carroll's hand in the choice of books, which may mean that the Churchill isn't as dire as it looks. Then the sports prizes were handed out, at even greater length. They let me sit down for assemblies, which is nice, but as everyone else is standing it does mean I can't see, not that I especially want to. The teachers, who are lined up at the sides of the hall, can see me quite easily if they look, so I don't dare read. Looking at everyone's backs in their identical uniforms I can compare heights and wrinkles and how their hair falls down their backs, but that's about all. It's surprising how much variety there is in something that's at first glance identical, a row of uniformed backs. I gave the girls in the row ahead marks for posture and neatness, and mentally rearranged them by height and by hair colour.

Scott won the cup, in a narrow victory over Wordsworth. I'm supposed to be very excited about this but as far as I'm concerned it's right up there with arranging people by the shades of their hair.

I went to the library afterwards to give Miss Carroll her chocolates. She seemed very touched to have them. She gave me what I'm sure is a book, wrapped.

I found Deirdre and gave her the soap box. I hadn't wrapped it because I hadn't thought to buy wrapping paper, but I put it in a pretty bag from the shop where I bought the scarves and things. She didn't open it, but she thanked me very nicely. She gave me a thin wrapped present. It also feels like a book. I wonder what on earth it could be? I'll have to read it and say I like it whatever it is.

Then it was all down to waiting for cars. Some girls weren't being picked up until this evening, poor dabs, but Daniel came for me just at one, not the first, but quite early in the process. Everyone was rushing about and shrieking even worse than normal. I'm sure he thought it was Bedlam.

Daniel drove me back to the Old Hall in time for tea—very dry mince pies, almost as bad as school food. His sisters were delighted about Scott winning the cup. They opened a bottle of champagne to celebrate. I thought it was horrible, and the bubbles got up my nose. I'd had it before, at Cousin Nicola's wedding, and I didn't like it then either. Daniel offered to mix mine with orange juice and make something called a Buck's Fizz, but I declined. If there was one thing that was going to make it worse it was horrible orange juice. Really, I only like to drink water. Why do people have such a problem with that? It comes out of the tap for free.

It's the solstice, the shortest day. After today the darkness starts to roll back a bit. I won't be sorry.

It's nice to have a door I can shut and a bit of privacy. I went to bed early. I thought about thinking about Wim while I masturbated, because that breathless feeling is definitely sexual, but it felt intrusive, as well as hard to imagine. There's also the Ruthie thing, which, whatever the ins and outs of it, gets in the way. So I just thought about Lessa and F'lar and Nicholas in the sea. It's funny that *Triton* has so much sex in it but is so unerotic. And—because I'm still thinking about connections between them—there's sex in *The Dispossessed* too, but not the sort that makes you feel breathless. I wonder why that is? Is there a way Fowles wrote Nicholas in the sea that's essentially different from the way Delany wrote Bron and the Spike having exhibition sex? I think there is, but I don't know what it is.

Saturday 22nd December 1979

The aunts took me shopping in Shrewsbury. They wanted me to get something nice for Daniel. I told them I'd already bought him *The Mote in God's Eye*, but they just laughed and said they were sure he'd like it. They bought him—in my name—a charcoal-grey jacket with lots of pockets. It looks like the kind of thing he wears, but honestly I'd never have bought it, and he'll know that. At least I got some wrapping paper. They took me for lunch in a posh department store called Owen Owens. The food was overcooked and slimy.

When we got home, I offered to make scones, in as deferential and polite a way as I could. They really didn't want me to, I could see that, but I can't quite see why. I can cook, I've been able to cook for years. I can cook a lot better than they can. They can't think it's beneath me, because they do it themselves. Maybe they don't want to let me into their kitchen, but I wouldn't mess it up.

I hardly saw Daniel today. He was working at something. I've borrowed a great pile of his books and am working my way through them. I wish the light in here was better.

I don't think I am like other people. I mean on some deep fundamental level. It's not just being half a twin and reading a lot and seeing fairies. It's not just being outside when they're all inside. I used to be inside. I think there's a way I stand aside and look backwards at things when they're happening which isn't normal. It's a thing you need to do for doing magic. But as I'm not going to do any magic, it's rather wasted.

Sunday 23rd December 1979

Church. The aunts inspected me when I got up as if I'd be on display, and one of them suggested that I should find something a little smarter. I was wearing a navy blue skirt and a pale blue T-shirt, with my school coat on top. It wasn't a cold day, though it was raining. I thought I was fine. I gave in though, and went up and put on a grey pullover. I don't have many clothes that aren't uniform. I left most of my clothes when I ran away, obviously.

Apart from the inspection, church was normal enough. St. Mark's is a nice old stone church, with gothic arches and a crusader tomb that's probably one of their ancestors, but I didn't go and look. It was an English service, as I'd expect, and a normal enough Advent sermon. There was a crib set up in the church already, and the hymns were carols. The vicar talked to us nicely afterwards, and they introduced me as Daniel's daughter. Daniel wasn't there. I wonder why not?

He was there for lunch, overcooked roast beef with oversalted potatoes and carrots. I wish they'd let me cook. I can understand why they wouldn't want me to cook Sunday dinner right off, but they could have let me make some scones. Three more days. This is as bad as school. Worse, because no book club and no library to disappear into.

I went for a walk after lunch, despite the rain and my leg, which actually isn't too bad today, just grumbling, not screaming. It's just like around school, not real countryside, just farms and fields and roads, no wild, no ruins and not a fairy in sight. I can't think why anyone would choose to live here.

Monday 24th December 1979, Christmas Eve

The Russians have invaded Afghanistan. There's a terrible inevitabil-
ity to it. I've read so many stories with World War III that sometimes
it seems as if it's the inevitable future and there's no use worrying
about anything because it's not as if I'll grow up anyway.

Daniel brought home a tree and we decorated it, with brittle
Christmas cheer. The decorations are all very old and valuable,
mostly glass. They're exquisite, and very magical. I was almost afraid
to touch them. Even the lights are antique—Venetian glass lanterns
that used to hold candles but they've been refitted for electric bulbs.
Two of the bulbs had gone and I changed them. I miss our old Christmas decorations, which Auntie Teg will be putting on the tree even
now. She'll be doing it on her own, if they're only letting Grampar
out for the day. I hope she can get it to stand up all right. The trouble
we've had getting trees to stand up! Last year we had to tie it to the
cupboard door. But it's better not to think about last year, the worst
Christmas of all time. Of course, the good thing about that is that no
matter how awful this is, it can't even compete.

Our Christmas decorations are also old, mostly, though some of
them are new, bought in our lifetimes. They're mostly plastic, though
the fairy that goes on the top is china. The Old Hall tree doesn't have
a fairy, which seems strange. It has Father Christmas on the top.
Ours don't match, except in being such a mixture they do match,
and we have lots of tinsel, not thin silver strands, big thick twists of
it. I hope it isn't too much for Auntie Teg to do all on her own. I hope
my mother doesn't turn up there tomorrow like the bad fairy at the
christening. At least that won't happen here.

I have wrapped all my presents and put them under the tree. My
paper's nice, dark red with silver threads. We lit the lanterns when
everyone had put their presents under—and another bulb went, and

I changed it. Then we lit them again and admired it. I put my presents from Deirdre and Miss Carroll under it too.

Christmas is a time when people ought to be at home. If they have a home, which I suppose I don't. But I wish I could be with Grampar and Auntie Teg, which is the closest I can get. When I'm grown up, I'll never go anywhere for Christmas. People can come and see me if they want, but I'll never go away anywhere.

They're playing a record of Christmas carols down there now, I can hear them through the floor. What am I doing here?

But it's worse in Afghanistan where the tanks are rolling.

Tuesday 25th December 1979, Christmas Day

This isn't going to be the entry I thought it was going to be, which would have been a list of boring presents.

I was woken by the sound of carols, their record again, which is carols from a cathedral. It's nice enough, I suppose, and I couldn't help having a kind of excited moment thinking it was Christmas Day, even if I am here. I went down and we all ate breakfast, cold toast and boiled eggs just like any day. I don't understand why they make toast that way. They make it in the kitchen and put it into a toast rack where it gets cold and crisp and disgusting. Toast needs butter right away.

After breakfast we went in and opened presents. They had a very fixed ritual about who opens what first, quite different from the way my family do it. We used to take turns opening one present each around a circle. They do it so each person opens all their presents and then the next person opens all theirs. I was last, because I'm the youngest.

They were pleased enough with their scarves, though I'd got the colours wrong and two of them swapped when they thought I wasn't looking. I still can't tell them apart. (Were Mor and I as alike as that? Would we still have been when we were forty years old?) They'd bought each other appointments for manicures and hair dos and that sort of thing. Daniel thanked me for *The Mote in God's Eye* and for the jacket. They bought him whisky, some special kind, and more clothes.

I had a great pile, far more than I'd expected. Deirdre had got me something I never heard of called *The Hitchhiker's Guide to the Galaxy*, which is no doubt science fiction of a kind, and Miss Carroll's thoughtful choice was *The Dispossessed*, which she knew I'd read but didn't own. Daniel gave me a pile of books, and one of these lockable notebooks, which is always useful. His sisters gave me clothes, mostly things I wouldn't be seen dead in, a box of Neapolitans, which I can certainly eat, and a small box which I could tell as soon as I touched it was powerfully magical. I didn't think anything though; after all, their tree ornaments were magical and they didn't seem to notice. I opened the box carefully, and inside were three pairs of earrings, which I could tell even without touching them were absolutely bursting with magic.

The first pair was a set of simple silver hoops, the second were hoops each with a tiny diamond, and the third were pearls dangling on silver. "The pearls were our mother's," one of them said. "We wanted you to have them."

"I don't have pierced ears," I said, as if regretfully, and offered the box back.

"That's the real present."

"We'll take you into town on Thursday morning and have them done."

"You'll have to wear the plain rings at first, and you can work your way up to the others." She smiled, they all three smiled with the same smile. With that same smile and their bland faces they looked like shop-window mannequins come alive and reaching for me, which is a bad dream I have sometimes.

"I don't want to have my ears pierced," I said, as politely and firmly as I could, but I know my voice quavered in the middle.

I had never thought about it before, but as soon as I did, it was quite obvious to me that having your ears pierced would stop you being able to do magic. The holes, the things in the holes, there they'd be, and it wouldn't be possible to reach out. I knew it the way I knew everything about magic. I didn't know it with my mind but felt it through my whole body, with an almost erotic tingling. I dropped the box and clapped my hands to my ear lobes.

"All teenage girls have it done now," one of them said.

"It's the fashion," another added.

"Don't be so silly, it doesn't hurt," the third said.

"You haven't had it done," I said, and it was true, they haven't, none of them, because of course they know what I know, and they haven't had it done because they do magic. They are witches, they must be, and they've been very clever up to now and I have been very stupid, because I hadn't guessed at all. I should have been suspicious because there are three of them, and I should have been suspicious because they wouldn't let me cook, and most of all at the way they all live here and do nothing and control Daniel. I totally missed it because they're bland and English and smile, the whole thing just went right past me because I thought they really were obsessed with Scott winning the cup.

They must have been horrified when Daniel brought me home. They sent me to Arlinghurst to get me away from magic, as well as away from them. It didn't work as well as they thought. They must have known when I did the magic about the karass, though they probably wouldn't have known what it was, only that I was reaching out. Now they wanted to control me entirely, which is what the earrings would have done.

"It wasn't the fashion then," one of them said.

"But all the girls have it done now . . ."

"You'll look lovely in our mother's pearls. It's our way of welcoming you to the family."

I looked desperately at Daniel, who was looking puzzled. I saw that he was my only hope. There are three of them and they're grown up, and presumably have no scruples about magic, any more than she does. Whatever it is they'd done to the earrings, they'd done it knowingly. The magic in them is directed at me personally, I could tell that now from holding the open box. They controlled Daniel in some ways, but they didn't want him to know about it, so this was all going over his head. "Don't let them make me have my ears pierced!" I appealed to him. I knew I was sounding hysterical, but I really was frantic.

"I don't see that Morwenna needs to have it done if she doesn't want to," he said. "She can wait a while and have it done in a year or two."

"We made an appointment."

"And she won't be able to wear Mother's earrings."

"And we wanted to welcome her to the family."

They sounded so bloody reasonable and adult and sane, and I knew I sounded unreasonable and childish and crazy. "Please," I said. I still had my hands at the sides of my head. "Not my ears."

"She's terrified," Daniel said. "The earrings can wait. She doesn't need them yet."

"You're just encouraging her to be silly."

"They'd look so lovely, especially now her hair has grown a little."

"It only hurts for a second."

Daniel looked puzzled. He's a weak man and he's not used to standing up to his sisters. He never has done it. They took over his life when he was younger, and they've probably been manipulating him with magic all this time. I think though, that they've kept it quiet and not done it directly. I don't know why. Maybe because of the puppet thing. Maybe they want him to love them. Not many people love witches. Look at my mother. Nobody loves her. They have each other, but would that be enough? I was sobbing and I kept looking at him pleadingly, because he is the one thing standing between me and them.

"There's no urgency, surely," he said.

"I won't, I won't," I said. I snatched up my books and ran upstairs.

"Typical teenage tantrum about nothing," one of them said.

"You have to be firm with her, Daniel."

"She's too used to getting her own way."

The door doesn't lock, but I have put a chair in front of it so nobody can come in. They came up and asked me to come down for Christmas dinner, but I didn't go. It'll be overcooked and dry anyway. I don't know what to do. Should I run away again? It worked last time, or it almost did. I don't know what they want. They seem sane enough, but so can she if you don't know her. They want to control me. They want to stop me doing magic. It's not that I want to do magic—in fact I swore I wouldn't. I swore I wouldn't except to prevent harm. I want to be able to prevent harm. This is harm. This is mutilation. I thought my leg was mutilation, but that's nothing. If I wore those earrings, I couldn't see the fairies. I don't know if the controlling thing would work, but having the holes would stop it. If it's true that my whole generation is having it done, that means a whole generation of women who won't see fairies. It doesn't sound so bad, it sounds like immunization, doesn't it, one little prick and away goes all the arcane side. But it is bad, because like immunization it only works if it's everyone. They won't do it, and nobody will be able to stop them.

Anyway, while most people can't see fairies anyway because they don't believe in them, seeing them isn't a bad thing. Some of the most beautiful things I've ever seen have been fairies.

I suppose I could get out of the window, though there isn't a convenient tree the way there is in school. Or I could walk out of the back door in the night when they're all asleep. I have the map. Only it's Christmas and there are no trains, and no trains tomorrow either. Also, I don't have any money, I spent it all on presents. I have 24p. Daniel would probably give me money, but he wouldn't want to hear anything against them, he probably literally can't hear anything against them. Also he's my father-of-record and my legal guardian. When I ran away before and they put me in the Home, it was him they found. If I run away, where can I go? I can't go to Grampar, he's probably back in hospital by now and anyway they won't let me live with him, or with Auntie Teg. I could try her anyway, but Auntie Teg's is the first place Daniel would look. The rest of the family let me down before, they knew about Liz and they still thought it would be all right to leave me with her. I won't be sixteen until June, six whole months, and where can I go on my own without a National Insurance Number and looking younger than my age?

I have to make it through the rest of today and tomorrow, and then I can go down to South Wales and talk to Auntie Teg and Glorfindel and see what I can do. If they'd leave me alone I can cope with school, at least for this year. When you're sixteen you can live alone. I could do what Janine said, get a job and do A Levels part time, like Wim. I could do that.

They must do everything in the kitchen and their rooms, the parts of the house I haven't seen. I have to stay near Daniel. He thinks I'm being irrationally hysterical, but he'll humour me. He's not too bad. I think he kind of likes me. They're eating down there, and drinking, and I'm going to go down and say I'm sorry I was hysterical but the thought of piercing my ears fills me with a terrible dread and fear and if they'll promise never to mention it again I'll promise never to run out of the room and barricade myself in my room. If I need to, I'll promise to go right away and never see them again after June. They are the ones paying for school, not Daniel. I could say I'll pay them back when I can.

I'm not absolutely sure they know I know—I mean know that it isn't just an irrational fear. In front of Daniel they'll pretend to agree.

Daniel's their weak point. Anyway, they can't actually do it until Thursday. Deep breath. I'm going down.

Wednesday 26th December 1979

On the other hand, how do I know they're evil? Why is that my assumption? Maybe they are exactly what they seem, except with a bit of magic, and they know nothing about me except the obvious. Maybe all they want is to make me into a nice niece. (A nice niece from Nice ate a nice Nice biscuit and an iced bun . . .)

I know having those holes bored would take me away from magic. I'm sure they know that, or they wouldn't be so adamant, but I'm not sure if they know I know about magic. Most people don't. For most people, it would be no loss. Though it's girls, boys mostly don't get their ears pierced. Can men do magic? I'm sure they can, but I don't seem to meet them. What I was thinking about vaccination, maybe they were thinking of it like that, to make me safe from the temptation of doing magic. I thought those earrings were to control me, but maybe they were to make me more like everyone else. They have a tame brother. Maybe they want a tame niece. In that case, they'd probably be okay with me going back to school and not trying again until half term, or even Easter. School is where they want me to be. School is insulated from magic, as I noticed right away, and I won't do any anyway.

I do want to go back to Arlinghurst, even though it's moronic and the food is awful and there's no privacy at all, because I have started to build my karass there. I have the book club, I have the library— both libraries. I can put up with everything else. I have been putting up with it. And I want to get my O Levels, and my A Levels if possible. I want to go to university and finally meet some people I can talk to. Gramma said I would find equals there, that it was worth pressing on.

She always said that when I was discouraged about maths or memo-rising Latin or something. Even if I get O Levels, well, O Levels are a qualification. Anyone without them is going to be assumed to be an idiot, and there won't be any jobs for them except idiot jobs. Being a poet, that doesn't matter, there aren't any qualifications for that, but I'm going to need to do something to keep food in the oven, and I'd rather it was something fun. I need O Levels at the very least. I need to either go back to Arlinghurst, which means staying on such terms with the aunts that they'll pay for it, or finding another school somewhere.

So anyway, yesterday.

I went down and apologised for running off—limping off is more like it. I explained that I appreciated they'd meant it kindly but the thought of having my ears pierced distresses me inordinately—they must have picked that up. They didn't try to persuade me any more, and the earring box had been taken away from my other presents. They said that we'd forget about it, and they brought me some cold turkey and stuffing, which was dry but not too awful. Then we played Monopoly, which one of them won, though I gave them a good game.

The weird thing about Monopoly was that you could see how long they'd been playing together, the four of them. They all had favourite pieces which they instantly grabbed. Their pieces, when I occasion-ally had to move them a few squares on my side of the board to save leaning, were full of the magic of use and fondness. In the pieces, I could tell them apart for the first time. They always dress alike, but the dog, racing car and top hat know. The other weird thing about it was how we were sitting there playing it like a normal family, only not, because I don't belong, but even leaving me out, they're not. Normal families have different generations, and they're all one gen-eration. Normal families have married people. Daniel's the only one of them to have married, and look who he picked! Normal families are not just forty-year-old children who are in charge now without having grown up. There were times in that game when they were squabbling with each other when I felt as if I was the oldest person at the table.

Afterwards we ate Christmas cake, though I just crumbled mine on my plate because it would be a really obvious thing to magic, because it has all those connections to everything. Anyway I don't like any fruitcake except Auntie Bessie's. Then I followed Daniel into his study and got him talking about the books he'd sent me, especially *Dune*. Arrakis is such a great world. You could feel it was real, with the different cultures. You don't see culture clash often enough in SF, and it's very interesting. Paul going into the desert to the Fremen is someone going right into another culture, and there are secrets both ways. Daniel was quite lively talking about this, and though he'd poured a glass of whisky, he only sipped it. He was smoking the whole time, of course. He asked me what I'd been reading and about the book club and what I'd like to borrow, and all the time I didn't say "Do you know your sisters are witches?" and he didn't say "So, why did you freak out about the earring thing?" We weren't saying those things so loudly you could almost hear them.

Then I got him on the subject of Sam, which is the most human he ever is. They must not be able to mess with Sam, maybe because of his religion? But Sam is a stable point for Daniel, a sane point. The more I was talking to him the more I was wondering how much they control him, what things he isn't able to think about, what things make him reach for the bottle. They have a tame brother. They have a man to manage the estate. That's when I thought that what they want is a Nice Niece. Because if they're not evil witches who want to take over the world—they're not insane, they're not like Liz—if they're pretty much what they seem to be, three women who haven't grown up properly living together and maybe using a bit of magic to arrange their lives the way they want, then that makes the most sense.

"Are we going to see Sam?" I asked.

"There isn't really time if you've told your Auntie Teg that you'll go down on Thursday," he said.

"We could do what we did last time," I said. "We could do it to-morrow."

"They wouldn't want me to be away on Boxing Day," he said, and I could see that they wouldn't. They have their Boxing Day rituals like their Christmas Day ones. They're his sisters and his employers and they have a magic hold on him; how can I compete?

I can look at Daniel now. I feel sorry for him. He's as kind as he knows how to be, as he can be in the limits of what he is, and he can't see the walls they've built around him. No wonder it was my mother he married, really. It would have to be someone else who had magic to get him away from them. Magic and sex, and maybe it took the getting pregnant too, because that would make a strong strong connection, yuck. No wonder they look so prune faced in the photographs. It didn't take them long to get him back though.

Then today, which was sunny and frosty, we all went for a walk on the estate. It was very feudal. I've never seen anything like it. Class, yes, class is everywhere, but not people touching their caps. We had lunch in a little old pub built literally into the side of a hill, called the Farrier's Arms. The lunch was great. I had steak and kidney pie which came in a bowl, with chips and a feeble winter salad. It was still the best meal I've had for ages. There were a lot of people there they knew, people kept coming over and saying hello. Then after we came back, lots of those people came around for mince pies and tea. They let me hand round mince pies. I played Nice Niece as well as I could, said I was enjoying school and coming third in the class. Several of the women had been to Arlinghurst, but only one of them asked about the Cup. I realised that meeting all those people was good, because they were the aunts' friends. If their friends have met me, Daniel's daughter, I can't just disappear without embarrassing them.

After they'd all gone, I offered to wash dishes, but they wouldn't let me. They're determined to keep me out of the kitchen. Daniel retreated into his study, and I retreated up here, supposedly to bed.

To Cardiff tomorrow, by train. I hope Auntie Teg meets me. She didn't reply to my letter. If not, I'll get the bus up the valley. I have the key to Grampar's house. I have to talk to Glorfindel, not that getting straight answers from fairies is the easiest thing in the world. But I have to try.

Thursday 27th December 1979

On the train, in the corner of a little carriage I have to myself, at least so far. The countryside is frosted as if it has been sprinkled with icing sugar. The sun peeps out of the clouds every so often as the train rushes along, and when we go around a bend I can see the Welsh mountains in the distance, and coming closer. I love the train. Sitting here I feel connected to the last time I sat here, and the train to London too. It is in-between, suspended; and in rapid motion towards and away from, it is also poised between. There's a magic in that, not a magic you can work, a magic that's just there, giving a little colour and exhilaration to everything.

I have not let them make holes in my head to hang jewellery from, and to take magic from me. And I am free, at least for now, at least as the train swoops through Church Stretton and Craven Arms, with Shrewsbury left behind and a long time yet before we come to Cardiff. There's a bit about this in *Four Quartets*, I'll see if I can find it when I have the book.

If there's an easier form of magic than making somebody do what they want, with things that want to do it too, I don't know what it is. They buy his clothes. They buy his shoes. They buy him glasses and whisky. They own the house and the furniture. He wants to drink the whisky, and the chair wants that and the glass, and of course nothing could be easier than making him drink so much he can't get up to drive me to the station. The only strange thing is that I didn't think of it myself. But I don't know that I could have stopped him, without magic, and even apart from the fact that it wouldn't be a good idea, I wouldn't do that, even if they do. If he loved them to start with, if he was grateful, they'd do anything to keep that. Probably over the years they've done more and more little things, not meant to hurt him, but never letting him go, binding him up in spider-strands of magic so that he stays, he does what they want, he has no will. It would take something very strong to get through that.

Poor Daniel. The only place where he's free is with Sam, and in his books. It's hard to use books for magic. In the first place, the more mass-produced and newer something is, the harder it is for it to be individually magical, rather than part of the magic of the whole thing. There's a magic of mass production, but it's spread out and hard to hold. And with books especially, books as objects are not what books *are*, it's not what's important about them, and magic works with objects, mostly. (I should never have done that karass magic, I didn't know half of what I was doing, and the more I think about it the more I see it. I can't be truly sorry I did it, because having people to talk to is worth more than rubies, more than anything at all, but I know I wouldn't have done it if I'd been wiser. Or less desperate.)

Anthea drove me to the station. I know it was Anthea because she told me so, though of course she could easily have been lying. That's very easy to do when you're twins. I should know. (I wonder if Daniel can reliably tell them apart. I should ask him about that.) Two of them stayed home to keep an eye on him, I think. "Daniel's a bit hung over this morning," one of them said, smiling as she put the rack of disgusting cold toast down on the breakfast table. "So Anthea will drive you to the station."

"I'm not having my ears pierced," I said, putting my hands over them again.

"No, dear. Maybe you'll be sensible about it when you're older."

In the car, Anthea didn't talk about the ear-piercing thing. I talked cheerily about school, about Arlinghurst and the prefects and

the houses, and tried my hardest to seem like I'd turned into Nice
Niece spontaneously without the need of any magical intervention.
It was hard, because of course I hadn't been doing it before, so perhaps I should have started more gradually if I wanted to be plausible,
rather than going into a full-blooded imitation of Lorraine Pargeter
right off. Her car is a silver thing, middle sized, I'm not sure what
kind, though if I were really Nice Niece I'd have checked to compare
it with the others when I got back to school. The inside has leathery
upholstery, and it's much newer than Daniel's car. There's a mirror
in the passenger side sun flap. I'd been in the car before, when we
all went shopping, but I had always sat in the back. I know they take
turns driving, and sitting in the front passenger seat. They're very
peculiar really. There are all kinds of things they could be doing.
They could be working on Dutch elm disease. They could see the
world.

When we got to Shrewsbury, instead of going to the station, she
parked outside a jewellers with a sign in the window that said "Ear
Piercing." "There's just time before the train," she said. "I've brought
your hoops."

"I'll scream," I said. "You won't get me in there without dragging
me."

"I wish you wouldn't be so silly," Anthea said, in that "more in
sorrow than in anger" voice adults use.

I didn't know what to say. I didn't know what she knew, how much
she knew about why I was objecting. It seemed to me, and it still
seems right, that it's best to keep as much as possible unspoken. If I
started talking about magic not only would she know, but she'd have
every reason to tell Daniel I was deranged.

"I absolutely will not have my ears pierced," I said, as firmly as
possible. I clutched my bag, which was on my lap, and which helped
to centre me. "I don't want to behave badly, I don't want to cause a
scene in the street or in the shop, but I will if I have to, Aunt Anthea."

As I was talking, I put one hand on the lever that opens the car door, ready to leap out if I had to. I had another bag in the boot, with books and some clothes in, but everything I really needed was in my bag on my lap. I'd be sorry to lose some of the books, but you can always buy them again if you have to. Heinlein says you have to be prepared to abandon baggage, and I was. I know I can't literally run, but I thought that if I leapt out of the car and hobbled down the street, she'd have to chase after me, and there might be people she knew and she'd be embarrassed. There were already some people about, though it was quite early. If it came to physically fighting, there was for the time being only one of her. I might have a bad leg but that also means I have a stick.

We sat like that for a while, and then she grimaced and turned the key and drove off. We came to the station where she bought my return ticket and then kissed my cheek and told me to have a good time. She didn't come up to the platform. She looked—I don't know. I don't think she's used to being thwarted.

Magic isn't inherently evil. But it does seem to be terribly bad for people.

Friday 28th December 1979

By the time the train got to Cardiff it was raining, and all the exhilaration of frost on distant hills was lost in city rain. Auntie Teg wasn't in the station to meet me. I thought she must be too cross with me not coming to help on Christmas Day to want to see me at all. I walked out of the station and across through the bus station to find the bus up the valley and realised that I still only had 24p, two tens and two twos in my purse, big as cartwheels and just as useless. I couldn't think how I could get some more money. I have a few pounds in the post office, but I didn't have the book. There are people I could borrow money from, but none of them were in Cardiff station today at lunchtime in the rain. And my stupid leg was stupidly hurting again. Fortunately, before I got to the point where I started hitchhiking, which I have done but only when I was running away, I spotted Auntie Teg's little orange car turning in to the car park. I limped across slowly to intercept her before she put money in the meter. She was very pleased to see me and didn't reproach me. She'd been expecting me to come on the next train. I think I probably caught the earlier one because of Anthea wanting the time to have my ears pierced.

This is the second time, the second time *running*, that I've got off a train and not been met and realised I can't cope. I have got to stop doing this. I need better organisation and I need more money. I need to keep emergency money in my bag. As soon as I get some, I'm keeping at least five pounds for that. And maybe I should keep a pound in the back of my purse too, in case I use the other, or only need a bit. Also, maybe I should start saving running-away money again, just in case. It would be lovely to have my life in order enough not to need it, but let's face it, I'm not there yet.

Auntie Teg lives in a little modern flat in a neat modern estate. It was all built about ten years ago, I think. There's a little curving parade of shops, including a terrific bread and buns shop, and blocks of six flats, each three floors high, set out with grass in between them. Her flat is a middle one. It isn't—I mean, I'd hate to live there. It's very new and clean and smart but it has no character and the rooms are all rectangular and the ceilings are very low. I think Auntie Teg chose it because it was what she could afford at the time and a safe place for a single woman. Or maybe because she wanted to make her own place something really different from home, with modern furniture and no magic. She had always, logically, sensibly, associated magic and fairies and everything like that with my mother, who is four years older than she is. Auntie Teg therefore wants nothing to do with them, any more than she does with Liz. She lives on her own with her beautiful but incredibly spoiled cat Persimmon. Persimmon goes out through the window, jumping down to the awning over the front door and from there to the ground. She can't get back in that way, though, she comes up the stairs and cries outside the front door.

I like the flat and don't like it at the same time. I admire it being so clean and neat with floppy brown Habitat sofas (too low for me, especially today), and blue-painted tables. I can see that the heat-grilles are efficient. When she first bought it, a little while before Gramma died, we were both terribly impressed with how modern it is. But really, I just prefer old things and clutter and fireplaces, and I suspect Auntie Teg does too, though nothing would make her say so.

"My" room here is small, with a bed and bookshelves with Auntie Teg's art books on them. There's a terrific pair of pictures by Hokusai on the wall—they're clearly part of a story. One is of two Japanese men looking frightened fighting a giant octopus; the other is of the same two men laughing and cutting their way through a huge spider-web. I don't know their names and I don't know their stories, but they have tons of personality and I like lying here looking at them and imagining their other adventures. Mor and I used to tell each other stories about them. Auntie Teg bought them in Bath, along with the brown and cream Moroccan blanket that hangs on the wall in the lounge.

Lying here writing this, every so often Persimmon cries outside the door to come in to my room. If I don't open it, she keeps on doing it. If I do get up and hobble over to the door, every step a minor victory, she walks in, looks at me disdainfully, then turns around and leaves. She's a tortoiseshell cat with a white chin and stomach. She sees fairies—in Aberdare where there are fairies, obviously, not here. I've seen her see them and turn the same look of disdain on them as she does on me, while keeping a wary eye to make sure we don't get up to anything. Auntie Teg has done an oil painting of her lying in front of the Moroccan blanket—the colours are wonderful together—where she looks like the loveliest gentlest most beautiful cat. In reality she likes to be petted for about thirty seconds, after which she turns on you and attacks your hand. I've had more bites and scratches from Persimmon than from all the other cats in the world put together, and Auntie Teg often has scratch marks on her wrists. Having said that, she adores her and talks to her in baby talk. I can hear her cooing now, "Who's the best? Who's the best cat in the world?" She might be in the running for most beautiful, with her lovely markings and aristocratic carriage, but I think the *best* cat would have better manners.

We're going up to see Grampar tomorrow. It's not like at half term, Auntie Teg isn't in school. It's not going to be easy to get time to go to find the fairies, though she is going away for a few days over New Year and I should have a chance then. Auntie Teg isn't old, only thirty-six. She has a boyfriend, a secret boyfriend. It's very tragic actually, a bit like *Jane Eyre*. He's married to a madwoman, and he can't get divorced from her because he's a politician, and anyway he feels an obligation to her because he married her when she was young and pretty and sparkling. In fact, he was Auntie Teg's childhood sweetheart and kissed her on the way back from her twenty-first birthday party. Then he went to university and met his mad wife, though she wasn't mad yet, and married her, and only later realised that he'd really loved Auntie Teg all along, and by then it was clear that his wife was mad. I'm not sure this version is quite accurate. For instance, his wife's father was someone who could help him get a parliamentary seat. I wonder if there was some self-interest going on. And would it really ruin his career to get divorced and remarry? It would much more ruin it if it came out that he was involved with Auntie Teg. However, she says she's happy as she is, she likes living alone with Persimmon and having a few days with him now and then.

I got to help make dinner. You can't imagine the pleasure of wiping mushrooms and grating cheese when you haven't had a chance to do it for a long time. Then eating food you have cooked, or help cook, always tastes so much better. Auntie Teg makes the world's best cauliflower cheese.

It's also very nice to relax and be looked after for a bit.

Saturday 29th December 1979

Not much of this year left. Good. It's been a rotten year. Maybe 1980 will be better. A new year. A new decade. A decade in which I shall grow up and start to achieve things. I wonder what the eighties will bring? I can just remember 1970. I remember going out into the garden and thinking that it was 1970 and that it sounded like yellow flags flying, and saying that to Mor and she agreed, and running up and down the garden with our arms stretched out, pretending to fly. 1980 sounds more rotund, and maroon. It's funny how the sounds of words have colours. Nobody except Mor ever understood that.

Grampar liked the elephant, and Auntie Teg was really pleased with the dressing gown. She waited to open it until we went up to Fedw Hir and we had a little Christmas around the bed. They gave me a big red polo-neck pullover, and a soap-on-a-rope, and a book token. I didn't tell them about the ear piercing. There's no point upsetting them needlessly. It had already been legally established that they have no rights with me—the fact that they brought me up counts for nothing. Any mother, however evil, and any father, however distant, that's the court system, and aunts and grandparents nowhere.

Grampar hates Fedw Hir, you can tell, and he wants to get home, but I don't know how we can manage it when he can't walk without help. Auntie Teg was talking about people coming in to get him up and put him to bed. I don't know what that would cost. I don't know how it could be arranged. It's such an awful place, though. They're supposed to be giving him therapy, but it doesn't seem to do any good. So many of the others are so clearly just waiting to die. They look so hopeless. And he looked like that at first. When we went in he was sunk down in the bed, I expect having a nap, but he looked small and pathetic and only half-alive, not like Grampar at all.

I was talking to him about when he taught us to play tennis, and we went up to the Brecon Beacons and played on the uneven ground up there and afterwards on flat ground it was easy. I remember the skylarks singing high above and the tufts of bracken and the funny tufted reeds we used to call bamboo shoots. (They're not bamboo, really, not anything like, but we had a toy panda and we used to play that they were and he could eat them.) Grampar used to be proud of how fast we could run and how well we could catch a ball. He'd always wanted a boy, of course. It's not that we wanted to be boys, it's just that boys have so much more fun. We loved learning to play tennis.

And I thought all that was wasted, all that time practising up there, because Mor is dead and I can't run and neither can Grampar, not any more. Except it wasn't wasted, because we remember it. Things need to be worth doing for themselves, not just for practice for some future time. I'm never going to win Wimbledon or run in the Olympics ("They never had twins at the Olympics . . ." he used to say) but I wouldn't have anyway. I'm not even going to play tennis for fun with my friends, but that doesn't mean playing it when I could was a waste. I wish I'd done more when I could. I wish I'd run everywhere every time I had the chance, run to the library, run through the cwm, run upstairs. Well, we mostly did run upstairs. I think of that as I haul myself up the stairs to Auntie Teg's flat. People who can run upstairs should run upstairs. And they should run upstairs *first*, so I can limp along afterwards and not feel I'm holding them up.

We called in to see Auntie Olwen, and then Uncle Gus, and Auntie Flossie. Auntie Flossie gave me a book token, and Uncle Gus gave me a pound note. I haven't forgiven Uncle Gus for saying what he said, but I took the money and said thank you. I've put it into the back pocket of my purse, where it can be a start on my emergency stash. There's a very comfortable wing chair in Auntie Flossie's. Otherwise, I found all the chairs very difficult. I don't know why people make them so low. Library chairs are always a lovely height.

Sunday 30th December 1979

Leg a bit better, thank goodness. In fact it was well enough that as I was walking through the bus station an interfering busybody asked me why I needed a cane, at my age. "It was a car accident," I said, which usually shuts people up, but not her.

"You shouldn't use it, you should try to manage without it. It's obvious you don't really need it."

I just walked on and ignored her, but I was shaking. It might seem as if I don't need it, walking along on flat ground, but I need it if I have to stand still, and I really need it for stairs or broken ground, and I never know from one minute to another if I'm going to be the way I am today or the way I was yesterday, when I can hardly put my weight on my leg at all.

"See, you're walking really fast now, you don't need it at all," she called after me.

I stopped and turned around. I could feel my cheeks burning. The bus station was full of people. "Nobody would pretend to be a cripple! Nobody would use a stick they didn't need! You should be ashamed of yourself for thinking that I would. If I could walk without it I'd break it in half across your back and run off singing. You have no right to talk to me like that, to talk to anyone like that. Who made you queen of the world when I wasn't looking? Why do you imagine I would go out with a stick I don't need—to try to steal your sympathy? I don't want your sympathy, that's the last thing I want. I just want to mind my own business, which is what you should be doing."

It didn't do any good at all, except for making me a public spectacle. She went very pink, but I don't think what I was saying really went in. She'll probably go home and say she saw a girl pretending to be a cripple. I hate people like that. Mind you, I hate the ones who come up and ooze synthetic sympathy just as much, who want to know exactly what's wrong with me and pat me on the head. I am a person. I want to talk about things other than my leg. I'll say this for Oswestry: English standoffishness means I don't get as much of that there. The people who have asked me about it there, both whether I really need it and what's wrong, have been acquaintances, teachers, girls in school, the aunts' friends on Boxing Day, people like that.

It took me ages to calm down. I was still overheated and nervous when the bus went round the narrow corner to the bridge in Ponty- pridd. If it didn't make it, I thought, if we all fell to our deaths, that awful woman would be the last person I talked to.

I had lunch with Moira, which was my ostensible reason for go- ing up to Aberdare today. Moira says my voice has got posher, which is absolutely horrifying. She didn't say "more English" because she's my friend and a kind person, but she didn't have to say it. School must be rubbing off on me. I so don't want to sound like the other girls there! I don't know what to do about it. The more I think about it the odder my voice sounds in my ears, but I hadn't noticed be- fore, I was just talking. There are elocution lessons. Are there anti- elocution lessons? Not that I want to talk like Eliza, but I really don't want to open my mouth and get filed as upper-class twit.

Moira's had a good enough term. It was surprisingly hard to find things to talk about. I can't remember what we used to talk about; nothing, I suppose, gossip, school, the things we were doing together. Without that there isn't much there. Leah's broken up with Andrew and Nasreen is seeing him, and her parents are flipping out, appar- ently. Leah's having a party on January 2nd, in the evening, so I'll see them all there.

After lunch I went out of Moira's house onto Croggin Bog and walked across. Heol y Gwern is the only proper road across it, of course, but I went off that right away. Croggin, well, properly it's spelled Crogyn, is big: It's an upland bog, it's the whole shoulder of the hill. There are older paths running through it, not as old as the Alder Road, but they've been there a long time. It's a bad time of year for it, and it's been a wet winter, but it isn't really dangerous if you know the way, or even if you don't if you follow the alders. Mor and I got really lost in Croggin Bog once, when we were quite small, and got out purely by alder-recognition. Anyway, it isn't quicksands, it's just wet and muddy. People are more scared of it than they need to be. There was also the time I went into it in the dark not long after Mor died and deliberately tried to get lost, but the fairies helped me out. They say marsh lights, willow-wisps, lead you astray and into the worst bits of bog, but that time they took me pointedly to the road right by Moira's house. I went in dripping and Moira's mother made me take a shower and dress in Moira's clothes to go home. I was afraid of getting into trouble, but Liz was fighting with Grampar and didn't even notice.

There's a good story about when they built those houses. They were building them along Heol y Gwern, and they started to build little short streets off it, into the bog, with new houses, because they wanted a proper estate for people to live. The problem was that the bog didn't want the houses. The real story, which I had from Grampar who remembers when it happened, is that they'd built the foundations for a house and they left it on the Thursday before Good Friday, and when they went back on the Tuesday after Easter Monday, they had completely sunk. The way I heard the story though, is that they'd built the whole house and when they came back after the weekend only the chimneys were sticking up above the bog. Ha! They stopped building up there after that and built the new estate in Penywaun instead, and I'm glad. I like the way the bog is, with the little stunted trees and the long grasses and rushes and sudden unexpected flowers and moorhens on the standing water and lapwings slow-flapping to guide you away from their nests.

What I wanted today was a fairy, and there are often fairies on Croggin. I didn't see a sign of one, and even when I came out of the bog by the river and into Ithilien I couldn't find any. I checked Osgiliath and the other fairy ruins in the cwm on my way back to town, the long way around, on the dramroad. There's an old smelter there,

and some fallen cottages, or I think that's what they are. It's so hard
to imagine them bustling and industrial. I did spot the occasional
fairy out of the corner of my eye, but none of them would stop or
speak to me. I remembered how Glorfindel wasn't findable after Halloween. There have been other times like that, times we couldn't find
them, times when they don't want to be found. They always found
us. I tried calling for him, but I knew that was pointless. They don't
use names the way we do. I might wish it worked the way it does in
Earthsea where names have summoning power, but it doesn't, names
don't count, only things do. I do know, I think, how to call him with
magic, but that wouldn't be magic to prevent harm, so I didn't really
consider it for more than a second.

I tried sitting down, though it was very chilly, and waiting for the
pain in my leg to ease off, in case that was keeping them away. It
wasn't very bad today though. It shouldn't have been that, I don't
think. It was too uncomfortable to sit for long, and there was a bit of
rain in the wind. Going through town was miserable, all the shops
boarded up that I can remember as active places, more all the time.
The Rex is shutting down, there won't be anywhere to watch films in
Aberdare any more. There are tattered "for sale" signs everywhere.
There's litter lying on the streets and even the Christmas tree outside
the library looks forlorn. I caught the bus back to Cardiff in time for
dinner with Auntie Teg.

I don't know what I'm going to do if I can't find them. I really need
to talk to them.

Tuesday 1st January 1980

Happy New Year.

Nice to wake up this morning in Grampar's house, and on my own.

Auntie Teg has gone off somewhere with Him for New Year,
which she pretty much always does. I could have gone too, she asked

me, but I didn't want to. I'd only be in the way. Yesterday morning we drove up to Aberdare and saw Grampar, and then she went off and I was promptly grabbed by Auntie Flossie. I had wanted to go to find the fairies, but instead I found myself enacting "Three French Hens" in Auntie Flossie's New Year Party. The cheer was a little forced, and I found myself aching for bed long before midnight, but I've had worse days. I've collected another four pounds fifty in clenigs, and six chocolate coins. And I had half a glass of champagne at midnight. It was nicer than Daniel's champagne, or maybe it's one of those things that grows on you.

I'm going to get up and cook myself breakfast and then have another try at finding the fairies. It's a new year, maybe I'll have better luck.

Wednesday 2nd January 1980

Yesterday morning, I really wanted to find some fairies. For a change, I went up through Common Ake. It's Heck's Common really, called after a Mr. Heck, but everyone calls it Common Ake. It's a common, it doesn't belong to anyone, the way most of the country was before the Enclosures in the eighteenth century. It's hard to imagine Aberdare as a farming valley with nothing really here except St. John's, and only the main road running through from Brecon to Cardiff, no other streets at all, all the coal and iron undisturbed underground. I had to learn a modern poem in Welsh once for an Eisteddfod that ended "*Totalitariaeth glo,*" the despotism of coal. I picked up a little piece of coal as I went. They often find fossils in it when they're digging it up, ancient leaves and flowers. It's organic, it was an organic sludge pressed down by the rock to make seams of carbon stuff that burns. If it had been pressed more it would be diamonds. I wonder if diamonds burn, and if we'd burn them if they were as common as coal. To the fairies, they'd be the same, plants changed by time to rock. I wonder if fairies remember the Jurassic, if they walked among dinosaurs, and what they were then? None of them would have had human shapes. They wouldn't have spoken Welsh. I rubbed the coal in my fingers, and it flaked a bit. I know what coal is, but I don't know what fairies are, not really.

There's a spot on Common Ake we used to call the Dingly Dell. It's one of the oldest of our names, older than the ones from *The Lord of the Rings*, and writing it down now I feel simultaneously slightly embarrassed and fiercely protective. The Dingly Dell is a place where there used to be a quarry or a surface mine or something and the ground drops abruptly on three sides, making a little amphitheatre. There are trees on the steep sides, and blackberry bushes. I think we went there first with Grampar blackberry picking when we were quite small, I remember eating more than I put in the basket, but then that went for most years. We felt quite bold when we first went all the way there on our own.

Today the brambles were winter-dead, and the rowans leafless. A pale sun shone from a distant sky. A cheeky robin perched near me as I stepped in and cocked his head. They put robins on Christmas cards, and sometimes on Christmas cakes too, because they don't go away in winter. "Hello," I said. "How nice to see you still here."

The robin didn't reply. I didn't expect it to. But I was immediately aware that there was someone there. I looked up, expecting to see a fairy vanishing, hoping to see Glorfindel, but what I saw was Mor, standing back against the fallen leaves near the slope of the hill. She looked—well, she looked like Mor, obviously, but what I was really aware of right away was how she didn't look like me. I hadn't noticed that at half term, but now I did. I've grown, and she hasn't. I have breasts. My hair is different. I am fifteen and a half, and she is still and always fourteen.

I took a step towards her, and then I remembered her clutching me and dragging me towards the door into the hill, and stopped. "Oh Mor," I said.

She didn't say anything. She couldn't, any more than the robin. She was dead, and the dead can't speak. As a matter of fact, I know how to make the dead speak. You have to give them blood. But it's magic, and anyway, it would be horrible. I couldn't imagine doing it.

I talked to her although she couldn't answer. I told her about the magic and about Daniel and his sisters and about getting away from Liz and about school and the book club and everything. The strange thing was that the more I was talking the further away she seemed, though she didn't move, and the more different from me she was. Nobody could tell the difference between us, but of course we always were different. Since she's been dead, I'd almost forgotten, or not forgotten, but not thought about her as her distinct self so much, more about the two of us together. I'd felt as if I'd been torn in half, but really it wasn't that, it was that she had been taken away. I didn't own her, and there were always differences, always, she was her own person and I'd known that when she was alive, but that had blurred in all the time since when she hadn't been there to defend her own rights.

If she'd lived, we would have become different people. I think. I don't think we'd have been like the aunts and stayed together all the time. I think we'd always have been friends, but we'd have lived in different places and had different friends. We'd have been aunts to each other's children. It's too late for that now. I'm going to grow up and she isn't. She's frozen where she is, and I'm changing, and I want to change. I want to live. I thought I had to live for both of us, because she can't live for herself, but I can't really live for her. I can't really know what she'd have done, what she'd have wanted, how she'd have changed. Arlinghurst has changed me, the book club has changed me, and it might have changed her differently. Living for someone else isn't possible.

I couldn't help asking her questions. "Can you go under the hill next year?"

She shrugged. Clearly she didn't know either. What happens under the hill? Where do the dead go? Where is God in all this? They talk about Heaven like a family picnic.

"Are the fairies looking after you?" I asked.

She hesitated, then nodded.

"Good!" That made me feel a bit better. Living with the fairies in the Valley wasn't the worst way of being dead I could imagine, not by a long way. "Why won't they talk to me?"

She looked puzzled and shrugged again.

"Can you tell them about the aunts, and what they want to do?"

She nodded, very definitely.

"Can you ask them to talk to me? I'm so worried about doing magic and what it does."

"Doing is doing," a voice said behind me, and I spun around and there was a fairy, one I'd never seen before, nut brown all over and knobbly like an acorn cup. His skin was all wrinkles and folds, and he wasn't the shape of a person, more like an old treestump. The thing that astonished me was that he'd spoken in English, and that was exactly what he'd said, those very words. They're cryptic enough, I suppose.

"But what about the ethics?" I said. "Changing things for people without their knowing it? You may be able to see the consequences of what you do, but I can't."

"Doing is doing," he said again. Then he wasn't there, but there was a thump, and where he had been was a walking stick the same colour as he was, carved with a horse's head handle.

I bent awkwardly to pick it up. It was the right height for me, and the handle fit my hand comfortably. I looked back at Mor, but she had gone too. The wind was blowing into the dell, rustling the dead leaves, but it was empty of presence.

I brought both sticks back to Grampar's, the fairy one and my old one. I'm going to leave my old one, which was his anyway, and keep this one. I suppose it might vanish at sunrise, or turn into a leaf or something, but I don't think so. It has a heft that seems to make that unlikely. I'll tell people it was a Christmas present. I think perhaps it might have been. I like it.

Doing is doing.

Does it mean that it doesn't matter if it's magic or not, anything you do has power and consequences and affects other people? Because that might well be the case, but I still think magic is different.

Leah's party tonight.

Thursday 3rd January 1980

Back in Auntie Teg's. Hung over. I wish the water in Cardiff didn't taste so dreadful. I brought a big bottle of Aberdare tap water back with me, but I have drunk it all.

We didn't do anything at all today, just came back to Cardiff and sat around eating chocolate cake and petting Persimmon (for her allowed time) and reading. It was lovely. Auntie Teg looks as exhausted as I am.

Leah's party last night was weird. There was punch, made with red wine and grape juice and tins of fruit cocktail, and later with added vodka. It tasted disgusting, and I think most of us were holding our noses and drinking it. I don't know why I bothered. I got drunk, and I suppose it was nice to have soft edges instead of hard ones, but it just made me stupid really. People do it as an excuse, to have an excuse, so they can deny responsibility for their actions the next day. It's horrible.

I don't want to write about what happened. It's not important anyway.

On the other hand, is this a complete and candid memoir or just a lot of angsty wittering?

It started off on the wrong foot. Nasreen was wearing a red sweater identical to mine, though she looked much better in it. "We're twins!"

she chirped enthusiastically, and then realised what she'd said and her face fell about a mile.

It's not quite a year, just about nine months, since I was living here. We've all grown up in that time, and it's as if they've learned some rules I haven't learned. Maybe it's because I was away, or maybe I was just reading my book under the desk the day when people were talking about how you do this stuff. Leah was wearing eyeshadow and lipstick—and even Moira was. Moira offered to put some on me, and she did, but we don't have the same colour skin. I normally look like a white person, like Daniel I suppose, but when you put me next to someone who really is white, and Moira is exceptionally pale, you can see that the underlying colour in my skin is yellow, not pink. Grampar used to say every time one of us got a sunburn that we were ridiculously pale and we'd have to marry black men to give our children a chance, and he was right—compared to him especially and to the rest of our family, we were very pale. I don't think you'd notice, if you didn't know, that I had ancestors closer to Nasreen's colour than Moira's. But Moira's makeup looked ridiculous on me anyway, and I wiped it all off.

Then I was talking to Leah about Andrew for ages, and afterwards to Nasreen about Andrew, for ages. Leah was over it, mostly, and interested in somebody else, an older boy called Gareth who has a motorbike. Nasreen was in the middle of a huge saga of fights with her parents about Andrew on which I had to be brought up to speed. Andrew doesn't seem significant enough to make all that fuss about if you ask me. But nobody did ask me, so I spent a couple of hours making a fuss about him. When he arrived, which Leah's parents had solemnly sworn to Nasreen's parents he wouldn't do, he spent the rest of the evening with his arm around her very self-consciously. Leah's parents had gone out until eleven o'clock, to the theatre in Cardiff with her younger sister.

There were a number of people there I didn't know very well.

One boy tried to put his arm around me, and I let him. Why not, I thought, because I'd had a few glasses of the stupid purple punch by then, with its little floating half-grapes and bits of pear and peach. It's nice to have someone near and warm. He was one of Gareth's friends, so he must have been sixteen or seventeen. His name was Owen, and as far as I could tell he'd never read a book in his life and had no interests apart from motorbikes and girls and music. He likes the Clash, who I've never heard of, and Elvis Costello. Leah must like Elvis Costello too, because she was playing some very loudly. I really miss out on music because we're not allowed any at school. I like the idea of Rock against Racism, but I don't like the actual music very much. He asked me what music I liked and I said Bob Dylan, which disconcerted him totally. I could tell he'd heard of Dylan but didn't know a thing about him. Oh well. He was a bit put off by the walking stick and left me alone for a bit after he saw it—I got up to go to the toilet. Later, after Moira had assured me he didn't have a girlfriend and wasn't he lovely—not a patch on Wim, I thought, and Wim has a brain, too.

Anyway, later Owen came back to me and started cuddling me again, and I didn't stop him. I was enjoying it, in a very much physical-only way. The thing is, I know that the others at least pretend to be in love with their boyfriends while they're going out with them. They're sort of rehearsing for grown-up relationships. They're temporarily exclusive, and playing at romance. I didn't, don't, want to play that game. Owen didn't make me in the slightest bit breathless, nor did I especially like him. But he was warm and male and solid and interested, and he did make me curious and desirous of more body-contact. So when he suggested he show me his bike, I went outside with him. It was only a Moped, 50cc, but he was very proud of it and told me all sorts of things about it. I'm not even sure those things go up hills.

You'd have thought the night air would have sobered me up, but it seemed to make me more drunk. When he started kissing me I liked it, and kissed him back, which he seemed to find a bit disconcerting. (Maybe I was doing it wrong? Books do not say, but I was doing it exactly the way I have seen in films.) He had his arms around me and he started running them over me. Now this did make me a bit breathless, and actually very turned on.

So we went back inside and into a little room which is actually Leah's father's study. There's a sofa in there and we sat down on that and started cuddling. It was dark—there was a light in the hall, but we didn't put any lights on in there.

Why is writing about sex more private and worrying than writing about anything else? There are things in this book that could get me *burned at the stake*, and I don't worry about writing them.

Anyway, we cuddled for a bit and then Owen put his hand inside my knickers, and I liked it, and I thought I was being selfish just sitting there and not reciprocating, so I put my hand on his leg, and moved it to his penis—and I know perfectly well what a penis is, I have had baths with my cousins, and played doctor with them as well, when we were young enough that there weren't all these stupid rules of etiquette. Anyway, Owen had a penis just as you'd expect, and he was excited too, but as soon as I touched it, through his trousers, he took his hands off me and practically leapt away.

"You slut!" he said, standing up with his hands clenched defensively in front of it, as if he thought I was about to grab for it. Then he rushed out of the room. I sat there for a minute, my cheeks burning. I couldn't understand it. I still can't understand it. He wanted me. I thought he did. I thought I was acting like a normal person, but evidently not. There's something I'm just not seeing about this even now, because I still do not get it.

Leah said to me when I went back that I should watch out for Owen because he had wandering hands. Was I supposed to stop him? Was he expecting me to put up resistance instead of cooperating? That's *sick*. The whole thing is sick, and I want nothing to do with it.

I want the infinite series of bars in *Triton*. Or even just the three

real bars. That I could cope with. This is completely beyond me. At
least I won't ever have to see him again, probably.

Friday 4th January 1980

Into Cardiff this morning to spend my book tokens in Lears. I love
Lears. It's huge—two floors, with a whole wall of SF, and some Amer-
ican imports. I got another issue of *Destinies* and *Red Shift* and *The
Einstein Intersection* and *Four Quartets* and *Charisma* by Michael
Coney (who wrote *Hello Summer, Goodbye*) and, wonder of wonder
miracle of miracles, a new Roger Zelazny book in the Chronicles of
Amber series! I squealed out loud when I saw it. *Sign of the Unicorn*!
It has a horrible yellow cover, but bless Sphere forever for publishing
it and Lears for stocking it!

I would rather have *Sign of the Unicorn* than all the boys in the
Valleys.

This afternoon we went for a run on the Beacons to see if the wa-
terfalls were frozen. They weren't, it isn't anything like cold enough,
though they do freeze for a few days some winters. There was no ice
cream van in the lay-by, and Auntie Teg remarked on this as if she
really thought there would be. I love the mountains. I love the kind
of horizon they make, even in winter. When we went down again,
towards Merthyr first and then over the shoulder of the mountain
to Aberdare, where Auntie Teg walked, once, when she was still in
school, it felt like nestling back down in a big quilt.

My new walking stick is still with me. Grampar is the only person who has noticed it, when we went to see him tonight on the way
back. He said it's hazel wood. I said I'd bought it in the market with
Christmas money. He said it was a lovely piece of work and I should
get a rubber ferrule to protect the end, and I could get one of those
in the market too. He was looking much more alert today. Nobody
could be doing more than Auntie Teg to try to get him out of there.

Saturday 5th January 1980

On the train I read *The Sign of the Unicorn*, all of it in one gulp, so I can leave it with Daniel when I go back to school. The thing I really love about those books is Corwin's voice, so very personal, making light of things, joking about them, and then suddenly so serious. I also love the Trumps and the Shadows, and the Hellrides through Shadow. (I think I'll always call Kentucky Fried Chicken Kentucki Fried Lizzard Partes from now on.) I don't think he has done as much with Shadow as he could. If you can walk through it and find shadows of yourself, there are lots of things you could do with that.

I finished it at Leominster, and after that read *Four Quartets* again and got drunk on the words. I could just copy out pages and pages of it. Sometimes it's hard to figure out what it means, but that's part of the joy of it, putting the images together into coherence. There's a story in there just the same as there is in "Young Lochinvar," but it isn't on the surface much at all. I'm so glad I have my own copy. I can read them again and again. I can read them again and again *on trains*, all my life, and every time I do I'll remember today and it will connect up. (Is that magic? Yes, it is a sort of magic, but it is more just reading my book.)

Shropshire remains horribly flat and unmountained. It looks miserable in the January drizzle. The sky is so low you feel as if you could reach up and poke it. I can imagine feeling claustrophobic and acrophobic at the same time.

Daniel met me without any problem. He was early, sitting in the Bentley reading *Punch* when I came out of the station. He was very apologetic about not driving me to the station when I left. It's so hard to know what to say. I could say it didn't matter, even though it did. What difference does it make if he feels guilty after the fact? "Don't apologise, just don't do it again," I said. He winced.

I had brought a Twelfth Night cake with me. I made it and Auntie Teg iced it. There was no direct and deliberate magic in it, except the thought of the Three Kings, and T. S. Eliot's poem about them, but just the fact that we'd made it with her bowls and spoons and our hands made it magically real. I suppose the sisters noticed that, because they produced their own, and said I should take mine to school and give slices to all my friends. In school, it's going to practically glow with magic. I didn't say that. I ate their sawdust cake and smiled and tried being Nice Niece for all it's worth. I made out that I was terribly excited to be going back to school and longing to know what the other girls got for Christmas.

It occurred to me sitting there eating tea and smiling so much my face felt sore, that they haven't tried to do anything to me magically. I mean the earrings were an attempt, I suppose, but they tried to use their authority as adults and their physical ability to drive me to the shop and so on, they didn't try to coerce me magically, or make it so I had always wanted earrings or anything. I wonder how much they know and how they learned it. Did they learn it from the fairies? Or from someone who learned it from the fairies? Theoretically, I could teach someone who had never seen a fairy all the magic that I know.

I was thinking about the Jurassic fairies in between reading *Four Quartets*, and I wondered if fairies are a sentient manifestation of the magical interconnectedness of the world. I remember once in Birmingham, when I was running away, I saw a fairy standing on the corner of the street. It was raining, and the pavement was wet and shiny, and there he was, looking quite unconcerned. I went up to him, he saw me, nodded and vanished. I saw that just where he was there was some grass growing through a crack in the pavement.

Sunday 6th January 1980

I always forget how loud school is. My ears are ringing.

I read *The Hitchhiker's Guide to the Galaxy* in bed last night. I intended to read it quickly to be able to thank Deirdre for it, but it turns out to be hilarious and also wickedly clever, so I could thank her sincerely, because I'd never in a million years have picked it up for myself, as it looks like total tosh. I wonder if the book group have read it?

What the other girls got for Christmas, notes for a Nice Niece to report: the richest ones got Sony Walkmans. They couldn't bring them back to school, of course, because we're forbidden music. Moira and Leah and Nasreen couldn't believe that, they thought it the worst deprivation of all. They live with the radio on. Sony Walkmans are apparently very portable cassette tape players with headphones that fasten to your belt, so you can listen to a tape while walking along. I admit that is quite nifty, even if their choice of music might not be mine. Lots of them got music, even if they didn't get a Walkman, lots of them mentioned records and tapes. Lorraine got a skateboard, and her brothers taught her how to use it. It's apparently almost as good as skiing. Other popular presents include clothes, perfume, make-up kits with little mirrors in the lid—also banned in school, but some of them smuggled in anyway—and soap-on-a-rope, which makes me like mine a little less.

Deirdre admired my new walking stick. She asked if it was Irish. I said no, Welsh, which it is, and she said it must be a Celtic thing. I just agreed. She was glad I'd liked the book, and I was glad I really had. She was pleased with her soap set, or so she said.

I gave the cake to the kitchen and told them to give slices to all of Lower VC. It's a big cake, and I could see that if they cut it thinly there ought to be enough. I didn't care if people didn't eat it. In fact, when it was handed round after supper, most people did eat it, though a few of them looked at me cautiously when they did. My thoughts about those kings bringing gold and frankincense and myrrh and the warning about Herod aren't going to hurt them, but I can't tell them that. Sharon gave her slice to Deirdre. I don't know what Jews think about Jesus. Do they think he was just a weird kid that kings happened to go up to with presents and who mistakenly thought he was the Messiah? Or do they think he's just a myth? I can't ask Sharon, but I could ask Sam. Deirdre found the bean, in Shagger's slice, and was thrilled to bits. The king bean and the poetry competition are probably the only things she's ever won. I don't know if they do Twelfth Night cake in Ireland.

I can feel this place closing round me like quicksand.

Book club on Tuesday!

Monday 7th January 1980

I went out to look back at the school and breathe this morning, and the grounds were full of fairies. I expected them to vanish as soon as they saw that I could see them, but they kept going about their business though they took no notice of me, barely moving out of my way. Most of them were the hideous warty kind, but there were some elf-maiden types among them. I tried speaking to them in Welsh and English but they ignored me. I wonder what's up?

Letter from the hospital with an appointment for Thursday morning with a Dr. Abdul. I've shown it to Nurse and Miss Ellis, and I'll go, though I can't see what good it'll do. My leg's been a bit better this last few days anyway. The Orthopaedic Hospital is in Gobowen, which means a bus into town and then a bus out there.

Miss Carroll was very nice to me, inquiring about my holiday and whether I got any books. I asked if she did, and she did, books and book tokens, just like me. She's not all that old. I suppose she wanted to become a librarian because she loves books and reading. I wouldn't mind that, if I could be in a real library, but a school library would be horrible, especially here.

Tuesday 8th January 1980

Book club tonight!

This term's book for English is *Far from the Madding Crowd*. I've been reading it all day when I have reading time. Hardy's very long-winded, though not technically as long as Dickens. There's a horrible scene where a fallen woman called Fanny Robin drags herself along a fence while actually giving birth. I think the rest of the book is too slight to support that scene. The happy ending is like a nightmare—Bathsheba and Gabriel Oak married and "whenever I look up, there you are, and whenever you look up, there I am." Talk about stifling! Gramma liked Hardy, but I can't. I've tried, but he's too depressing and too trite at the same time. He makes things happen neatly, and sometimes they're horrible things, but they're always very pat. I hate that. He could have learned a lot from Silverberg and Delany.

We're also going to be reading *The Tempest* and some Keats. I've already read both. The good bit about *The Tempest* is that we'll be going to see it in Theatre Clwyd in Mold, a school trip. I expect everyone will giggle and be annoying, but a real play in a theatre! I've never seen *The Tempest*. I've only seen *Romeo and Juliet*, in the Sherman Theatre, with Auntie Teg, and *A Midsummer Night's Dream* with school, in the New Theatre. I expect Mold theatre won't be at the level of Cardiff theatre, but who cares. I wonder how they'll do Caliban? I always see him like the first fairy I saw here, all warty and spider-webby. I wonder how they'll do Ariel?

In history we're doing more of the boring old Nineteenth Century, ugh, all Acts and Ireland and unions. Give me history with some fun in it! In French we're going to learn the subjunctive. People say it's hard, but it isn't in Latin. In Latin we're starting on Book I of Virgil's *Aeneid*. I love it so far.

> A nation hostile to me
> Is sailing the Tyrrhenian sea
> Carrying to Italy Troy and her conquered gods!

Though I think "Etruscan sea" scans better?

Wednesday 9th January 1980

Book club last night. I got there a little late because the bus wasn't on time, but they hadn't started, and Janine had saved a seat for me opposite the bust of Plato.

Great meeting, led by Mark, who's a tubby middle-aged guy with huge thick glasses and a little beard. We talked about the Foundation Trilogy. The best bit was where we all really got into psychohistory, whether it's possible. I don't think it is, because of chaos. I don't think it would take a mutation like the Mule, or rather, I think ordinary people are just as unlikely to keep on track. (You could do it with magic, maybe. But not to the level Hari Selden supposedly did it. I didn't say that.) Then Wim compared it to *The Lathe of Heaven* and some Dick books with manipulated history. Then I wondered if you could write a story where a secret society have been manipulating history all along for mysterious ends?

"Who's been around long enough?" Greg asked.

"The Catholic Church?" Janine offered.

Pete snorted. "If so, they haven't been doing a very good job of it. They controlled half the world, and they lost control."

(Janine and Pete are back together. They were holding hands under the table. I don't know if she's forgiven him for supporting Wim or whether she's come around to Hugh's view of things. I couldn't ask, even when we were just chatting at the end, because Wim was there.)

"Unless it's actually a secret inner cabal whose goals are not the church's ostensible goals," I said.

"Templars?" Keith suggested.

"Secret alien technologist Templars!" Wim put in.

We were a long way off the Foundation books. But that was all right, that was how it bounces. It's so nice to be with people who have read the things I've read and whose minds go to those sort of places. The idea of secret alien technologist Templars manipulating all of history for mysterious ends—maybe to get people to go to the moon, where they have a cache or something, as in *The Sirens of Titan*?—is just so wonderful.

At the end, I told everyone about *The Sign of the Unicorn*, but couldn't lend it to anyone because Daniel still has it. I'll ask him to send it. Almost everyone was excited, and the two or three people who hadn't read the first two—and they're in for a treat—got told about them. Only Brian doesn't like Zelazny. Greg says he'll order it for the library, but not until April because they're out of money for book purchase until the new financial year. If I was rich, I'd donate lots of money to libraries.

"Meanwhile, people can get it through interlibrary loan," Greg said, and smiled at me.

"That reminds me," I said. "What else has Zelazny written?"

Tons, apparently, but almost none of it in print. Greg's going to put ILL for it all through for me. He's one of the nicest people I know. You can't tell at first because he's very closed down, but underneath he's lovely.

Next week, Cordwainer Smith! Terrific.

Wim came up to me as we were all leaving. "Did you say you hadn't read *The Dream Master*?" he asked.

"That's right," I said.

"I could lend you that, if you don't want to wait for it to come. If you like, I could meet you here with it on Saturday."

So I'm meeting Wim in the library at half past eleven on Saturday for him to lend it to me.

Nobody who offers to lend me Zelazny could be as black as he's been painted.

Thursday 10th January 1980

In hospital, in bed, in traction, in terrible pain, excuse appalling handwriting. This had better help.

Friday 11th January 1980

I feel kidnapped. I came to the hospital yesterday morning for an outpatient appointment. The doctor, Dr. Abdul, looked at my x-rays for five minutes, poked at my leg for two minutes, and said I needed a week in traction. He told his assistant to make a date for it, found there was a bed available right now, telephoned Daniel and the school, and the next thing I knew here I was on the rack. It really feels like being on the rack. It's hard to do anything. Writing is very hard. I'm doing it forwards, because backwards is just too difficult, even with all the practice I get. I keep pouring water on myself when I drink. Even reading is hard. My leg is held out on this thing, elevated on white metal bars, strapped in place, stretched agonisingly so it hurts like hell every second, and the rest of me is forced flat. I can hardly move at all. I have read all three books I had in my bag, one of them twice. (Clement's *Mission of Gravity*.) I should have brought more, but I only had three because I know about hospital waiting times.

Pain, pain, more pain, and the indignity of bedpans. I have to press a button for a nurse when I want a drink or a bedpan, and sometimes they don't come for ages, but if I count on that and call early, they seem to come right away. To add insult to injury there's a television at the end of the ward. It's unavoidable, and even more unbearable than usual as it's constantly tuned to ITV, so there are adverts. I wonder if hell is like this? I'd definitely prefer lakes of sulphur and at least being able to swim about in them.

All the other patients have visitors between two and three, or six and seven, which are visiting hours. This is the second day I've watched them all troop in with flowers and grapes and odd expressions. I watch them compulsively, as well as I can watch anyone from this angle. I'm not expecting anyone, and indeed, I don't get anyone. Daniel could come. It's not all that far, and he knows I'm here. I don't expect they'll let him though.

I won't be able to meet Wim tomorrow and he'll think I didn't show because I have heard bad things about him.

A woman at the end of the ward has started to scream, short staccato cutoff screams. They're putting screens around her bed so the rest of us can't see what they're doing to her. This is definitely much worse than the way most people describe hell.

Saturday 12th January 1980

Still on the rack.

Miss Carroll came in towards the end of visiting time last night with a pile of light paperbacks. They're from the school library and therefore not ordinarily terribly exciting, but right now they seemed like manna. She couldn't stay long. Nobody told her I was here, but when she hadn't seen me she went to find out what had happened. She came as soon as she knew. I almost cried when she told me that. I had no idea how hard it is to blow my nose in this position. She promised to tell Greg where I was, and he can tell Wim and the others. She's coming back tonight with more books.

Dear God, if you are there and care and can bless people, please bless Alison Carroll with your very best blessing.

She brought me three books by Piers Anthony, the first books in two different series. I think she chose them because they're at the beginning of the alphabet and she was in a hurry. I hadn't read them, because, frankly, they looked like crap. I'm beyond the stage of reading the whole library in alphabetical order, though I'm glad to have done it once. I'm enjoying these anyway. So far I've read *Vicinity Cluster*, and *Chaining the Lady*, and I'm about to start *A Spell for Chameleon* which is fantasy. I was right, they are crap really, but they hold my attention and don't require all my brain, which when half of my brain is sending me messages like "Ow, Ow, Ow" or "Remove leg from rack soonest," is actually an advantage. I had weird "hosts" universe dreams last night, about transferring into alien bodies. All of them had bad legs, though; even when I was in a ballerina's body she had to dance with a walking stick. I suppose that was the pain coming through even when I was asleep. Last night I read myself to sleep and then they woke me up to give me a sleeping pill.

Sunday 13th January 1980

Miss Carroll came back last night with more books and a bunch of grapes, and Greg came this afternoon, bringing Janine and Pete, and more books. Also, while they were here and we were talking about Piers Anthony, who Pete likes, and Greg compared to Chaucer (!), Daniel turned up. I didn't notice him at first, because I wasn't obsessively looking over at the door at other people's visitors because I had three of my own for a change. He came sidling up to the bed looking embarrassed. I could see that he wasn't sure if he should kiss me or not, and in the end he didn't. He had also brought books, and a big card from his sisters, and more grapes, little red ones. I don't know why people bring grapes. Are they supposed to be specially healing? Janine brought a Mars Bar, which was rather more welcome, though messy to eat. The food in here is just beyond horrible.

At first, conversation was awkward. I introduced Daniel to the others, and it was clear nobody knew what to say. Greg even said that maybe they ought to go. Then, fortunately, Daniel said he'd brought my *Sign of the Unicorn*, and it was a case of deciding who got it first, and we all talked about books until the end of visiting time when the nurse rang the bell and everyone all had to go. I didn't ask Daniel if he was able to wait for another hour at visiting time tonight, but he evidently didn't as it has come and gone with no more sign of him. Still, it was very nice of him to spare me his Sunday afternoon.

The books Greg brought are all my this week's ILL arrivals, which he stamped out to me in my absence without my cards. He was joking that this was a standard library service, but of course it isn't. Unfortunately, they're all hardcovers and terribly difficult to read at this angle. I can hold a paperback above my head sideways in one hand, but not a hardback. I have Mary Renault's *Return to Night* and I can't even read it. Still, just looking at the spine on my table is something.

A week would be until Wednesday. That would be three more days of agony and hell.

A nurse comes round and offers me painkillers every four hours. "Only take them if you're in pain," she says. How could anybody be hooked up like this and not be in pain? I take them, but they barely take the edge off.

I'm sleeping really badly, weird dreams and waking up often because of the pain and disturbances in the ward. The sleeping pills, which they insist I take, make me fall asleep but don't make me stay asleep.

Monday 14th January 1980

Last night, or early this morning, my mother tried the night attack again. I woke up and could not move, and I knew she was in the room, hovering above me. It's never dark in the ward, there's always a light at the nurses' station and little lights along the floor, and someone had their reading light on down at the end. There was enough light that I should have been able to see her, but I couldn't, only feel her presence very strongly. There was so much pain that I couldn't think what to do. I tried to remember what had worked last

time, and of course it was the Litany Against Fear, so I did that, and
it worked again. As I calmed down and got control of myself, I could
move, as much as I can anyway on the rack, and then she was gone.

How did she know I was here and vulnerable? Why didn't my protection spell hold? It shouldn't make any difference where I am.

I saw Dr. Abdul this morning, for the first time since he hooked me
into this contraption last Thursday. He poked at my leg, making me
scream, dammit, and said I was coming along well. Then he moved off
down the ward to his next patient. I am nothing like so confident that
I am coming along well. It feels as if it is making everything worse.

I suppose it might feel like that anyway and be working. He's a
doctor. You have to get three As at A Level to even start to train to be
a doctor. (Do they have A Levels in Pakistan? I suppose they might,
because they used to be British, they were part of British India when
Grampar's grandmother left there. But did they have A Levels then?
Nasreen would know, because her father must have done them.) Well
anyway, Dr. Abdul would have had to have got the Pakistani equivalent of three As at A Level before he even started training. He'd have
to be clever and diligent and know what he was doing. He wouldn't
strap someone to a contraption just for nothing.

Why does the Litany Against Fear work?

Miss Carroll came in at evening visiting time, with books. They're
more Josephine Tey mysteries, which seem just about right, and paperbacks thank goodness. She says she misses me in the library, and that
they mentioned my name in Prayers.

Tuesday 15th January 1980

Still on the rack, and feeling really down.

I'm missing book club, and because I know everyone is there, and
Miss Carroll came yesterday, I know I won't get any visitors.

Grampar and Auntie Teg don't even know I'm here, or they'd

have at least sent a card. So how does my mother know? There's no magic here. There are no fairies, there's nothing—I thought school was purged and neutral, but it's nothing to this hell ward.

I've read all the Tey. *Brat Farrar* is especially good. But what is a pit in Dothan? Is it from the Joseph story?

Only one more day on the rack. I'm starting to wonder if sadists could get three As at A Level, but if Dr. Abdul was a sadist he'd come around and gloat more. It's clear he's entirely indifferent. He didn't look at my face at all, and barely even at my leg, it's just the x-rays that interested him. I'm trying to see this as a good thing. Three As at A Level is starting to seem like a very small thing to hold so much weight of trust.

Wednesday 16th January 1980

They're not letting me out until Dr. Abdul sees me, and he doesn't come in until tomorrow.

At afternoon visiting, Wim came. He brought *The Dream Master* and *Isle of the Dead*. He came in wearing a leather jacket and looking really awkward, even more awkward than Daniel did. I was suddenly very aware that I was wearing a stupid hospital gown with stains on it where I'd spilled my food (it's very hard to eat neatly when horizontal) and that my hair hadn't been washed for more than a week. I felt touched that he'd come all the way out here to see me, even more so than with the others.

"Greg mentioned last night you were here," he said. "I thought I'd bring these. Though it looks as if you don't need them." He gestured to the piles of books on the bedside table.

"I've read most of these," I said.

He raised his eyebrows.

"There is nothing else at all to do in here," I said.

"Looks pretty grim," he agreed. "How's the food?"

"Awful."

He laughed. "My mother's one of the cooks here."

"I'm sure her food at home is much better," I said.

"No it isn't," he said. "She's not much of a cook. Though she says herself the food here is appalling, so it must be really bad. That's why I was asking."

"It's not all that different from school food," I said.

"I'd have thought they'd have fed you well at Arlinghurst, from what they're charging," he said.

"So would I, but it's all awful. Spam and custard."

"I've brought you some NASA astronaut ice cream," he said, and produced a packet from his pocket.

I held it up where I could see it properly. It was black with a picture of a rocket ship and it did claim to be astronaut ice cream, just like that eaten on the Apollo missions. I looked at Wim in awe. "Everyone else brought grapes. Where did you get this?"

He looked a bit shy, if such a thing is possible. "My cousin brought some back from Florida. He brought quite a few packets, this is the last one. It isn't that nice, it's more the idea. I was saving it for an appropriate occasion."

I stopped turning the packet over and looked right at him. "You have a cousin who went to America?"

He smiled at me, and I got that breathless feeling again. "America's real, you know, it's not just in science fiction. Greg's been there. He went to a Worldcon in Phoenix. He met Harlan Ellison!"

"What's a Worldcon?"

"A world science fiction convention. It's five days where people get together and talk about SF. Last year it was in Brighton and I went. It was brill. It was beyond brill. You can't imagine."

I thought I *could* imagine. "Like book club multiplied?"

"Multiplied geometrically. Robert Silverberg was there. I talked to him! And Vonda McIntyre!"

I could hardly believe I was sitting in the same room as someone who had talked to Robert Silverberg. "Where is it this year?"

"Boston. It's usually America. Goodness knows when we'll ever have one in Britain again. But there are British cons. There's one at Easter in Glasgow. They don't have all the American writers, of course. But it's not just the writers. It's the fans as well. You wouldn't believe the conversations I had in Brighton."

"Are you going to Glasgow?"

"I'm already saving up for it. I went to Brighton on my bike, and slept in a tent, but I'll need money for at least a share of a hotel room in Glasgow at Easter, and it would be nicer to go on the train." He looked eager and animated.

"A hotel room. Trainfare. And how much is the ticket?"

"They call it membership," he reproved me. "I've already bought mine. It was five pounds."

"I wonder if Daniel would pay all that. I wonder if he'd agree to me going. I wonder if I could persuade him to go too. He'd enjoy it."

"Who's Daniel?" he asked, shifting away from me without getting out of the chair. "Your boyfriend?"

"My father," I said. "He reads SF. He met Greg and Janine and Pete on Sunday, and we all talked about books the whole time. He'd enjoy a convention, I'm sure he would." I was much less sure his sisters would let him go. It wasn't the kind of thing they'd want at all, doing something he wanted to away from them. They probably wouldn't approve it for me either, not if they wanted me to be Nice Niece. I'd have to find some way of getting round them.

"You're so lucky," Wim said, surprisingly.

"Lucky? Why?" I blinked. I am not in the habit of thinking I am lucky, even when my leg isn't strapped to a rack.

"Having a rich father who reads SF. Mine thinks it's childish. He was okay with it when I was twelve, but he thinks reading at all is sissy and reading kid stuff is babyish. He roars at me whenever he catches me reading. My mother reads what she calls nice romances, sometimes, Catherine Cookson and that sort of thing, but only when he isn't in the house. She doesn't understand at all. There are no books in our house. I'd give anything for parents who read."

"I only met Daniel this summer," I said. "My parents are divorced, and I was brought up mostly by my grandparents. They didn't have any money, but they did read, and encouraged us to read. And Daniel isn't exactly rich. His sisters are, and they give him money but they keep him on a tight rein. They're paying for me to go to Arlinghurst so they can get rid of me, I think. I don't know if they'd let him have enough money to go to Glasgow, because they wouldn't want him to go. They might let me go."

"Where's your mum?" It was a natural question, but he asked it with an elaborate casualness that seemed rehearsed.

"She's in South Wales. She's—" I hesitated, because I didn't want to say either that she's a witch, or that she's mad, though both of those things are true. There isn't a word that means both, really, and there should be. "She's insane."

"You told the girls in school she's a witch," Wim said, tossing his hair back from his face.

"How do you know that?"

"I've got a girlfriend who works in the laundry, and she told me."

My heart sank at the news he had a girlfriend. He was two years older than I was, he couldn't possibly be interested in me and I knew that, even if he had come to see me and seemed to be paying a lot of attention to me. I knew at once that his girlfriend must be the girl I'd seen at the end of term wearily bundling uniform shirts into the washing machine. In a way, it was gratifying that he'd asked her about me.

"Let them hate me as long as they fear me," I quoted. "It's what Tiberius—"

"I've read *I, Claudius*," he said. "You told them your mother's a witch so the girls would be afraid of you?"

"They're awful bullies," I explained. "They all knew each other and I didn't know anyone, and my voice isn't like theirs, and it seemed like a good strategy. It's mostly worked, too, though it is a little lonely."

"She's not a witch then?" He sounded oddly disappointed.

"Well—actually, she is. A mad witch. An evil witch like in stories." I didn't want to talk about her, I didn't want to tell him what she's like. It's hard to describe her anyway.

He leaned forward and looked into my eyes. His eyes are very blue, as blue as the sky almost. "Can you read minds?"

"What?" I was startled.

"You know, like in *Dying Inside*." He stayed where he was, just inches from me, looking into my eyes intensely. As far as breathless goes, it's amazing I didn't suffocate, even knowing he does have a girlfriend.

"No! I don't think anyone can do that," I said in an odd sort of squeak.

"I just wondered." He sounded tentative and uncertain, as if he wished he hadn't asked. He didn't move away. "It's just, the first time I saw you, I felt as if you were seeing right into me. And when I heard you'd said your mother was a witch, I thought—you know, did you ever read so much SF that you start thinking you don't know quite what's impossible any more? Where you're ready to start admitting hypotheses that you know are screwy, but . . ." he trailed off.

The first time I saw him, all I can remember is thinking how gorgeous he was. If he thought that was some kind of mystic communication, he was completely wrong. The bell rang for the end of visiting time.

"She is a witch," I said quickly, as he started to get up. "And there is magic."

He leaned forward over me, urgent. "Show me."

"It isn't like it is in books," I said, not much above a whisper, though with the clatter of visitors leaving there wasn't much chance of being overheard.

"Show me anyway."

"There isn't anything to see. And I've sworn not to do it except to prevent harm!" Even as I said it I heard how feeble an excuse it seemed. His face closed down and he straightened up. "I might be able to show you something, though," I said, desperate to have him believe me. "I don't know if you'll be able to see it. You'll have to wait until I'm out of here."

"You're not having me on?" he asked, suspicion clear in his voice.

"No! Of course not!"

"All right," he said, ungraciously. "Thank you."

"Thank you for coming and for bringing the books," I said.

I watched him walk out of the ward, and then I've spent all the rest of the day eating the astronaut ice cream (very peculiar stuff) and writing down every word of the conversation, even though writing is so awkward, so I won't forget.

I don't have to do magic. If he'll come into Poacher's Wood, I can probably show him a fairy. He believes, he does believe, at least, he believes something. But standing in the wood with fairies I can see and he can't if it comes to that is going to be very awkward, because he's going to think I'm mad or lying, and either would be pretty awful.

Oh well.

Thursday 17th January 1980

It didn't feel this bad even right after I did it.

They took more x-rays. Dr. Abdul wanted to talk to Daniel, and seemed cross that he wasn't there, as if I kept him in my pocket. They let me go, eventually, insisting I take a metal stick instead of using my perfectly nice fairy one. I only just made it to the bus stop, and then from the bus stop to the other bus stop. It's a good thing there are walls to sit on. It was never this bad before. I think they've made it worse, I think they've wrecked it forever and that's what he wanted to tell Daniel and wouldn't tell me.

I'm back in the library. Miss Carroll thinks I should be in bed. She brought me a barley sugar and a glass of water, even though eating in the library is strictly forbidden.

Pain, pain, PAIN.

Friday 18th January 1980

In bed in the San. Lying down with pillows and no rack is wonderful. Lying still doesn't hurt all that much. I never appreciated school food before either. Of course, one good thing about hospital was visitors. Nobody can visit me here except Deirdre and Miss Carroll. They'd have a fit at Janine or Greg, and probably expel me if Wim came, not that he would.

I'm catching up on the school work I missed, well, I've done it all except the maths. I don't have maths brain anyway, and somehow I can't keep the numbers straight when there's all this pain. In geography, we are doing Glaciation. I have done this before, so I have no trouble with it. In fact, it's boring, yes, glaciers, cwms or corries, terminal moraines, u-shaped valleys. Deirdre hadn't heard of it before and confessed to nightmares about it. I was very good and didn't tell her the story of Clarke's "Forgotten Enemy."

I won't be able to go to town tomorrow, but I hadn't arranged to meet anyone anyway. Miss Carroll will take my library books back and collect any new ones. Maybe by Tuesday I'll be all right. Or as all right as I was before.

I want my mobility back. I feel trapped. I hate this.

Return to Night is excessively and unsubtly Freudian. It does have some good bits though.

Saturday 19th January 1980

Daniel came to see me, which was a surprise. He put his head around the door. "Who do you think I've brought?" he asked.

I hoped for Sam, but I guessed right that it was his sisters. I was surprised that it was only one of them. "Hello, Aunt Anthea," I said, which made her jump. It was just a guess of course, but a guess based in experience. Usually if there's just one of them, it's Anthea, who is the oldest.

"I just couldn't resist coming to see the old place," she said.

"I'm surprised the others could resist," I said, as Nice Niece as I could be.

"There wouldn't have been room in the car, dear."

Now Daniel's car, like most cars, like every car in the world apart from maybe Auntie Teg's little orange Fiat 500, holds four people. Even Auntie Teg's car, which we call Gamboge Gussie the Galloping Girl—Gussie because the registration number starts GCY—can hold four, it's just a bit of a squash, especially if any of them are tall. So that was when I realised that they'd come to take me back with them.

"To convalesce," Daniel said.

It seemed to me that it would have been more use if Daniel had come on a weekday and talked to Dr. Abdul, but it seemed he'd spoken to him on the phone—I wonder who initiated that call? In any case, it seemed as if the school thought it would take me a little while to be back in class, and I'd be better off being nursed at home. Well, that might be the case, for people who have homes. I tried every argument I could think of to stay in school, including a few outright Nice Niece ones, like not wanting to miss the hockey match against St. Felicity's, but none of them held water.

I found myself being helped down to the car. That sort of help is actually a hindrance. If you ever see someone with a walking stick, that stick, and their arm, are actually a leg. Grabbing it or lifting it or doing anything unasked to the stick and the arm are much the same as if you grabbed a normal person's leg as they're walking. I wish more people understood this. A number of girls saw me leaving, and of course Nurse knows, so I expect someone will tell Miss Carroll and she'll think to tell Greg who will tell the others. "The others," I say, and I do mean Janine and everyone as well as Wim. But I should admit that mostly I mean Wim. I think I have a bit of a crush on him. And I stupidly left his Zelazny books, which I was saving, in school, so I can't even read them.

Sunday 20th January 1980

There's half a gale blowing, and it feels as if it could shake the Old Hall down. It bangs against the windows and creeps through the cracks and whistles down the chimneys. Lying here I can feel the whole house singing with it, as if it were a sailing ship.

I have plenty of books, and Daniel comes up now and then to ask if I want more. I have pillows, and I'm not hooked to a rack. I can hobble to the bathroom. I have a decanter of water, a real decanter with a proper crystal stopper. They bring me meals, which are no worse than school meals. (If there's magic in the food it's the magic of the Old Hall going on as it always has without any disturbance, that's all I can feel.) I have a radio, which plays the news, and the Archers, and Gardeners' Question Time and, to my surprise and delight, *The Hitchhiker's Guide to the Galaxy*! It's terrific as a radio play. I suppose I could retune the radio away from Radio 4, which Grampar still calls the Home Service, to Radio 1, which people used to call the Light Programme. The only advantage of this would be annoying the aunts, because Radio 4 might have other unexpected gems like HGttG, whereas all Radio 1 would have would be pop music. Most of the time I just read anyway.

How long am I going to be stuck here?

I hobbled downstairs for supper, which is what they call dinner when it isn't formally served. It was macaroni cheese, overcooked and on the edge of inedible. They all sat there eating it and making inane remarks, nodding and smiling. I played Nice Niece. Actually I'm longing to talk to Daniel about the possibility of Glasgow at Easter, but I want to do it when there's no chance of them hearing.

Afterwards, I asked if it would be okay to phone Auntie Teg. They couldn't very well say no, with Daniel right there, so I called her. She was horrified to hear about the hospital and that she hadn't known, and didn't believe that it seemed to have made things worse. She always tries to look on the bright side and find every silver lining, which is very nice sometimes, and there's nobody in the world better to celebrate with, but isn't very useful at the moment. She said she'd explain to Grampar why I hadn't been in touch and give him my love. I hope it doesn't upset him—but it won't, she'll probably say it's making me better and soon I'll be running again. I wish it was. Even when my leg isn't actively hurting there's a kind of an ache all the time now. I'm sure it's worse.

The phone is in the corridor, and on a sort of table with a padded bench attached. I was sitting on the padded bench while I talked to Auntie Teg. After I put the phone down, I wondered who else I could call, while I was here and everyone else was out of the way. The trouble is I don't know numbers. There'd be no point trying to call Greg at the library on a Sunday night anyway. I don't know anyone's home number, not even Janine's. There was a phone book next to the phone, a homemade one, with people's numbers written in, not a big Yellow Pages type book. I flicked through it, not seeing anyone I knew, until I came to M, and there was Sam, his address and also his telephone number.

His landlady answered right away, and she remembered me. "The little granddaughter," she said. I'm not little, and it feels weird thinking of Sam being my grandfather. I already have Grampar, the position isn't vacant. I like Sam though.

After a moment he came to the phone. "Morwenna?" he said. "Is there something wrong?"

"Not exactly wrong, only I'm at the Old Hall convalescing and I thought of you and wanted to speak to you."

"Convalescing from what?" he asked, so I told him the whole thing and how I thought it had made me worse. "Maybe, maybe," he said. "But sometimes healing hurts, had you thought of that?"

"They won't tell me anything," I said. "Dr. Abdul wanted to talk to Daniel, he wouldn't say anything to me. I could be dying and they wouldn't tell me anything."

"Daniel would tell you, I think," Sam said, but he didn't sound sure.

"If they'd let him," I said.

Sam didn't say anything for a moment. "Maybe I'll come down and see you," he said. "I have an idea. Let me talk to Daniel."

I had to call Daniel then, and explain, and he sent me off to bed and talked to Sam for a while. Then he came up and told me Sam was coming to see me tomorrow, on the train, and he'd pick him up in Shrewsbury.

It seems odd to think of Sam going anywhere, and odder to think of him here, but he's coming tomorrow! Daniel says he's getting to be a very old man and seldom goes anywhere, so I should think it a privilege, which I do.

Monday 21st January 1980

Sam brought me a tiny bunch of snowdrops from his landlady's back garden. "They're just starting," he said. Despite the long journey by train and then car—Daniel met him in Shrewsbury—they were in very good shape and had that special scent. Mor used to love snowdrops. They were her favourite flower. We planted some on her grave, I wonder if they're out yet? One of the aunts put mine into a tiny crystal vase that matches the decanter and I have them on my bed-side table.

Sam also brought some more Plato—*The Laws* and *Phaedrus*, which I've been wanting because it's the one they read in *The Charioteer*. They're not new, he's clearly had them a while, but he must have spent ages rooting around to find them. He also brought a little blue Pelican paperback book called *The Greeks* by H. D. F. Kitto, which he says will give me context. It'll give me context for Mary Renault as well as Plato. I hope it's interestingly written. I still haven't started the Churchill history I got for a prize.

The other thing he brought was a pot of comfrey ointment, which smells very weird. "I don't know if it'll help, but I brought it anyway," he said. I rubbed some on my leg and it didn't help at all, except for making it smell peculiar, but I appreciated the thought.

Sam's real thought though was that I should have acupuncture. There's a kind of magic about Sam, not real magic, but he's very solidly himself. It would be hard for any magic to find somewhere to start doing anything to him. It was interesting to see him with the aunts; he's impeccably polite to them but he treats them as if they're not important, and they don't know how to deal with that. He has no cracks for them to get into. If they'd suggested acupuncture, which involves sticking needles into people, I'd have resisted as hard as I could. As it was, they were very opposed to the idea.

"It's silly Chinese superstition, you can't possibly believe in it," one said.

"Morwenna's terrified of needles, she wouldn't even have her ears pierced," another put in.

"What good could it possibly do?" the third finished.

Even this kind of thing doesn't bother Sam. "I think we should try it. What harm could it do? Morwenna's a sensible girl, I think."

He had found a place in Shrewsbury, and written the address down. He wanted to go there right away, but the sisters managed to persuade Daniel that we should phone for an appointment. He made an appointment for tomorrow morning.

Sam spent the afternoon in my room, talking to me. He's an old man and he's had a strange life—imagine finding out your whole family had been killed. It would be as if Wales sank under the sea this minute and only I was left out of everyone. Well, Cousin Arwel's in Nottingham, but just the two of us out of everyone I grew up with. It was just like that for Sam. When he went back after the war they were all gone and strangers were living in his house, and the neighbours pretended not to know him. He saw his mother's bread-bin on the neighbour's table, but she wouldn't even let him have that.

"And they mean nothing to you," he said.

"Not nothing."

"They're strangers. Even I am a stranger. But my family were your cousins. They're talking, different governments have been talking for years about giving some compensation. But how can anyone compensate me for my family? How can they give you back your cousins that you never knew, and your cousins who were never born, the ones who would be your age now?"

That made me feel it. I could write a poem about that. "Hitler, give me back my cousins!"

I think Sam's a bit sad that I'm not Jewish, that his descendants won't be. But he didn't say so, and he isn't reproachful about it at all. He said he didn't stay in Poland because he could feel the dead everywhere, as if they could come around any corner. I understand that. I almost talked to him about magic, then, about the thing I did to have a karass, about Mor wandering around with the fairies. I might have if there had been time. But Daniel came in and said they should be going to catch the train, so I said goodbye.

Sam kissed me, and he put his hand on my head and said a blessing in Hebrew. He didn't ask, but I didn't mind. At the end of it he looked at me and smiled his wrinkled old smile and said, "You'll be all right." It was remarkably reassuring. I can hear it now. "You'll be all right." As if he could know.

I can smell the snowdrops. I'm so glad he came.

Tuesday 22nd January 1980

Sam was right about the acupuncture.

It is, in fact, magic. The whole thing is. They call it "chi," but they don't even pretend it isn't magic. The man who does it is English, which surprised me after all the fear of wily orientals the aunts tried to put into the procedure. He was trained in Bury St. Edmunds, which is in the Fens, near Cambridge, by people who had been trained in Hong Kong. He had framed certificates, like a doctor. On the ceiling was a map of the acupuncture points of the human body. I got to look at it a lot, because most of the time I was lying on the table with huge enormous needles stuck in me, not moving.

It doesn't hurt at all. You can't feel them, even though they're really long and they're really stuck in you. What did happen was that when the last one went in, the pain stopped, like turning off a switch. If I could learn to do that! One of them, in my ankle, he put in slightly the wrong place first, and I did feel it, not real pain, but like a pinprick. I didn't say anything, but he immediately moved it to a spot a fraction of a centimeter to the side and I couldn't feel it. It's body-magic plain enough.

Even if it just turned the pain off for the hour I was there, it would have been worth the thirty pounds, to me anyway. But it wasn't. I'm not miraculously cured or anything, but I hobbled up the stairs to his room and I walked down them, no worse than before they put me on the rack. He wants me to go every week for six weeks. He said that today he was just doing what he could for the pain, but if he saw me regularly he might be able to see what was wrong and do something about it. He admired my stick—I've been using the fairy one, as it seems to give me more strength than the metal one, as well as being less ugly.

"Take me back to school," I said to Daniel as we walked back to the car. A pale wintry sun was shining and the rose-gold buildings of Shrewsbury were flushed with it. If we'd set out right away, I could have been in school in time to go off to book club as normal after prep.

"Not until we see how you are tomorrow," he said. "But how about a Chinese meal, as Chinese medicine seems to agree with you?"

So we went to a restaurant called the Red Lotus and ate spare ribs and prawn toast and chicken fried rice and chow mein and beef in oyster sauce. It was all delicious, the best food I've had for years, maybe ever. I ate until I was full to bursting. While we were eating I told Daniel about the convention in Glasgow, Albacon, this year's Eastercon, and about what Wim had said about the Worldcon in Brighton and how he'd met Robert Silverberg and done nothing but talk about books for five days. He said he didn't think his sisters would let him get away at Easter, but he agreed that I could go, and said he'd pay!

In a way, I would like to rescue Daniel from his sisters. He has been good to me, and I suppose it might be his duty as a father, but why should he feel any of that? I would like to rescue him, but I don't think I can, and I think that trying would provoke war with them, whereas if they think I won't interfere they might leave me alone. Trying to rescue Daniel I might entangle myself. I am my own priority here, I have to be. They're not going to agree to him going to Glasgow. It's good that they agreed to acupuncture and a meal in a Chinese restaurant, and they probably wouldn't have if it hadn't been for dear old Sam.

With the bill, they brought us fortune cookies. Mine said "All is not yet lost," which I thought very cheerful. It's just like the line in the *Aeneid, Et haec olim meminisse iuvabit*, "even these things it will one day be a joy to recall." At first, you think how awful, and then you realise that it's true, and not a bad thing. Daniel's just said "You like Chinese food," which is undeniable. Getting one that said "You are an awful father" would have been unkind.

In the car, when I was putting my seat belt on, Daniel looked at me seriously. "You still seem to be feeling the benefit of the acupuncture."

"I am," I said.

"You should come once a week for six weeks, the way he said."

"Okay." I finished fiddling with my seat belt. Daniel threw his cigarette end out of the window.

"I won't be able to come to school and collect you and drive you here and back, not every week. Maybe sometimes."

I could immediately see that they wouldn't let him. He put the car in gear and pulled out of the car park, and all the time I didn't say anything, because what could I say.

"There's a train," he said after a while.

"A train?" I'm sure I sounded sceptical. "There isn't a railway station. There might be a bus."

"There's a railway station in Gobowen. When my sisters went to Arlinghurst they went to it, and were collected there by the school. Everyone used trains then."

"Are you sure it's still there?" But it wasn't in the long list of Flanders and Swann "Slow Train" stations that had been closed by Beeching, so it probably was.

"It's on the route to North Wales, to Welshpool and Barmouth and Dolgellau," he said. The only one of those places I'd heard of was Dolgellau, where Gramma and Grampar had been to visit an old vicar who'd moved there, before I was born. North Wales is like another country. You can't even get there from South Wales, you have to go to England and out again, at least if you want to go on trains, or on good roads. I suppose there are roads through the mountains. I've never been there, though I would like to.

"All right," I said. "That means a bus into town and a bus out to Gobowen, and then a train."

"I'll be able to take you sometimes," he said, lighting yet another cigarette. "What would be the best day?"

I thought about it. Definitely not Tuesdays, because I might not get back in time for the book club. "Thursdays," I said. "Because Thursday afternoons I just have religious education and then double maths."

"It seems from your marks that maths is the thing you least ought to miss," Daniel said, but with a smile in his voice.

"Honestly, it doesn't matter if I'm there or not, it just doesn't go in. The maths I do know I know from phys and chem. Maths class might as well be taught in Chinese. It makes no sense to me. I think that bit of my brain is missing. And if I ask her to explain again, it doesn't make any more sense."

"Perhaps you ought to have extra tutoring in it," Daniel suggested.

"It would be money down the drain. I just can't do it. It would be like teaching a horse to sing."

"Do you know the story about that?" he asked, turning his head, and incidentally blowing smoke at me, yuck.

"Don't kill me, give me a year, and I'll teach your horse to sing. Anything might happen in a year, the king might die, I might die, or the horse might learn to sing." I summarised. It's in *The Mote in God's Eye*, which is probably why it was in his mind.

"It's a story about procrastination," Daniel said, as if he was the world's expert in procrastination.

"It's a story about hope," I said. "We don't know what happened at the end of the year."

"If the horse had learned to sing, we'd know."

"It might have become the origin of the Centaur legend. It might have gone to Narnia, taking the man with it. It might have become the ancestor of Caligula's horse Incitatus who he made a senator. There might have been a whole tribe of singing horses and Incitatus was their bid for equality, only it all went wrong."

Daniel gave me a very strange look, and I wished I'd saved this for people who would appreciate it.

"Thursdays, then," he said. "I'll call and arrange it when we get home."

If it was a story about procrastination, it would have a solid moral about the man dying at the end of the year. I like to imagine their survival.

> And at year's end they broke the stable door.
> The man and horse, together, gallop yet
> Beyond the sunset's end, the pounding hooves,
> Both harmony and beat for their duet.

Wednesday 23rd January 1980

A tiny sprinkle of snow this morning, not enough to wet a Hobbit's toes, and melted before breakfast.

I am back in school, which is noisier than ever, so noisy it echoes.

The Dream Master turns out to be a novel version of "He Who Shapes," which is a variation on, or the other way around, Brunner's *Telepathist*. I don't know which was written first, but I read the Brunner first. The very idea of working with dreams is odd. *The Dream Master* is a good book, but a very unsettling one. You wouldn't guess it was written by the same person who wrote the Amber books, which are such fun.

People seem a lot friendlier to me than before. Sharon said hello and welcome back when I went into English after lunch. Daniel insisted on seeing how I was after I woke up, and didn't drive me back until mid-morning. I'm still the same. The cold made my leg do its rusty weathercock thing, but that's so much better than it was before the acupuncture that I almost don't care.

I haven't forgiven Sharon for turning her back on me. I'll be polite and nice, but I won't go out of my way not to call her Shagger when everyone else does. Deirdre, however, who stuck by me, gets my ever-lasting loyalty, and the word "Dreary" will never pass my lips. Oddly, though I am limping worse than ever, everyone seems to be calling me Commie today. Maybe going into hospital had given them a new respect for me. Nobody has come around gushing though, thank goodness.

It's really nice to see Miss Carroll again. She doesn't bother me when I'm reading, or writing in here, but she always has a few kind words when I pass her desk. I'd got almost used to this library, all the wood, and the lovely bookshelves, but seeing it now I am struck again with how brill it is. I'd like to have a room like this in my own house, when I have a house one day, when I'm grown up.

Isle of the Dead is very odd. I love the idea of making worlds, and the alien gods, and the aliens, and the whole setup. I'm just not sure about the actual story.

Thursday 24th January 1980

Tonight we are going to see *The Tempest* in Theatre Clwyd in Mold. Nobody else seems the faintest bit excited about this, so I act as if I don't care either. Deirdre says she hates Shakespeare. She has seen *The Winter's Tale* and *Richard II*, when they were set plays, and she hated both of them. This makes me think the company might be aw-ful, because *Richard II* at least should be terrific acted. "Sit upon the ground and tell sad stories of the death of kings."

The new friendliness seems to be lasting. Did they think I was faking it with the leg before? Or has something else happened? I deal with it in an offhand way, as if it's normal, but always cool to them, because if I give away anything they could throw it in my face.

I am reading *The Lord of the Rings*. I suddenly wanted to. I almost know it by heart, but I can still sink right into it. I know no other book that is so much like going on a journey. When I put it down to write this, I feel as if I am also waiting with Pippin for the echoes of that stone down the well.

Friday 25th January 1980

The first thing that was wrong with the Touring Shakespeare Company's production of *The Tempest* was that they cast a woman as Prospero. She was very good, but the play just doesn't work with a mother. The whole thing is set up with male in opposition to female: Prospero and Sycorax, Caliban and Ariel, Caliban and Miranda, Ferdinand and Miranda. Though I suppose doing it that way made Prospero and Antonio a male/female thing. I suppose the way it really didn't work was in Prospero and Miranda's relationship. It didn't work as mother and daughter to me, at least, not and keep Prospero sympathetic. I read him as a man who is remote, and good to bother with a toddler, but a woman like that would be too unnatural for sympathy. Which isn't to say I think women should be stuck with childrearing, but—how interesting that what comes out as doing the best he could in a man looks like neglect in a woman.

Though Prospero was in fact neglectful however you look at it. He must have been the world's most crap Duke of Milan, and he would be again. I can certainly sympathise with spending your whole time in the library reading your book instead of bothering with what you're supposed to be doing. But there's absolutely no indication that he won't do the exact same thing once they get back. In fact, he'll be worse, because he'll want to catch up on everything his favourite authors have written while he was stuck on the island. Antonio was probably a much better Duke. Sure, he was a conniving bastard, but he'd keep everyone happy because it would be to his own advantage. The people were probably horrified to see Prospero back, drowned books or not.

Very little of this will be going into my formal response essay on seeing the play. But what's really not going in is what I thought about the fairies, which is that they were brilliant, and surprisingly lifelike.

Ariel did not speak, she sang all her lines. She was wearing something white, maybe a bodystocking, with veils all around that drifted about when she moved or gestured. She had a shaved head, also with a veil. When she went free at the end, all the veils fell away and we saw her face for the first time, and her expression was most convincingly like a fairy. I wonder if the actress knows any? Singing was a good way of getting across how oddly they communicate, well done Shakespeare, well done Touring Company. Shakespeare must have known fairies, probably quite well. He just did what I do and translated the things they say into the things they would have said.

Caliban, well, what is Caliban? I read it thinking he was a fairy, fishy and warty and odd. But seeing it made me think. His mother, Sycorax, was a witch. We don't know about his father. We don't see Sycorax at all. Was Prospero his father? Is he Miranda's half-brother? Or was he there when they got there, as he says, offering welcome, to be made into a servant? He wants to rape Miranda ("I had peopled else this isle with Calibans"), but that doesn't make him human, or his mother either, necessarily. He could be human, or half human, he's pokable and hittable in a way fairies aren't. There was a lot of hitting and cringing last night. What I believed about that particular Caliban, about (I have the programme) Peter Lewis's Caliban, was that he was between worlds. He didn't know where he belonged.

Shakespeare must have known some fairies. I know I said this about Tolkien, and actually I do still think Tolkien did as well. I think lots of people do.

What I love about Shakespeare is the language. I came home on the coach quite drunk on it, and had to ask Deirdre to repeat everything she was saying because I hadn't caught it the first time. I don't know what she thought. We had a conversation about what Miranda and Ferdinand's married life would be like, and how she would cope with Italy after an island. Would it keep on seeming a brave new world?

Deirdre thought it would as long as she was in love. Can you imagine though, confronting a whole world when you have only known three people, two of them not quite people and one of them remote Prospero? Imagine coping with fashion and servants and courtiers! Deirdre thought Prospero very cruel not to teach her. But maybe teaching her magic would have been more cruel.

Prospero breaks his staff and drowns his books because you can't bring magic back home with you. If he had brought it back, would he have become like Saruman? Is it power that corrupts? Is it always? It would be nice if I knew some people who weren't evil and used magic. Well, there's Glorfindel, but I'm not sure fairies count. Fairies are different. The other interesting contrast with Prospero is Faust.

Letter from Daniel saying the acupuncture is arranged for Thursdays and paid for, saying he'd written to the school asking for me to be allowed to go, and enclosing ten pounds for trainfare and lunches. When I get change, I'll put half of it into my running away/emergency fund.

Saturday 26th January 1980

I made it to the library, but Greg wasn't there. It isn't his Saturday to work. I took my huge pile of books back and collected what was waiting for me. I was wishing I'd arranged to meet someone, but of course I hadn't because I wasn't here on Tuesday. I was hoping I'd be able to see Greg and ask him the subject of this Tuesday's meeting.

I wandered down to the bookshop, where there was no sign of anyone. I didn't buy any books. It was drizzling in a very discouraging way. I sat in the cafe and ate a honey bun and read, looking up now and then to watch the rain. They always say it's lovely weather for ducks, but the mallards on the pond looked as miserable as anyone. The drakes are starting to get their spring colours though. Maybe it's spring rain. They'd have been glad of it in the Dead Marches, I thought.

I bought a couple of buns for me and Deirdre—there's really no point wasting money on Sharon, even though she is speaking to me again.

The junk shop was open, and I looked through their books. I didn't see anything appealing except a folding cloth (canvas I think) map of Europe, with Germany huge and no Czechoslovakia. I think it must be from the war, or right before. Somebody had drawn a pink line on it in felt pen, but otherwise it's in really good condition. The country colours are sort of pastels, not hard colours like they would be now. I couldn't resist it, as it was only 5p. I don't know what I'm going to do with it. But maps are brill.

I walked slowly back up into town, looked through Smiths, which is usually a total waste of time, but today I was rewarded with a copy of *Isaac Asimov's Science Fiction Magazine*! I wonder where that came from. I do hope they'll start getting it regularly. I bought it, and also a packet of Rollos, which I would happily share with Frodo and Sam if I could, but I can't. I also bought a card for Grampar, one with the sea and a sandcastle that reminds me of summer holidays, and will remind him too.

Gill was at the bus stop. "No boyfriend today?" she asked.

I looked her straight in the eye. "Not that it's any concern of yours, but Hugh's just a friend, not a boy friend. He goes to the book club."

"Oh. Sorry," she said. I was amazed that she believed me. It's a good thing it wasn't Wim she'd seen me with, or I wouldn't have been able to say that with such conviction, even though it would have been equally true.

Sunday 27th January 1980

The way to be popular in this school is to go into hospital and come out again. Or maybe it's to have someone say you're brave—I know Deirdre's been saying that. Maybe they didn't actually believe there was anything wrong with my leg before? Or maybe they feel sorry for me? I hope not. I'd hate that. But anyway, seven buns today, counting my honey bun. Two iced buns, two Chelsea buns, an iced cupcake and an eclair. I couldn't eat them all, and gave one of the Chelsea buns to Deirdre. I hadn't done anything to make this happen, not just no magic but nothing at all. It's very peculiar. I asked Miss Carroll about it and she said it was probably just that I'd been in hospital and come out and hadn't made a fuss, and I'd been mentioned in Prayers and now was there and was in people's minds when they went bun-buying. Maybe. It seems very odd to me.

I wrote a cheerful letter to Sam telling him what a terrific idea the acupuncture was. I haven't even started the books he gave me, so I didn't mention them. I also wrote to Daniel, mostly about seeing *The Tempest*, and to Auntie Teg, telling her about the acupuncture and the play. I sent the card to Grampar.

I'm up as far as the Battle of the Pelennor Fields, which may be the greatest thing ever written.

Monday 28th January 1980

Aujourd'hui, rien.

That's what Louis XVI wrote in his diary on the day of the storming of the Bastille.

I helped Miss Carroll stamping and shelving some new books. They all looked awful, being of the category of books about teenagers with problems—drugs, or abusive parents, or boyfriends who push for sex, or living in Ireland. I hate books like that. For one thing they're all so relentlessly downbeat, and despite that you just know everyone will overcome all their problems in the end and start to Grow Up and Understand How the World Works. You can practically see the capitals. I've read half a ton of Victorian children's books, because we had them lying around at home, *Elsie Dinsmore* and *Little Women* and *Eric, or Little by Little* and *What Katy Did.*

They're by different authors, but they all share the same kind of moralising. In the exact same way these Teen Problem books share the same kind of moralising, only it's neither so quaint nor so clearly stated as the Victorian ones. If I have to have a book on how to overcome adversity give me *Pollyanna* over Judy Blume any day, though why anyone would read any of them when the world contains all this SF is beyond me. Even just within books written for children, you can learn way more about growing up and ethical behaviour from *Space Hostages* or *Citizen of the Galaxy*.

I've written my *Tempest* response, and most of Deirdre's, for her to copy out in prep. To make them different, I've made hers mostly about Miranda, and mine mostly about Prospero. She's doing my maths in return. I just can't cope with all these simultaneous equations, especially as I've missed some explanation.

Finished LOTR, with the usual sad pang of reaching the end and there being no more of it.

Tuesday 29th January 1980

Book club tonight, but I don't know the subject.

Wednesday 30th January 1980

The subject was Tiptree! I'm so glad I knew she was a woman in advance, because it would have been an awful shock to have discovered it when everyone started saying "she." I haven't read all of Tiptree, only the two collections, and I can see I'll have to rectify this. Having said that, there was no problem having enough to talk about, because we talked for ages about "The Girl Who Was Plugged In," such a brilliant story, and "Love Is the Plan, the Plan Is Death," both of which I know really well. Harriet led it, which was nice, except that I remembered she'd also led the one on Le Guin, which made me wonder if there was something going on there. I mean, why have both of her sessions been on women writers, when none of the sessions done by the men have been?

Keith really doesn't like Tiptree, he thinks she's anti-men, and did even when he thought she was a man. He thinks "Houston, Houston" is a horror story. I don't think that, though I can understand men feeling threatened by it.

It was Pete's birthday, so we all went to the pub afterwards for a little bit. Brian asked a funny question he said he'd heard at work. "Which would you rather meet, an elf or a Plutonian?" I had to think about it for a moment, because the question is really about the past and the future, or about fantasy and science fiction. I've met plenty of elves, though they're not exactly elves. Not like Tolkien's elves. I said a Plutonian, and so did everyone eventually, except Wim, who said elf and stuck to it.

Next week Wim's doing Zelazny. I gave him back the two books he'd lent me, and he gave me *Doorways in the Sand* and *Roadmarks*.

He asked me if I could meet him on Saturday. I said I would, and I said maybe he could meet an elf. He looks as if he wants to believe, but isn't quite sure about it. "Where?" he said.

"We can go looking in the Poacher's Wood, so why not meet in the little cafe across from there?" I said.

"Those woods belong to Harriet," he said. "Hey, Harriet, is it all right if Mori and I go walking in your woods on Saturday?"

Harriet turned around from her conversation with Hussein and Janine about whether Tiptree was misogynistic and raised her eyebrows. "Certainly you may, William, though you may find them a little muddy at this time of year. It's too early for violets or primroses, I should think."

I hadn't known Wim's name was William, but I suppose it makes sense. I wonder why he isn't Will or Billy?

Meanwhile, Janine was giving me a look like the one Gill had given me when she saw me with Hugh. I wonder why Wim did that, making it open to everyone like that? Because we could have done it quietly without anyone else knowing. And if we're doing it so he can see a fairy, or see magic, which is what he thinks, then why would he want them to know? They won't believe it, even if he tells them. People just think you're mad, or lying. He might think I am if he can't see them. If there even are any. I'm not, no matter what he says, going to do magic just for the sake of it. Anyway, magic is always deniable, if you want to deny it, and he might well. Or did he want them to know I was going somewhere with him? Why? So if they disapprove of him, they'd disapprove of me too? Certainly that's what Janine did.

It's so complicated. I want lots of friends, not just one.

On the way back in the car, Greg warned me about Wim. He wasn't as specific as Janine and Hugh had been. He just said that Wim had had a girlfriend who thought she'd got into trouble, and I should be careful how I went.

"It's not like that," I explained. "He's got a girlfriend. He wouldn't be interested in me. I mean I have a bad leg and I'm kind of funny-looking and I'm getting fat because I never get any exercise and I eat all the time, while Wim's, well, Wim could have anybody."

"You've got a lovely smile," Greg said, which is what people always say. It's like an automatic programmed response, if ever I say I'm not pretty, which I entirely understand that I'm not.

"He's so much older anyway."

"Eighteen months, not sixty years," Greg said. "And I'm not blind. I'd say he is interested in you, and you in him. I've seen you looking at each other."

I couldn't say Wim was looking at me like that because he thought I could read minds like in *Dying Inside* (where did he get that idea from?) or that he wanted to go into the woods with me so he could see a fairy. "I'll be careful," I said.

It must be horrible for Wim if everyone he knows, knows, and everyone new he meets gets warned off him like that. That's what Hugh said. Hugh wasn't there last night, I don't know where he is. I haven't seen him for ages.

Thursday 31st January 1980

It was great walking away from school at lunchtime to get the bus. It felt like escaping. My leg didn't even feel particularly bad, which made it all the better, it was like putting one over on everyone. Two buses and a train, and I was in Shrewsbury, easy as that. The train's a little rattly local, not all that different from a bus. Most of the people who were on it had come from North Wales and had North Welsh voices and said "yes/no" at the end of all their questions just like people in South Wales making fun of them. "Shall I get us a cup of tea from the buffet, yes/no?" "Is this Shrewsbury we're coming to now, yes/no?" Delete where inapplicable. I didn't laugh, but it was a near thing. It's hard when someone is just exactly like a parody.

The acupuncture went well. It turned the pain off entirely while I was on the table. That's marvellous, it's just so nice not to have any pain at all, not grinding away in the background even, just no pain. I lived like that for years, but it's hard to remember. Pain oozes. Like my dream with the ballerina with the walking stick.

Afterwards I went to a cafe and had baked potato with egg salad and a tuna mayonnaise sandwich, and a double decker. I sat in a little booth with sides and read my book (Charisma, which is brilliant but weird), and felt safely alone and anonymous. It's not as if I'm me, it's just that I'm "person in crowd" or "schoolgirl reading book in cafe." They got me from central casting, and when I go there'll be another one. Nobody will notice me. I'm an insignificant part of the landscape. There's nothing that feels safer.

Then I walked back to the station, and on the way I passed that Owen Owens where I went shopping with the aunts. It's a department store, not just clothes, and I remembered noticing that there was a pen and paper department. I popped in to see if they had nibs for my pen. The problem with writing backwards with a fountain pen is that it destroys the nib—left-handed people have this problem too, going through nibs fast. Because I write in here a lot, and pretty much always backwards, I go through nibs. So I came in to look, and they did, so I bought one, which was good, but what was even better was I saw through that department to a book department.

Now I did know that some department stores have book departments. Harrods has one. My copy of LOTR in three beautiful volumes with the Appendices came from there, when Auntie Teg went to London. But Howells and David Morgans in Cardiff don't—probably because they can't compete with Lears—and I hadn't thought there might be one in Owen Owens. Well, joy and rapture, there it was. And, best of all, to my total astonishment, a new Heinlein: *The Number of the Beast*, NEL paperback January 1980, how new is that! I bought it right away, not even needing to go into my put-away money to get it.

I almost started it on the train, but I was very good and not only finished *Charisma* but started *Doorways in the Sand*. Having a whole fat new Heinlein I haven't read a word of is such a lovely feeling. Like a reward. I feel all bouncy and happy when I think of it sitting there waiting for me.

Friday 1st February 1980

Rabbits.

Had a severe warning from Miss Thackerly about cheating at maths. Deirdre and I had the same mistakes. She kept us behind after class and said she wasn't going to report us this time, and she wasn't going to ask who had copied whose work, but that if she ever caught us again we'd be looking at expulsion. I had no idea it was that serious. People copy each other's prep all the time. Deirdre has copied my Latin loads of times, and plenty of people copy Claudine's French. I suppose it's a case of not getting caught. I promised Miss Thackerly we wouldn't do it again—Deirdre was in tears and could hardly speak. Getting expelled would be awkward for me, but it would be the end of the world for her.

Letter from Daniel, with another fiver. I'll tell him about finding *Number of the Beast* when I write. It starts well.

Saturday 2nd February 1980

I was almost sorry I had such a big pile of library books, though of course they were all things I wanted and had ordered. Greg was there and stamped them out for me.

"There's a new Heinlein," I told him.

"*The Number of the Beast*," he agreed. "It's on the top of my list of things to order for the shelves as soon as April comes."

"It's wrong for libraries to have limited budgets," I said.

He snorted, and took the books from the lady behind me. I'm not wrong though. They could take the money from building enough nukes to kill all the Russians in the world and give it to libraries. What good does an independent nuclear deterrent do Britain, compared to the good of libraries? Somebody has their priorities wrong. I'm not really a commie, no matter what they call me, but I do think it might be instructive to look at library budgets in the Soviet Union.

The sun was shining in a watery way as I walked down the hill. I thought I was early to meet Wim but he was already there, sitting in the table at the window eating a toasted teacake and drinking coffee. He always looks so relaxed and at home wherever he is, I don't know how he does it. He was wearing a blue turtleneck just one shade darker than his eyes. I was conscious that I was, of course, as always, wearing school uniform. He looked like a student, like an adult, the way I would so much like to be, and there I was in a stupid gym-slip and a stupid hat, looking about twelve. I ordered and paid for tea and a honey bun, like always. I admit I did think of ordering something more sophisticated but I resisted the temptation.

"I'm surprised you came," he said, as I sat down next to him. His lips were greasy with the butter from the teacake. I'd have liked to have wiped it away. While I'm cataloguing what I'd have liked to do, I'd also have liked to feel his pullover to see if it was as soft as it looked. I don't often have to suppress this kind of urge.

"I said I'd come," I said.

"I thought Greg would have told you about me."

"So that's why you did it. I couldn't work that out." It came out before I thought about whether saying it was a good idea or not.

"You already knew?" he asked. "About Ruthie and all that?"

"Janine told me, ages ago, and also Hugh told me, rather more sympathetically." The waitress put down my tea and bun.

"Hugh's all right," he said, wiping his lips on his napkin. "Janine hates me."

"Greg did tell me as well, in very general terms."

"It's the trouble with a place like this. Everybody knows everybody's business, or thinks they do. I can't wait until I can shake the dust of it off my feet. I won't ever look back." He stared out of the window, stirring his coffee without looking at it.

"When will that be?" I asked.

"Not until after I take my A Levels. A year next June. Then I'll get a grant and be off to university."

"What A Levels are you doing?" I asked. I wanted to eat my honey bun, but on the other hand, I didn't want to have my mouth full. I took a smallish bite.

"Physics and chemistry and history," he said. "You wouldn't believe the flap there was. It's ridiculous only studying three subjects and trying to segregate arts and sciences."

"I made them rearrange the entire timetable so I could do chemistry

and French," I said. "At O Level, that is. I'm taking my O Levels next
year. Every time we have a French class in what is technically the
lunch hour, the teacher blames me, apologises to the others for the
fact that I'm inconveniencing everybody."

Wim nodded. "That must have been an impressive fight."

"I couldn't get them to do it for biology too. And Daniel, my father,
backed me up. And I suppose he *is* paying for it."

"My parents don't give a damn."

"I wish we had the education system they have in *Doorways in
the Sand*," I said. "Here it is, by the way." I got it out from under all
the library books and handed it over. He held it for a moment before putting it in his coat pocket. It looked very purple against his
blue jumper. "Did you know, there's a new Heinlein? *The Number
of the Beast*. And he's borrowed the idea of that education system,
where you study all those different things and sign up and graduate
when you have enough credits in everything, and you can keep taking courses forever if you want, but he doesn't acknowledge Zelazny
anywhere."

Wim laughed. "That's what they really do in America," he said.

"Really?" My mouth was full, but I didn't care. I felt embarrassed
that I'd been so stupid, but also thrilled it was true. "They do? They
really do? I want to go to university there!"

"You can't afford it. Well, maybe *you* can, but I never could. It costs
thousands every term, every *semester*. You have to be rich. That's the
downside. You can get scholarships if you're brilliant, but otherwise
it's all loans. Who'd give me a loan?"

"Anyone," I said. "Or if it's real, maybe they have universities here
that do it where you could go for free."

"I don't think so."

"Imagine studying a little bit of everything you wanted to," I said.

We just sat there for a moment, imagining it. "How come you're
reading Heinlein?" Wim asked. "I wouldn't have thought you'd like
him. He's such a fascist."

I sputtered. "A fascist? Heinlein? What are you talking about?"

"His books are so authoritarian. Oh, his kids' books are all right, but look at *Starship Troopers.*"

"Well, look at *The Moon Is a Harsh Mistress,*" I countered. "That's about a revolution against authority. Look at *Citizen of the Galaxy.* He's not a fascist! He's in favour of human dignity and taking care of yourself, and old-fashioned things like loyalty and duty, that's not being a fascist!"

Wim help up a hand. "Hold it," he said. "I didn't mean to stir up a hornet's nest. I just wouldn't have thought you'd be the type to like him, with liking Delany and Zelazny and Le Guin."

"I like them all," I said, disappointed in him. "It isn't exclusive, so far as I know."

"You're really weird," he said, putting down his coffee spoon and looking intently at me. "You care more about Heinlein than about the Ruthie thing."

"Well of course I do," I said, and then felt awful. "What I mean is, whatever it was with Ruthie, nobody says you did anything to deliberately hurt her. You were both stupid, and she was even stupider, from the best I can tell. That matters in one way, but good grief, Wim, surely in a universal sense Robert A. Heinlein matters a lot more however you look at it."

"I suppose so," he said. He laughed. I could see the woman behind the counter looking at us in a curious way. "I hadn't thought about it exactly like that."

I laughed too. The woman behind the counter and what she thought didn't matter at all. "From the distance of Alpha Centauri, from the perspective of posterity?"

"It could have been posterity," he said, more soberly. "If Ruthie had been pregnant."

"Did you really dump her because you thought she was?" I asked. I put the last bite of my bun into my mouth.

"No! I dumped her because she told everyone before she told me, so it was all over everywhere and I heard it second hand. She walked into Boots and bought a pregnancy testing kit. She told her mother. She told her friends. She might as well have bought a megaphone and stood in the market square. And then she wasn't even pregnant after all. I dumped her because of what you said, because she was stupid. *Stupid*. What a moron." He shook his head. "And then the shunning started. I might have been poison. They seemed to think that because I'd slept with her I ought to marry her and tie myself to her forever even though there wasn't even a baby."

"Why didn't you tell people that?"

"Tell who? The whole town? Janine? I don't think so. They won't listen to me anyway. They think they know something about me. They don't." His face was hard.

"But you have a girlfriend now," I said, encouragingly.

He rolled his eyes. "Shirley? Actually I've dumped her too. She's another moron, not quite as bad as Ruthie, but close. She's working in the laundry at the school, and she's quite happy to keep on doing that until she gets married. She was making getting married noises at me, so I broke up with her."

"You certainly get through them," I said, because I didn't know what to say.

"It would be different with someone who wasn't a moron," he said, and he was looking at me carefully, and I thought maybe he meant he was interested, but he couldn't be, not Wim, not in me, and I was feeling breathless enough without that.

"Let's go and see if I can find you an elf," I said.

He frowned. "Look, it's all right," he said. "I know you were just saying that because—well, I'd asked you a very strange question, and you were in a lot of pain on that thing and . . ."

"No, it is real," I said. "I don't know if you're going to be able to see them, because you have to believe first, but I think you nearly do. You don't have pierced ears or anything that would stop you. Just promise you won't get all sarcastic and hate me if you can't see them."

"I don't know what to think," he said, standing up. "Look, Mori, you kind of like me, right?"

"Right," I said, cautiously, staying where I was. He was way up above me, but I didn't want to be struggling to my feet.

"I kind of like you too," he said.

For an instant, I felt wonderfully happy, and then I remembered about the karass magic. I'd cheated. I'd made it happen. He didn't really like me, well, maybe he did, but he liked me because the magic had made him like me. That didn't mean he didn't really think he liked me now, of course, but it made it much more complicated.

"Come on," I said, and struggled to my feet, putting my coat on. Wim put on a scruffy brown duffle coat and went out. I followed him out onto the pavement.

There was an Indian woman with a baby in a pushchair just coming out of the bookshop as we came out. She was wearing a headscarf, which made me think of Nasreen and wonder how she was getting on. We waited for her to pass us and then crossed the road to the pond, where the mallards were chasing each other.

"You don't want to talk about it?" Wim asked.

"I don't know what to say," I said. I didn't want to tell him about the karass magic, and I couldn't think what was ethical, if I'd sort of accidentally bewitched him. It was a little bit exhilarating and a little bit terrifying, and it felt as if gravity wasn't quite as strong as normally, or as if someone had decreased the oxygen or something.

"I've never seen you at a loss for words," he said.

"Very few people have," I said.

He laughed, and followed me into the trees. "This magic thing, you're not making it up?"

"Why would I?" I didn't get it. "It's just that I really have sworn an oath not to do magic except to prevent harm, because it's so difficult to understand the consequences. Anyway, magic is difficult to show, because it's so deniable. You can say it would have happened anyway. And with the, um, the elves"—I didn't want to say fairies, it sounded too babyish— "not everybody can see them, not all the time. You need to believe they're there first, before you can."

"Can't you give me a charm so I can see them? Or teach me their names? I'm not like stupid Thomas Covenant, you know."

"A charm is a good idea," I said. I handed him my pocket rock and he rubbed it thoughtfully in his fingers. "This should help." It wouldn't exactly help him see the fairies, as all there was on it was general protection and specific protection against my mother, but if he thought it would, it might. "I haven't read the Covenant books. I saw them, but it compared them to Tolkien on the cover so I didn't want to read them."

"It isn't the author's fault what the publishers put on the cover," he said. "Thomas Covenant is a leper who mopes his way around a fantasy world most of us would give our right arms to be in, refusing to believe anything is real."

"If it's from the point of view of a depressed leper who doesn't believe in it, I'm glad I haven't read them!"

He laughed. "There are some great giants. And it is a fantasy world, unless he's mad, which he thinks he is and you can't tell."

We were quite deep in among the trees now. It was muddy, as Harriet had said it would be. There were a few fairies in the trees. "I don't know if you'll be able to see, but hold tight to that rock and try looking there," I said, pointing with my chin.

Wim turned his head very slowly. The fairy vanished. "I thought I saw something for a second," he said, very quietly. "Did I scare it off?"

"The ones around here are very easily scared. They won't talk to me. In South Wales where I come from there are some I know quite well."

"What's the best place to find them? Do they live in the trees, like in Lorien?" His eyes were darting about all over, but not seeing the fairies that were peeping back.

"They like places that used to be human and have been abandoned," I said. "Ruins with green things growing in them. Is there anything like that?"

"Follow me," Wim said, and I followed him downhill through a lot of mud and old leaves. The sun was out, but it was still cold and damp and the wind was freezing.

There was a stone wall about shoulder high, with ivy growing over it, and as we followed it along we came to an angle of wall, as if there had been a house once, and inside the angle where it was sheltered, snowdrops were pushing through the leaf mould. There was also a big puddle, which we stepped around. There was a half-height wall there, which we sat on, side by side. There was also a fairy, the one I had seen before on Janine's lawn, like a dog with gossamer wings. I waited for a moment, quietly. Wim didn't say anything either. Some more fairies came up—it really was just the kind of place they like. One of them was slim and beautiful and feminine, another was gnarled and squat.

"Hold the stone, and look at the flowers, and at the reflection of the flowers in the water," I said to Wim, quietly, not that it made much difference how loudly I spoke. "Now look at me." When he looked at me I put my hands on the sides of his face. I was trying to give him confidence. He wanted so much to believe, to see one. His skin was warm and just slightly rough where he needed to shave. Touching him made me feel more breathless than ever.

"He wants to see you," I said to the fairies, in Welsh. "He won't do any harm."

They didn't reply, but they didn't vanish either.

"Now look to your left," I said to Wim, letting go.

He turned his head slowly, and he saw her, I could tell he did. He jumped. She regarded him curiously for a moment. I wondered for a second if she'd enchant him and lead him away into wherever it is they go when they vanish, like Tam Lin. He put out his hand towards her, and she vanished, they all did, like lights going out.

"That was an elf?" he asked.

"Yes," I said.

"If you hadn't said so, I'd have thought it was a ghost." He sounded shaken. I'd have liked to have touched him again.

"They're not all that human-looking," I said, which was an understatement. "Most of them are kind of gnarly."

"Gnomes?" he asked.

"Well, sort of. The thing is you read things, and you see things, and they're not the same. To read about it, it all makes so much more sense, with Seelie and Unseelie courts, with gnomes and elves, but it's not like that. I've been seeing them all my life, and they're all the same whatever they are and whatever they look like. I don't really know what they are. They talk, well, the ones I know do, but they say odd things, and only in Welsh. Usually. I met one who spoke English at Christmas. He gave me this stick." I tapped it in the mud. "They don't call themselves elves, or anything. They don't have names. They don't use nouns very much." It was such a relief to have someone to talk to about this! "I call them fairies because that's what I've always called them, but I don't really know what they are."

"So you don't know what they are, not really?"

"No. It's not the sort of thing. What I think is that people have told a lot of stories about them and some of them are true and some of them are made up from other stories and some of them are muddled. They don't tell stories themselves."

"But if you don't know, then they could be ghosts?"

"The dead are different," I said.

"You know? You've seen them?" His eyes were very wide.

So I told him about Halloween and the oak leaves and the dead going under the hill, which meant I had to tell him about Mor. I was getting cold by this time. "So how did she die?" he asked.

"I'm freezing," I said. "Can we go back to town and maybe get a hot drink?"

"I won't see any more elves or whatever today?"

I couldn't understand why he couldn't see them now. "Look carefully by the puddle," I said.

He turned his head slowly again and saw, I think, one of the gnarled gnome-like ugly fairies that isn't human at all except for the eyes. He blinked.

"Did you see it?" I asked.

"I think so," he said. "I saw its reflection. If it's there and you can see it, why can't I see it? I believe you, I really do. I saw the other one."

"I don't know," I said. "There's ever such a lot I don't know about them. I can't see them if they don't want me to."

The fairy was smiling in an unpleasant way, as if it could understand. "Let's go," I said. "I'm getting chilled through."

It was hard to stand up from the wall, and hard to walk for the first few steps. Sitting on walls is better for my leg than standing up, but not very good for it all the same. Wim offered to help, but there's nothing that helps, really. He put his hand on my arm, my other arm, my left arm. "Can I at least take your bag?" he asked.

"If you have a bag, you could take the books," I said. "But I have to keep the bag."

"Are you telling me your bag is magic?" he asked.

We both looked at my bag, bulging with library books. You couldn't find anything less magic looking if you tried. "It's sort of part of me," I said, feebly.

He didn't have a bag, but he took some of the library books anyway and carried them under his arm. "Now," he said, as we came out of the woods. "Some real coffee, not that Nescafe swill."

"What do you mean, real coffee?" I asked.

"In Marios, they have real filter coffee. They make it from coffee beans. You can smell them grinding it and roasting it."

"The smell of coffee is great. The taste, however, isn't," I said.

"You've never had real coffee," he said, confidently and correctly. "Wait and see."

Marios was one of the brightly lit neon cafes in the high street where the girls from school hang out with their local boyfriends. The tables were full of them. We went to sit at the back where there was a small table free. Wim ordered two filter coffees. There was a juke box playing "Oliver's Army," very loudly. It was horrible, but at least it was warm. He put my library books on the table, and I put them back into my bag.

"How did she die?" he asked again, when we were sitting down.

"This isn't the place," I said.

"The wood wasn't the place and this isn't the place?" Wim asked. He put his hand on my hand, where it was lying on top of the table. I gasped. "Tell me about it."

"It was a car accident. But really it was my mother," I said. "My mother was trying to do something, some huge magic, to get power, to take over the world I think. The fairies knew and they told us what to do to stop it. She tried to stop us, and one of the things she did was to try to use things that weren't real, things coming at us. We just had to keep on. I thought we'd both die, but it would have been worth it, to stop her. That's what the fairies said, and that's what we were prepared for, both of us. There were all those things that were magic, that were illusion. I thought it was like that, when I saw the lights, but it was a real car."

"Jesus, how awful for the driver," Wim said.

"I don't know what he saw, or what he thought," I said. "I wasn't in any state to ask."

"But you stopped her? Your mother?"

"We stopped her. But Mor was killed."

The waitress interrupted me by putting two red cups of black coffee down on the table. One of them was slopped into the saucer, onto the packets of sugar. Wim paid, before I could offer to.

"And then what happened?" he asked.

I couldn't, of course, tell him about those awful days after Mor was killed, the bruise on the side of her face, the days when she was in a coma, the time when my mother turned off the machine, and then afterwards when I started to use her name and how nobody challenged me, though I'm sure Auntie Teg knew, and probably Grampar too. We might have been identical, but we were different people after all.

"My grandfather had a stroke," I said, because however unbearable that was it was the next bearable thing to say. "I found him. They used to call it elfshot. I don't know if she made it happen."

I tried my coffee. It was horrible, even worse than instant coffee if that was possible. At the same time, I could see how it could become an acquired taste if I tried hard to like it. I'm not sure it would be worth the effort. After all, it's not as if it's good for you.

"So what are you going to do about her?" Wim asked.

"I don't think I need to do anything. We stopped her. Her last chance was Halloween."

"Not if your sister didn't go under the hill like she was supposed to. Not if she's still there. She could use that again. You have to do something to really stop her. You have to kill her."

"I think that would be wrong," I said. The other girls from school were all getting up, and I knew it must be time for the bus.

"I know she's your mother—"

"That has nothing to do with it. Nobody could hate her more than I do. But I think killing her would be the wrong thing to do. It feels wrong. I could talk to the fairies about it, but if it would have helped, I think they would have told me to do it already. You're thinking about it in the wrong sort of way, as if it was a story."

"This is just so damn weird," he said.

"I'm going to have to go. I'll miss the bus." I stood up, leaving the rest of my coffee.

He gulped his own coffee. "When will I see you?"

"Tuesday, like always. For Zelazny." I smiled. I was looking forward to that.

"Sure, but on our own?"

"Next Saturday." I shrugged my coat on. "It's the only time there is."

We started walking out of the cafe. "They don't let you out of there at all?"

"No. They pretty much don't."

"It's like prison."

"It is in a way." We walked down to the bus stop. "Well, Tuesday then," I said, as we reached it. The bus was there, and the girls were pouring onto it. And then—no, this needs to be on a line of its own.

And then he kissed me.

Tuesday 5th February 1980

It took me until today to finish writing up what happened on Saturday.

I'm not sure I really like *The Number of the Beast*. There's a lot to like about it, but it's all over the place as far as plot goes, and as far as location goes as well. I've never read Oz or the Lensmen, and I'm not quite sure what they were doing there.

Apart from that, the main excitement has been that all the girls who were on the bus have been asking me nonstop about "my boyfriend," where I met him, what he's like, what he does, and so on and on and on. Some of them who were in the cafe know about his reputation and have warned me about him—what, seventeen-year-old boy had sex with girlfriend, shock horror! It's such a weird mixture of puritanical and prurient. The girls who have local boyfriends say they're not serious about them, and some of them have what they call serious boyfriends at home. What they mean by serious is just what Jane Austen would have called an eligible parti, a boy of the same class who they might marry. They're slumming with the local boys, and the local boys mostly know that. It's vile, they're vile, the whole thing is vile and I don't want to think about Wim in the same breath as that.

The real difference is that we're not of different classes. Wim and I are both of a class that expects to go to university. I don't know what his father does, but that his mother works in the hospital kitchens while I go to school here is irrelevant. Well, maybe not irrelevant, but not the point. Anyway, I'm not sure if Wim is my boyfriend, and even if he is it isn't at all the thing they're talking about with their serious and not serious. I'm only fifteen. I'm not sure I ever want to get married. I'm neither messing around while waiting nor looking for some "real thing." What I want is much more complicated. I want somebody I can talk to about books, who would be my friend, and why couldn't we have sex as well if we wanted to? (And used contraception.) I'm not looking for romance. Lord Peter and Harriet would seem a pretty good model to me. I wonder if Wim has read Sayers?

But that's also almost irrelevant, because there's also the ethical thing of the magic. I should probably tell him, and then he'd hate me, anybody would.

I've asked Nurse to make me a doctor's appointment. She didn't ask what for.

Wednesday 6th February 1980

Zelazny meeting last night. Wim thinks Zelazny's the greatest stylist of all time. Brian thinks style is unimportant compared to ideas, and he thinks Zelazny's ideas are ordinary, except for Shadow. It's funny how people divided on that one. I think if we'd voted for whether style matters or only ideas, the division would have been really different from whether Zelazny has good ideas. I think he does, and I think both matter, which isn't to say that the Foundation books suck because they have no style, or Clarke either. Zelazny can get where he's all style and no substance—I can't forget *Creatures of Light and Darkness* after all, which almost put me off him forever. But mostly he keeps the balance.

We talked about Amber and what's going to happen, and we talked about the kind of wisecracking voice he uses in those and in *Isle of the Dead* and *This Immortal* and we talked about whether it was actually science fiction or fantasy. Hugh thinks the Amber books are fantasy, and so is *Isle of the Dead*, because despite the aliens and everything, world-building is talked about in such magical terms. "That's condemning him for being poetic!" Wim said.

"Saying it's fantasy isn't condemnation," Harriet said.

So, a good meeting. Afterwards Wim said to Greg, "Do you have a recent *Ansible*?"

There's a magazine, a "fanzine" called *Ansible*! It's for information about what's going on in the SF fan world, it's funny, and it's so exactly what I would have called it that I love the author, Dave Langford, sight unseen without meeting him. Ansibles are from *The Dispossessed* and they're faster-than-light communication devices. Brilliant. All the details about Albacon in Glasgow at Easter were in Greg's copy, and I copied them down, and all I have to do now is get the money from Daniel when I see him, probably at half term, which is at the end of next week, and send it off.

Walking out of the library, Wim held my hand. "Are you sure I can't see you until Saturday?" he said. "Will you be locked up in school the whole time?"

"Well yes, apart from going to Shrewsbury Thursday afternoon for acupuncture," I said.

"What time are you going?" he asked.

"On the half-past one train—but don't you have to work?"

"I work mornings and go to college in the afternoons," he said. "That's how I came to see you in hospital, remember? I can skive off tomorrow afternoon if I want to. Nobody cares."

"Skive" is like "mitch," it means "skipping school." That's what they say around here. The first time I heard it I had no idea what it meant.

"You'll care when it gets to the exams," I said.

"I won't even notice," he said. "I'll meet you in Gobowen railway station, all right?"

Greg drove me back to school, as normal. "So, I was right," he said.

I blushed. I don't think he saw in the darkness. "Sort of," I admitted.

"Well, good luck."

"Hot jets," I replied.

Greg laughed. "I've always said that what Wim needs is a girlfriend who could quote Heinlein at him."

Has he always said that? Or does he only think he always said that because I did the karass-magic? Greg existed before I did it. I know he did. I met him in the library. But he never said a word to me beyond not letting me join the first day and then taking my interlibrary loan cards. Was the book group, and SF fandom, there all the time, or did it all come into being when I did that magic, to give me a karass? Was there *Ansible*? I know they think there was, that there were conventions going back to 1939, and certainly science fiction was there all the time. There's no proving anything once magic gets involved.

I'm going to have to tell Wim. It's the only ethical thing.

Thursday 7th February 1980

I set off from school with even more of a sense of escaping this week, even though it was raining, the kind of irresistible damp drizzle that gets through every crack. If I had clothes of my own here I could have changed into them before leaving, but I don't so I couldn't. Arlinghurst wants its girls to be recognisable at all times. If they could make us wear the uniform in the holidays they would. At least the coat is good and solid, and the hat might be awful but it does keep the rain off, mostly.

Wim was waiting in Gobowen station. It's not much of a station, more like a bus shelter beside the line with a ticket machine and a couple of empty hanging baskets. He was sitting in the shelter with his feet up on the glass, folded up like a paperclip. His bike was chained to the railings outside, getting wet. There was a fat woman with a child sitting next to him, and a balding man with a briefcase, all in raincoats. Wim was wearing the same duffle coat as before. Next to him, the other people looked as if they were in black and white while he was in colour. He didn't see me for a moment, then the balding man saw me and made a fuss about getting up to give me his seat, so Wim noticed and smiled and got up instead. It was funny, we were kind of shy with each other. It was the first time we'd been alone together since Saturday, and we weren't really alone, they were there, but they didn't quite count. I didn't know how to behave, and if he did—and he should, as he's had a lot more practice—he didn't show it.

The train came, people got off, and then we got on. It was only a two-carriage train, and again full of people from North Wales with their funny singsong voices and yes/no questions. We managed to get a double seat because a nice lady moved across to give us one. We couldn't really talk about anything, because she was sitting across from us, along with a worried young man with a cat in a carrier on his lap. The cat kept crying, and he kept trying to reassure it. It must be awful taking a cat to the vet on the train. Or maybe he was moving. He didn't have much with him except the cat, but maybe you wouldn't. Or perhaps, worst of all, he had to give the cat away, and he was taking it to a new home. If so, though, he'd probably have been crying too, and he wasn't. The funny thing about the man with the cat was that Wim didn't notice him at all. When I said something about him, after we were on the platform in Shrewsbury walking along, he didn't know what I was talking about.

I don't think Wim goes to Shrewsbury very often, for all that it's so near. He didn't know where anything was. He didn't know there was a bookshop in Owen Owens. I had to go for acupuncture first, so I left him in a cafe—a shiny coffee bar, all chrome and glass, after he'd rejected the one with the nice booths where I went last time because it didn't have real coffee. I never knew before Saturday that there were any kinds of coffee but Nescafe (or Maxwell House, but they're the same), granulated coffee you make with boiling water. It seems a funny thing to be fussy about.

The acupuncture went well again. The acupuncturist says the traction might well have done it some violence (that's the word he used) and been unwise. I'd use considerably stronger language than unwise, but I suppose it is my leg, and just any old leg to him. I looked at the chart the whole time I was on the table, memorising where the points are and what they affect. It could be really useful to know. Just pressing them might help. I can feel the magic, the "chi" when the pins are in, moving smoothly around my body with a jump like a spark-gap where the pain would be. I'm going to try it without needles and see if I can drain the pain out. The easiest thing would be to put it into something, like a rock or a piece of metal, but then anyone picking it up would get it. The acupuncture just drains it out into the world, as far as I can tell. Good trick if you can do it.

Afterwards I went back—faster down the stairs than up them!—to where I'd left Wim. I sat down opposite him. The coffee machine let out a blast of coffee-scented steam. "Let's go somewhere else," he said. "I'm sick of this place."

Once we were out of there he cheered up. He held my hand, which was nice, though it would have been nicer if it had left me with a free hand. We went to the book department, and didn't find anything, but it was nice to look and point things out to each other. He's much more picky than I am, and also likes some things I don't, like Dick. He despises Niven (!) and he doesn't like Piper. (How can anyone not adore H. Beam Piper?) He's never read Zenna Henderson, and of course they didn't have any. I'll borrow them from Daniel to lend to him.

After that, I insisted I would buy him lunch, though it was mid-afternoon by that time. I was starving. We found a fish and chip place with a sit-down part, and we sat down and ate fish and chips and white bread and butter, and I had truly awful tea so stewed it was dark orange, and Wim had a Vimto, which he said he hadn't had since he was eight years old. That made him smile. He also ran his finger over the back of my hand, which was nicer than holding hands walking along, and much more comfortable. It made me feel all shivery.

The chip shop wasn't full, so when we'd finished eating we ordered another Vimto and a lemonade—the tea was too awful even to pretend to drink. We sat there in the warm and dry while our coats steamed gently on the backs of our chairs. We talked about Tolkien. He compared it to Donaldson, and also to something called *The Sword of Shannara* which I haven't read, but which sounds like a total crap rip-off. And then by degrees we got to talking about the elves. "They could be ghosts," he said.

"The dead can't speak. Mor couldn't speak when I saw her." I managed to say her name perfectly normally, without even a quiver.

"Maybe not when they're newly dead. I had a thought about that. When they're newly dead, they can't speak, and they look like themselves. And you can make them speak using blood, like in Virgil, you said, right? Later, they draw life from things that are alive, animals and plants, and they get more like them, less like people, and they can speak, with that life."

"The way they speak really isn't much like people, not even dead people," I said. "What you're saying makes sense, and it would fit perfectly in a story, but I'm not sure it feels right."

"It would explain why they like ruins," he said. "I went back there afterwards, on Saturday. I could sort of see them, out of the corner of my eye, when I was touching your rock." He touched his pocket when he mentioned it. I liked the thought that he was carrying around something I'd had so long. It won't really do anything except protect him from my mother—but goodness knows, that can't be a bad thing.

"You should be able to see them," I said. "They're all over."

"They're ghosts," he said. "You just think they're fairies."

"I don't know what they are, and I don't know that it really matters," I said.

"Don't you want to find out?" he asked, his eyes gleaming. That's the spirit of science fiction.

"Yes," I said, but I didn't really mean it. They are what they are, that's all.

"Well, what do you think they have to do with?"

"Places," I said, very sure. "They don't move around all that much. Glor— my friend did magic to make me come down to South Wales at Halloween, he didn't come here and speak to me."

"Well, that's like ghosts, lingering where they come from."

I shook my head.

"Will you teach me magic?" he asked next.

I jumped. "I really don't think that's a good idea."

"Why not?"

"Because it's so dangerous. If you don't know what you're doing, and I don't mean you, I mean anyone, anyone who doesn't know enough, it's so hard not to do things that have wide-reaching effects and you don't know what." This was the perfect opportunity to tell him about the karass spell, and I knew it, but when it came to it, I didn't want to. "Like George Orr in *The Lathe of Heaven*, only with magic, not with dreams."

"Have you done anything that's like that?" he asked.

So I had to tell him. "You're not going to like it. But I was very lonely and very desperate. I was doing a magic for protection against my mother, because she kept sending me terrible dreams all the time. And while I was at it, I did a magic to find me a karass."

He looked blank. "What's a karass?"

"You haven't read Vonnegut? Oh well, you'd like him I think.

Start with *Cat's Cradle*. But anyway, a karass is a group of people who are genuinely connected together. And the opposite is a gran-falloon, a group that has a fake kind of connection, like all being in school together. I did a magic to find me friends."

He actually recoiled, almost knocking his chair over. "And you think it *worked*?"

"The day after, Greg invited me to the book group." I let that hang there while he filled in the implications for himself.

"But we'd been meeting for months already. You just . . . found us."

"I hope so," I said. "But I didn't know anything about it before. I'd never seen any indication of it, or of fandom either."

I looked at him. He was rarer than a unicorn, a beautiful boy in a red-checked shirt who read and thought and talked about books. How much of his life had my magic touched, to make him what he was? Had he even existed before? Or what had he been? There's no knowing, no way to know. He was here now, and I was, and that was all.

"But I was there," he said. "I was going to it. I know it was there. I was at Seacon in Brighton last summer."

"*Er' perrhenne*," I said, with my best guess at pronunciation.

I am used to people being afraid of me, but I don't really like it. I don't suppose even Tiberius really liked it. But after a horrible instant his face softened. "It must have just found us for you. You couldn't have changed all that," he said, and picking up his Vimto, drained the bottle.

"I wanted to tell you, because there's an ethical question about why you like me, if you like me because of that," I said, to make it perfectly clear.

He laughed, a little shakily. "I'll have to think about that," he said.

We walked back through the wet streets to the station, not hold-ing hands. But on the train, which was much emptier going back, we sat together, and our sides touched and after a moment he put his arm around me. "It's a lot to take in," he said. "I always wanted the world to have magic in it."

"I'd prefer spaceships," I said. "Or if there has to be magic, then less confusing magic, magic with easy rules, like in books."

"Let's talk about something normal," he said. "Like, why do you have such short hair? I like it, but it's really unusual."

"That's not normal," I said. "We used to have long plaits. Gramma used to plait it, and then after she died we used to do each other's. When Mor died, I couldn't do my own, and in a fit of, well, furious grief I suppose, I cut them off with scissors. Then my hair was horribly uneven, and my friend Moira tried to even if off, cutting a bit off each side, until I had practically none. Since then, I've kept it short. It's only just got to be the same length all over. It used to be really spiky."

"You poor old thing," he said, and gave me a squeeze.

"Why do you have long hair? For a man, I mean."

"I just like it," he said, touching it self-consciously. Hair the colour of honey, or anyway, of honey buns.

In Gobowen, he unchained his bike. "See you on Saturday," he said.

"In the little cafe by the bookshop?" I asked.

"In Marios, so I can get some decent coffee," he said.

I think it's important to Wim to be seen in public with me. I suppose it has to do with the Ruthie thing and his feeling of being a pariah.

We kissed again before I got on the bus. I could feel it right down to my toes. That's magic too, in a way, the same as the "chi" is.

Friday 8th February 1980

Aujourd'hui, rien.

People were telling riddles at lunch today, and I asked the question about whether you'd rather meet an elf or a Plutonian. Deirdre didn't know what a Plutonian was. "An alien from the planet Pluto," I said. "Like a Martian, but more so."

"An elf, then," she said. "How about you, Morwenna, which would you rather be?"

It was a typical Deirdre mix-up between "meet" or "be," but in a way it's a more challenging question. Which you'd rather meet is about worldview, past and present, fantasy and science fiction. Which you'd rather be is—I keep thinking about Tiptree's "And I Awoke and Found Me Here on the Cold Hill's Side," which manages to be both.

Doctor's appointment made for Monday.

Saturday 9th February 1980

Wim seems to be inherently early, except for the time when he had a puncture and was late for book group, the first time. He was waiting in Marios when I got there, and had even ordered me a coffee.

He looked through my library books, tutting or nodding at them. Mary Renault's *The Persian Boy* had come in, and he wanted to know what I saw in historical fiction, and when I said I'd already read it, what I saw in re-reading. Several girls I knew were in the cafe, with local boys, including Karen, who kept looking over at us and smirking.

"Could we go somewhere else," I said after a while, when Wim had finished his coffee.

"Where?" he asked. "There's nowhere to go. Unless you want to go ghost-hunting again?"

"I don't mind, if you do," I said.

Just then Karen came over to the table. "Come to the toilet with me. Commie," she said.

Wim raised his eyebrows at the name, but I was just relieved she hadn't called me "Crip" or "Hopalong" in front of him.

"Not right now," I said.

"No, come," Karen said, making faces. She put her hand on my arm and pinched me quite hard. "Come on."

It was easier to go than to make a scene. Karen wasn't my friend, exactly, but she was Sharon and Deirdre's friend. I sighed and went off with her. The toilets were painted red and had a mirror with a row of bright bare lightbulbs over it. Karen checked her make-up in it— although make-up was just as strictly forbidden on Saturdays as any other day, she was caked in the stuff.

"Craig, that's my boyfriend, says he saw your boyfriend with another girl at the disco last night; Shirley who works in the laundry at the school."

"Thank you," I said. "I could hardly go to the disco with him, could I?"

"You don't care?" She sounded incredulous.

I did care, of course I did, but I wasn't about to let her know that. I just smiled and pushed the door open and went back to the table.

Wim was still there, which I had briefly wondered about. I sat down and took his hand, because I knew Karen would be watching. "Let's go," I said.

"What did she say to you?" he asked.

"You know better than I do that in this town everybody knows everybody's business," I said. I stood up and put my coat on.

His face fell, but he also had a look of calculation. "Mori, I—"

"Come on," I said. I wasn't going to talk about it in there, in front of an over-appreciative audience.

"How is this supposed to work anyway if I can only see you at book club and on Saturday afternoons, and for a couple of hours on Thursday hanging around in Shrewsbury?" he asked, belligerently, as we walked up the hill, past Smiths and BHS. "You couldn't ever go to a party with me."

"I can see that," I said. "I can't help being stuck in school. Maybe it isn't going to work."

"So you could break up with me because I went dancing with Shirley?" He looked down at me inquiringly.

"More because I don't want to be humiliated about it, than because you did. I mean, obviously, even if I wasn't stuck in school I couldn't go dancing."

"It isn't that," he said, very quickly. "I don't care about dancing especially, it's just something to do."

"And you don't care about Shirley either, she's also just something to do?" I asked, cattily.

"Or I could break up with you because I can hardly ever see you and it's too inconvenient," he said, in a strange musing tone.

We had come to the corner by Thorntons, where we'd turn down if we were going to the bookshop and Poacher's Wood. I stopped, and he stopped too. "Are you supposed to be making any sense?" I asked, exasperated. Boys are weird.

"Do you agree that we could break up right now, on this corner, and never say a kind word to each other again?" he demanded. The wind was blowing his hair back, and he had never looked more gorgeous.

"Yes!" I said. I could imagine it all too well, saying things at book group about books and never looking at each other.

"Then it's all right. If we could break up right now then whatever magic you did didn't make it destiny that we would be together," he said.

"What?" Then I got it. "Oh."

He grinned. "So if we're not together because the magic forced us to be, that's all right."

It was the most backwards way of looking at it that I could imagine. "So, what, you were doing a *scientific experiment* with Shirley in the disco?"

He did have the grace to look a little abashed. "Sort of. I hate the idea of being forced into things. I hate the idea of True Love and Finding the Right One and you know, being tied down, marriage, and the thought that the magic had made me—"

"Wim, I admitted I kind of like you," I said. "When *you* asked *me*. I did not and would not say anything about destiny, true love, marriage, ever after or any of that crap. That is not what I am looking for, that is not what I want. I want friends, not True bloody Love. I don't plan to marry ever, and anyway not for years and years."

"That's you," he said, starting to walk again, so I started to walk too, downhill now. "That's not the magic. I like you, I really do. But I thought if we *could* break up, and you agreed we could, then it wasn't doing that, and it would be all right."

"So you don't actually want to break up?"

"Not if you don't," he said.

What I know about magic that he doesn't is how tricky it is, and how much easier it is to get people to do things they want to do anyway. It would only prove anything if we did break up, not if we just agreed that we theoretically could. But . . . I didn't want to. "I don't want to," I said.

"What did you say to her?"

"Who?" I asked.

"Little Miss Hitler, back in the cafe?"

I snorted. "Her name's Karen. I said obviously I couldn't go to a disco, and then I just smiled. I didn't want to give her the satisfaction." We were coming down to the bookshop, and he stopped again.

"Then just keep smiling. I won't see Shirley again."

"I don't care if you see Shirley, as long as I know about it," I said. ". . . I think." I was really clear on the theory of this from Heinlein, I wasn't quite so sure about the practice.

"She's a moron," he said, which was very reassuring. It's nice to be wanted for something real.

We crossed into Poacher's Wood, and walked down to where the ruined walls are. The snowdrops were dead. There were leaves coming through, but no other flowers yet. The place was swarming with fairies, mostly gnarly treelike ones, who didn't pay any attention to us. Wim could sort of see them, he said he could see them sideways.

We sat on the wall for a while, looking at them. Then when we started to get up, he happened to brush against my walking stick, and made a choking sound. "Now I can really see them," he said. He sat down again beside me, holding the stick on his lap. "Man," he exclaimed, rather inadequately.

Ages afterwards, after he'd been watching the fairies for a long time, I said it was time to go, and reached for my stick back. Without it he was back to only half-seeing them. "I wish I knew what they were," he said, as we walked back up into town. "Could I have that stick? I mean, do you have another one of those?"

"I do, but the other one is metal and hideous, and this one gives me strength. The fairies gave it to me."

"Maybe they gave it to you so I could see them," he suggested. "All of those colours and shapes." He sounded drunk. They were just fairies, and not even doing anything especially interesting.

"Maybe," I said. "I need it now, anyway."

He took my hand as we went through the trees.

"I'm sorry about the dancing thing," he said. "I don't mean Shirley, I did that on purpose, I mean the actual dancing. I wasn't thinking about that, and I wouldn't want to make you feel bad about not being able to do it."

"That's all right," I said, though it wasn't. My leg is about back to where it was before the traction wrecked it. I have good days and bad days. They said it was going to keep on being like that. Maybe the acupuncture will help, and maybe I can learn to do it myself, and that would help, but I'm not going to be dancing any time soon.

It was almost time to catch the bus, so we walked on through town. "So, Tuesday night, Thursday afternoon and next Saturday? If that's all that's on offer, then I'll take it," he said.

"Next weekend is half term," I said. "All of next week is. So Saturday's out."

"Are you going away?"

"I'm going to spend one night in the Old Hall with Daniel, and then go down to Aberdare for a few days, to see Auntie Teg and my grandfather."

"And kill your mother?" he asked. "No, I know, but I could. That wouldn't be against any ancient prohibitions."

"In the ancient prohibitions I've seen, I wouldn't even be able to share a meal with someone who had killed my mother, whatever I thought of her," I said, though I was mainly going from Mary Renault, and not any actual ancient prohibitions. Funny how nobody teaches ancient prohibitions any more. "Anyway, there's no need."

"I could come down with you."

"Don't be silly, where would you stay?" I asked. "Anyway, you have to work. I'll see you when I come home."

"I'll miss you," he said, and kissed me very gently for a long time.

Well, at least it isn't boring.

Sunday 10th February 1980

There was a frost this morning. When I woke up and looked out of the window everything was crisply outlined in white. It had melted by the time we went to church.

The sermon was all about giving thanks, and how we shouldn't just skim through our blessings but choose two special things to give thanks for. So, mentally, when it was prayertime, I gave thanks for Wim and the interlibrary loan system.

I wrote to Auntie Teg saying I'd be there next Sunday. I hadn't bought a card for Grampar yesterday, or last week either, because Wim distracted me both times. I'll take one with me.

My new worry about Wim is that it's the possibility of magic that he wants, not really me.

Monday 11th February 1980

The Persian Boy is so wonderful. It might be her best book. Stimulated not by it directly but by the general thought of her books, I have also raced through the *Phaedrus* and started *The Laws* and got a bit bogged down.

Miss Carroll seems to approve of me reading things that aren't SF. She started a conversation about ancient Greece, and mentioned the possibility of me doing an O Level in Greek while I'm doing my A Levels. I don't know if I'm going to be doing A Levels here or what, but if I am and I do, that would be a really good plan. I don't think they'd let me do what Wim's doing and keep mixing arts and sciences. Besides, I'd like to do English, history, and Latin, which is a very usual and conventional mix. I'd like to keep on with either physics or chemistry too, but as Miss Carroll pointed out, not having the maths would make that difficult. I might just scrape a pass in maths, if I'm lucky, but that's the best I can hope for.

At the doctor's, I asked if I was seeing him in confidence, and he said of course. Then I asked if he'd give me a prescription for the Pill. He asked if I was sexually active, and I said not yet, but I was thinking of becoming so. He looked at my date of birth and tutted a little, but he gave me the prescription. He said I'd have to take it for a whole month before it would work, that I had to start taking it on the day after a period, and that if I missed one pill after that I'd be okay, but no more than that, and I should take them at the same time every day. I picked the prescription up in Boots on the way back. I also bought a packet of condoms (be prepared) and a bar of Cadbury's Dairy Milk, which was more to disguise the other things than because I wanted it, though I ate it anyway.

I'm keeping the pills and the condoms in my bag, because there isn't anywhere else safe.

Tuesday 12th February 1980

Deirdre nearly got caught copying my Virgil today. There are two verbs, "progredior" and "proficiscor" and they're both weirdly in the passive all the time, and they both start "pro" and one means "advance" and the other "set out" and I always confuse them, and I did in my prep, which Deirdre had copied. Miss Martin, who's very sharp, gave us both a stern look when Deirdre read that bit aloud, and she said that mistakes with passive verbs seem to be catching, and then she had Deirdre come up to the front and do the next bit, the bit we hadn't been set to prepare. She didn't make too bad a muck of it, so I thought we'd got away with it. Then she made me construe the next part, again unseen. After class, while the bell was ringing and everyone was charging off down the corridor for physics, she stopped me and said "Did you and Deirdre co-operate a little on that piece of Virgil, Morwenna?"

"She was a bit stuck," I said, which was the truth, and sounded much better than saying she copied all of mine.

"She'll never learn if she doesn't learn to learn on her own," Miss Martin said, which sounds like an aphorism, and maybe is one in Latin, where it would be about three words, no six, maybe seven.

Letter from Daniel saying he'll collect me on Friday and it's fine to go to Aberdare on Sunday, also saying I might get a surprise before that. I wonder what he means? Maybe he's sent books separately?

Book club tonight, talking about *Pavane*.

Wednesday 13th February 1980

Hussein led the meeting, and we didn't just talk about *Pavane*, but also Brunner's brilliant *Times Without Number* and Dick's *The Man in the High Castle* (which I haven't read) and Ward Moore's *Bring the Jubilee* and the whole idea of having para-history. We also mentioned *Up the Line* and *Guardians of Time* and Christopher Priest's *A Dream of Wessex* (must order!) which Wim says is brill. There was a question of whether they were really SF, which they obviously are, and whether there was a difference between the kind of "paratime" thing, like *Lord Kalvan of Otherwhen* and a book like *Pavane* which is all in one universe where things went differently.

We kept coming back to *Pavane* and the way *Pavane* covers such a span of time, which, Greg says, is what makes it SF, the perspective. Then Brian mentioned the Lord Darcy books (I adore Randall Garrett!) and asked whether they were SF, which was a cheat, as they're obviously fantasy, except that they're not at all like fantasy, and they are exactly like SF. Harriet said she felt they belonged rather with things like Dunsany's club stories and tall tales, they were whimsical. I disagreed (probably talking too much and too vehemently) because I think the way in which they're like SF is the opposite of whimsy, they're taking magic and treating it as another bit of science, especially in *Too Many Magicians*.

Janine doesn't seem to be speaking to me, or Pete either. They'll get over it, Wim says. I hope so.

Hugh looked a bit confused. Greg thinks—he said in the car—that Hugh thought he and I would automatically become an item, because we were the same age. I never heard anything so stupid in my life, and said so, because while I like Hugh I never thought of him in that way for two seconds. Greg just laughed and said these things sort themselves out, and had I read McCaffrey? I don't know what that has to do with anything, but we talked about Impressing dragons all the rest of the way back.

Wim's meeting me in Gobowen again tomorrow. He seems to think this isn't very often to see each other, but I think it's loads. I need time in between to think—and to write it all down! I don't suppose he does that.

It has just belatedly occurred to me that tomorrow is Valentine's Day. I don't suppose he'll take any notice of it—or will he? I don't have the foggiest. Miss Carroll thinks he might, and that I should have something ready to produce if he does. The problem with that is that I don't have anything. She suggested a book—well, she would!—and that would be a terrific idea if there was time to go to a bookshop. I could make him a card. Well, except that nobody would want a card I'd made. I could write him a poem, or more to the point, write out neatly one of the poems I have already written about him. But what if he didn't like it? I've never talked to him about poetry, I have no idea whether he likes it or not. If he didn't hate Heinlein I could give him *The Number of the Beast*, but he does, so I can't. I don't have anything else new, and he probably has everything I have here.

If I leave school a little bit early, I can go to the bookshop on the way to the station, I suppose.

Thursday 14th February 1980

Well, that was awkward.

Daniel's "surprise" was turning up to drive me to Shrewsbury. I can't think why he did it today, when it's half term tomorrow, but I shouldn't expect him to make sense. He was sitting outside in the car, looking very pleased with himself, like the cat who got the cream. I stopped still when I saw him, absolutely convulsed with horror.

Wim was meeting me in Gobowen station. I had no way of

contacting him to tell him what had happened. If I didn't meet him, I wouldn't see him until after half term. He'd think I'd dumped him, and on Valentine's Day too.

The alternative was to tell Daniel about Wim. I thought about that as I got into the car. The problem there was that I hadn't said anything about him at all up to that point, because as usual my letters to Daniel had been exclusively about books. It was an excruciating situation. I couldn't possibly ask Daniel to turn around and leave me alone, which would really have been what I'd have preferred.

"I managed to get away," Daniel said. "We can go to the Chinese restaurant again."

"That's lovely, but," I said, and stopped.

"But what?" he asked, starting the engine and driving down the drive, between the two dead elms, which look terrible again now that the other trees are starting to think about getting leaves. "I thought you'd be pleased." He sounded really pathetic.

"I'm supposed to be meeting a friend in Gobowen railway station," I said. "Do you think we could go there and collect him and take him with us?"

Daniel's face went oddly blank, then he smiled. "Of course," he said, and did a U-turn in the road, which was, fortunately, deserted.

After that, I couldn't possibly say I wanted to go to the bookshop first.

"Is this a boyfriend, or just a boy-type friend?" he asked.

"Sort of a boyfriend. Well, actually a boyfriend, yes." I was tripping over my own tongue in embarrassment.

"So, tell me about him?" Daniel sounded encouraging, but also bewildered.

I didn't know quite what to say. "His name's Wim. I met him in the book group. He's seventeen. He likes Delany and Zelazny. He's doing English, history, and chem for A Level, at the college, while working part time. I'm thinking of doing that myself next year, if I need to."

"Why would you need to?" Daniel asked.

"I'll be sixteen in June," I said. "You won't have to support me. I could live on my own."

"I'll support you for as long as you want to be in full-time education," Daniel said, not having read *Doorways in the Sand* or *The Number of the Beast*.

"Did you know there's a new Heinlein?" I asked, having remembered it.

"You told me on Sunday," he said. "I'm looking forward to it, even if it isn't his best."

At that point, we were at Gobowen station. It was deserted. For once, I'd got somewhere ahead of Wim, because he was expecting me to come by buses around two sides of a triangle, while in fact I'd come by car down the third side. "He'll be here soon, he's always early," I said. Daniel parked neatly on the forecourt.

"How long have you been seeing each other?" he asked.

I added it up. "Almost two weeks," I said.

To his credit, Daniel didn't say anything about how I should have told him, or that I was too young, or anything like that. "Yet another new role," is what he said, but he was smiling. "I feel absurdly nervous."

"Well how do you think I feel?" I asked.

He laughed, and just then Wim came freewheeling into the station yard, hair blowing around his face. "Is that him?" Daniel asked.

"Yes," I said, feeling more proud than I had any right to be. I got out of the car, which Wim hadn't been paying any attention to at all. He isn't a very noticing person.

Daniel got out too. "We can put the bike in the boot," he said.

"Wait here while I explain to him," I said.

I walked over to Wim. Daniel leaned on the car, smoking a cigarette and watched. Wim saw me, saw the Bentley, and then saw Daniel, I saw him registering. "Wim, my father turned up unexpectedly to take me to acupuncture. I had no warning at all either. Do you want to come to Shrewsbury with us, in the car?"

He looked very surprised. "In the car? With your dad?"

"He doesn't mind. If you'd like to. But we wouldn't be on our own, and we can't talk about magic or anything, because he doesn't know anything about it."

"Anything for a weird life," Wim said, quoting Zaphod. Then he kissed me, a little tentatively, but still bravely considering that Daniel was standing right there. He pulled a packet out of his coat pocket and handed it to me almost defiantly. "Happy Valentine's Day."

I opened it right away. It was three books! Theodore Sturgeon's *A Touch of Strange*, with a lovely cover of a woman's head and the moon, Christopher Priest's *Inverted World*, and something I'd never heard of by an author new to me, *Gate of Ivrel* by C. J. Cherryh. I was overwhelmed. "Oh Wim, that's lovely. And I haven't got any of them. I didn't have a chance to buy you anything yet, but I did make this for you." I pulled the poem out of my pocket. I'd written it on nice blue paper Miss Carroll had given me, in my best handwriting. (It's the one that starts "To drag yourself over the dry rock of the deserts of the mind.")

He read it, and I waited while he read it, watching him, very conscious of Daniel waiting behind me. Wim blushed and pushed it into his pocket. I don't know whether he liked it or not.

Then I introduced him to Daniel, and they shook hands like a pair of judges. Things got a little easier when they cooperated in getting the bike into the car boot. Then we all climbed back in and started off for Shrewsbury. I realised as we did that the two of them were going to have to spend an hour together without me while I was having acupuncture. Has anything ever been awkwarder? It served Daniel right for not telling me, but poor Wim didn't deserve it at all.

In the car, we talked about Zelazny, a subject of deep and unfailing interest, and then we talked about *Empire Star* and how it could be just an ordinary adventure except that it isn't. I felt that Daniel and Wim were starting to like each other through all this, though of course Wim was sitting in the back so they couldn't exactly see each other. We came to Shrewsbury, early for my appointment. We had a little look at the bookshop, and Wim and Daniel had an argument about Heinlein, very much the argument that Wim and I had had, though at greater length. I was on Daniel's side, and both of them knew it, but I tried to bite my tongue and not say anything and just look at the shelves. When he wasn't looking I bought *Sign of the Unicorn* and *Cat's Cradle* for Wim, and gave them to him when we got outside.

Then I had to leave them together. They agreed to come to the clinic and meet me afterwards. I have never felt so apprehensive having acupuncture, not even the first time when I was afraid of the needles. I just tried to get my mental breath back when I was on the table, I didn't concentrate on the diagram or the magic or anything. It didn't seem to do me as much good as sometimes, or maybe I was better when I went in and didn't notice the difference the way I sometimes do.

They were waiting for me when I came out, both leaning against the wall. Next to Wim, Daniel looked old and saggy. When I came up to them they were talking about Wim's experiences at Seacon in Brighton and his hopes for Albacon in Glasgow. "I wish I could go," Daniel said.

"Why don't you?" Wim asked.

Daniel just shrugged, looking defeated.

We went to the Chinese restaurant, where we ate essentially the same as last time, Wim and I fumbling with the chopsticks, and talked mostly about Silverberg, with digressions into all the things we'd mentioned on Tuesday night in the *Pavane* talk. Daniel had read everything except *A Dream of Wessex*. I could see him and Wim being impressed with each other, which was lovely, and very strange. When Daniel went to the bathroom, Wim took my hand. "I like your dad," he said.

"Good," I said.

"You're so lucky," he said again.

"I suppose I could be a whole lot less lucky," I said. Most people wouldn't think Daniel much of a father, but there are far worse people. Then I remembered the last time Wim had said that and what we'd been talking about. "Oh, this is priceless, he said he'd support me until I finished in full-time education. But he hasn't read—"

Wim burst out laughing, just as Daniel came back, so we had to explain to him. Fortunately, he thought it was funny too.

Wim's fortune cookie said "You have been given a gift," Daniel's said "Fortune favours the brave," and mine said "The time to be happy is now."

Then Daniel drove us back. He asked Wim where he wanted to be dropped, and Wim said anywhere in cycling distance was fine, so he dropped him by the roundabout. I got out while they were getting the bike out, and boldly asked Wim for his phone number. "I could call you next week when I'm away," I said. "And it would have been useful this afternoon."

"No it wouldn't, I was coming from work," he said. But he gave it to me, and Daniel wrote it down too. Daniel then gave Wim his card—he would have a card!—in exchange. Wim and I hugged, and kissed very decorously, then Daniel drove me back to school in time for prep.

Friday 15th February 1980

Sharon was picked up first, as usual. There are a whole lot of advantages to being Jewish if you ask me. There's also the whole pile of things to watch out for. I must remember to ask Sam what happens if you break the rules.

Daniel was one of the first of the regular parents though. "I liked your young man," he said as I got into the car.

"He liked you too," I said, putting my seat belt on.

"I thought we might ask him to tea tomorrow, at the Old Hall. If he came to Shrewsbury on the train, we could meet him there. You two could go for a walk or something, and then we could all have tea."

Daniel sounded so tentative and hopeful that I couldn't really say no. Also, I knew that Wim would like it. He'd like to see the Old Hall, and he'd like to see the aunts, because he knew they were magic. He wouldn't be afraid of them, because he isn't afraid of anything. Also, I wanted to see Wim, of course I did, even in less than ideal circumstances. "Terrific," I said. "But have you asked your sisters?"

"Anthea suggested it," he said.

"I thought they might not approve of me seeing a town boy," I said.

"Well . . ." Daniel hesitated. "They did say that in their day it wasn't done, but I'm sure they'll change their minds when they meet Wim and see how intelligent and well-spoken he is."

Well-spoken is code for *middle class*, by the way. I've figured that one out since I've been at Arlinghurst. Somebody or other once said that the British class system was branded on the tongue. Wim has a Shropshire accent but he uses grammar correctly. He sounds like an educated person. He doesn't sound stuck up and pretentious like the girls in school, but I suppose I'm glad he counts as *well-spoken* enough for Daniel. It's so stupid that this sort of thing counts!

I had dinner with all of them, and had to answer lots of questions about school and Wim and more school. I was Nice Niece as best I could be. Everything went smoothly. Ear piercing was not mentioned.

After dinner, I rang Wim. Someone I assume was his mother answered, but got me Wim quite quickly. I was relieved he was there. He could easily have been at a disco with Shirley. "What are you doing tomorrow?" I asked.

"Why?"

"Daniel was wondering if you'd like to come here to tea. You could come to Shrewsbury on the train, and we'd meet you."

"I thought you were going down to South Wales?" He sounded very far away.

"Not until Sunday," I said. "But it's all right if you don't want to come. You don't work Saturdays, do you?"

"I do, but only in the morning."

"Well, it's up to you." I didn't want to push.

"Would I get to see you?" he asked. "On our own, I mean."

Bless him. "Daniel said we could go for a walk or something. And they leave me alone a lot of the time."

"So, what should I wear? For afternoon tea at a manor house?"

It was so sweet that he worried like that! "Just what you always wear would be fine," I said. "It's not a formal black-tie dinner."

"Will the sisters be there?" he asked.

"Definitely."

"What a treat!" he said, his voice dripping with irony.

"Well, see you tomorrow. On the one o'clock train?"

"Tomorrow it is."

After he'd put the phone down I felt cold and lonely and wandered around from room to room for a while. Daniel was drinking in his study and the sisters were watching television in the drawing room. It almost makes it worse that I'm going to see him tomorrow than if it wasn't for a week. I'd braced myself for that.

Saturday 16th February 1980

The sun was shining and Wim showed up at the station in a collar and tie, which made him look younger, more like a schoolboy. I didn't say that, of course. Daniel accommodatingly drove us to Acton Burnell castle. The castle is a ruin, covered in new spring grass and ivy.

"There's nobody else here," Wim said when we got out of the car.

"Well, it is February. Hardly grockle season," Daniel said.

Wim raised his eyebrows. "Tourists," Daniel said. "We get a lot of them in the summer. Now, you can walk back from here. It's not much over a mile. Or, if you don't feel like walking, call from the phone box, Morwenna, all right?" There was a red phone box right there by the castle gate.

"All right," I muttered. He meant if my leg fell off, of course. I shouldn't be churlish with people who want to accommodate me, really. It's crass.

The outwall was fallen, the moat was full of nettles, and you could just about tell what's what in the keep if you'd seen a proper castle like Pembroke or Caerphilly where everything is marked. There were fairies everywhere, of course, which was why I'd suggested it.

I've noticed before that there are two kinds of people for going round castles. There are the ones who say "And here's where we'd put the boiling oil and here's where we'd put the longbowmen," and the ones who say "And here's where we'd put the settee, and here's where we'd hang the pictures." Wim turned out very satisfactorily to be of the first camp. He'd been to Conwy and Beaumaris with his school, so he knew about castles. We fought a very successful siege (and had a few cuddles in corners out of the wind) before he even asked about fairies.

"Tons of them," I said, sitting down in a windowseat so that he could have my stick and see them. I looked out through the cross-shaped arrow slit, but the view so attractively framed was of pylons stretching out wires over neat Shropshire fields, and the red telephone box down below.

Wim sat beside me, with my stick across his lap and watched them for a while. They didn't take much notice of us sitting there. When we were children the fairies would play games with us, hide and seek, mostly, and other chasing games. The ones in the castle seemed to be playing games like that with each other, moving in and around the rooms, keeping out of each other's sight, dashing through doorways ahead of entrances through broken walls. Not having the stick didn't stop me seeing them, of course, so Wim and I sat there and wondered aloud what they were doing. Then one of them, a tall, impossibly tall, fairy woman, with long hair mixed with swan feathers, swept through the fallen wall, saw us and stopped. I nodded to her. She frowned and came over and stood before us. "Hello," I said, and then in Welsh "Good afternoon."

"Go," she said to me, in English. "Need. In—" She gestured.

"In the Valleys?" I asked. I was used to guessing games when it came to fairies and nouns. "In Aberdare? In the vales of coal and iron?"

I could feel Wim looking at me.

"Belong," she said, and pointed at me.

"Where I come from?" I asked. "I'm going tomorrow."

"Go," she said. "Join." Then she looked at Wim, and smiled, and drew her hand down the side of his face. "Beautiful." Well, he was. She swept on, out of the doorway, and a parade of warty grey gnomes came in through the hole in the wall and followed her out without a glance in our direction.

Wim stared after her, awestruck. "Wow," he said, after a while.

"Do you see what I mean now about hard to have a conversation?" I asked.

"Impossible, yes," he said. "Fragments like that, you wouldn't know if you were making up the right half or not." He was talking quite distractedly and still looking after her. "She really was beautiful."

"She meant that you were," I said.

He laughed. "You're not serious? No, you are serious? Jesus!" He peered after her, but she was out of sight.

"You are beautiful," I said.

"I get zits," he said. "I cut myself shaving. I'm wearing a stupid tie. She—"

"Have you read 'Firiel'? In *The Adventures of Tom Bombadil*? The end of that? That's what you're feeling."

"Tolkien really knew what he was talking about," Wim said.

"I think he saw them," I said. "I think he saw them and dreamed them into the elves he wanted. I think they are his dwindled remnant."

"Maybe he saw them when he was a child, and remembered them," Wim said. "I wish I knew what they are really. You're right, they're not ghosts, or not only ghosts. They're definitely not aliens either. They're not substantial. When she touched me . . ."

"They can be more substantial sometimes," I said, remembering the warmth of Glorfindel beside me on Halloween.

"What did she mean? Go, need, in, belong, go, join."

I was impressed that he'd remembered so precisely. "I think she meant I should go to the Valleys because I'm needed there for something. Maybe you're right about my mother, or maybe it's something else. I'm going tomorrow anyway."

"Half the time I can't believe it. What you told me about your mother and magic and all of that. And then something like her." He turned to me and put his arms very tightly around me. "If you're going to go and save the world, I want to come."

"I'll phone you every day," I said.

"You need me."

I didn't ask what earthly good he'd be, because that would have been cruel. "I did it on my own before."

"You got mashed up and nearly killed before," he said. "Your sister did get killed."

"There's nothing she can do like that now," I said. "I don't even think she wanted to kill us then. And this—this isn't unusual. Or it's only unusual in that it's in English, and here, where they don't usually bother with me. Maybe it's because we're closer."

"Not unusual!" Wim looked at me as if that was the oddest thing he'd ever heard. "And closer to what?"

"Wales?"

"Closer for values of closer that mean further away. The Welsh border is only a couple of miles from Oswestry."

"Okay. But they want me to do something, and I'll do it, or I won't do it, and it'll work or not, and I'll survive or not," I said.

"I'm coming with you."

"I'm not going to Elfland to have adventures," I said. "I'm going to South Wales, where, in between seeing my slightly peculiar relatives, they probably want me to do something that seems pointless, like dropping a flower in a pond or a comb in a bog, which will have repercussions down the way."

"A comb in a bog?" he echoed. "What did that do?"

"It made somebody go away and die," I said, looking away guiltily, sorry I'd mentioned it.

"Are you always going to be doing this stuff?" he asked.

"I don't know," I said. "I always have. But I'm less use now. And I think—I think children might be better at it because there are fewer shades of grey."

"I could help," he said.

"I'll see. If I think you could help, I'll let you know and you can rush down then."

He settled for that, thank goodness.

We walked back across the fields to the Old Hall. There's a footpath, which Daniel had shown me on the map, and which was easy to find, all except for one bit where a sign had been taken down. It's all boring fields and crops around here.

The aunts were very nice to Wim, in a revoltingly patronizing way. They asked him what his father does. I was rather surprised to discover that he's a farmer. Wim isn't the way I imagine a farmer's son at all. His mother works part time cooking at the hospital. He has two younger sisters, eight and six, called Katrina and Daisy. I hadn't heard any of this, while he knows everything about my peculiar family. I knew I talked too much!

The food was awful, heavy fruitcake, dry scones, watery tea and, because it was High Tea, dry slices of ham. The bread was good, Daniel brought it back from Shrewsbury.

They did not attempt any magic on Wim, I'm sure I would have noticed. They approved of him, and of me being with him. It was normal, which was what they wanted from me. Nice Niece would have had a boyfriend, and if he wouldn't be exactly like Wim, Wim would do. As long as I was going to grow up and go away and not rock their world, they could put up with me. They weren't evil, after all, they were just odd in a very English way.

I went to the station with Daniel to drive Wim back. "Remember, phone every day, and if you need me, I'll come straight down. I can be there in three and a half hours," he said. It's so sweet of him, really it is. I'll see him again in just over a week.

Sunday 17th February 1980

On the train.

Inverted World is weird. I'm not sure it's even science fiction. It doesn't make sense in the end. To begin with, I thought I really liked it, but now I'm not sure at all.

Auntie Teg is meeting me in Cardiff station. But if she doesn't, I'm fine. I've got six pounds seventy-two. There's a way that money is freedom, but it isn't money, it's that money stands for having a choice. I think that's what Heinlein meant.

This train line skims along the Welsh border all the way. One day I must go to North Wales, or even over the Welsh border Wim says is only a couple of miles from Oswestry. It's marked on my map, now I know. I wish they taught us maps in geography instead of stupid Glaciation all the time. Though I suppose Glaciation helps me see the landscape, or at least where the glaciers have been down it. In some parts of the world the glaciers came so often the mountains were worn down to stubs and everything is like a flat lake bottom except with plugs sticking up where volcanic cores of mountains were left. That would be cool to see, but I'm glad it didn't happen here. I love the mountains the way they are.

Sweeping past Abergavenny (and over the border into Wales) there's a sudden rush of primroses along the embankment. I must remember to tell Grampar. The daffodils will be out in Cardiff, well in advance of St. David's Day.

I'm adding this in Auntie Teg's flat, just before bed.

We went up to see Grampar for visiting time. To my horror, when we got there, Auntie Flossie was there, which would have been all right, but with her was Auntie Gwennie, one of my least favourite people in the world. There's not much that's worse than a ward full of senile and dying old men, but there she was. Auntie Gwennie knows nothing about tact, and nothing about kindness. She's rude and annoying and prides herself on speaking her mind. She's eighty-two, but it isn't because she's old and impatient that she does it. Gramma used to say she was the same when she was six years old.

"So, why have you walked out on Liz?" was Auntie Gwennie's greeting to me.

"Because she's insane and impossible to live with," I said. You have to stand up to her, or she walks all over you. "What were the family doing thinking it was a reasonable place for me to live?"

"Humph. And how are you enjoying living with your good-for-nothing father?"

"I don't see much of him, I'm away at school," I said, which I admit was a bit of a cop-out.

We had, of course, managed to sort of keep it from Grampar that Daniel was involved at all, but of course now it all came out. Trying to get onto a calmer topic, Auntie Teg mentioned the plans she's working on to get Grampar out of Fedw Hir in the summer holidays, when she'll be able to fill in if the arrangements don't work out. Auntie Gwennie immediately suggested that Auntie Teg should give up teaching and sell her flat and move back to Aberdare to look after Grampar full time. I don't think so! If nothing else, imagine when he dies! I can't believe people, selfish people too, like Auntie Gwennie, think other people ought to sacrifice themselves entirely like that. She says things, and you just stand there because you can't believe that what she's said really came out of her mouth. Grampar did tell her not to be so daft, that's the only satisfaction.

However, Auntie Gwennie did tell one very funny story about how she lost her driving license, which I want to record. She's eighty-two, remember. She was driving from Manchester, where her awful daughter lives, to Swansea, where she lives. She was on the Heads of the Valleys road, which is an A road, with two lanes in each direction, but not a motorway, and the speed limit is therefore sixty. She was doing ninety. A policeman stopped her—a young whippersnapper of a policeman, she said. "Do you know how fast you were going, madam?" he asked.

"Ninety," she responded, accurately but unrepentently.

"Are you aware that the speed limit on this road is sixty?" he asked.

"Young man," Auntie Gwennie said, "I have been doing ninety along this road since before you were born."

"Then it's high time you had your license taken away from you," he said, fast as lightning, and he did it too, so she has to go on the train!

Unlike me, she hates trains. "I can't abide trains. I hate Crewe station. I can't bear changing platforms there. You have to go all the way to Platform 12 for the Cardiff train, up the stairs and then down them again! I'm never doing it again! No, Luke, this is the last time you'll see me. I won't come down to South Wales again until I die, and then it'll be my coffin changing at Crewe!"

I burst out laughing at that, which, I'll say this for her, she didn't mind at all.

I rang Wim, and told him I'd made no progress yet. I'd better go and see if I can find Glorfindel tomorrow. I told Auntie Teg about Wim and she wanted to know everything—not what his father did and what A Levels he's doing, but what he's like. I told her he's gorgeous and he sort of likes me. She wants to meet him. I said he wanted to come down, and she immediately started fussing about where he could have slept. Her funky brown sofas are much too short for visitors.

Monday 18th February 1980

I went up to the cwm. I didn't tell Auntie Teg any lies, though I didn't tell her all the truth either. I said I wanted to go up to the cwm and have a wander about on my own. I went up past the library. There's never anybody about up there. I don't know why not. The river runs along beside the dramroad, and it's as pretty as anything, especially right now with the beech trees starting to come into leaf. There's no colour like that very early green. There were big clouds in the sky, scudding along up the valley as if they had an urgent appointment in Brecon. In between the sun made everything almost glow with green.

When I came to Ithilien, Glorfindel was there, and Mor, and the fairy who gave me the stick, and loads of other fairies, many of whom I know quite well. I'm not going to get into this impossible thing where I try to record conversations again. What Glorfindel said was that I needed to open a gate so that Mor could live with them and be one of them, and also to give them a way to use the magic that they know. "Then are you ghosts?" I asked. I knew Wim would want to know the answer, and I wanted to know myself for that matter.

"Some," he said.

Some of them are? "Then what are the rest?"

"Being," he said.

Yes, well, I knew that. They are beings. They exist. They're there and they know about magic and they live their lives that are not like our lives. But where did they come from? Are the ones who speak the ones who were human, once?

The gate he wants me to open has to be opened with blood, of

course. And there's something more, something I didn't understand.
I asked about my mother and he said she can't hurt us, or she won't
be able to hurt us ever after I've done this. That definitely means I'm
doing it to prevent harm. It's not the place in the Labyrinth, thank
goodness, because that's a long trudge. It's just down in the old Phurnacite. I can get the bus almost all the way there. Using blood for
magic is always risky, but Glorfindel knows what he's doing. He always has. The weird thing is that he knows it and yet needs me to do
it, because he can't really move things.

It was odd seeing Mor among the fairies like that, as if she was
half a fairy already. I felt really strange. She seemed so remote. She
wasn't growing leaves or anything, but I wouldn't have been surprised if she was.

This evening, I phoned Wim and told him everything as best I
could. "What are the risks?" he asked.

"Well, getting too caught up in the magic, or making the magic
wider than it should be."

"What do you mean getting too caught up in it? You mean dying?" His voice sounded exasperated, at the other end of the line.

"I suppose I do."

"You suppose! Look, I'm coming down."

"There's no need," I said. "It'll be fine. He knows what he's doing."

"You're much more confident than I am."

Telephone conversations are so inadequate, so lacking in expression and gesture and everything. I'm not sure I managed to reassure
him properly.

The thing with dying, well, with death really, is that there's a difference between being someone who knows they can really die at any
time and someone who doesn't. I know, and Wim doesn't. That's all
there is to it. I wouldn't wish on anyone that awful instant when I
realised that the headlights coming towards us were *real*. But without that understanding people think there are dangerous things that
can kill you, and everything else is safe. That's just not the way it

works. We were past the dangerous bit that we knew could kill us and just crossing the road. I don't even think she wanted to kill us. We were more use to her alive.

I need to do it at sunset, which according to the *Western Mail* is half past five.

Tuesday 19th February 1980

I went up the valley on the bus after lunch. Auntie Teg had to go in to school for a meeting and then was coming up to meet me at Fedw Hir for seven o'clock visiting time. I got off the bus at Abercwmboi, by the ruins of the Phurnacite. I was early. I was wishing I'd arranged to do something else in the afternoon, like meet Moira and Leah and Nasreen. I thought about ringing them, but then I thought about Leah's party, which is the last time I saw them, and how they weren't really friends any more, just people I knew. They'd want to hear about Wim, and trying to talk about him in their terms would cheapen what I really feel about him.

There was a sign on the rusty iron railings at the top of the Phurnacite road. "Land Reclamation Project. Mid-Glamorgan County Council." It lifted my heart, because it reminded me of the march of the Lords of Gondor. We had called this place Mordor, and it had fallen. There were no hell-flames now. Some of the trees were showing a little spring green. No fairies were about. My leg was hurting a bit, probably enough to keep them away.

The chimneys were cold and all the windows were broken. It was pathetic, a five-year ruin, not yet crumbled enough to seem like a fairy fortress. The sign about dogs was hanging at an angle. The dogs, if there ever had been dogs, were gone with the workers. The dark pool still looked evil, though there was grass around the edge now. I walked around to the other side of the factory where I could lift up my eyes to the hills and sat in one of the alcoves. I wanted to rest so that my leg would get down to a normal quiet background pain the fairies could put up with. I read *A Touch of Strange*, which is brilliant, and beautifully written, though a bit weird. It's short stories. I'm glad at least one of the things Wim gave me is good.

After I'd finished it, instead of starting *Gate of Ivrel*, I tried to see if I could get the pain to go out of my leg the way acupuncture does. It isn't really magic, except that it is. It's not magic that reaches into the world and changes things. It's all inside my body. I thought, sitting there, that everything is magic. Using things connects them to you, being in the world connects you to the world, the sun streams down magic and people and animals and plants grow from sunlight and the world turns and everything is magic. Fairies are more in the magic than in the world, and people are more in the world than in the magic. Maybe fairies, the ones that aren't lost dead people, are concentrations, personifications, of the magic? And God? God is in everything, moving through everything, is the pattern that everything makes, moving. That's why messing with magic so often becomes evil, because it's going against that pattern. I could almost see the pattern as the sun and clouds succeeded each other over the hills and I held the pain a little bit away, where it didn't hurt me.

Glorfindel came first, and then all the others behind him. I'd never seen such a parade of fairies, not even last year when we had to stop Liz. Looking at Glorfindel with my insight about magic and everything, I decided I should stop calling him that, stop trying to fit him into a pattern I'd found in a story. The name wasn't his, not really, though names are such useful labels. The fairies were all around me, surrounding me, very close. Nobody had told me to bring anything special, and I hadn't, but I was ready.

The sun was starting to sink behind the hills. Glorfindel, without speaking, led us all back to the pool. I should have known it would be there. I stopped beside it. Mor came up to me. She looked so young, and also so remote. I could hardly bear to look at her. Her expressions were like a fairy's expressions. She was like herself, but she'd moved away from who she was, into magic. She was more fairy than person already. I took my penknife out, ready to cut my thumb for the magic, but Glorfindel—I can't think of him any other way—shook his head.

"Join," he said. "Heal."

"What?"

"Broken." He gestured at Mor and me. "Be together."

The fairy who had given me my stick came forward.

"Make, stay together," Glorfindel said. "Stay."

"No!" I said. "That's not what I want. That's not what you want either. Halfway, you said, at Halloween. I could have done that then if I'd wanted to."

"Stay. Heal. Join," Glorfindel said.

The old man fairy touched my stick, and it became a knife, a sharp wooden knife. He mimed plunging it into my heart.

"No!" I said, and dropped it.

"Life," Glorfindel said. "Among. Together."

"No!" I started moving away from the knife, slowly, because of course, it was also my stick, and without it slowly was the only way I could move. Mor picked it up and held it out to me.

"Beyond dying," the old man said. "Living among, becoming, joining. Together. Healed. Strength, reaching, affecting, safe always, strong always, together."

"No," I said, more quietly. "Look, that's not what I want. Last winter, maybe, right after it happened, but not now. Mor knows. Glorfindel knows. I've gone on. Things have happened. I've changed. You might see me as half a broken pair, and you might see my death as a way of tidying up loose ends and getting more power to touch the real world, but that's not how I see it. Not now. I'm in the middle of doing things."

"Doing is doing," he said, which I found much less reassuring than before. "Help. Join. Act."

Mor held out the knife, blade towards me. There were fairies all around me, tangible substantial fairies pushing me towards the knife. The knife I knew was substantial. I had been leaning on it for weeks. I had been making a magical connection with it, as it had with me.

"No. I don't want to," I insisted. "A little blood and magic to help Mor, to help you, if it would help you, yes, I agreed to that, but not to death."

What would Wim think? Worse, what would Auntie Teg think, who had no idea about the fairies, who would think I'd come up here without saying a word and killed myself? And how about Daniel? "I can't," I said.

I tried to move backwards, away, but they were pressing against me, pressing me forwards towards the knife.

"No," I said, again, firmly. They were all around me, and the knife was closer than ever, and the knife wanted my blood, my life, tempting me to become a fairy. If I was a fairy I could see the pattern of the magic all the time. There would be no more pain, no more tears. I would understand magic. I'd be with Mor, I'd be Mor, we'd be one person, joined. But we had never really been that, and that would be all. I took a step backwards and started speaking as calmly as I could. "No. I don't want to be a fairy. I don't want to join. I want to live and be a person. I want to grow up in the world." The calmness helped, for the same reason the Litany Against Fear helps, because fear is something the magic uses. And rejecting it in my heart helped even more, because the other thing it was using was whatever of me did want to become a fairy, had always wanted that.

In front of me was Mor, the knife, and behind her the pool. All around me were fairies. I reached out to the knife with my hand. Whatever else it was, it was wood, and wood loves to burn, burning is in the pattern of wood, the potential fire that is the sun's fire. The sun was setting, but the wood leapt to flame, and I was flame, I was a flame contained in my own shape for a moment, and then I was a huge flame. The land here knew flame. Here the hell-flames had burned, here coal from the mines had been processed to lose its smoke and poisons. Coal wanted to burn, knew burning even more than wood. The fairies fled from me, all but Mor, who was holding the burning knife and connected through it to me. We were two huge mirrored shapes of flame.

I didn't have an oak leaf, and we weren't near the door to death, but I was fire and she was fire and I had the pattern and I loved her. She was not me, but she was in my heart, she always would be. "Hold tight, Mor," I said, and, though she was flame she smiled her real smile, the smile she used to smile on Christmas morning when Gramma was alive and we would wake up to see the balloons hanging in the hall that meant Father Christmas had been and there were stockings waiting to be to opened. I opened a space between the flame and where death fell in the pattern, and I hurled her through it, knife and all, and then I closed it up again and sank down, dampened the flame until I was in my own shape again.

I was still burning, still flame, but I knew how to stop, how to return to the flesh which is what I am. It would be easy to forget, to be consumed in the transformation. I reached for flesh, and with flesh came pain. I was not even singed, but my leg was protesting having my weight on it.

The fairies had backed off, but they were still all around me. Glorfindel looked rueful and the old man looked angry. "Goodbye," I said, and took several slow steps backwards, up hill. The sun had set while I was talking and everything was dusky shadows. The fairies were melting away. I turned around slowly.

And there she was, of course, on the road in the twilight. Auntie Gwennie must have told her I was around, and she'd probably followed the commotion among the fairies to find exactly where.

She hadn't changed at all. She looks like a witch. She has long greasy black hair, darkish skin, a hooked nose and a mole on her cheek. You couldn't typecast someone more like a witch—though of course the Sisters are witches too, and they're impeccably blond and

County. She was wearing typical clothes for her—that is, whatever things had come up when she'd counted through her wardrobe by threes. It found things that were the most magically charged, or that was the idea. It also found things that were incredibly mismatched and unsuitable for the season, in this case a huge knitted patchwork jumper and a long thin black skirt.

"Mama," I said, hardly above a whisper. I was terrified, far more so than I had been of the fairies and the knife. I have always been afraid of her.

"You've always been the one like me," she said, conversationally.

"No," I said, but my voice cracked and it came out as a whisper.

"Together we could do so much. I could teach you so much."

I remembered how we had tormented her once, when she was at her maddest. We must have been ten or eleven. She had pushed me down the front steps because she had sent me to the shop for cigarettes and I had come back empty-handed because they wouldn't sell them to me. I was bleeding, and Mor was picking me up and we saw a big black bird flap slowly across from the cemetery gates—it was probably a crow, but at that age we called them all ravens. It's the same word in Welsh, anyway. "Once, upon a midnight dreary," Mor began, and I joined in, and she, Liz, my mother, had retreated into the house, and then into her room, as we'd gone on reciting Poe's *Raven* louder and louder.

I had seen the pattern of the world. I had sent Mor through to where people are supposed to go when they die. I had been flame. My mother was a pathetic patchwork witch who had used magic so much to meddle in her own life that she had no integrity left and was nothing but a coil of hatreds consuming themselves in futility. We had already hedged her power, with the help of the fairies.

"I have nothing to say to you," I said, loudly, and took a step forward.

I took another step, which was making my leg hurt quite a bit, but I ignored that, ignored her. I could tell that she was doing something

magical, something aimed at me, but my protections, the ones I had made at school, held, and it drained harmlessly away into the ground, the way the pain does in acupuncture.

I took another step and passed her. She reached out and physically grabbed me. Her hands were like claws.

I turned and looked at her. Her eyes were terrifying, just like always. I took a deep breath. "Leave me alone," I said, and shrugged her off.

She reached up to hit me, and I realised she really was reaching upwards. I was taller than she was. I pushed her, using the momentum of her own movement and the turning of the world. She fell. I took another step on beyond her, up the hill. I couldn't run, I could barely limp, but I kept on limping upwards.

"How dare you," she said, from where she had fallen. She sounded really surprised. Then she was drawing on magic again and like the time when Mor died, she sent illusory monstrous shapes swirling around me as I walked. Then, we'd ignored them as best we could. Now I took hold of them and drew them around me. They were sad hollow things without fear to feed them.

I heard a ripping sound, and turned, and gasped with horror. She had taken out the one-volume edition of *The Lord of the Rings*, which was hers, but the first one I had ever read, and torn out a page. She threw it at me, and it became a burning spear in the air between us. It was dark enough now that it lit everything up with strange extra shadows. I dodged it. She tore another page. I could hardly bear it. I know books are only the words, and I have two copies of it of my own, but I wanted to go back and grab the book from her. The spears weren't as bad as the violation, they wouldn't have been even if they'd hit me. How could she use books against me? But I could see how it would seem the obvious thing.

I could do the same. I drew the illusion monsters towards me and gave them a push towards her. They changed and became dragons and huge alien turtles and people in spacesuits and a boy and girl in